Gemma Amor

FIRST DATE

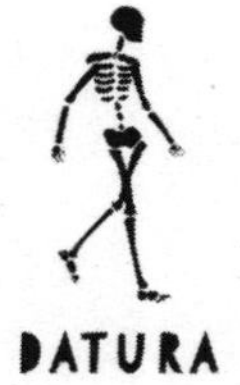

DATURA BOOKS
An imprint of Watkins Media Ltd

Unit 11, Shepperton House
89-93 Shepperton Road
London N1 3DF
UK

daturabooks.com
Love at first fright

A Datura Books paperback original, 2026

Edited by Dan Coxon
Cover by Alice Claire Coleman
Set in Meridien

ISBN 978 1 91552 380 8
Ebook ISBN 978 1 91552 381 5

Printed and bound in the United Kingdom by CPI Group (UK) Ltd, Croydon CR0 4YY

The manufacturer's authorised representative in the EU for product safety is eucomply OÜ – Pärnu mnt 139b-14, 11317 Tallinn, Estonia,
hello@eucompliancepartner.com; www.eucompliancepartner.com

9 8 7 6 5 4 3 2 1

For the lovers.

Actually, no. For me, for once.

TRIGGER WARNINGS

Sexual violence
Torture
Explicit content
Violence towards women
Graphic descriptions of bodily harm
One reference to abuse of a child

Prologue

Water is noisy, even still water, although Amandine realised there was no such thing. The water around her naked, bound body moved constantly. It crackled and popped, licked and burped, slopped, slapped, sighed and even fizzed as if it could not help itself, a thick meniscus of ice latticed with odd, spear-like patterns jostling up against the edges of the jetty she lay upon. With a chorus of birds settling to roost for the night and rippling reeds moving in sinuous, percussive accompaniment to the watery diatribe, Hickling Broad gave out such an assortment of sounds it felt symphonic. Mistle thrushes worked mottled throats to release fluted goodnight songs in anticipation of the dark. Bitterns made odd, booming calls to each other as they waded through mud on stilted legs, lifting clawed feet fastidiously high, dancing a polka. Marsh harriers screeched as they wheeled overhead. The broads performed a cold rhapsody neither Amandine nor Connor – whom she was tied to, knee to knee, ankle to ankle, face to face, for all the world like lovers lying in bed, warm and satiated instead of starved and frozen, blood-crusted, abandoned – could enjoy in the circumstances.

Perhaps if they were warmer.

Amandine doubted she would ever feel warm again.

The weak winter sun had sunk down beyond the 1,500-acre expanse of man-made waterways and marshland acting as Amandine's prison, as if wearied by the act of another day served. A bitter breeze chased in a northerly direction towards the remains of a drainage structure called Stubb Mill, the top of which was just visible above the feathery reed tips. The mill had fallen into disrepair long ago. Proud sails now reduced to a broken windshaft and a single jagged sail stock thrust upwards out of reclaimed land once drained and mined for peat. Other skeletons of past agricultural endeavours lingered nearby: slumping mills and desiccated barns, muddy foundations, an old stone cross boundary marker.

And a boathouse.

This particular boathouse, roofed with drooping, moss-infested thatch, was accessed via a rickety, rotting, green jetty that connected to a boardwalk raised six feet above the surface of the broads. The walkway, jetty, and house were built for reed cutters who transported bundled crops inland using the waterways.

Now, it was the favourite haunt of a pair of otters, and a man who had recently adopted it as his own.

It was also Amandine's prison. She could feel slimy wood beneath her. Old nails, jagged splinters. Rough knots and ridges.

It can't get worse than this, she thought drowsily.

It can't.

That's when it started to snow.

FRIDAY

Sunset

After a long, bitterly cold day, during which two lovers died with fingers stubbornly intertwined – until those fingers were removed, diligently, one by one, with a freshly sharpened pair of drop-forged carbon steel secateurs by a man who was not from around these parts – dusk finally fell.

Evening's birth came slow and painful after.

There weren't many places the man felt comfortable, or at peace, but this ramshackle hut on stilts and algae-slick jetty was one of them. His discovery of the boathouse, of the walkways and waterways and vast, high skies around it, had opened up opportunities he'd previously only been able to dream of.

It had broadened his horizons, literally and metaphorically.

He stood now at the very end of his jetty, on the last available plank, observing the dwindling light from behind smeared and spattered aviator lenses that rested at a skewed angle across his nose. The glasses caught the final bleed out-glow of the sun, giving him an otherworldly appearance: instead of eyes, he sported two burning triangles on his face. There was a sticky clot of blood stuck to his left eyelid, a gluey mass that made him blink funny, lopsided, like he was drunk, but he let it be. He liked the feel of it there. It aroused him. His dick felt hard as rock. If he had been less encumbered by his outfit, he would have pulled it out, then and there, and fed the broads his seed.

Access was, however, hampered by layers of clothes. An old-fashioned, wrinkled tux nestled under a once-white disposable coverall. He had the hood pulled up tight over his head. Over the coverall, which was drenched with blood, nylon waders rose right up past the waist, hoisted by elasticated braces. Beyond this assembly, a bowtie cut into his neck. It was too small, or perhaps his neck had just gotten larger since he bought it. His wife told him not to wear bowties for this precise reason, but he had long since stopped taking anything she said with any degree of seriousness.

Finally, in one rubber-gloved hand, the man held a single rose, the stem denuded of thorns. The rose had come from a bouquet that lay dying, ungifted in the boot of his car.

Roses are red, as the saying went.

So are the insides of people.

The man took a deep breath. Expelled it. His breath came out thick in the frigid air, forming a blush cloud around his head. Dragon's breath, but instead of fire, he breathed out panic, relief, elation, disgust, desire. He was every emotion a man could feel all at once, and also none.

Because he'd done it.

He'd finally done it.

His senses felt amplified by the cold.

He could smell mud, ice, wood rot, mould, still water, and mildew.

He could also smell blood and faeces.

And feel his own semen, crusted on the folds of his chin.

It was not an unpleasant sensation.

He was happy, he realised, suddenly. The sunset was beautiful, if a little unsure of itself. But then it was always beautiful, out on the broads. He imagined himself regent of this darkening kingdom, monarch of the reeds, sovereign of the glassy land.

Out here, there was enough space and peace to finally be himself.

Out here, he could escape judgement and scrutiny, and act as he'd always wanted to: without witness.

He looked down at a large blue plastic rubble sack that rested beside him. It leaked blood from a slit on the bottom. Liquid dripped through the gaps in the jetty planking and into the murky water below.

Inside the sack, jumbled, disassembled human remains.

Or at least, most of the remains. There was a nicely manicured hand sitting in a cool box in the boot of his car parked two and a half miles away. The man was glad it was as cold as it was. The hand would travel better, keep longer.

He'd held onto a few other trophies: a toe. An ear. A few matted clumps of hair.

Nothing that would take up too much space.

Easily stored anatomy.

What was left in the sack were the unwanted parts, like a bag of discarded Lego. Well-used. Pre-loved. Slot the pieces together, see what you can make. A fleshy jigsaw puzzle, dozens of possible permutations of build-your-own-person, if you were so inclined.

The man in the coveralled tux and bowtie was not.

It was time to say goodbye.

He tucked the rose into his coverall collar, bent and grabbed the neck of the bag, pulling the bulky object forward until it teetered on the very lip of the jetty.

Then, with a grunt, he kicked the sack over the edge, down into the water.

The resulting loud splash shattered any temporary illusion of peace that may have settled around him as night fell. Small, scared birds burst from the reed beds in chirruping clouds, scolding him. The pair of otters playfully squeaking and splashing in and out of the weed-garlanded groynes holding the jetty and boathouse aloft slid out of view. A heron barked.

The bag of body parts sank quickly below the surface of the water.

The man imagined cold, black liquid infiltrating the sack and embalming the dismembered parts within, spilling into open mouths and invading orifices with an unforgiving inevitability.

They only had themselves to blame, he thought.

He wiped his hands on his wader legs, observing the large ripples that emanated from the point at which he'd dumped the sack. The only visible marker of a couple who had, by all outward appearances, been very happy together, until he'd met them.

Soon enough, the ripples smoothed, leaving a small trail of bubbles that rose from the tied neck of the blue bag as it let out the last of its air.

The bubbles eventually stopped, too. The waters became glassy, a reed-punctured mirror once again, the broad's surface capturing the death of the day and echoing it back to the sky above, infinite quietus, and the self-appointed King of the Broads smiled to himself in satisfaction.

Later, he would be given a new name:

Lone Diner.

Binding Power

In preparation for her date, Amandine dipped her finger into herself, gathered a dollop of fresh period blood and wrote a word on her belly with it, a Miracle Word. She'd read in an article online that the blood had some sort of binding power. That there was magic in it. That if you had sex with someone while on your period you tapped into a deep, primal, feminine power that created a special bond with the other person inside of you.

She knew that was bullshit, just like most of the things she read, but she found the notion intriguing enough to try anyway. It couldn't hurt, could it? Amandine was jaded, disillusioned with dating and romance in general. She had been alone for a long time and had reached that phase of single life where she had to admit that, while doing the same thing over and over again and expecting different results each time wasn't exactly tantamount to insanity, it certainly wasn't a winning strategy, either.

So, maybe a little magic blood would make all the difference. Who knows?

Her finger dragged across her soft skin, carefully scrawling the Miracle Word, but she felt sheepish and ashamed as she marked her stomach, almost checking over her shoulder to see if anyone was watching – which was absurd, because she lived alone.

You need to stop listening to pathetic advice written by copywriting bots, she told herself, crossly, as she wrote. *Get yourself some real-life, non-artificial friends instead.*

Easier said than done, though, wasn't it?

Meeting new people.

And keeping them.

Which was precisely why she read so many articles.

It wasn't that she couldn't strike up a conversation, or that she struggled to get attention on either of the two dating apps she was signed up to. She enjoyed sex and flirting, and had gotten good at cutting to the chase when it came to what she wanted and how – *grab my hair, now squeeze my throat, lightly, not choking, just enough that I know you could, now slap my ass, that's perfect, now slow, now fast, gentle, bite just here, not too much...* The mechanics of sex and intimacy were simple enough if you were clear and straightforward about it.

The problem wasn't the sex. The problem was getting the connections she made to stick *outside* of the bedroom. She was beginning to think, after a string of unfortunate encounters, that she had bad taste in people. She repeatedly seemed to go for the wrong type. The ones who came across as genuine at first, then proved not to be.

Like the guy who had introduced her to his friends after their third hookup. She'd been excited by this gesture, knowing it was significant to meet a man's friend group, thinking this would catapult their arrangement out of a casual sex thing and into a proper relationship, but it didn't take long before the evening turned sour. The lads, who'd been drinking all day and were completely past the point of sensibility by the time she joined them, had been nice enough to begin with. As more drinks were consumed, however, they started to wink at each other and make stupid, wildly dramatic moaning orgasm sounds mid-conversation. Amandine realised her date had been making fun of how loud she was during sex to all his friends. The mockery ramped up as the evening wore on, progressing to hurtful remarks about her pubic hair, of which she apparently had too much, and the size, shape and consistency of her labia and breasts – both of which were evidently lacking on all aesthetic fronts, and even the presentation of her arsehole, which was unladylike, according to the men. She left the bar in tears, furious at the childishness of it all.

Then there was the man who'd sent flowers, texted sweet things, seemed so mild and nice-mannered and, honestly, a little vanilla until they'd slept together, whereupon mid-thrust, while he was inside her, face all screwed up in concentration, sweat pouring off him as if he had a fever, he pulled back, panting, and asked her quite seriously if he could push her down the stairs then jerk off on her, because he "had a thing" for it. He wanted it to look like an accident, he said. She did her best to remain calm and politely declined – changing the lock on her front door the day after, just to be sure.

After him, there had been the smart, funny, personable business owner with the raging cocaine addiction. They'd been in his car, driving to a country pub on the way to their first in- person date, when he slowed for a junction, pulled out a small vial, tapped it out onto his knee, and nonchalantly snorted several large piles of white powder. When the junction was clear of traffic, he drove on, pedal to the floor, oblivious to Amandine clutching the door frame white-knuckled beside him as he grew increasingly agitated and angry at other cars on the road, swearing and gesticulating the whole way. Amandine had been forced to hide in the toilets when they eventually arrived at the pub. When a barmaid came in to use the bathroom, she asked her to call a cab to take her home. The last she saw of that date, he'd been rubbing his left nostril and sucking frantically on his lower lip while he texted someone. His dealer, presumably.

After that, there was the florist who hated his ex-wife, yet spoke about her endlessly, mistaking Amandine for a therapist he didn't have to pay for. He cried a lot during foreplay and struggled to get hard.

Then there was the architect who pretended to be separated from her wife when she was, in fact, firmly married. "I'm not ready for a committed relationship," she'd said. The woman's wife had used a location-tracking app to gatecrash their cosy evening in an Airbnb that Amandine had paid for.

After that disaster, which was over nine months ago, Amandine had almost given up hope of finding a life partner. Almost. The honest ones were taken, she feared. She wasn't getting any younger. Most people her age were married, had kids, were focusing on their careers. Amandine was doing none of these things. She was pinballing from one exhausting day to the next, feeling her own loneliness like a lead-lined jacket weighing her down, and she longed for a safe person to help carry the load. She'd been longing since the day her parents died, although she knew she could never replace them.

The yearning meant she kept trying, though. A small part of her hoped that if she held the doors open long enough, eventually the right person would walk in. Then, perhaps she'd get a decent night's sleep for the first time in nearly ten years.

She just had to keep trying, was all.

And really, she thought, as the minutes ticked by and that evening's date crept closer, she only had herself to blame for her disastrous love life.

She should know better, she told herself. Be less naive. Learn to spot the signs. The red flags.

The internet, in that regard, was her one true ally.

Celery

The same article that extolled the virtues of sex while menstruating also told Amandine to eat celery before her date, because it minimised bad breath. She therefore chewed on a long crunchy green stick as she wrote on herself, wincing when the stringy celery threads got stuck between her teeth, snagging her gums.

Other nuggets of wisdom from the article: stuff your bra with rolled-up socks to make your cleavage pop (she wasn't keen on that idea, what if one fell out mid-entree?), maintain eye-contact as much as possible (this wasn't really an option for Amandine, for whom prolonged eye-contact was tantamount to torture), and make sure to use your date's first name as many times as possible in conversation to build a deeper connection with them.

Amandine would have been okay with that last one, if it weren't for the fact that she kept forgetting his name.

It just wouldn't stick.

That wasn't his fault. So far, the man had come across as an okay guy. More than okay, really – halfway decent, from what she could glean from their text exchanges. A little needy, perhaps, but otherwise decent.

But then, they always did seem that way at first.

She was willing to give him a shot, however, if for no other reason than he seemed very keen on her. She grew somewhat used to him being there in the background, a potential conversation in her pocket. They had chemistry, when she let herself lean into it. And he was attractive, in a tired sort of way. His WhatsApp profile picture displayed what was clearly his signature smile: lopsided, self-conscious, anxious crinkles puckering the skin around his eyes. Too many teeth, but it wasn't an aggressive display, just a little awkward. He was thinning slightly at the hairline, which was uneven, rising higher on one side than the other. He tried to disguise this feature with caps, or flopping his parting to one side. His neck was thick: he worked out. He was handsome enough for her to say "yes" without too much hesitation when he finally asked her out for dinner.

It was just a shame she kept forgetting his name.

Part of this was because she'd stored his number in her phone as 'C' and had thought of him as such from then on.

The main reason, though, was that Amandine had very poor short-term memory.

In fact, she had very poor short-term everything: memory, temper, focus, patience, appetite. It made for a tiring day-to-day existence.

If he invited her for a second date, she would be able to remember his name better, she was sure. After she'd put a voice to it, and facial expressions. Personality. Intent. Once she'd made a judgement. Names tended to stick better when she knew she'd have to use them on more than one occasion.

Until then, she would have to fake it.

She'd written another word on her skin, this one in biro on the inside of her wrist. Not a Miracle Word.

A Reminder Word.

CONNOR.

That should do it.

She looked at her other wrist. The remnants of yesterday's Reminder Word were just visible on top of her blue, prominent veins:

CELERY.

She sighed and shook her head.

I'd better not mix them up, she thought.

Connor

To say that Connor was excited for his date was an understatement.

Connor was almost beside himself with anticipation.

He hadn't been on a real date for a long time, not after the last shit show, and he had no idea what to expect anymore. What did women want, these days? He'd always been told they were the romantic gender, but he'd met at least a dozen over the past year who wanted a quick fuck and nothing more. The world had become adamantly no-strings since his last relationship ended. It confused him, and dating – or the idea of it, at least – made him ambivalent. Asking and answering the same questions over and over, hoping eventually that some of them would stick. Manufacturing an endless supply of feigned interest. Wondering when the right time was to suggest sex without looking like a complete fucking creep, or, worse, wondering how to get *out* of sex without hurting someone else's feelings. Or, having sex with a woman he didn't really like because he was horny, and feeling gross about it after; or because *they* were horny, and he was lonely enough to not know how to turn away from that.

Then there were the depressing, let-them-down-gently texts, both sent and received. The sinking, miserable feeling in the pit of his belly when someone he liked, who he thought liked him back, faded slowly away after a date, never to be heard from again.

Or, even worse, having to be the ghost himself. Executing the slow, cowardly fade, melting away like cigarette smoke blown out of a window. It usually happened when someone gave him the shivers, or was far too invested in him after an unreasonably short amount of time and wanted him to meet their parents or children or best friend or dog. These requests evoked a knee-jerk *RUN, CONNOR!* response in him, because commitment was a terrifying enough prospect with someone you knew well, let alone an almost complete stranger.

Yes, dating made him tired. The simple act of meeting and getting to know someone had become highly complicated. He'd found it easier, after much analysis, to stay single than to put himself through the excruciatingly slow interrogation process that came with figuring out who a new prospect was, exactly. What they liked, what they didn't like. What their tastes and preferences were. What they felt about things that were important to him, whether their politics and persuasions aligned with his... the repetitive, crushing hammer of disappointment to the heart when he realised the burgeoning connection was going nowhere. It was all so fucking exhausting. Like sitting a series of exams over and over, yet never quite achieving the necessary grades.

Friends would text: *How's it going?*

And he would reply: *Bullshit, mate. It's all bullshit.*

They would answer with: *Yeah, but I bet you're getting a ton of pussy* – and he'd sigh and throw his phone to one side in disgust. The grass was always greener with people who weren't single. They never seemed to appreciate what they had, painting his life as something to aspire to, when really, he was just incredibly fucking lonely. It had come to the point where he felt as if life was something that happened to other people, and he was a mere bystander.

Tonight, though, he had nothing but good feelings about the woman he was meeting.

Hence his excitement.

Her name was Amandine.

He scrolled through the few pictures he had of her on his phone as he psyched himself up for his evening. Statuesque, Amandine was probably an inch or two taller than him, if not more, with big eyes, big hair, and big tits, and she had a look about her that was quietly confident but also reserved. As if she were holding herself back. She didn't smile much, but that was part of the charm. She came across like a hard woman to please, and for Connor, that represented a challenge.

And he'd always liked a challenge, no matter what form it took.

A mutual acquaintance had introduced them virtually. From the word go, Amandine had been different from the other women he'd met. Intriguing. She was not a big texter, for one thing, which was a massive relief at first because neither was he, not really.

Or at least, he'd thought he wasn't.

When she did drop him a message it was always about something real, something interesting or funny or a bit weird, and it made a change from the usual *hey, how's it going?*, or, *hey, how are you feeling today?*, as if he had a fucking clue, or, *hey, so I was just wondering, what are we? Are we okay?* missives. Amandine only got in touch when she had something genuinely logistical or interesting to talk about, and never once felt the need to question the nature of their conversation, which had made life a lot easier and safer to navigate.

At first.

They continued a light-hearted back-and-forth for a while. Connor caught himself staring at his phone periodically throughout the day, hoping for her message icon to pop up.

When it didn't, he started to get moody, then annoyed with himself, which led to a nasty feedback loop of mounting insecurity, wondering whether she'd lost interest in him. He would try and work it out in the gym, but this always made it worse, because the gym was a cold warehouse on an industrial estate only ever occupied by old men in tracksuit bottoms, the occasional bodybuilder, or spotty teens trying desperately to broaden their chest or arm span with the wrong exercises, and Connor would look around himself, depressed, and think *What the fuck am I doing this for? There's nobody to see.* And he would feel as if he was wasted, as if he would wake up one day at the age of seventy or eighty without ever being fully seen, or appreciated, physically or otherwise.

Then, when Amandine's replies did eventually arrive, hours, sometimes days after his initial texts, his whole mood shifted back into the realm of the positive. He started daydreaming about taking walks in the park with her. Trips to the cinema, long drives, whole days in bed together, nights where he made her moan, then made her laugh, which was how he knew he liked her more than most of the other women he was simultaneously texting in a lacklustre way – he was building a fantasy life with her in his head without even realising he was doing it.

The fantasy was dangerously alluring. Amandine made him feel good about himself. She made him feel desirable, young, and horny – and his testosterone levels rocketed whenever she texted. When he wanked to her, his dick felt larger than it ever had before.

Connor felt himself growing invested in Amandine with an alarming, intoxicating rapidity. Her stand-offishness was tempered by unpredictable flashes of warmth that fascinated him, and with that fascination came a certain degree of hope that he might, at last, be able to get off the treadmill of romantic uncertainty his life had become. He opened up to her, told her that he wanted what most people wanted: someone who *got* him. Someone who gave him that feeling in the pit of his belly, like a kid the night before Christmas. Amandine did that. She was a Christmas Eve girl. When she reached out, Connor felt ten years old again.

Amandine would never reply to these statements in any truly reciprocal way, but there were hints that she might feel something similar. Carefully chosen words, a strategically placed emoji. Never an affirmation, but always the potential of one.

Those hints kept him going.

That she was playing hard to get also turned him on, which was pathetic, he knew, but he couldn't help it. He was a sucker for the chase. He wanted to be an itch that she scratched, and then kept on scratching, until he was well and truly under her skin.

It took him several weeks to realise that, sadly, this would not be the case.

Rather, *she* was the itch, and he longed to dig his nails into her beyond the *tip-tap-tap-tip* of his phone screen.

Eventually, it got to the point where Amandine (or the idea of Amandine that he'd built in his head) was all he could think about. He thought about her from the moment he woke (checking his phone before doing anything else) until the moment he reluctantly went to sleep with his phone volume up loud and within easy reach in case she decided to late-night text him, which she never did. He built up a precise understanding of her daily routine and became twitchy on the rare occasions she deviated from it. He knew when she woke, when she showered, when she ate breakfast, when she watched movies, when she exercised, when she cleaned her house or went grocery shopping or did her admin. He pictured her going about her day as he went about his, building up a false sense of intimacy with her spectre that he told nobody about, not even his dad.

After a while, he came to understand that he needed Amandine in his life in order to function in his. He wanted to make a life raft out of her and nestle into her sturdy, secure bow.

He was aware this sort of dependency was unhealthy, but the whole thing had become too exciting for him to pay heed to any cautionary inner voice. Especially when Amandine unexpectedly sent him a naked selfie one evening while he was eating his microwave dinner in front of the TV. He was toast after that. He'd nearly choked on opening it. Her tits were spectacular: full and round, a little low, big enough to pass the pencil test, and the nipples were dark and perfect. He set the picture as his phone screensaver for a day, before someone in the post office had seen it and given him a funny look while he was depositing a cheque for his dad. He'd changed it back to her WhatsApp profile picture after that, knowing it created the impression, to anyone glancing at his lock screen, that she was his girlfriend. He liked people thinking that. In his mind, she was, anyway.

He'd returned the favour with his own selfie, posing carefully in the right light, taking the shot from down below his balls so his shaft looked huge, gripping the base of it tight so the veins stood out. He'd been impressed with how he looked in the picture, but Amandine had been characteristically close-mouthed about it – beyond her initial reaction, a shocked open-mouthed emoji. This response had sent him into a huge doom spiral of insecurity about his body, which then, strangely, made him more attracted to Amandine.

It was then that he realised he had it: a bad case of the feelings.

With enormous restraint, he managed to keep most of this neediness out of his ongoing communications, not wanting to scare her off. It was a struggle not to blurt the depth of his emotions.

I want to use the L-word, he thought about saying, but never did.

Constantly swallowing down an enormous globe of want, his jaw and fingers ached from the effort of holding himself back. He played the game as patiently and slowly as he could, marinating in the drawn-out frisson, privately torturing himself on a sometimes-hourly basis, imagining, during the quiet periods where her phone was inactive or in flight mode, that she was on dates with multiple other men, because why should she not be? She was gorgeous. He made frequent, semi-jokes about her host of boyfriends, which she either ignored, laughed off or replied to with eye-rolling emojis – a response he found both reassuring and infuriating. It was not the explicit *no, Connor, I am not seeing anyone else at the moment* reply that he wanted.

Eventually, unable to handle the uncertainty of it all, he'd struck up the courage to ask her out on a real-life, in-person date. No sexting after that first, amazing tit shot, which was very hard for him. His preferred approach was sext first, fuck later, because it meant he could vet the women with compatible sexual proclivities, gamifying their eventual tryst.

But not so with Amandine. No more nudes, no grubby video calls late at night so they could rummage, frantically, long-distance, phone hand shaking as the other worked to bring them individually off, only to hang up and clean up and feel empty and dissatisfied and twice as alone after. No phone dates, or even phone calls beforehand.

No. Connor wanted a good, old-fashioned sit-down dinner date with candles and flowers and all the trappings. He wanted to sit across a table from Amandine and look her in the eyes and try to coax a smile from that serious mouth in person.

And he would do his best, while looking at her, not to tell her he thought he was falling in love with her already.

Decision made, heart racing, hands sweating, Connor had finally typed a message and invited Amandine out for an evening meal.

Like a date? she'd replied, after an excruciatingly long time.

*Not *like* a date,* he'd typed, more confidently than he'd felt.

*An *actual* date.*

And dinner's on me.

Sure, she replied, seventeen hours later, during which Connor was convinced he had almost died five times over, *But I'm an *actual* freak in real life.*

Me too, he'd sent back, *don't worry. We can be freaks together over steak and ice cream.*

Her sign-off had been abrupt, and typical, and infuriating:

This lukewarm response left Connor intensely dissatisfied. He forced himself to sit with the feeling. Being this hungry and anxious for someone was a good sign, he reminded himself. All or nothing, life is short, carpe diem, et cetera.

Still, he couldn't wait to lock her down, take her off the table. He knew other men were circulating, how could they not be? He had to get the ball rolling as quickly and convincingly as possible.

Connor booked a table at the fanciest gastropub he could find, a place that prided itself on being "the most romantic restaurant in Norfolk", and then immediately worried that he would terrify Amandine by taking her there – as if he was planning on proposing right out of the box. There weren't many other choices for first date venues in the area, not without driving a long way from where they both lived, which he didn't think Amandine would be comfortable with. The pub he'd chosen was remote enough as it was.

Amandine didn't seem to mind. She shot him a thumbs-up emoji in response to the date, time and location, and, just like that, Connor had an *actual* date. His first real, non-hookup date in years.

After they'd settled plans, he deleted his dating apps.

Even if it all goes tits-up with her, he told himself, *I can't do it anymore.*

It's just too depressing.

He hoped it wouldn't go tits-up. He was ready. To not be lonely anymore. For a relationship, a real relationship, with someone he could count on as a teammate. He wanted that more than anything. Someone to tackle the world with. He was tired. He hoped for more from his life.

He hoped she did too.

Looking forward to it, he'd sent Amandine, unable to help himself from sending one last message. *Really.*

She replied: *Me too,* with another *:)* after.

Then she switched her phone off.

Clean Up

The man eventually grew tired of standing out in the cold and dark. It was getting late. Coming back to finish off tomorrow was not an option, either. Tomorrow, he planned on taking a rest day. He missed his office, his computer, his chair, the sepulchral quiet of his house after his wife had gone to bed.

Besides, he had unfinished business to attend to online.

He shifted his weight from foot to foot as he unwrapped the elastic band of a head torch from his wrist, jamming it down over his scalp and clicking on the light. The reeds in front of him suddenly jumped into view, illuminated by the concentrated beam, thin white stalks contrasting against the night sky and black water like a barcode across his vision. A pair of reflective yellow dots glowing among the stems quickly vanished: wildlife of some sort, perhaps a mouse or a water vole.

He sniffed. A long string of snot had worked its way down from his right nostril, swinging like a sticky pendulum. He left it there, dangling. No point in wiping it away. There was no one around to see, to poke fun at him. The otters didn't give a fuck. Why should he?

That was the beauty of the broads. He was as alone as a person could be in twenty-first-century Britain.

And because of that, it was all too easy to dissociate, out among the hissing, crackling reeds. Everything felt so far from civilization and modernity. It was like he was on Mars, a real-life Dr Manhattan, done with humanity's shit. The wetlands had a heavy, alien atmosphere, especially at night. A restorative wildness.

It also meant that screams were easily absorbed, swallowed by the wide, open reserve.

The perfect place, all things considered, to dispose of a human body.

Or two, for that matter.

A steady stream of bubbles still rose up from the sack he'd tipped into the water, popping as they reached the surface of the broad. The man lingered to be sure nothing else bobbed to the top, even though he'd weighed the sack down with bricks before pushing it into the water.

When it was clear that nothing was coming back up, he allowed himself to relax.

He'd done a good job, he thought.

The man marked this affirmation by hurling the rose he still held into the reeds with cold disdain.

Then he turned and walked the short distance down the jetty to the boathouse. The wooden planking widened out to a crude loading platform, punctured by two large anchoring posts that stuck up like telegraph poles. The posts were actually old tree trunks thrust through the platform and deep into the mud below, festooned with slippery mooring ropes, weather-bleached from their original vibrant blue, intertwined with brand-new bloodstained nylon ropes.

An axe, a saw, and a pair of secateurs lay in coagulating pools of blood on the boards between the posts.

Lumps of flesh, hair, and skin glistened in the beam of the headtorch.

Messy, the man thought.

He tackled the nylon rope remnants first, cutting them free from each post with a small penknife, bundling them into tight knots and lobbing them into the broad. He gagged repeatedly as he did so, annoyed with himself for his sensitivity. Chopping up the bodies hadn't been as bad as he'd anticipated, but something about the ropes got to him. Maybe it was their texture. Rough, synthetic, but coated with slime that set his teeth on edge.

He wouldn't use ropes next time, he noted. He'd use cable ties instead. He'd bought a large packet from a hardware store yesterday on a whim. They sat in his car, waiting, along with the bunch of flowers, now one rose down, and the cool box with the hand sitting in it, and other tools, accessories, weapons. He supposed the contents of his car boot constituted, if he thought about it, some sort of intent for a repeat performance, but he found it best to not analyse his own behaviour too much, not while he still had things to do. So what if he'd bought zip ties and a new supply of large blue rubble sacks too? It didn't mean anything. Being prepared for any eventuality wasn't the same thing as premeditation.

The man used buckets of marsh water to sluice the platform down until he was confident most traces of human life had been washed off, like tiresome graffiti. It was so cold that the water iced over even as he scrubbed the planking with his feet. The slick sheen transformed the jetty boards into a lethal runway. He would have to be careful walking back in the dark, else he'd fall headlong into the broad. A wet man could get hypothermia easily in temperatures like this, as well he knew, if the shock of falling in didn't kill him. Water didn't have to be deep to be deadly.

Which gave him an idea for next time.

An idea he filed away, intending to come back to, work on, refine.

Ideas don't mean intent, either, he told himself.

They're just ideas.

Doesn't mean I'll act on them.

But if he did choose to, there was no margin for error.

Not if he was going to make a habit of this.

Finally, happy to be almost done, his body aching with labour, he shed his coverall skin like a snake peeling back its own outer layer in one long piece, turning the plastic shroud inside out, sloughing off his gory self and emerging renewed from under it.

Beneath the moult, his dishevelled tux, food-stained shirt, scuffed leather shoes with worn-down soles, wonky bowtie, smudged glasses, and glaring head torch would have made for an incongruous image against the backdrop of shimmering waters and wide, star-studded sky – if anyone had been around to see him.

But they weren't. Which was the whole point.

Within moments of being released from the coverall, the man's body reminded him that his biological needs had long been ignored. He pissed urgently over the side of the jetty into the water where he'd thrown the sack of body parts. The relief was immense. He imagined his urine sinking down, infiltrating the bag, swilling around the tender bits of the couple who had made fun of him with such monstrous self-satisfaction. That felt like a long time ago, now. The imagery gave him satisfaction as he shook the final drops away and tucked himself back in.

The man then scrunched the discarded coverall into a tight wad and set it on fire with a disposable lighter he kept in his left tux pocket. The suit caught easily, shrivelling up into a tiny, crumpled blob in seconds, all traces of violence melted away in a few sticky blinks of an eye. The molten plastic went the way of the sack: off the jetty and into the water, propelled there by his toe. Some of the melted coverall stuck to his shoe, like chewing gum. He would fix that later, when he was home.

For now, he considered this night a job done.

Finally.

It had taken him a lot longer than he'd anticipated.

It had taken them a lot longer to die than he'd anticipated too.

But it was finished.

He left the platform and the boathouse without looking back, waddling along carefully like a penguin, arms and hands out to each side for balance.

He'd return soon enough, no need for farewells.

The jetty and house squatted patiently among the reeds after the man's departure, waiting for wildlife to return. Before long, a soft white barn owl swooped in from a nearby bed, landing on a knot that protruded from one of the anchoring posts, now stripped of their ropes. Head cocked, huge eyes soaking up the night, the owl pecked at the post and pulled a long, snarled clump of blond human hair from a jagged splinter just beneath the knot, gathering it up in its beak efficiently, like a fisherman reeling in a line.

Then it took off, the hair trailing behind it.

No Such Thing as Normal

Amandine knew there was no such thing as "normal", not really, but she was beginning to suspect there was something profoundly wrong with her. Some cognitive issue that was rapidly getting worse. Memory loss was only a small part of it. Life in her thirties had become a great deal more difficult than it ought to be, to the point where her days had deteriorated into a chaotic sequence of disorganised events, half-finished tasks, missed opportunities, clumsy accidents, easily avoided misunderstandings, and constant distractions. She didn't seem to be able to complete any single task in one go, interpersonal relationships and friendships had become nigh-on impossible to maintain, and she found herself moving around her house as if wading through fog, day in, day out. She would often wander from one room to another and forget what her purpose for doing so was. She also caught herself zoning out with alarming frequency, especially in pressurised situations or occasions when she was due somewhere.

As if her body was willing, but her brain was not.

Like now, for example.

Instead of getting ready for her date, she was still furiously daydreaming, staring into space, grinding her celery like a cow chewing the cud, *crunch-crunch-crunch*. Her terrible memory was busy trying to sort through the terabytes of received internet wisdom offered by the hundreds, if not thousands, of listicles and articles and thirty-second videos she'd scanned in preparation for this date. She was aware that deep diving to the extent that she did was a very real demonstration of not being able to see the woods for the trees, but she couldn't seem to help herself. The content she craved offered something she didn't otherwise have access to: immediacy, and the illusion of support. If her brain had an itch, she could scratch it, right away, by simply unlocking her phone screen.

This was important to Amandine, a woman who spent vast quantities of time alone. Through circumstance at first, later through choice.

Advice was hard to come by, especially when both your parents were dead.

She examined her index finger, used as a crude pen to write the Miracle Word on her body. Crimson-tipped now, the nail ridged with her own blood-ink.

Well, that won't do, she thought. *Can't shake hands like this.*

She stood up to go to her ensuite bathroom, intent on cleaning her finger, and promptly got lost in another thought-loop.

Periods.

People either wanted to talk about them in detail, or not at all.

This dichotomy fascinated her.

There was a wealth of misinformation online about a woman's bleeding, most of it masquerading as advice. Amandine had read and seen all sorts of wild and wonderful things: bleeding was the sign of the devil; bleeding was only supposed to happen twice a year, not once a month; bleeding was supposed to be an egg-cup of fluid a day, no more, no less;

inserting a tampon inside yourself was tantamount to having sex and taking your own virginity; sanitary products were behind global warming; you couldn't get pregnant during your period; bleeding should last exactly seven days every month without fail; period pain was a myth; cramps were "tricks of the mind"; you shouldn't bathe during your time of the month; you couldn't go camping in the woods because bears would smell your blood from miles away and come looking; you shouldn't touch flowers while bleeding because they would wither and die; washing your face in your first menstrual blood would give you a good complexion...

She'd also read that menstruation was a "gift" linked to the lunar cycle, that her body had formed a sacrosanct bodily pact with the moon that enriched her life with special meaning, significance, and a unique energy, and that she had a pre-ordained path to walk, if she chose, a bloody path towards a "ferocious type of feminine power".

She'd laughed at that phrase. What was so fucking special and ferocious about bleeds so heavy she could barely walk, cramps so severe she spent days of her life bent in half, mood swings so violent she could barely function, ruined underwear, stained jeans and bedding...

She didn't believe in menstruation as a gift, or in ancient lunar cycles, nor did she subscribe to the idea that her natural bodily functions were shameful, in any way. Inconvenient, sure. Messy and painful, definitely. But never shameful.

But she *did* believe in the power of words, which is why she daubed herself.

It felt, now she'd done it, like making a pact with some higher power, a strange contract of sorts. Amandine found that after the Miracle Word was written, her nerves subsided, a little.

An alarm sounded on her phone, wrenching her out of herself. One of many she had to set throughout the day, for this precise reason.

She cancelled the alarm with an untainted thumb and finally went to wash her hands. Then, she sat naked at her vanity table, patting eyeshadow onto her lids with a soft brush as she waited for the sticky word to dry on her belly.

I wonder what he is like, she thought, working powder into the creases of her lids.

I wonder if he will like me.

She glanced at her wrist.

If Celery will like me.

She giggled.

It didn't much matter if he liked her, not really.

What mattered was whether *she* liked *him.*

Amandine had cautiously low expectations. Sure, they'd been texting back and forth for a while, but that was no way to assess a person's true nature. She considered texts low-value exchanges, didn't place much importance on them. It was the easiest thing in the world to shoot someone a message. In the moments between his texts, she hardly thought about Connor at all. It was hard to get excited about a little round speech bubble. She preferred to keep her energy for real-life interactions, because they demanded so much more from her. Meeting new people was hard, and faintly traumatic every time she did it. She tended to judge books firmly by their cover and preface, always had. Face value was important to her.

The problem with this approach was that other people were often not as they first presented themselves.

Especially when it came to sex, dating, and love.

But the internet validated her. She could find dozens of first-hand accounts from other women just like her with a few swipes of her thumb. It seemed to have all the rulebooks governing "normal" people's conduct, motivations, and behaviour. She'd done a lot of reading in the wake of her string of failed dating attempts and learned a lot of lessons.

As a result, Connor, although he didn't know it, was going to have to work much harder to get her approval than he might have if they had met several years earlier.

Vet this one thoroughly, she told herself. *Protect your peace.*

That was what the girls on TikTok said, at any rate.

Red flags, they called it in the various relationship-advice communities she subscribed to. Buzzwords that generated endless social wisdom she could scroll through when bored, depressed, lonely, or overstimulated. *Ten Red Flags You Shouldn't Ignore.* She never liked the expression, it implied *red flags to a bull,* like it was animalistic of her to react to shitty behaviour with anger, coldness, or firm boundaries, even when provoked.

A depressing concept, flags.

Depressing, but necessary.

She would prefer it if she didn't have to think this way, in terms of potential harm, before even shaking hands with another human being.

She would prefer it if she was allowed to think of love in terms of signs, instead.

Some people, she mused, had signs coming out of them like way posts, and they either pointed in the right direction or the wrong one.

They rarely, if ever, pointed the way she was walking, but she was willing to keep on the path. One foot in front of the other, until she found her footsteps doubled.

The flags, she was beginning to understand, were necessary.

They stopped her wandering off the path and over the edge of a cliff.

Not that she thought Connor gave off any cliff-edge vibes.

But you can never be too careful, she thought.

She remembered that, later.

Nerves

Connor grew increasingly nervous and agitated as the date grew closer. He showered twice, shaved, took a shit, and cranked out an anticipatory wank, looking at Amandine's picture, propping his phone up against the taps on his bathroom sink so he was hands-free. Her breasts taunted him, teased him. He imagined them in his hands, heavy and pliable, the nipples jumping to life under his attentive thumbs.

Can't go on an important date with a live round in the chamber, a friend texted, helpfully. *It'll help you last longer, too, when you get down to it.*

Connor took this advice, resenting himself thoroughly as his cum squirted into the sink, but it did help calm his nerves a little.

He showered again after. Then he scrubbed the sink until it gleamed and gave himself a routine pedicure and manicure. *Short fingernails,* he thought to himself as he clipped and buffed. *Don't want to scratch any delicate skin.*

Change lock screen! his brain shouted at him, suddenly, as he finished trimming his cuticles.

He shook his head at his own stupidity.

Fucking hell, Connor.

Imagine turning up for a first date with her face plastered all over his phone lockscreen. She would think he was a psychopath.

He changed the screen to a picture of the night sky, black with stars.

That was close.

Outfit choice proved tricky. He wanted to look as if he'd made an effort, but not too much effort. He wanted to be smart, but not like a salesman. He didn't know if Amandine would dress up or not. He considered texting her so he could match her mood, but restrained himself. Too much communication before the date would spoil the magic, he reminded himself, even though he ached to ask her how she was doing.

He settled on a nice suit jacket, with new jeans, new shoes, and a crisp shirt tucked in at the waist, finished off with a brand-new tie and cufflinks.

Fuck, he thought as he studied his reflection in the mirror.

He looked like the preppy best man at a friend's wedding.

Panic surged again.

He texted a picture of his outfit to his friend.

Too much? he asked, aware he was testing the boundaries of this friendship by asking for sartorial feedback.

His friend was accommodating.

Better to try too hard than look like you don't give a shit.

Good point, Connor typed. *Cheers, mate.*

No worries, came the response. *Amazed you managed to find anyone to go on a proper date with you, tbh. She doing Care in the Community?*

Smh, Connor replied, then immediately began to worry that Amandine was indeed only going on a date with him because she felt sorry for him. This sent him sliding down a helix of anxiety that he only barely managed to halt by telling himself that women didn't shell out for taxis and go to restaurants in the middle of nowhere out of pity. Instead, they made excuses.

But what if she couldn't think of an excuse? a small voice whispered.

What if she's too scared to tell you she's not interested?

What if she stands you up, instead?

What if what if, he answered himself. Work with certainties, not what-ifs. It was advice he'd picked up from an Instagram reel about anxiety, about not "feeding the beast". It had popped up as if intended for him and him alone, interrupting the scrolling parade of women in Lycra at the gym doing squats (#shesquatsbro, #glutes, #gymgirls, a collection of related hashtag variations he had a genuine addiction to) that he only watched partly out of horniness, partly because he found the repetitive motion of flesh comforting, soothing.

Don't feed the beast.

What will be, will be.

You can't control the actions of another, only yourself.

Thoughts are not facts.

The mantras only partly helped his Amandine-induced nerves.

Connor sealed his look with a few slaps of aftershave, something he never wore unless it was a special occasion. It was musky, a little strong. He liked it. It smelt like he cared, he thought. It was ceremonial.

He hoped Amandine appreciated the effort.

Then, fully dressed and ready to go, he looked at his watch, thinking he surely didn't have much time before he had to leave the house.

His watch told him he was two whole hours early.

His heart sank.

Fuck, he thought, despairingly.

What now?

His stomach was a mess, his mounting nerves playing hell with his guts.

Another wank?

He settled on research instead, pouring himself a cold glass of milk and sinking into his couch, phone at the ready.

Might as well be prepared, he thought, even though he'd carried out these digital detection exercises many times already.

Connor looked up Amandine's name first, so he had something to talk about, right off the bat. Amandine, as far as he could ascertain, was a French name. It loosely translated as "much loved". He wondered if he should brush up on his wines, but didn't want to come off as one of those wine tossers, not if she was the expert anyway.

He tried, once again, to find her on all the usual social media platforms, but he'd searched before, to no avail, and this attempt was no different. She either used an alias he didn't know about or simply didn't do social media, which seemed wild to him, but also fitted with her reticent demeanour. She didn't share information lightly. A search of all the usual dating apps had brought up nothing before he'd deleted them, which was some small comfort, although it was entirely possible that she was, again, using another name. He'd tried dozens of different approaches to locate her digital self: mileage radius, age, interests, height, hair colour, build… Amandine remained a ghost, at least in the dating app dimension.

Finally, Connor tried reverse image searching Amandine's profile picture on Google. The browser brought up nothing of use. However, he did glimpse a news preview as he opened the new browser tab:

Concerns grow for missing local couple last seen two weeks ago.

Connor found himself clicking the link, needing the distraction – then immediately wished he hadn't.

The headline image was of an attractive couple in their thirties, taken while they were on vacation. Behind them: an azure sea, palm trees, a deep burnished glow all around. They were bronzed by the sun, relaxed and happy in the photograph. The man's arms circled the woman's waist from behind, and his chin rested comfortably on her shoulder. She was holding her phone out in front of her to take the selfie, which, instead of being a snapshot of a lovely, shared experience, had now morphed into a chilling memorial photograph announcing their absence from the world.

Beneath, a caption read:

Police have updated their appeal for any information as to the whereabouts of Elise Ridgeway (32) and fiancé Thomas Clarkson (35), last seen…

Connor sourly thumbed the corner 'x' and closed the news story down. He was not in the mood for it.

He was not in the mood for anything except Amandine.

He put his phone down, making a mental note to charge it before he left, but then got distracted by what he thought was a smudge of dirt on his neck. He stood up and studied his reflection in his floor-length mirror. His agitation increased. He felt like he wanted to climb out of his own skin.

Fuck it.

One more won't hurt, he told himself, *if I'm quick.*

I have to do something.

He stripped off and took a final shower, just to be on the safe side.

He had to make a good impression. It was vital that he did.

You've got one shot at this, he thought, as he came once more with a desultory groan and collapsed against the shower wall, heart pounding, head against the cool, wet tiles.

He'd die if he fucked it all up again.

Now What

With the couple finally disposed of, the man from out of town relaxed as he walked back to his car, enjoying the bite of the air on his skin. It was the coldest weather he could remember, a record-breaking winter freeze. His bones ached. His fingers and nose were numb now that he was no longer occupied with strenuous labour.

Still, the burn of frost felt good. Oddly cleansing. He was used to fuggy, over-recycled air in his own house. His wife had the heating on almost all year round, creating a hot, headachy cocoon they both slobbed around in, and he realised, as winter's fingers slipped through the gaps in his clothes, how much he hated it. His home was like a horrible sweaty womb that he had been breached in for far too long.

Well, that's changing when I get back, he thought.

It was all changing for him, now.

He took a few deep breaths, inviting the ice into his lungs. It had been horribly hot inside the synthetic coverall. He could smell himself even more strongly now he'd disposed of it: sweat, the dried remains of old food. Blood. A little vomit. Ejaculate. He would have to get everything dry-cleaned before he got home. Or perhaps burn it all, to be extra safe, but he was loathe to do that. This was his favourite suit.

He was still feeling a lot of things all at once as he picked his way carefully along hoar-slicked boardwalks, slipping occasionally and righting himself by holding his arms out rigidly like a gymnast on the beam. Emotions and thoughts slithered and writhed inside him like a knot of eels. His heart thundered along in his chest as if he'd run a race. His skin prickled with a rare form of angry excitement, tempered only by the sharp pain that occasionally made itself known in the left side of his chest.

Heartburn, he told himself. *Indigestion.*

He felt his gloved hands shaking.

A slow sensation of disappointment crept across him the closer he got to his car. The sight of it in the distance felt jarring. It was a means of transport back to reality. Back to the mundane. It was a prison van headed for a town called anticlimax.

Now what, he thought.

His brain cycled through various options. Only an hour ago, he'd been sure he was heading home after the night's deeds. But what waited for him there felt impossible to return to. Too ordinary. Too commonplace. Stifling. He wasn't the same man he was a week ago, two weeks ago. He couldn't bear the thought of opening the door and seeing his wife's face in profile, lit by the TV. The smells that would greet him, cat litter and microwaved food and the godawful joss sticks she insisted on burning. He could predict, word for word, the conversation they would have on his arrival. The routine that would follow. They would eat something soggy and reheated and watch something inoffensive on one of the many streaming platforms they subscribed to, and they'd sit side by side without really touching (that part suited him just fine). Then, his wife would heave herself up and start the laborious process of putting the plates in the dishwasher and calling the cats in from outside.

Getting ready for bed, he would grind his jaw at all the familiar noises she made while doing so: the scrubbing of teeth, the hawk and spit of toothpaste, the extravagant blowing of her nose, the rustling of paper, the pebbly plops of her shit hitting water, the flushing of the toilet, the running of the tap, the fapping together of soapy palms…

His misery grew and grew the more he thought about it. As did his conviction that perhaps now was *not* the right time to go back. If he did, he was not sure he would be able to control himself around his wife, and he needed her, if only to continue to bask in the illusion that he was a normal sort of man. An ordinary, unremarkable, very married man with an ordinary, unremarkable sort of existence. Killing her would solve nothing and only curtail his new-found creative freedom before he'd had a chance to fully explore it.

In that moment, he felt as though he could do it. It wouldn't take much, after all: a quick slip down the stairs, or perhaps a push down in a full bath, or even something crushed into a drink …

He'd be fucked if he did, though.

A dead body in the city was different to a dead body sinking to the bottom of a marsh.

Despite this knowledge, the urge was there. He thought maybe it had always been there, hiding.

No, now was not the time to return home.

Sure, he missed his computer. A pang of regret hit him every time he thought about it. He had a layered, complex world in his PC that he'd carefully cultivated. Thousands of threads of nastiness woven across multiple platforms: Facebook, X, Instagram, Reddit, Discord, Mastodon, 4chan, 8chan, other very highly specific chans, Substack – where he was particularly fond of creating fake profiles and having conversations with himself on the bottom of certain people's blog posts – Pinterest, YouTube, Tumblr, BlueSky, Twitch, TikTok, Threads, Quora… He'd spent years crafting hundreds of various personalities to enable him to watch, stalk, annoy, leer at, and harass a select list of individuals who deserved it, for a number of reasons. He used a wide variety of third-party sites and apps to enable him to do his work in an almost automated fashion, but it all paled in comparison to being out in the formative cold with a pair of actual, real-life audience members. People he could finally influence. Injure. Get a real response from. The usual sneer aimed at people like him, the anonymous legion who lurked in the shadows, was that he and his ilk were too chickenshit to do anything harmful to another person in real life. That they hid behind screens but could never venture beyond that.

Well, he'd proved that theory wrong, hadn't he?

He had delivered a wonderful performance out on the broads that night. He had been witnessed. Paid attention to. He hadn't realised how fundamental that part of him it was – the need to be seen. To not be ignored. To make an impact. His urges had grown more intense as the years progressed, as his body dragged him towards middle age, like a set of black holes slowly expanding inside of him and swallowing all the other, more rational parts of his psyche. He was sure there was a term for it, the expanding. He was sure there were many words for what he was, all of them pejorative: *troll, incel* – that one pissed him off; he was anything but – *fakecel, 4chan stan, chud, keyboard warrior, rage farmer, lurker, loser, edge lord, sociopath, narcissist…*

But why waste time on words when there was a world of opportunity out there waiting for him?

The migration of his desires from an almost exclusively virtual existence to the wide, salty Norfolk Broads had transformed him. He felt like a moth wriggling from a cocoon. He had made a great leap, and he could not leap back.

Not now.

Out here he was himself, at last.

And it was surprisingly, shockingly easy to follow one's true nature, that much he had just proved.

Now that he knew this, he could see himself doing it all over again.

He spat off to one side.

One step at a time.

First, he needed a good, long sleep. His whole body ached with exertion. Until recently, he'd led a largely sedentary life. He blamed his wife for this, for her propensity to make everything "nice and cosy". It had been suffocating him slowly, he saw that now. He sometimes had violent dreams about sinking into his couch, his wife sinking beside him, mid-show, trays on their laps tipping up like capsizing boats, both of them drowning in foam and fabric, the couch stuffing rising up like surf and invading their insides, filling up their organs, squeezing them to death …

The man wobbled on the uneven planking. He was having a hard time getting his limbs to coordinate. His mind felt as if it had suddenly untethered like a floating balloon, soaring high up above him. A weird, loud buzzing sound built up in his ears.

He had to get to the car before he fainted.

You're just tired, he told himself. *You've been busy.* A wild little bubble of mirth fell from his lips, turned immediately into a sobbing sound. He swallowed it before it could fully take flight.

No time, no time.

A little driver-seat nap would do just fine, set him right.

Only an hour or two, at most, then it would be time to set off again. It couldn't be later than five or six in the evening, despite how dark it was.

The night was young yet.

He'd make sure to set an alarm, so he didn't waste any of it.

Rented Heels

Perhaps I should give up on the notion of love altogether, Amandine told herself as she finished the celery stick, brushing her teeth and flossing. She then carefully applied expensive Mac tangerine-tinted lip gloss to her pouting mouth, concentrating hard on not going over her lip line.

Perhaps there is just no one out there for me, and that's okay.

The idea didn't make her as sad as it should.

Because life is about more than love, maybe?

It's only our biological programming that…

Then why was she getting ready for what was more than likely to be another humiliating evening of misunderstandings and awkwardness?

Why put herself through this at all, if she didn't believe in love?

Naivety?

Pride?

Fear?

"Stop it," she scolded herself out loud, abruptly marching over to her wardrobe. "I know what you're doing. You're talking yourself out of it before you've even left the house."

She yanked open the wardrobe doors and eyed her reflection critically in the full-length mirror stuck to the inside-left door panel.

Tall, solemn-faced, square-shouldered. She worried that her feet were too big to be feminine. She grimaced at the cellulite that stippled her thighs, at the stretch marks at the backs of her knees. Her hands were large, the fingers too long in her opinion. She'd shorn her pubic hair down to the skin, which felt irritated, but she couldn't bear the thought of any more humiliation on that front, even if she hated the way the soft parts of her looked now. Exposed, embarrassed. A small, white string protruded from between her legs, hardly the most attractive accessory, but the timing couldn't be helped. She suspected Connor would be disappointed, but undeterred. A surprising number of men didn't care about all that, she had learned.

Her tits looked good, she conceded.

The Miracle Word on her belly glared at her in reverse.

EVOL, it read.

It didn't look or feel very miraculous when viewed backwards. It looked angry, accusatory. Like *RED RUM* in the mirror in that movie. She had forgotten that words got flipped in reflections. Levography, they called that.

Is it less powerful back to front?

Should I wash it off?

She shook her head.

"Behave," she admonished. "Get dressed."

Another alarm dinged across the room.

Amandine checked her phone.

Twenty minutes before she needed to leave.

No time left to waste.

She chose an outfit that was revealing but not *too* revealing, pretty and feminine but not *too* girly or prudish, fun and frivolous but not *too* quirky, because the internet told her men didn't like quirky women, or overtly sexual women, nor overtly girlish women; *it is a fine line*, the experts said, *between Whore and*

More, and Amandine had often thought, well, what the fuck *do* men like if they don't like any of those things? But she did as instructed. After all, they were the experts, which Amandine, still single at thirty-three, accepted that she was not. She found other people's expectations confusing, along with the fact that a person could say one thing (*you look nice, I really see this going somewhere*) and mean another thing entirely (*I'm not going to call you after we fuck*), which seemed like a colossal waste of energy to her, but this is why she leant on external advice so much.

She thought, when she was assembled, that the internet would be proud of her. Her choice of outfit was deliberately designed to disguise the fact that she struggled with socialising, and the effect was immediately convincing, even to her eyes. Her cotton dress, new and fashionable, was emerald green and dipped at the neckline to show some cleavage, *but not the whole meal*, as advised. The hem ended just above the knee, and she paired it with dark, sheer stockings and a small, knitted cardigan that would just about fit underneath a new (second-hand) leather jacket. To her wrist, she buckled a delicate silver watch (once belonging to her mother). The leather strap conveniently concealed the biro Reminder Word scrawled underneath. She further accessorised with a simple chain around her neck (given to her by her father), before finishing off the look with tiny silver hoops in her ears. From each hoop, a small silver heart dangled.

She checked the time on her phone again and slid into a pair of high heels, wincing. She didn't usually go for heels, being tall enough as it was, and found them somewhat idiotic, changing the way she walked, stood, held herself, but these had cushioned pads sewn into the soles to protect the balls of her feet, and ankle straps that prevented the shoes from slipping off every time she lifted a leg.

Besides, Connor had mentioned he had a thing for heels, so she thought she'd oblige.

She took an experimental step forward, wobbled, but soon got used to balancing her weight differently, and, as she paced experimentally around her room, she found that on this occasion she quite liked the sensation of being larger than usual. It made her feel more powerful.

The bloody Miracle Word had dried now, but she could feel the skin underneath the word tugging. It felt tight, a little crusty when she moved. Her dress caught on the blood, making her aware of a faint snagging sensation.

A person should always have secrets, she thought.

Amandine took a deep breath. She was, despite telling herself otherwise, nervous. Her mind was filled with a dozen competing thoughts, noises, feelings, sounds. Overwhelm loomed – which, in turn, made her suddenly angry.

Rather than ruminate any further, she snatched up her handbag and made her way downstairs. She went step by step carefully, conscious of not wanting to twist an ankle before she'd even left the house. *So much danger wrapped up in the simple act of appearing presentable,* she fumed. The anger she felt as she hobbled down each step swelled and turned outwards. Would *he* be putting himself in a similarly idiotic position, tottering around like a tortured bird on stilts? Squeezing himself into a padded bra? Plucking and shaving and moisturising and blow-drying and exfoliating and applying war-paint and…

No, he would not.

He might be wearing a tie, perhaps some nice leather shoes, but otherwise he would be comfortable, wouldn't he?

He would arrive in a thick winter jacket, chosen for the weather rather than aesthetics. Her own quilted, comfortable winter coat was a dreary colour, well-worn around the hood and completely engulfed her. Practical, but not sexy. Not viable Date Night gear. The internet had expressly forbidden her from wearing it, so she was prepared for a freezing, uncomfortable evening travelling to and from the restaurant.

The injustice of this got to her. Mainly because she allowed it to. She was in the mood to be unsettled, to ruffle her own feathers.

"It's not fair," she muttered, clinging to the handrail for dear life and realising she should have waited until *after* the stairs to put her shoes on. Rookie mistake.

Her mood plummeted the further down she teetered.

Then, she missed the last step and overshot, her leg coming down too fast at the end of the stairs. Jarring pain shot unexpectedly up both her shins. She kicked back her right foot reflexively to try and rub her leg, and the heel of her shoe caught on the hem of her dress, tearing a hole in it before she managed to unhook herself.

"Oh, go and get *fucked*!" she shouted.

The words were eaten by the silence of her empty house. Another mirror, this one hung in the hallway, presented the image of a woman of indeterminate age who was dressed nicely in everything except facial expression.

Amandine saw her own twisted features, realised she was winding herself up, like a mechanical toy.

Getting your knickers in a twist over nothing.

Stop it, Amandine. Stop.

She sucked in a deep breath, held it while she checked her makeup again, smoothing down her hair with clammy, shaking hands. Then she twisted to get a better look at the hole in the dress. From what she could see, it was small, near the hem at the back – barely noticeable at all, especially if sitting down. She could tuck that part of the skirt beneath her. Her date would be none the wiser. Rented heels, holey hems. Tiny deceptions, easy to maintain.

The bigger deceptions: I'm a normal person; I have a normal lifestyle and appetites and opinions and…

Just get through tonight.

"He'd better fucking appreciate the effort I've gone to," Amandine said to her reflection.

And she wished, for the dozenth time that day, that her mother was still alive to talk to instead.

Decisions

Connor decided at the last minute to match Amandine and get a taxi. He needed to drink on this date. If he drove, he'd have to leave his dad's Skoda at the pub and schlep all the way back to get it the next day. Cars left in quiet pub car parks overnight tended to get broken into, but Connor was less concerned about that and more concerned with getting lucky post-date.

He admitted to himself that this was a tactical move: if he came without his car, it meant he could persuade Amandine to share a cab home. To split the cost, he'd tell her. If she ended up at his place, so much the better. If she didn't, he would tell the driver to drop her off first, and then Connor would have her address, so he could send her flowers the next day and hopefully seal the deal. Win-win.

Connor imagined waking up alongside Amandine in the morning, naked and perhaps a little hungover. He imagined rolling to her, spooning, hands travelling around her ribcage to cup her spectacular breasts, pushing his erection into the small of her back, nudging her legs apart, feeling the wetness of her against the tip of his...

Jesus, Connor!

Wine would help.

He would buy a nice expensive bottle from the pub to bring home and hope it would lower some of her defences. He looked around, wondering if his place was tidy enough. The house he shared with his dad reeked of bachelor-pad despair, sparsely furnished and decorated in a dull, low-maintenance fashion. Standard Ikea furniture, magnolia-white walls, beige carpet.

Don't get ahead of yourself, sonny, Dad's voice warned him as he checked his taxi app on his phone.

You might not be getting intimate with anyone after this date but your own right hand.

Again.

Before he ordered his ride, Connor shot his dad a text. He hadn't heard from him for a while, and they liked to check in on each other when he was away.

Off out on a date, he typed, no further details provided. *When do you get back?*

The reply came almost immediately.

Not for another week, at least.

How come? Connor had been expecting him back in two days.

Delayed by a supplier. A right shitshow here.

Shame, Connor said, and he meant it. He missed his old man when he was off on his business trips. The house felt so quiet without him. He'd never been very good at being alone.

Good luck for the date! His dad sounded pleased for him.

Thanks! Connor said, exclamation mark for exclamation mark.

Then his dad spoiled it.

Don't scare her off like the last one, eh? ;)

Connor composed a tetchy response. Deleted it.

The old boy had a point, he supposed.

A Nap

The car was no warmer on the inside than it was on the outside, as the man discovered when he slid into the driver's seat. Shivering, he fired the engine, whacked the heater up to maximum and adjusted his seat so it leaned as far back as possible. He was tired enough to sleep standing up, but this was better.

Despite his exhaustion, the building warmth, the rattling, hypnotic idle of the engine and the strange chemical smell that began to leak out of the glove box, sleep eluded him. His brain was having a hard time letting go of the day's events. As he closed his eyes, he saw a flashing succession of images and recollections: hands bound and bloodied, tears sliding down filthy cheeks, otters playing, reeds rippling, flesh separating beneath a blade's press, glazed corneas, frost-crisped hair, sunrise, sunset, icicles, a severed hand in a cool box...

The image of the hand jerked him awake. He had forgotten all about that.

He sat up, switched off the heat, suddenly worried he'd sped up the hand's decomposition. Climbing out of the car, he went round to the boot and struggled with the faulty catch.

The boot popped eventually. Inside, he saw the large blue plastic cool box he'd bought from a supermarket ten miles down the road. Next to it lay a dry bunch of roses wrapped in cellophane, price sticker still attached. Next to that, a canvas tool bag held a curved saw-like tool with a serrated edge and a stubby handle, a spare pair of secateurs, some blue rubble sacks, a hacksaw with a brand-new blade, zip ties, another coverall, still sealed in its cellophane wrapper, a pack of surgical gloves, and some disinfectant wipes.

Behind the tool bag lay a long, old-fashioned duck-hunting shotgun. 'Wildfowling' they called it round here. The gun was an antique, but it still worked. Looking at it always gave him a thrill. He'd been after a weapon like this for a while and had finally worked up the courage to go into a hunting shop in a small town he'd detoured through last week. The owner of Wisbech Gun & Tackle had been very helpful, at first. "A heavy pellet will kill at sixty yards," he'd said, showing off the range of guns and shot types proudly, "but you have to be damn good with your aim. Small shot will kill something smaller and closer, at about ten yards, but ruin the bird for the table."

"Ruin?"

"Fill them full of shot," the store owner explained. "Makes for an uncomfortable dinner if you have to keep spitting them little balls out. I've cracked a few teeth in my time."

"Oh," the man had said. He hadn't thought of that. He just assumed if you pointed a gun at a living thing and shot them with it, they died, and that was that.

"You need to strike a balance with load, shot type, and choke…" The owner prattled on for several minutes without drawing breath.

When he stopped, the man asked the question he'd been meaning to ask all along.

"So, what if you're shooting something… larger than a bird?"

"You'd need a special..." The owner stopped, choosing his next words carefully. "What exactly are you thinking, target-wise?"

"Deer," the man said, noncommittally. "My friend has a place up in Scotland..."

The store owner relaxed.

"Oh, well, for deer I'd recommend something entirely different, you want the..."

The man zoned out again until the store owner started talking about a gun licence, which, of course, he didn't have. He'd taken off pretty fast after that, aware suddenly that there was CCTV rigged up in the shop and kicking himself for not having checked earlier.

Later, he Googled local wildfowling clubs, and found, to his delight, several adverts for used guns on their websites.

One, in particular, seemed too good to be true:

FREE TO A GOOD HOME!

Single barrel 12g shotgun.

Licence holders only.
Location: Stiffkey, Norfolk.
Collect in person only.
Email: enquiries@marigoldfarm.aol.com
Please send your name, telephone number and a legible copy of your SGC – Front sheet only!

An SGC was a Shot Gun Certificate. It turned out to be an easy document to forge. The email accepting his faked certificate and confirming the collection address came back so poorly spelled and clumsily typed, the man suspected he was likely dealing with a pensioner, or at least someone not used to a computer.

His suspicions were confirmed when he drove out to the remote farmhouse on the edges of Stiffkey to collect the gun. He was greeted by an elderly woman who treated him like cavalry to the rescue. She'd been trying desperately to offload her recently deceased husband's stash of hunting weapons, but nobody, she complained, seemed to want them, for love nor money.

"Oh, thank goodness you're here," she'd quavered, showing him into a large, dusty shed full of tackle and hunting paraphernalia. "I've been trying to get rid of the damn thing for months."

She unhooked a long, inelegant weapon from some brackets on the shed wall and almost shoved it at him, along with a dozen boxes of something called "Fiocchi 12 Gauge 2-3/4 Inch Shell, 6-Shot".

It had been that easy. She hadn't wanted money. She hadn't wanted to see his licence. She just wanted the gun to be gone.

On his way out, the man spotted something hanging on the wall of the shed.

"What's that?" he asked, his hands sweating with excitement. He kept his voice flat, disinterested.

The old woman had squinted at the tool he'd pointed to. "Oh, my husband used to help his brother out with reed cutting every year. That's a weed hook, a Silverline. Good one, not a speck of rust. You can take that too, if you like. I don't need it, do I?"

The man nodded and unhooked the curved, serrated tool from its bracket. He hefted it in his hand, thought about swiping it right, planting it hard into the vulnerable old lady's neck, then dragging back to the left, wondering what the hook's teeth would feel like as they ripped through wobbly flesh and gristle and cartilage.

"Oh, and these need a good home," the old woman went on to say. The man realised two things: that she was not in the slightest bit afraid of him, and that he would need to leave before she foisted the entire contents of her husband's shed on him. "These are brand new, never used." She had pulled a pair of secateurs out of a plastic trug resting on a table. "Think you can find a use for them?"

The man nodded. The secateur blades were wickedly sharp, as he found when he thumbed one experimentally and nicked himself. He had a pair already, but these were, as yet, unused.

"I'm fairly sure I can find plenty of things to do with those," he said, smiling.

When he bid her goodbye, he looked the old woman earnestly in the eyes.

"You should be more careful with who you let in here, you know. There are some strange people out there."

The old woman had flapped a hand at him in dismissal. "Oh, I'm too old to care much about that sort of thing," she said. "Who would be interested in an old leather boot like me?"

The man said nothing but had hidden behind a large bush after their goodbyes and watched her go back inside. She really was very vulnerable out here. She lived entirely alone in that massive old farmhouse. The nearest neighbour was a good mile or so down the road. If something were to happen to her...

It could be a good base, he told himself. *If you need one.*

It was useful to have options.

Several YouTube tutorials later, the man had a loaded shotgun in the boot of his car. You could get anyone to do anything with one of these pointed in their face, he reasoned. A stocked promise, violence-in-waiting. So was the weed hook.

But the weapons were not why he was here, staring into the boot.

The man flipped up the lid of the cool box, peered in. His head torch beam lit up several blood-smeared plastic zip-lock bags lying at the bottom.

He took out the largest bag, smiling as he felt its familiar shape.

Back in the driver's seat, he carefully extracted the woman's hand from its plastic shroud and examined it closely. The hand seemed fine, mostly. The ragged flesh around the severance site was more discoloured than he liked, already, and the skin had taken on an odd texture in parts, but otherwise, the fingers were still elegant and slender, the nails red and shiny – she'd had one of those expensive gel manicures where the polish never seemed to chip or flake off – and the engagement ring sat snug on the ring finger, a little tighter than it had been before he'd met her. He doubted she minded now.

With a happy sigh, he slid his hand into the disembodied one, holding it so he looked to be shaking on an important business decision, then loosened his grip, attempting to entwine his fingers with the dry, dead digits like he'd seen lovers do countless times in countless places: on television, at the cinema, in real life. He imagined the woman the hand had belonged to, gazing at him in wonder and fright. He had been able to see his own significance in her eyes before she died, and it had made him feel twenty feet tall.

"Can't resist me now, can you?" he grunted, basking in the remembrance.

And yet, she could. Even in death, her flesh refused to cooperate. The hand stubbornly withstood his manipulations. He had to forcibly bend her fingers to accommodate him.

When he was finally entangled, he groaned loudly in comfort.

Strangely, he didn't enjoy holding hands with his wife. Avoided doing so whenever possible. She was often clammy and clingy, but this...

This felt different altogether.

He laid their intertwined hands carefully on his lap, enjoying the weight on himself. Then he wrapped his free arm tight around his ribs to conserve heat.

For now, the man didn't care. He was warmed internally by the glow of his own accomplishments. He leaned back, felt sleep coming for him, fast and hungry. He closed his eyes, fell into oblivion quickly, the severed hand resting on his crotch, it's touch cold and stiff and comforting, just the way he'd always imagined it.

Everything is Fine

Amandine tried to fight off an encroaching panic attack. Her chest felt as if it was going to explode. Her fingers tingled. She felt cold and started to shiver.

You're being an idiot.

You're being a coward.

You haven't even met him yet.

Give the man a chance, she told herself.

She breathed out, slowly, slowly, slowly, counting, trying to ground herself.

Fine.

You're fine.

But was it fine?

It didn't feel fine.

Something felt wrong.

She wasn't sure what, but there was a mounting sense of dread and foreboding.

A warning going off somewhere deep inside.

Perhaps it wasn't too late to cancel.

She pulled out her phone. Her trembling finger hovered over the text messages that filled her screen. He'd sent quite a lot over the last few months. She'd never thought about it much before, but now that she looked…

She scrolled up and up.

Her sense of dread intensified.

There were hundreds of texts. On average, three or four to each one she had sent. Paragraphs in reply to her single sentences. Memes. Gifs. Emojis. Links. Songs. Voice notes. There seemed to be no end to him trying to get her attention. Her thumb worked the screen. She'd been roundly oblivious to how intense his approach was, perhaps because she only checked her phone once or twice a day.

Or perhaps…

She accepted the possibility that perhaps she'd turned a deliberate blind eye to Connor's neediness.

Why?

Because she didn't hate him as much as she'd hated the others?

Because she couldn't face the despair of knowing she'd wasted energy on yet another shitty person?

No, that wasn't fair. It was more than that. She liked him, genuinely, or at least she *thought* she liked the version of himself he had shown so far.

She was suddenly shocked at how much of his pushiness she'd seemingly glossed over, for the barest of reasons: because he'd shown a modicum of decency, because he was attractive, halfway charming, and vulnerable, too. Because he could string together a coherent, engaging text.

Because she was lonely.

Now she felt as if she had been manipulated into this date.

Is that why she was on the verge of panic?

Or was she overreacting?

She hated that she could not trust her own sense of reality.

Trepidation rising, she reversed her scrolling, searching for Connor's most recent text.

Look forward to meeting you then, he'd said. Civil and polite.

You too, she'd replied.

Smiley face emoji.

Wink face emoji.

There was nothing immediately obvious to worry about, not from the words on her screen. But something about the inanely grinning round yellow faces made her skin crawl.

The panic did not subside. If anything, this second-guessing of everything made Amandine feel worse.

It's not too late, she reasoned. *To cancel.*

All it would take was one text.

One message.

I'm sorry, something has come up.

I'm sorry, I'm sick.

I'm sorry, I fell down the stairs because of the stupid fucking idiotic shoes I wore to try and impress you and broke my neck.

I'm sorry, a plane crashed into my house.

Everything is on fire.

I have herpes.

Or maybe the truth.

I'm sorry, but I can't come tonight because I'm scared.

Of something going wrong.

Of you being a creep.

Of not actually liking you in person.

Of realising that nobody will ever really suit me, or understand me, and I don't want to pretend anymore, I don't want to settle.

Frowny face emoji.

"For god's sake, Amandine!" She slapped herself hard across the face. "Stop it!"

The slap was loud. A shocked Amandine gazed back from the mirror.

A red mark began to spread across her carefully applied makeup.

Fuck.

"Oh, no, no," she moaned, grabbing a powder compact from her bag and patting it hastily over the redness.

No, no!

If you cancel, the internet will be disappointed in you.

She stopped patting her face, pulled up a browser on her phone and typed frantically into the search bar.

The article that popped up at the top of the search results read:

7 Times You Should Not Feel Guilty About Cancelling a Date.

Here we go, she thought. *Let's see if there's a valid excuse here.*

Reason 1: When you've had the longest week, ever.

Amandine sighed, because she hadn't. She'd had a week exactly like the one before and the one after. Boring, quiet, insular. Nothing taxing.

Not really a valid excuse.

Reason 2: When you have nothing to wear.

Amandine looked down at her outfit. No dice.

Reason 3: When tea sounds better than vodka.

Amandine rolled her eyes.

Reason 4: When you'd rather be sweaty.

This one produced a twinge of guilt for the gym membership she paid for but never used.

Reason 5: When you just really want alone time.

Amandine was always alone. She wanted the opposite of alone time, hence agreeing to the date.

Reason 6: When you're just not into him.

She chewed her lip over that one. How did she know if she was into him or not until she'd met him? Wasn't that the whole point of going out to dinner with someone?

Reason 7: When your girlfriends call.

Amandine swiped the article away petulantly. She didn't have any girlfriends. If she did, she might not be such a nervous fucking wreck all the time, she thought.

"It's fine," Amandine said out loud, realising she couldn't come up with a good enough reason to cancel the date at short notice beyond this odd crawly feeling in her stomach and fingers.

Fine.

She did not cancel.

Instead, she opened the notes app on her phone and drew another Miracle Word, in capital letters, like she always did, on a fresh notepad screen. She had to do it with her index fingertip, rather than type the word, or it wouldn't count.

STRENGTH, it said, the writing childish and wobbly.

The Miracle Word worked, like always. The panicky feeling subsided, a little. She closed the notepad app, went to open another. A weather warning notification from the Met Office slid across the screen.

Yellow Warning: Snow and Ice, it said. *Extreme Cold.* She thumbed it away.

Another notification took its place: a news app.

Concerns grow for missing couple last seen…

Exasperated, she flicked that away too and finally got to the app she needed.

A few taps later, and another notification.

Your driver is on the way.

There, she told herself.

Now you HAVE to go.

Taxi ordered, she loitered by the front door, checking and rechecking that she had everything.

Keys.

Purse.

Money.

Phone.

Address of the restaurant.

Tampons.

Rape alarm.

You never know, she thought.

Change of plan

The man slept for an hour. Once awake, he masturbated. Relieving himself was a grind. He was tired and sore from the hard labour he'd put his body through. The freezing temperatures didn't help much either. There were swirling, fern-like frost patterns on the car windows, glittering as his head torch beam bounced off them.

He pushed through the discomfort, knowing it was necessary.

His post-nap orgasm was perfunctory, tactical. Three-handed.

The severed palm was easy to wipe clean.

Ignoring the surge of self-hatred that always followed the expulsion of his gouting ropes of yellowish-white ejaculate (he'd been caught doing it once as a teenager, over a snipped-out picture of a Page Three girl he'd swiped from a friend at school, and had never recovered from the look of revulsion on his mother's face), he set about scraping the ice off the windscreen and side windows with an old CD case lid, cursing as the night bit at his fingers and ears and nose. He had no memory of it being this cold, ever. It was all over the news, *a record-breaking freeze*. The homeless and elderly were dying in droves. Pipes were bursting in the streets. The sea had frozen in places along the coastline. Winter crops were destroyed.

He wondered if the waters of Hickling Broad could freeze over entirely. The remains he'd dumped wouldn't rot, he realised, in temperatures like this. They would sit there, perfectly preserved, until spring. He might have to fish them out and deposit them somewhere else.

But that was a problem for another day.

The man got back in his ancient Nissan and fired up the engine. A scented air freshener hanging from the rear-view mirror leaked out a weak approximation of pine. His wife had given it to him for Christmas. The words LOVE BUG were printed on it.

The brilliant glare in the narrow strip of mirror reflection gave him a moment of confusion. He'd left his head torch on. He pressed the button, so the light dimmed rather than clicked off. This afforded him a clear view of his own reflection.

His glasses and the skin of his face were the wrong colour, a mottled red.

The penny dropped.

You forgot your face, he thought, annoyed.

He reached into a pocket on the driver-side door and pulled out another packet of half-dried disinfectant wipes, giving his face and neck above his bowtie a thorough going-over until it was presentable.

Better.

His glasses were still smeared and spattered with blood, though. He spat on the lenses and rubbed them, right eye, left eye, on the fabric of each of his dirty trouser legs.

Holding them up to the light, he made a face.

Good enough.

He clicked off his head torch, put the car into reverse, and slowly backed out of the concealed patch of land he'd parked in. He saw no other cars or people, but then he didn't expect to. He fancied, not for the first time, that he was the only living creature left on the Earth, and half-thought he might find, on leaving Hickling Broad, that this fancy was in fact reality, that the silence was now permanent. That all the residents of the villages, towns and cities had gone away forever, leaving only him, and the birds in the sky, and the severed hand lying on the seat next to him, *riding shotgun*, he thought, chuckling to himself. It was an intoxicating idea, that he owned the world now, and was free to do exactly as he liked.

The meek shall inherit the earth, except, he long longer wanted to be meek.

He wanted to be more.

He hauled the Nissan around with a clumsy three-point turn, gears crunching in protest at each point, then headed off into the countryside along a potholed, winding road patched with ice that made his wheels spin if he drove too fast.

At the end of the road there was a blind junction. He usually turned right here, towards the A-road that would take him to the city, but he wasn't ready for that. So, he turned left, towards the coast. It was difficult driving, the night was thick, and the roads were rarely lit beyond the odd, ancient lamp sporadically placed near a layby or passing place. He had to rely on the cat's eyes running down the middle of the road to make sure he didn't steer off the tarmac, and was grateful for the high, thick hedges running along each side of him. When the hedges broke up, he glimpsed the bright spots of deer eyes in the fields through the gaps, and the bobbing, white flash of rabbit's tails, all of whom bounded away as his roaring, stuttering engine approached.

What was that song his grandfather used to sing?

Run, rabbit, run, rabbit, run, run, run…

He hadn't gone too far before he spotted the pub.

It was called the Boat Inn. It looked like one of those once-smoky, sleepy country boozers that had since been solidly gentrified. *Gastropubs,* he thought, shaking his head in disgust.

The closer he got, the more he hated the building: the brickwork in the headlight beam was clean and well-pointed, the glowing window casements newly painted, the roof sharply thatched with freshly cut reeds and topped with a trio of pheasants fashioned from hay and wire. Hanging baskets would be full of flowers come the summer. Fairy lights adorned the bushes surrounding the car park, the trellises on the walls of the pub, and even wound up the chimney stacks, so the whole thing looked like a tacky Christmas display. It gave off a twinkling faux radiance that blotted out the starlight with a ruthless, gaudy efficiency.

The man sneered, slowing as the pub drew near.

A sandwich board standing by the roadside caught his eye. It, too, was framed with fairy lights, so he could easily read the words written there in bright pink chalk:

Norfolk's most romantic pub!

Underneath: *Rooms Available.*

The man felt his guts roil in response.

He was starving, he realised. A good home-cooked pub meal would set him right, he thought. Thick-cut chips. A burger. Sauce in sachets. Tons of vinegar. A good IPA.

Well, why not, he thought, and veered off into the car park.

Maybe he'd get a room for the night, too.

He made sure to put the hand back in the cool box. With the boot once again open, he hesitated briefly, then snatched up the bunch of dying roses in their cellophane before slamming the door down. Perhaps he'd find someone to give them to, inside. Perhaps not.

Roses are red, violets are blue…

People fucking suck, and so do you.

Can't Get the Service These Days

The pub foyer was empty when he entered. A reception desk near the front door sported a vase full of dried flowers, more fairy lights, and a small brass service bell with a heart-shaped handle on top. He could smell woodsmoke and chip-fat, and bleach from the toilets.

The man picked up the bell and rang it without pause.

"Alright, alright, I'm *coming*!" came an irritated reply from the bowels of the building, which was low-ceilinged, and full of narrow passageways. As such, the man couldn't see who had answered until she popped out of a small, squat door behind the desk counter. Only when she was fully present did he stop ringing the bell.

"How can I – oh!" the young woman said, squinting and holding up her hands to block out a light that suddenly shone on her face.

The man had clicked his head torch to the brightest beam while he'd been waiting.

"Sorry," he mumbled, enjoying her discomfort. He clicked off the beam and pulled the contraption off his head, pocketing it. "Forgot about this." The lie went unanswered. The woman was now looking at his forehead, frowning. He could feel where the strap had been, knew it had left a mark, for the band was tight. Messed up his hair, too, no doubt.

Good, he thought. He knew he looked weird. He liked it when the first impression people had of him was confusing. Confusion meant abdication of control, an empty seat into which he could slide.

He felt the familiar hot-sewage surge of excitement flood his nervous system.

The girl clicked her tongue, annoyed. "Almost blinded me," she remarked.

"You serving food?"

"This is a pub, sir," the girl quipped.

He laughed humourlessly, shifted his weight from foot to foot.

"I was thinking of eating, if you had a table free, and then maybe… a room for the night?"

"Sure thing." The girl turned to a large, low shelf behind her. She was dressed, he saw, in waitress whites over a short black skirt and sheer black tights, with black sneakers finishing the outfit. She bent over and he got a good, long look at the gusset of her white thong showing under the gossamer tights. There was a small soft bulge there that he longed to jam his fingers into. He'd rip through the tights first, because it was better that way.

The girl pulled a large reservation book off the shelf and brought it back to the counter, opening it up.

"We've got two nice singles, one with an ensuite," she said, "and a double, breakfast included. Or there's the honeymoon suite if you're meeting someone?"

Her eyes went to the dying roses clutched in the man's hand.

He hid them behind his back, not really understanding why he did this.

"Honeymoon suite sounds fine," he replied. It would save him having to sleep in his car during the coldest night of the year. "How much?"

"Room rate is two hundred and thirty pounds a night," the girl replied, cheerfully.

The man scowled. *Fucking daylight robbery.*

"Maybe I'll eat first, then decide," he said eventually, trying not to lose face.

"Sure thing."

The reservation book snapped shut with a loud, disapproving noise.

The girl looked at him strangely from beneath lowered lashes. Wrinkled her nose, flared her nostrils.

A second later, he understood why.

She'd got a whiff of him.

He moved closer. *Sniff it up, bitch,* he thought, pleased at her reaction.

Her hand went reflexively to her mouth as she struggled to conceal her disgust.

He did smell ripe; he was willing to concede. It hadn't been as bad or noticeable outside in the fresh air, but in the bleached sanctum of the spick-and-span pub, he was more obvious.

"Table for two?" the girl asked, in a strangled tone. Her expression was faintly disbelieving, as if she couldn't countenance that a person could reek as much as he did.

"One," he corrected. "Will you be serving me?"

The girl plastered a cold, tight smile on her face.

"This way, please."

The familiar arousal welled up in him as she stalked off. *Hoity-toity,* he thought, staring at her retreating arse.

Did she think she was too good to serve him?

That he wasn't good enough to eat in this fancy fucking over-the-top, poncey pub?

Did a little dirt and grime mean he wasn't good enough for all the fairy lights?

He was being nice, wasn't he?

What more did these fucking people want?

He fell into a rich fantasy about spanking the girl with a plank of wood as she showed him to a small, poorly appointed table in the middle of a deserted dining room overlooking the edges of Hickling Broad. He'd hoist her up and lay her across his lap and thrash the shit out of her, and if he had his way, he thought, pulling out his seat, she'd never walk straight again.

"No problem," she said. "I'll be back in a moment with–"

"Can't I take that one over there?" he interrupted, pointing to a much larger table next to the large glass viewing window that overlooked the marshes.

"That one's reserved," the waitress muttered, oblivious to the violent play still rolling in his mind. "Drink?"

"Pint of IPA." He felt like grabbing her, his fingers itched, but he managed to keep a lid on it as he sat down.

"We've got Malt Coast and that's it," the waitress replied, curt and cold.

She left before he could approve the beer.

Phone is Weapon

The man pulled out his phone. Usually, the girl's rudeness would have bothered him far more, but luckily for her, he was still sated from his excursion to the broads.

He swept his fingers over a cracked screen encrusted with gunk. He'd need a new phone soon. His wife kept telling him so, which was partly why he resisted, but she was right. He'd abused this one too much.

There were a variety of things on his device to keep him occupied as he waited for the waitress to return with his beer and a menu. He loaded up his favourite porn site, scrolling through all the newest uploads on the home page, letting the previews autoplay before refining his search with his trusty, well-worn, "safe to view in public" keywords, which erred on the tame side: *swingers, anal, vintage full movie, game of thrones, chastity, oiled, cuck, domination, humiliation, golden showers, men cumming compilation, whips, first time, orgy, dogging, fake taxi, tied up, delivery man, facial, edging, bound, captive...* He found these terms soothing, like a nursery rhyme or a lullaby. He tapped through each video that came up in twenty-second bursts, his attention not held for any longer than that. This was appetiser porn for him, amuse-bouche they called it (*amused bush*), or was that something else? It didn't matter. It staved off boredom and helped pass the time. The stuff he *really* liked, that really got him going, was on his PC at home, on a special hard drive (his "get hard drive"), under encryption.

But this would do while he waited.

He kept the volume down, and the screen brightness low, idly rubbing his left inner thigh with one hand while he manipulated his phone with the other. He skirted around his cock half-heartedly, a fiddly gesture more than anything, and found, after ten minutes, that he wasn't really in the mood to get hard. There wasn't an audience, for one thing. Besides, his stomach was too angry at him. He hadn't eaten in nearly twenty hours.

He shut down the porn and started his next familiar ritual.

Checking up on the women he called "his favourite things to hate".

The man opened the newsletter of a self-professed "up-and-coming model and artist" he liked (he'd once left a comment on a post of hers along the lines of *I'm up, and I'm coming*, but she hadn't found it funny), who he'd first discovered on Instagram. She was a conundrum to him. She didn't seem to have many real talents beyond having spectacular tits and being very good at social media, and he was both fascinated and angered by this. She presented a wholesome, pleasant, and humorous persona alongside carefully staged, gratuitously needy selfies, and he wasn't fooled by it for a moment, but it nevertheless got under his skin, and the skin of many others, apparently: her various social accounts had hundreds of thousands of followers, and she had been able, by her own admission, to quit her boring office job and go full time with her art and other pursuits as a result. Those other pursuits being: wearing the makeup and clothes that people sent her and staying in hotels that invited her free of charge in exchange for posting about them on her accounts. An "influencer", they called that. Influencing what? A whole generation of new, vacuous, talentless bitches to do the same thing?

But then why wouldn't they? He hate-scrolled to her last post. Attractive people always had it easier; it was a basic law of the universe. Society was willing to overlook mediocrity when it came packaged with perfect breasts and milky skin and big green eyes. If he had been more aesthetically blessed, he might have tried to capitalise on it too. He wished she'd ease up on the humble, self-deprecating captions. Whenever she tried to minimise her success or beauty it felt like an insult. A deception. Did she really think that humble bragging worked on people? She was undoubtedly a bitch, behind the scenes, that much was glaringly obvious. Everybody knew social media was all fake, so why bother lying?

He had tried to point this out to her several times, but she had him blocked on most channels. He had so many alt accounts it didn't matter; he could always keep an eye on what she was up to.

And what she was up to wasn't very nice, it turned out. He was certain, on reading, that she'd written her latest newsletter post about him specifically, but she'd been clever about it. Lots of layers and hints and subtleties to unpack, as if she thought she was intelligent enough to deceive him.

He snorted, read and re-read the post five times, knowing it word for word already, but examining each sentence carefully anyway, finding nothing new beyond what he already understood: that she was getting tired of his harassment of her, and was skirting around the edges of threatening him with a lawsuit if he didn't cease and desist.

Good luck with that, he thought.

He exited the post and flicked over to her Instagram, using his latest fake profile to view the account. Her most recent selfie was as gorgeous and painfully executed as ever: she was in her house, by a window, where the natural light was best, as all vain bitches seemed to know, and smiling as she held up an artwork print. The caption read: *Available now on Redbubble!* The art was worse than mediocre, a mishmash of badly drawn leaves and glittery stars, but she was cleverly posting with a considerable amount of cleavage on show so it would sell.

He zoomed in on the selfie, specifically homing in on the reflection in her eyes. He was sure the striped lines he could just about make out across her irises meant she had venetian blinds hung in the window, which helped him out enormously, because he was almost certain he had her precise street address figured out, having sleuthed for hours and hours on her various accounts while his wife slept soundly in the room next door to his study.

He zoomed in further, as far as he could go, and as he stared at the grainy block of colours on the screen, he knew he was right. A surge of victory welled up inside him, and he smiled.

Definitely venetian blinds in the windows.

All he had to do now was take a drive down that street and eliminate the houses without blinds in the windows, and he'd narrow it down even further.

Keep posting, slag, he thought to himself, relaxing back in his seat as the welcome warmth of the pub sank into his bones. *You'll dox yourself eventually; I know you will.*

He couldn't resist leaving a comment under the selfie: *gorgeous face, awful body, you should lose some weight to even out the difference imo.*

Seconds later he was blocked again, as he knew he would be.

It didn't matter. Creating a new account took moments.

The miserable waitress showed no signs of arriving with his beer anytime soon, or the menu, so he came out of the model's Instagram and scrolled through the stories of several other women on his hit list who had also blocked him. One story in particular appealed to him: a dark-skinned woman was winking playfully up into the camera's lens, her mouth open, the tip of her tongue caressing one of her incisors. She had one hand arched across her breastbone, drawing attention to her cleavage and the perfect round swell of her tits.

The man grabbed a screenshot, then went into the settings of his phone and changed his lock screen to this new selfie, feeling a like he had put the woman in a tiny, flat cage for his own pleasure. She would have no idea he owned her image in this manner, that it would stare out from his phone every time he picked it up. He liked that; he liked the ease of it. In the old days, he'd tried to take his own photos, from a distance, of course, even bought a miniature video camera to film women going about their business as he went about his, but these days that wasn't necessary. The stupid creatures were so intent on documenting every moment of their own lives that their images, moving or static, had become fair game, prime digital real estate, and what he did with them was up to him.

It wasn't that he wouldn't prefer something more meaningful, as far as associations went. He had tried to reach out to women the old-fashioned way. They always replied at first, typing out responses full of emojis of blushing faces with hearts around them or hands templed in gratitude as he flattered and complimented, but the replies invariably dried up as he continued his attentions, and he could never fully understand why. He knew he was saying all the right things: *you're so beautiful, you're so talented, I love your hair/eyes/smile, you must have so many men in your dms, can I show you my dick, here's a photo of my cum in the palm of my hand, I was thinking about u,* but they always stopped interacting.

That left him only one option: to hassle, and to creep. He couldn't figure out another way to get to these women. If he ignored them, they didn't notice. If he flattered them, they politely accepted the compliments then ignored him anyway. If he messaged every day, their replies grew terse and annoyed and dwindled off and eventually stopped abruptly like a plugged leak before he was blocked.

He'd tried other things: sending gifts, comments, replies, tags, emails, dms; he'd tried to play the pity card more than once, to no avail – *I don't socialise well* (true), *I'm an alcoholic* (not true), *I'm lonely* (partially true), *I have dyslexia* (he didn't), *I'm autistic* (he wasn't)... He'd even read up about something called rejection sensitive dysphoria, which he was certain was bullshit, but sounded good on screen, and gave him a convenient justification for lashing out when he didn't get what he needed. *It's not my fault, I have a disorder, you should be nicer to me...*

Concurrent with his private efforts to foster relationships with strangers who didn't want any part of him and made this painfully obvious, he spread a deceptive layer of harmlessness across the publicly available virtual version of himself like glossy chocolate spread on toast, crafting long and detailed Facebook posts about his wife and how much he appreciated her, how much she supported him, despite his *many disadvantages and challenges in life*. Women seemed to like men who were openly romantic with their spouses, he knew. As a tactic, it wasn't working, but he kept the façade running anyway.

Then he remembered: it was his wedding anniversary tomorrow.

Shit.

He jumped over to his Facebook profile, started typing, realising as he did so that his fingernails had a deep crimson stain under each of them. Ten red crescent moons, trapped on the ends of his fingers.

Ten years together, he gushed, jabbing his phone screen with practised ease, choosing a succession of pictures from his camera roll to attach to the post where he thought he looked fine, but his wife looked as awkward and unphotogenic as ever. He almost, accidentally, uploaded a picture from a different, more explicit folder by mistake, but as soon as he saw the blood and the body parts lying spaced out across the wooden jetty, he deleted the image, removing it from the post within seconds of realising what he'd done.

He replaced it with a nice, innocent shot of himself and his wife with their two cats, who he hated, but the world at large didn't need to know that.

He captioned this last one: *The only type of pussy that's good for anything,* then deleted the description, knowing his joke wouldn't be appreciated or understood, but chuckling to himself anyway. He replaced the wording with *Love U, Mrs. D, xxxx.*

Then he hit "post".

The waitress came back after that.

The man ignored her as she set his drink and the menu down, sending her away with a supercilious grunt after she'd read the specials out to him as quickly as possible.

He leaned back in his chair, studying the menu. He felt accomplished. He was warm, comfortable, the few gulps of beer he'd taken already going right to his head. He had a phone in hand, and it was cold outside, bitterly so, but he was okay, inside, about to be fed.

He pushed the menu back onto the table, deciding he would take his time. The pub was deserted, and he had no place to be, no plan to stick to, nobody to answer to.

Might as well settle in for a bit. He wasn't going anywhere for a good long while, he thought.

Introductions

Amandine arrived at the restaurant ten minutes early and hobbled across the car park unsteadily in her heels. There were only two cars in front of the pub, a small Ford and an ancient, filthy, rusty Nissan with frosted up windows. Amandine wondered if one of them belonged to her date.

I don't imagine so, she told herself. *I bet he'll be late. Twenty minutes, at least. They always say "traffic", even though there never is any, not out here.*

She was surprised to find, however, on entering the pub and navigating the maze of corridors inside, that she was wrong. He was already seated in the snug bar, which was in a separate part of the pub to the restaurant, waiting for her with his back turned. Despite the limited view she had, she could see he had made an effort: suit jacket, tie, new shoes, what looked like a fresh haircut – although it was hard to tell from the back of his head.

Amandine, who still wrestled with waves of nerves and trepidation, was relieved to see the man appeared to feel as outwardly nervous as her, perhaps more so, if the leg-twitching and finger-twiddling was anything to go by.

See? Don't make assumptions about people you haven't met yet; it isn't fair.

Unprepared for his punctuality, she gave herself a moment to gather her feelings. Then she approached quietly and tapped him lightly on the shoulder.

He turned, startled. His face lit up.

"Amandine?"

She pushed a hand awkwardly at him.

He consciously stilled himself, visibly stamping down his nervous tics. The leg stopped bouncing; the fingers ceased their anxious motion.

"Connor," she confirmed, still holding out her hand. "It's nice to meet you."

She didn't even need to look at her wrist to remind herself of his name, she thought, proudly. *How about that.*

They shook. His skin was warm and dry, a little rough, but she didn't mind that. She was glad he didn't try and kiss her on the cheek or do anything more than the handshake.

"What did you do to your face?" he said, frowning.

Amandine winced, scrambling for a lie.

I slapped myself to stop having a meltdown, she thought, but instead she said:

"Oh, it's nothing. I was wearing heels, and I sort of… fell down the stairs a bit."

Not a lie, but it wasn't exactly the truth, either.

Connor's eyebrows shot up his forehead.

"Jesus, are you okay?"

Amandine nodded, making it clear she didn't want to talk about it anymore.

"Fine and dandy," she said, coolly.

"I wasn't sure you would come," Connor said, a moment later.

Amandine coughed nervously. Was she that transparent?

"Why?"

"Well," he countered, trying to make a joke, "I could be anyone, after all. A serial killer! You never know."

Amandine's stomach lurched.

Connor winked and laughed, then immediately looked stricken and squeezed his eyes shut as his own words sank in. Amandine could see him mentally kicking himself in the awkward silence that followed.

I fucked up already, his expression said.

And at first, she was inclined to agree.

Who makes jokes about things like that? His words left a sour taste in her mouth. But it was obvious he was embarrassed, squirming in his seat like a kid caught short, his face a deep, beetroot red.

"I didn't mean that, I wasn't thinking straight."

Amandine tried to give him the benefit of the doubt. It was such an absurd thing to announce that she could have said it herself.

Words tumbled over themselves as Connor continued to apologise.

"Amandine… ah, Jesus, I get nervous, I try to make jokes… Fuck! I'm off to a good start, eh?"

Amandine chewed on her bottom lip.

Still not too late to cancel, she thought.

Another failed date, Amandine. Another disaster.

No. Stick it out. Give it a chance. You've only just arrived.

At least she was not the only socially inept one.

"Are you?" she asked, semi-seriously.

He looked confused.

"Am I what?"

"A serial killer?"

Connor sunk his head in his hands comically. "I'm a fuckin'

idiot is what," he said. "Just forget I spoke. I'm rusty. We should call it a night right now."

Amandine made a decision, pulled out a bar stool, and sat down, making sure to arrange her dress so the hole in the hem was hidden in the folds of fabric beneath her.

"It's fine," she soothed. "So am I. Rusty, I mean. Not a serial killer."

Connor let out a huge breath of relief. Then a laugh.

"Let's start again. Would you like a drink?"

"Yes, please. A martini, if that's okay."

"Of course it's okay! At this point you could order a magnum of fucking champagne and I wouldn't complain about it."

Amandine dipped her head. "I'm not really a champagne kind of girl, to be honest."

"Good. I hate the stuff."

"Too many bubbles," Amandine said.

"Too many fucking bubbles," Connor agreed.

He beckoned to the bartender, who came immediately: there was no one else to serve. Amandine was grateful for this. Overly loud places made conversation especially difficult for her.

"How can I help?" the bartender asked.

It was a risk, ordering a cocktail in a country pub in the middle of nowhere, but Amandine had a feeling about the place, judging by the bottles she could see behind the bar.

Connor gestured to Amandine. *Ladies first,* his motion implied.

"I'd like a martini, please," she said. "Extra dry, three olives."

The bartender nodded. Amandine could tell the "extra dry" part of her order amused him.

"One gin in a glass, coming up," he said, with a wink. Amandine smiled.

The barman looked at Connor. "Another lager for you, sir?"

Connor pushed his half-empty beer glass to one side. "I'll have what she's having. It sounds good."

Amandine cocked her head to one side. "You like martinis?"

"Never had one in my life," he said, "but you seem to know what you're doing, so I'll give it a try."

She studied his face as openly as she dared while they waited for their drinks. He had a beard, which she liked, and a strong profile, a heavy brow, fierce eyes, a prominent nose with a pronounced bump on the bridge, more noticeable in real life than on his WhatsApp profile picture, and thick hair tucked back behind his ears. He was very handsome, she realised. Far more so than his photos implied. He took care of himself, was groomed. He was about thirty, give or take, nicely dressed but not too flashy. No evidence of a wedding ring hastily removed. A small tattoo on his inner left wrist, a symbol of some sort, she couldn't see it clearly under his sleeve.

Maybe it's my name, she thought, and her mouth twitched. The reminder word tingled on her wrist.

There were old piercing holes in his earlobes, leftover evidence of a misspent youth, he said. A slightly toothy smile lurked beneath the beard, awkward but genuine, nervy, a little anxious, just like her own. She didn't mind the toothiness, in person. It made him more approachable.

Amandine assessed him, and then, to her amazement, her stomach lurched.

Gut feeling?

But a good one this time, which rarely happened.

And suddenly she felt very shy.

Get a grip

When Connor saw how tall Amandine was, he felt a little sting of disappointment. He knew she was tall, but seeing how tall in person made him feel instantly less attracted to her. Dreams of manhandling her evaporated quickly. If anything, she could manhandle him.

Still, she smelled good.

Clean, fresh, a light scent of something floral, sweet, but also a little musky.

His brain tried to figure out how he was feeling as he took in her outfit, her hair, her eyes. He kept his gaze steadfastly away from her breasts, but he was acutely aware of the cut of her dress and exactly how much flesh was on display. In his mind, he suddenly saw himself burying his face in her cleavage, teasing each tit out from their bra cups, fingering the nipples until they were hard, mouthing them until they were harder, and…

Jesus fucking Christ on two sticks, Connor. Get a grip.

She told him it was nice to meet him.

Then he saw her stiletto heels, expensive, accentuating her ankles and calves, and his nerves finally got the better of him, and he made a joke about being a serial killer, and immediately wanted to throw himself into the sea.

She dealt with it calmly, blinking then laughing it off, but he remained angry with himself for a good while after the off-colour quip had faded from the conversation.

Why are you so fucking stupid, Connor? he asked himself, over and over as Amandine talked.

His dad's text came back to haunt him periodically: *don't scare her off like the last one.*

Connor cleared his throat. *Go away, Dad,* he thought. *You don't understand.*

It'll be different, this time.

I know it will.

A Rose Without Thorns

"This is for you," Connor said, suddenly remembering.

He pulled a single red rose from the barstool next to him and handed it to her. Amandine took it. All the thorns had been clipped off the stem so she would not prick her fingers.

What's the point of that? she thought. *A rose without thorns is not truthful.*

She thanked him anyway, blushing a little performatively. Nobody had ever given her a rose before, and it made her feel faintly giddy, thorns or no thorns.

He seemed pleased by her reaction.

"Amandine," he said, hesitantly. "That's an unusual name."

"It's French," she replied. This did not seem to surprise him. "My father is from Brittany. My mother is originally from London but lived in France for a while as an exchange student. They met by a canal when they were both eighteen."

"That's young."

She shrugged. "It wasn't back then. A different time, I guess. Where are your parents from?"

"The clue is in my name, too," he said. "My folks are about as Irish as they come. I haven't lived there since I was a small lad, though. My dad brought me over here when I was three. I've never been back, although I'd like to."

"You've lived here ever since?"

"You mean out in the arse end of buttfuck nowhere? Yeah, unfortunately."

They both laughed then, because it was true. Out here, it often felt like a frontier to Amandine. A collection of small villages that time had largely forgotten, lurking on the edges of the marshy, reed-lined wilds of Hickling Broad. Hickling itself was the largest of the lot, mostly full of second properties now, the small sleepy parish fast becoming a holiday home destination for rich Londoners to escape to during the summer. For those who did not fall into that category, it was a quiet, weird, rather dislocated life – especially during the winter months. A difficult place to grow up in. It was hard to get anywhere interesting without a car. For young people, the area didn't offer much, jobwise or otherwise: a windmill, mostly intact; a ruined priory; a small windsurfing club; two pubs; marshes, creeks and ponds and waterways for miles; and when that ran out, fields, farmland, mud, ditches. Fenland. To the east of all that: coastline. Sandy beaches. That part was okay. You could get a decent tan, at least.

Career prospects, however, were minimal, unless you wanted to work on the land pulling gunky daffodils or Brussels sprouts or onions or lettuce or do night shifts in a sugar beet or dog food or paper factory, or try your hand at reed cutting.

Minimal prospects, and minimal opportunities to meet new people.

"May as well be living on the moon," Amandine said.

Connor nodded. "My dad loves it. But he made all his money years ago, so he doesn't have to think about the practical ramifications of his son living in the back of beyond. As long as he's fishing or birdwatching when he's not away for work, he's happy."

"What does he do?"

"He runs an agricultural consultancy firm."

Amandine nodded politely. "Interesting."

Connor looked at her. "It's really not. It's about as fucking boring as you can get, but then who am I to comment? I'm thirty and I just lost my job."

"Oh." Amandine wasn't sure how to respond. "I'm sorry."

Her date shook his head, working hard to hide his bitterness and not quite managing it. "Nah, don't be. It was a shitty sales role. Real boiler room stuff. Targets and stupid rules and dinging a stupid fucking bell every time someone was persuaded to part with their money. I hated it. I would have been better off working on the land, like everyone else around here does. You know there's a syndrome associated with this area, right? It might be an urban myth–"

"Don't you mean a rural myth?"

He deferred to her. "Rural myth. It's called Fen Syndrome."

Amandine shook her head. "I've never heard that."

Connor rubbed his palms on his thighs. "Too much sky out here, apparently. And the land is too flat. Farmers and workers out in the fields go mad, eventually. They keep thinking the sky is going to collapse on them."

Amandine sat up straighter. "Oh, I've heard of that! There's a name for it. Um…" She pulled out her phone, googled it. "Casadastraphobia!"

"Wow. I couldn't repeat that after a drink."

"I'm not sure I could repeat it without one."

He grew a lopsided grin. "There's a fucking name for everything, now," he went on. "Even the existential dread of being squashed by the sky."

"Right? Remember the nursery rhyme… what was it… Chicken Licken!"

Connor put on a high, chickeny voice. "'Goodness gracious me!' said Henny-penny, 'the sky's a-going to fall; I must go and tell the King!'"

Amandine stared at him, a grin illuminating her own face.

"Impressive chicken voice," she said, trying to control her expression.

Connor crumpled again with embarrassment. He shook his head in despair.

"Why do I blurt shit out the way that I do? Jesus. You've got me all… all…"

"Discombobulated?"

He let out a short, sharp breath.

Amandine stepped in while he was searching for the right response.

"No, I'm intrigued. Do you remember all the words to Humpty Dumpty, too?"

Connor continued to squirm. "You must think I'm a *complete* fucking special case."

"No," she said, kindly, wanting suddenly to reassure him. "I don't."

Their eyes locked. A moment was had.

What is happening here? She thought.

Amandine could see Connor searching frantically for a way to proceed.

"My dad also told me that in the old days, men used to walk around on stilts. Through the marshes and peat bogs. The bottoms of the stilts would swell up, so they didn't sink. I always liked that idea. An army of men with long, thin legs marching around like giants or fucking Slenderman or something."

"Interesting," Amandine said, and she went to some effort to make this sound sincere. Really, she just wanted him to keep staring at her in that hungry, yet oddly vulnerable, way.

It made her feel powerful. Attractive. He wanted her, and he was having a hard time hiding it.

She liked having that effect on someone.

She bit her lip, very deliberately.

Connor began to sweat.

The couple were interrupted by two martinis placed discreetly in front of them.

Amandine lowered her gaze and sipped gratefully, enjoying, as she always did, the cold, sharp hit of the drink upon first taste.

Connor followed suit, and his face lit up.

"Wow," he said, taking another sip. "That is *good*."

She nodded, pleased. "Not as good as my dad used to make, but yeah, this isn't bad."

The bartender acknowledged the compliment with a brief dip of his head, clasping his hands. Then he retreated to a discreet distance.

They drank their martinis in companionable silence, the conversation falling into a natural lull, but the temporary change of pace didn't feel awkward.

I think this date is going to be okay, Amandine thought, finally allowing herself to feel optimistic, even cautiously excited.

I really think this is going to be okay.

Her dress snagged gently against her Miracle Word, and Amandine hoped it wasn't flaking off too quickly.

She thought it might be working, after all.

Tomato Soup

"What's the soup of the day?" the man asked the waitress, who scowled at him. The soup of the day was clearly written in capitals on a chalkboard on the wall directly next to him.

He held his ground, forcing her to spell it out for him.

"Tomato," she said, quietly seething.

"Does it come with bread?"

"Yes."

"What type of bread?"

Her face took on a mutinous expression. "Sourdough," she said, moodily. "Rustic style sourdough bloomer, thick cut. We serve it with freshly churned butter direct from a local supplier."

"What kind of tomatoes?"

"In the soup?"

"Yes."

"Er… roasted vine, I think."

The man scrunched up his face. "Sounds too fancy for me. You don't just have a tin of Heinz sat in the cupboard, do you? With white bread. Pre-sliced. Margarine, not butter. Can't stand the stuff."

The waitress blinked. "You want… tinned soup instead of the fresh?"

"Yes."

She let out an exasperated sigh. "I don't think we can do that, sir. If it's not on the menu, then…'

"You can go and ask, though, right?" the man said. He took out his wallet, laying it on the table and tapping it idly with his index finger. The implication was clear: *you want tips, you do as I ask.*

She hesitated, obviously needing the potential extra money just enough that she was willing to put up with him.

"I'll go ask," she said, darkly, and the man marked it up as another win as she turned and stomped out of the restaurant once again.

He could hear conversation in the snug adjoining bar, now. A woman's laugh, a man's deep undertone. They'd be in here soon, he thought, sitting at the table he wanted for himself, by the window. Making eyes at each other and filling the space with their revolting, moronic flirtations.

He decided to leave them a little present before they arrived. He went quickly across to their table, bent over each place setting, and scratched at his head frantically with his bloody fingernails, really digging them in, raking his scalp repeatedly. Huge flakes of dandruff came off in a thick, abundant shower, landing all over the tablecloth, the side plates, the cutlery, and in the glasses. The light was low and romantic, candlelight and more fucking fairy lights, and as he stood upright again, he knew they wouldn't be able to see any of the flakes until it was too late.

Satisfied, he went back to his seat and waited.

Patience was a virtue, his mother had told him repeatedly.

If that was the case, he was the most virtuous man alive.

Lone Diner

After their martinis, Connor and Amandine moved to their table. The back of the restaurant sat up on stilts above the banks of Hickling Broad, surrounded by reeds and black water lit by artfully positioned floodlights. Outside, a large, decked area rigged with lights and a pizza oven waited for warmer weather. The pub was largely empty now as the couple moved through it, only a skeleton staff on hand. One waitress, the barman and a chef, Amandine supposed. Winter staff.

The cavernous dining room with exposed oak beams holding up the ceiling did have one other lone diner sitting three tables over from theirs. He had a bowl of tomato soup in front of him and was slurping at it messily as they were shown to their table by the smartly dressed waitress.

Amandine and Connor nodded to the other diner in acknowledgement as they passed.

"Evening," Connor said, pleasantly.

His cordiality was met with a palpable contempt. The man, who had thick, bushy eyebrows and greasy hair tied back in a ponytail, glared at Connor over the rims of his glasses – which were filthy, Amandine saw – for a few moments too long as they walked by.

Connor blinked.

The lone diner put his head back down over his soup, his phone illuminating his dry, wind-chapped face as he shovelled hot liquid into his mouth, which he opened comically wide, like a gulping fish at the surface of a pond. Thick rivulets of orange stuff dribbled down his chin, plopping onto the tablecloth and back into the bowl below.

"Rude," Amandine whispered, once they were safely past him. She was confused by the man's hostile reaction, but more revolted by his messy eating habits.

"Maybe he's been stood up," Connor whispered back conspiratorially. "People only really come here on dates, after all. Where's his?"

Amandine shot the other diner a final look back over her shoulder. On the man's table, in front of him, still wrapped in cellophane, was a bunch of red roses. They looked a little worse for wear, as if they hadn't been near water for a while. Amandine could see the supermarket label stuck to their plastic shroud.

"Look at the flowers," she whispered, turning back. She hid her words behind her hand, like a child divulging a secret in the playground. "Red roses."

Connor looked, let out a "huh" as if to say, *See?*

"Either way, there's no need to be rude," Amandine concluded, sniffing her own red rose.

Connor pulled Amandine's chair out for her, and they sat. The waitress handed them each a menu and departed with a surly flick of her hair.

"Fuck him," Connor replied, quietly. He flicked a flake of something white from his napkin, frowning, then laid it neatly across his lap.

"No, thanks," Amandine shot back, and there were more shared smiles.

Fuck Them

The man watched the couple weave through the restaurant on their way to the table and instantly hated them. The way they smiled at each other, the way they walked close and matched each other's stride, even though the woman was taller than her date and clearly struggling in her high heels. The smell they gave off: perfume and aftershave. The sparkle in their eyes. The way they showed off their teeth. The single red rose, which felt like a personal insult. He hated them so much he thought his heart was about to explode in his chest. A pinching, grasping nastiness stippled him all over. The man stopped slurping soup and massaged his left pectoral with a sweaty hand until the stabbing pain that had suddenly erupted there subsided, which it always did, after a bit of persuading.

Slightly out of breath, he glared at them with renewed spite, as if they were wholly responsible for his aches and pains.

The couple, oblivious to his discomfort, had the audacity to say "hello" to him as they passed, which unleashed a special flavour of rage that flared up like acid reflux. He could detect the sneer in their voices, the pity in their tone as they saw him sitting alone with his soup and his phone and his dying bouquet.

He began eating again, slurping angrily, deliberately letting soup dribble down himself and splatter across the table linen.

Making a mess felt necessary. Creating work for others was one of the many ways in which he protested the encroaching decay he saw all around him: the decay of manners, of common decency, of values he'd held dear for so long.

The woman looked back at him over her shoulder. The man froze, spoon midway to his lips. She locked eyes with him for a brief, hot moment, then, unable to hold his gaze, lowered hers to the roses sitting on the table in front of him.

Her mouth turned down, forming a pink crescent of sympathy.

That sealed it for him, that little moue of commiseration.

He knew, then, why he was here. In this pub. On this night.

Why he'd turned left instead of right at the junction.

Why he hadn't gone home.

It was because he was *meant* to be here. He was meant to meet her.

And he knew he would not be happy until he'd wiped the blush from her cheeks. Slapped the pity clean out of her eyes.

Her date's, too.

He wondered what the woman would look like. Cold, wet, and desperate. He wondered how her makeup, so carefully applied, so artfully and deceitfully plastered on, would smear once he'd pushed her face into bog water a few times. Makeup was a sure sign that a woman was a liar, his father had told him when he was eight years old. *They use it to hide the ugly,* he remembered hearing, and that had sunk in deep. *Never trust a woman who uses makeup.* His mother never wore it, and his wife never wore it. On the few occasions she'd tried, for a friend's wedding or the rare date night they might take out of the house, he'd ordered her to take it off. She always complied good-naturedly. He wished often that she wasn't so placid. Sometimes, he wished she'd push back, so he'd have a better reason to put her in her place.

But she never did.

The woman turned away, continued to her table. Her date, who was good looking and well dressed – too well dressed, as if he was compensating for something – pulled back the chair for her. The woman sat down gracefully, delicately sliding her long legs under the low tabletop. They were mismatched, height-wise, but neither of them seemed to mind.

The man felt sick, witnessing this display of old-fashioned "chivalry". He remembered trying to do the same to a girl he'd had a crush on in college, once, at a bar. She'd laughed at him. The sound of her contempt, and that of her friends, who all joined in, had stayed with him ever since.

Really, they only have themselves to blame, he thought.

He resumed his soup, dividing his attention between the couple, who had opened their menus, and his phone, which showed a succession of videos he'd filmed out in the marshes earlier. He'd created a special folder, called it *Elise & Thomas*. He kept the volume on silent as he played each video in order. The moving images calmed him as he finished his soup.

One video in particular.

On screen, a woman wept, tied to a post on a jetty surrounded by rippling reeds. Grey clouds pressed down from above, a dense, dark ceiling that seemed too low to be real. It was raining, almost sideways, verging on sleet, and soon it would turn to snow.

The unsteady camera rushed in uncomfortably close, then pulled back to show the whole jetty, and a man tied to another post nearby. The woman's fiancé.

The camera went back to the woman. Both lovers were drenched, shivering. Her lips were blue. Her eyes were puffy and wild. There was ice in her hair and on her eyebrows. She was weak, on the point of giving up. She would be the first to go. Her fiancé would succumb nearly a full day later, from blood loss. He had freed his bound hands somehow before he died, probably by twisting and rubbing – another argument for cable ties – and crawled the short distance across the platform to his fiancée. The man had found them the next morning, frozen to the floorboards, eyes unseeing, hands intertwined like they were on a date.

The phone camera jerked around chaotically, capturing a blurred flash of a boot connecting with soft, marbled flesh.

Use a tripod next time, the man thought. He was rubbing himself again, had started without realising it.

The woman in the video threw back her head and howled.

Just beyond the phone's glaring screen, another woman seated at a dandruff-dusted table by the pub's large picture window threw back her head, tossed her nicely styled hair over her shoulder, and laughed prettily.

Table Talk

It felt good to be facing each other, now that they had broken the ice.

"This is a nice place," Amandine said. The reeds outside the window moved in eerie, rippling patterns, their fluffy tips tickling the night sky. It was soothing to look at, almost hypnotic.

Connor stared at them too, then up at the stars that were making their timid way out into the night.

"It's packed with tourists in the summer. You can never get a table."

"I kind of prefer the off-season feel, to be honest with you. It's more…'

"Intense," he finished, nodding. "Intimate. I know what you mean."

They agreed to order starters before the mains. An extra course would extend their date by a good half hour or so, and this mutually implied decision gave them both enough confidence to relax, although maybe the martinis helped with that too.

Amandine started to tell Connor about herself. Haltingly at first, in dribs and drabs, information teased out by his gentle questioning, and then to larger degrees with more detail and colour thrown in as she warmed up.

She told him about her quiet upbringing, how her mum was a big presence in her life, her father less so, as he was away a lot with business. Both were dead now, although she glossed over that part. Amandine still lived in her childhood home, and knew she was lucky to own a house at her age but wished it hadn't come at the cost of losing both parents. She missed them, she said, especially her mum, who had been kind and vivacious and extremely funny and clever, with beautiful skin that went nut-brown in the summer. She had a raucous, joyous, room-filling laugh, liked to sing and made wonderful bread.

Talking like this was a new experience for Amandine, who spent most of every day in silence, to the point where she sometimes forgot the sound of her own voice. Once she started opening up to Connor, however, she found it was hard to stop. A faucet had been turned.

She told him about her life as a kid on the beaches and in the wetlands, a childhood probably not that dissimilar to his, messing about on boats, crab fishing, swimming in the sea and creeks, foraging samphire. Losing her virginity behind the post office. Occasionally, she would get the bus to town to see a movie, but when she got older and spent more time online, she didn't do that as much. School was challenging. Amandine found it hard to fit in, was bullied for being 'different'. She was smart, imaginative, like her mum, and preferred books, her computer, and her own company, to people her own age.

Connor seemed surprised by this.

"Really? You look like someone who would have lots of friends."

Amandine shook her head. "No. I struggled to get people to understand that I was not, um, being strange for the sake of it, you know? I just couldn't help it. I was myself, and other children didn't seem to enjoy that very much. The expression 'too much' was used a lot around me, I recall. But I was never too much for my parents."

Talking about them like this began to stir long-suppressed feelings of grief in Amandine. She sank into silence momentarily, her attention once again on the reeds.

"I bet you liked climbing trees," Connor countered, trying to cheer her up and bring her back into the room.

The waitress, who had already asked them twice if they would like more time to order, yawned pointedly off to one side of the room before disappearing again.

They both ignored her.

"I did," Amandine said, a little dreamily. She slowly turned back to the conversation at hand. "I loved climbing trees. I still do."

"Me too."

Connor didn't strike her as an outdoors type of person, but then she told herself that she wasn't going to be so quick to judge on this date. Even if he might just be saying what she wanted to hear.

He asked her then how she would feel if he ordered a bottle of wine, telling her firmly that it didn't matter how expensive it was, he would pay.

"But you probably know more about wine than I do," he admitted, looking at the wine list as if it intimidated him.

She pulled a face. "Why? Because my father was French?"

He spread his hands. "I guess?"

Amandine shook her head, feigning disappointment in him. "Give it here." Connor handed her the wine list. She went back and forth over a South African Meerlust and a Pinot Noir, before choosing the Saint Emilion premier Grand Cru, Chateau Ausone, the second most expensive bottle on the list.

"I trust you," he said. "The martinis were a good judgement test."

"You like other people to make decisions for you?" Amandine leaned back in her chair.

He was almost too quick to reply.

"Not at all. I just like to learn from others. I don't know shit about wine, but then I grew up around here, didn't I? The best we have in the refined alcohol department is a strong IPA."

"Fair," she acknowledged. "I don't mind beer, though. Good beer."

"You could have said before you ordered the second most expensive bottle of red off the menu," Connor teased.

Amandine lifted her chin. "You told me to."

"I did. I'm just messing around."

"Hmmm," Amandine said, narrowing her eyes.

"Hmmm." Connor put on a good-natured parody of her expression.

The wine arrived. Amandine held out her glass for the taste test, then stopped, frowning and picking a small white crumb of something out of the bowl. Then another, and another.

"Is yours like this?"

Connor peered into his wineglass, grimaced. "Yep."

"A dirty glass is no way to enjoy a good wine," Amandine said, collecting Connor's glass, handing both to the waitress.

"I'll get you some fresh ones," the waitress said, puzzled and embarrassed. She came back moments later with two clean glasses, giving them an extra polish at the table with a fresh white cloth for good measure.

Amandine waited for the wine to glug out, then sipped.

"S'good," she said, nodding to the waitress, who went on to pour for them and ask for the third time if they needed longer to decide on their food.

Amandine realised she was hungry.

"No, I'm ready now," she said. Connor seemed to enjoy her assertiveness; his eyes gleamed with approval.

She ordered the scallops to start. Connor went for the whitebait. When you grew up by the sea, you ordered seafood off the menu; they both knew that.

"So, tell me," Connor said, when the waitress was dispatched. "Tricky question. When was your last relationship?"

Amandine drew a deep breath. She'd known this was likely to come up, so she had prepared a lie. At the last minute, she opted for the truth.

The truth was always better, she told herself, even if it was awkward.

"Can I tell you something?" She shifted around in her seat.

Connor's face said: *Oh god, here it comes. I knew this was too good to be true.*

"Uh oh," he said out loud. "What is it?"

"I've never, ah… I've never been in a relationship," Amandine confessed, awkwardly. "Not a real, long-term relationship, at any rate."

Shock widened his eyes.

"Never?"

"Nope. In fact…"

She bit the bullet. Connor was going to get the entire truth, not a diluted form of it.

"In fact," she said, shyly swirling wine around in her glass while secretly gripping the stem so fiercely she feared it might break, "this is the first proper date I've ever been on."

Connor looked stunned.

"Hold up," he said, raising a hand in disbelief. "What?"

"This is my first ever real romantic date. That hasn't been a disaster, I mean. Yet."

He sat back in his chair.

"Ever? A beautiful woman like you?"

"I swear."

"Nah, come on, Amandine."

She felt herself going red and shrugged.

"I mean, I've been out for drinks and things but... it never felt like a date. More of a means to an end. Hookups, you know? They weren't dates. We never talked, not like this. Just polite ways of passing the time before the deed. Like we were just getting the pleasantries out of the way until... ah...'

"I get the picture."

"Well. I just haven't dated properly, okay? Romantically. Dinner. Candles. Roses. This is coming out all wrong. I'm not a virgin or anything, it's important you know that. I suck cock like a trooper."

Connor choked and sprayed his wine everywhere, spattering the white tablecloth with bright red dots.

"Sorry," he apologised, while Amandine giggled.

"I do, though," she insisted. "Zero gag reflex."

It took Connor a moment to gather his composure.

"Well, that's good to know. But you're telling me... that this is your first ever *date-date*. Proper, like?"

"Yes. Don't make me feel any more embarrassed about it than I already am."

"No, no, I just..." He looked at her, really looked at her. "I guess I just feel lucky it's with me."

She rolled her eyes. "Don't patronise me. I know it's odd. I'm thirty-three years old. I get it. But I don't know what to tell you. I just... I've just never quite figured out the whole romance thing."

He liked that. "It was my wit and charm, right? In my text messages."

Don't remind me about the text messages, Amandine thought, reliving a moment of discomfort as she remembered just how many he'd sent her in the weeks before their date. She chose not to call him out on this just yet because, in person, it was different. He didn't seem creepy. He was sweet and funny.

Nobody's perfect, she told herself. *You were right not to cancel the date.*

"I mean, you can string a sentence together," she said out loud, "which definitely helps. But it was more than that. I don't know exactly, I just felt something intriguing. It was how you communicated."

Connor sipped his wine.

"I am usually very shy with women," he confessed, reluctantly. "I imagine that's the main reason I'm still single."

Amandine was relieved the spotlight had shifted to him. "You've had other relationships, though?"

His tone shifted. "One. A serious one. She broke my heart."

"I'm sorry."

"It happens. Love, right?"

Amandine shrugged. "I wouldn't know," she said quietly.

Sorry Date

The Lone Diner thought his soup tasted like liquid shit. They'd found him a tin, as requested, but it wasn't Heinz. It was some supermarket own-brand filth, almost certainly out of date. It had a sour tang that lingered at the back of his throat.

He sucked it down with spiteful dedication anyway. He took grim pleasure in building up another layer of food sediment on himself, thinking of his body as a work of art, a canvas of splattered fluids and secretions. He could smell himself particularly well, even through the artificial fug of soup-steam and cheap toasted white bread. He was potent and he hoped his odour would waft over to the couple by the window.

They were locked in an intense conversation, sipping what looked like expensive wine – he could tell by the pleased pursing of lips that happened after each taste. The man was showing off, ordering the fancy shit. It seemed to be working. The couple were leaning into each other across the table. The woman's face, lit from below by candlelight, was alternately beautiful and then not, her face carved with flickering shadows at the whim of the candle's flame.

Lone Diner went back to his phone. A different video now played. Filmed in darkness, the flash on. The bright glare made the subject squint. The man being filmed said something that Lone Diner couldn't hear, because the volume was down, but he had heard it a dozen times before. "Get that fucking thing out of my face," the slurred words commanded, but Lone Diner hadn't listened, had slammed the phone right up against the man's cheek, hard, so the lens was smudged with pore-grease. The camera retracted and there followed an awkward, fumbling motion as the lens was wiped as clean as it would get, under the circumstances.

Then, the secateurs came into view.

The bound man's mouth stretched into a wide, horrified O.

Lone Diner thumbed the volume up a notch, just loud enough that he could hear a rough zipping sound, accompanied by desperate protests and thrashing, then pitiful pleading. A limp, pale member jumped into view, ludicrous in the flash glare, like a naked mole rat, white with foreskin shrivelled and pink at the tip.

The secateurs opened. Sharp, curved blades pressed against veined flesh.

The man stopped thrashing. Went statue-still, except for the faint rocking motion his tears produced.

The camera swerved as the cameraman's grip renewed. His hands had been so cold, he remembered. Holding anything still under the circumstances had been almost impossible.

Tripod, he reminded himself again.

"Please," the captive in the video begged. "Please, I'll do anything."

Anything wasn't enough.

There was a distinct crunch, and a snip.

The screen filled with red.

A violent, tortured scream ripped out across the footage, so loud it was distorted by the camera's inadequate microphone.

The man smiled, thumbed down the volume again, and slurped his own bowl of red.

Never Been in Love

"You've never been in love, either?"

Amandine flinched at the directness of this. "No, not yet."

They let the silence that followed go on for a little bit. The information exchange had grown unexpectedly heavy. Neither of them really wanted to forgo enjoyment for brutal honesty at this stage of the date.

"You know what's funny?" Connor said, breaking the pause.

"What?"

"Your name. It means 'much-loved', or 'worthy of love'."

"Is that so?" Amandine replied, sipping more wine. Connor had a look on his face that confused her. An expression she couldn't quite look away from. Usually, she avoided the eyes at all costs.

But not his.

His felt exciting.

"Did you Google that?"

Connor laughed. "Guilty."

"Well, then you should know that Amandine is also a type of potato," she clarified.

They both leaned into the lighter mood.

Amandine wistfully gazed at the flame of the candle that flickered in the centre of their table. "Have you ever heard of Miracle Words?"

"Miracle words?" Connor didn't place the emphasis where she did, but that was because he had never said the phrase before.

She emptied her glass of wine; he poured some more. *He's trying to get me drunk,* she thought to herself. Poor Connor. He had no idea how high her tolerance was. He'd be out of pocket by at least another expensive bottle of red before it started to affect her in any significant way.

"It's something my grandma used to tell me when I was little," she explained, her tone soft as she relived some memories. "She used to say that certain words could perform miracles, if you said them with enough belief. She used to get me to stand in front of a mirror and say the word 'beautiful', over and over, repeat it dozens of times a day. Then she would make me write it down, over and over, in capital letters, until, eventually, I believed what the words said."

"My dad used to do the same," Connor said, around a mouthful of wine. "Only it wasn't at all miraculous. He just used to tell me: 'Women always leave,' again and again. After a while, I was left with no choice but to believe him. It was like brainwashing."

Amandine nodded. "I think if you hear something spoken out loud enough times, it becomes a reality, you know? Like how politicians end up believing their own lies after a while. It does feel like... programming, I guess. I didn't know anything about 'affirmations' or any of that bullshit. It just felt like a good thing to do – describe the world with Miracle Words."

"You still use miracle words?" He stared pointedly at her wrist, the one marked with the word CELERY.

Amandine laughed. "I've got your name on my other wrist," she confessed, moving her watch strap to prove the point. "I forget things easily."

The word CONNOR showed up in biro against her blue-veined skin.

He blinked.

"You were worried about forgetting my name?" Connor seemed more upset by this than she anticipated.

"You're missing the point," Amandine replied, feeling suddenly embarrassed. "As I got older, the Miracle Words changed. I don't care that much about being beautiful. But I care about other stuff. Being strong. Being capable. Being smart. Miracle Words help. I write the word down somewhere, I look at it, and it helps. Don't ask me how. I think it's magic, of a sort. Not that kind of nonsense magic you read about in books. But personal magic. Like when… when you really like someone. Which doesn't happen a lot."

Connor was still stuck on the Reminder Word.

"I can't believe you couldn't remember my name! We've been talking for months!"

Amandine shrugged. "I'm not normal in that way. And I liked you, so I didn't want to upset you by getting your name wrong."

"Do you often send naked pictures to men whose name you can't recall?"

She didn't like the bitter edge to the question.

"Again, you're missing the point," she said, quietly.

He reined himself in with visible effort.

"You really like me? Enough to tattoo yourself with my name, at least." Connor was trying to put a positive spin on it.

She waited a beat before replying.

"I think I do. Yes."

He let out a faint breath, cleared his throat.

"So, when you say 'like a trooper'," he asked, one finger rubbing his top lip carefully. "Fancy elaborating?"

Her laughter came up all the way from her belly and filled the empty restaurant.

The lone diner sitting three tables away lifted his head and glared at the couple in response. His posture was rigid, head-to-toe vehemence. A blank-eyed, dishevelled pillar of hate, with red soup on his chin.

The lovers, in the first flush of something new and exciting, did not notice.

First Course

"Well," Connor said, making room for the waitress to put food down on the table as the starters finally arrived. "I don't know about you, but this all feels easy. As far as first dates go."

"It does, doesn't it?" Amandine said, but she wasn't finding it easy at all. She was exhausted, hiding it as well as she could. The effort it took to present as "normal" always left her feeling like she'd been hit by a truck after any sort of physical interaction with another human. Even Connor.

"I feel like I'm talking about myself too much, though. Thank you." These last words were to the waitress, who deposited a basket of fresh bread on the table.

"You're not," Connor assured her.

"Promise?"

They were interrupted by a loud noise of disgust.

Amandine's eyes whipped over to the source of the exclamation, to find the lone diner staring at her over Connor's shoulder.

Now that he had her attention, the man rolled his eyes, as if he'd been listening to their conversation intently, and found it wanting.

Amandine frowned.

What the fuck is his problem?

The waitress slowly set down the last plate and whispered conspiratorially to Amandine, "Ignore him. He's really weird. I wish I'd never let him in."

Amandine nodded once.

The waitress departed, steering a wide arc that took her far away from the lone diner's table.

The man continued to leer over at Amandine and Connor, undeterred. His mouth worked, that gaping fish motion again. He was rolling a piece of white toast in his hand so that it formed a ball, then, using the ball to clean his soup bowl, shovelling the wet object into his mouth with relish as if it was a prize oyster. He chewed with his mouth open. Amandine could hear the noises his cheeks made as his jaws worked on the mush.

Connor's face moved back into her line of sight, partially blocking the other man from view.

Amandine, flustered, struggled to refocus.

"What?"

He said, "Can I touch you, Amandine?"

Amandine blinked, considered the odd, formal phrasing, feeling somewhat perturbed. The figure of the lone diner was still in her peripheral, making it almost impossible to concentrate on anything or anyone else. She shifted her body so that Connor's face completely blotted the stranger out.

Better.

"Touch me?" It felt like such a ceremonious, significant request that she wondered if she'd misread his intentions. Did he mean touch her, privately? Here, in the restaurant? She wasn't averse to the idea, but…

He offered no further explanation. Amandine felt suddenly as if she were being tested.

"Depends where," she said, eventually, and the uneasy feeling that had bothered her back when she was in her house before the date was suddenly back with a vengeance. It felt like someone was standing close behind her, breathing down her neck, even though she knew there was nobody but the other diner, a few tables away. If she'd had hackles, they would have been up.

Connor adopted a reassuring tone, shifting modes with startling speed.

"On the back of your hand," he said, eyes now innocent.

Amandine was sure he hadn't meant that at all.

Red flag, a voice inside her whispered.

Was it? It was incredibly hard to tell, with Connor. One minute he gave her butterflies, the next...

She had brought up cock-sucking, after all. Perhaps he was only working on her cues.

Amandine told herself to relax. So, he was horny, and disingenuous at times, and a bit of a chameleon, but that didn't mean he was bad, necessarily.

Give him a chance, Amandine, she reminded herself. *He's still doing better than all those other bin fires. No such thing as perfect.*

"I'm pretty sure I can cope with that," she said out loud, even if the thought of being touched right in that moment made her stomach churn.

Because deep down, in another circumstance, she would have loved to be touched. In the right way, by the right person. Just not while the weird man with the ponytail and soup all over his face watched them.

Conner, oblivious to the staring form of the lone diner behind him, gently laid his fingers on the back of her hand and let them rest there. It was a quiet motion, meant to build trust, she assumed. Faintly erotic but also controlling.

She felt suddenly as if she was a skittish dog being trained. She wondered what was next. Treats? A pat on the head?

But she also found, to her consternation, that she *liked* his touch. Well. Liked *and* hated it. It brought about a small physical awakening, like a sliver of sunlight pouring in through a crack in drawn curtains. He smelt good, she realised. Aftershave, a touch of hair gel, a hint of musk, something sandalwood.

Is this intimacy?

It made her deeply uncomfortable. She crossed and recrossed her legs. The food on her plate suddenly no longer interested her. She had a vision of herself straddling Connor on her couch, arms locked behind his head, breasts pushed into his face as she…

It was no good. The fantasy dissolved before it really got going. The prickly *you're-being-watched* sensation continued to play havoc with her nerves.

Amandine moved her head, seeking to defuse some of the intensity of the moment, and check on the other occupant of the restaurant. She saw with dismay that the lone diner had adjusted his seat position, putting him firmly back in her line of sight.

And he was gazing at her again with naked…

Disdain? Lust? It was hard to tell.

Red flag, the voice inside her whispered again.

A very real one, this time.

His stare made her feel seasick.

The moment with Connor soured.

Still, the other diner refused to look away. Aggression rolled off him in seething waves that Amandine didn't understand.

She returned a silent challenge of her own.

What?

Accompanied with a hand gesture.

In her brain, alarm bells rang loudly.

Red flag red flag red flag!

"Amandine?"

Connor didn't like that her attention was elsewhere. He seemed bemused, frustrated.

The lone diner continued to glare as if Amandine were directly responsible for spoiling his food, and beyond that, his entire life.

She straightened her back, tilted her head. Issued him another silent challenge. It flew across the restaurant like a bolt loosed from a crossbow.

What the fuck are you looking at, freak?

Connor finally glanced over his shoulder to where Amandine's focus was directed.

The man sitting a few tables away, who Amandine now privately and officially named Lone Diner, finally dropped his gaze and went back to his meal – *how long can a bowl of soup last?* – and his phone, which he pawed at, one-handed.

Amandine was not fooled. There was something about the way he was handling his spoon, scraping his bowl even though there was nothing left in it. He might not be looking their way anymore, but the man seemed hyper aware of them both. Probably still hoping to eavesdrop on their conversation while pretending he was otherwise occupied.

Connor turned back, confused.

"What was that all about?"

Amandine tried to compose herself.

She shook her head. "I honestly don't know. But it's like… we've offended him somehow. He keeps staring at me, and it's… I don't know. It's aggressive."

Connor shrugged. "Fuck him," he replied, a little too loudly. "He's not worth paying attention to."

The inference was not subtle: Amandine should be paying attention to her date, not another man in the same restaurant. She felt irritated by the dig, but the irritation was subsumed by the animosity of the previous encounter.

She shivered.

"Here," said Connor, shrugging off his jacket. "It's cold in here. Obviously, they're worried about the heating bill."

"Obviously," she murmured, but suddenly, she found she didn't want his touch anymore.

She had to stop herself from flinching when Connor laid his jacket on her shoulders.

How Dare She

How dare she.

How fucking *dare* she stare him down like that? Head all pushed back, looking down her nose at him as if he was shit on her shoe.

And what was that hand gesture?

All he had done was taken a friendly interest in her, nothing more.

Did she think he was obsessed with her or something?

He was allowed to look where he pleased, wasn't he?

He was allowed to eat his fucking soup and look at whatever the fuck he liked.

Stuck up bitch.

He would show her.

He'd fucking show her.

He'd show them both.

Edges

Amandine mentally tried to disconnect from her feelings of unease by drinking yet more wine. She could still enjoy the moment, she told herself, gulping down three huge mouthfuls, even if the edges had been rubbed off. Connor hadn't done anything definably wrong, she reasoned, not in comparison to some of her other dates. And he was a good listener – or he was good at faking it in order to get into her knickers. Either way, it had been nice to talk to someone – really talk.

Stick it out a bit longer, Amandine, she thought. *Make a judgement at the end of the night, not partway through. He's probably just as nervous and uncomfortable as you.*

She flicked a glance at Lone Diner, unable to help herself. The man was watching something on his phone again. The lenses of his smeared glasses were lit up by whatever he was looking at, a chaotic succession of colours and shapes, most of them flesh-toned, from what she could see. Amandine wondered if it was porn.

Lone Diner smirked.

He knew she was watching him.

He turned his screen so she could get a proper view of it. Three women, naked, exposed, writhing; she could tell what it was, even from a distance away.

Her eyes widened.

It is porn!

Lone Diner grimaced at Amandine, a tideline of soup thick on his teeth. His lips were wet and loose, and as she watched, he deliberately let a long strand of orangey-white spit spill out of his mouth.

Revolted, she thought suddenly of sperm, and almost gagged.

He was taunting her.

Obscene old fuck probably makes a habit of this, she thought.

Gets a kick out of it.

Like a flasher in a mac.

"You okay over there?" Connor asked, his voice once again edged with irritation. "I keep losing you."

"I..." Amandine was at a loss to explain.

"Is it him again?"

Connor looked back over his shoulder to where Lone Diner sat.

The screen abruptly flipped.

The man met Connor's enquiring stare with innocently raised eyebrows, an almost cherubic grin, and wiped the spit off his chin with the back of his hand.

"Fucking weirdo," Connor muttered, turning back.

"I really don't like him, Connor," Amandine whispered.

"Hey, you remembered my name!" There was only a trace of sarcasm in this response.

Amandine sighed.

"I'm serious. That guy... I don't know. He feels kind of... dangerous, to me."

"Dangerous?"

Amandine persisted.

"Yeah. How he sits, how he's dressed. Like he's completely out of touch with reality. And he's watching porn on his phone, you know. He just showed me his phone."

Connor scoffed. "Porn?"

"I know what I saw."

Connor flung another indiscreet look backwards, trying to make his own assessment.

"I don't know, he looks harmless to me. A bit gross, but harmless. He probably just gets off on making people uncomfortable, like most perverts. I bet he was bullied at school."

"*I* was bullied at school," she retorted, feeling like she was fighting a losing battle. "And it's more than that. He puts my back up. I can't explain it. He just feels like..." She wrinkled her nose. "Like a threat."

Connor laughed. "Not every middle-aged man with a ponytail, a bowtie, and a porn habit is a threat, you know."

Amandine bristled. "Ever heard of women's intuition?"

Connor sighed. "Yes, and I think it's a crock of shit."

Her eyebrows shot up her forehead.

Connor held up a hand to ward off her outraged response. "Now, don't be offended. I don't disbelieve in it."

She folded her arms.

"I just don't think its gender specific," he went on. "You don't get the monopoly on instinct just because you're a woman. Guys have a danger radar too, alright? And I am telling you, that dude over there is about as much threat as a wet lettuce." He laughed.

That's because you've never been in real danger, Amandine thought, *at least not from another man.*

"Danger radar? Like a physical response?" Her words came with a rime of frost.

Connor caught on. Something subtle shifted in his face.

"I guess," he said, more defensively now. "If I meet someone who makes me feel uncomfortable, it is quite physical, yeah.

Balled fists. Slow breathing. You become more aware, tense, ready. To run or to fight. Or just... to act."

"And you don't feel any of those things now? Genuinely?"

"Nah." Connor puffed up his chest. "I could stare that shit-stain down in a moment, just watch."

"No, please, I don't think you should–"

Connor turned, draping his arm over the back of his own chair so his entire upper body was twisted to face Lone Diner. Then he glared at the man, aggressively.

Lone Diner lifted his head.

The two men faced each other down for several long, hard seconds.

Amandine cringed, wanting the ground to swallow her up, unable to watch the gross show of ego suddenly playing out in 'Norfolk's most romantic pub'.

Lone Diner stopped smiling, went back to his empty bowl.

He didn't raise his head in their direction after that.

"See?" Connor said, turning back around in his chair. There was triumph in his voice. "Man's a complete pussy."

Fuck, Amandine thought, gulping down more wine.

They're both psychos.

The skin on her arms was mottled with gooseflesh.

It was going so well, too.

She made an assessment, then, a lightning-fast analysis of her present situation. Of the two immediate threats, Connor was definitely the lesser. She would have to use one to ward off the other, until she could reasonably call it a night and order a cab.

She picked up her chair and moved it so she was sitting next to Connor, fighting all her instincts to do the opposite, forcing herself closer to him, seating herself at a right angle to Lone Diner, instead of facing him.

"That's better," she lied.

Connor seemed pleased by her proximity. He relaxed.

Probably feels like he's won a prize, she thought, bitterly.

The fact that Connor represented her best chance of protection while Lone Diner was still in the room bothered her deeply. Two of them as a pair made less of an easy target than a woman by herself, she knew, but the date was over for her. A deep fatigue settled in her bones. She started to fantasise about climbing into her own bed. If she could find the right moment to slip out, she would. When the waitress came back, maybe. She'd ask her to show her where the bathroom was. Discreetly.

In the meantime, Amandine slid a calculated hand onto Connor's thigh, let it rest there. Connor sat up straighter.

Amandine was beginning to regret not cancelling the date.

Brass Monkeys

The waitress came to take his soup bowl away, her face thunderous. She was starting to piss Lone Diner off with her attitude. She made it obvious, as she moved towards him warily, her nose wrinkled, eyes downcast, that she thought she had better things to do with her time than serve him. She had not once come over to check to see if he was satisfied with his soup (he was not), choosing instead to hide in the kitchen or near the bar, scrolling on her phone.

When she did deign to visit him, she was grossly perfunctory: "Finished?"

She didn't even waste complete sentences on him and made sure to keep the table between them as a barrier while she spoke. Her body language reeked of hostility: jaw set, limbs stiff.

It made him angry.

What was her fucking problem?

What was everyone's fucking problem?

Roses are red, violets are…

Did she think he was blind?

Did she think he couldn't see what she was doing?

He was not devoid of feelings, or pride.

Why was it always the same?

His wife was the only person he'd ever met who didn't seem to feel uncomfortable around him. Indifferent, yes, but not uncomfortable.

The waitress, clearly, did not share this indifference.

"Ready for your main?" she intoned, flat and rude. She leaned over the table to collect his bowl, rather than move around to stand beside him and risk physical contact.

His anger threatened to burst like an ugly, acidic bubble.

Until he saw her tits. As the waitress leaned further across the table, Lone Diner was afforded a clear view of her cleavage, a flash of lacy bra. When she straightened up, bowl in hand, he realised her nipples were poking out beneath her crisp white shirt.

She's cold, he thought, remembering another chilled body from the day before. Skin like marble, breasts carved from…

"Maybe you should turn the heating on?" he remarked, staring at her nipples intently, hand once again rubbing his inner thigh. "It's brass monkeys in here."

"Sure," the waitress mumbled, turning to leave.

"It'll save you a shirt," the man continued.

"What?" She didn't understand.

"You're cutting your shirt, at the moment," he pointed out, openly staring at her chest and smiling broadly. It was slang for "your nipples are on show", something his father used to say to his mother on the rare occasion she wasn't modestly dressed.

Lone Diner reinforced the point by positioning his hands in front of his own chest, then holding both index fingers out straight, mimicking giant, erect nipple tips.

The waitress froze, looked down.

Her face twisted in shock.

There we go, he thought, smugly.

A response, at last.

"I'll warm them up for you in my mouth, if you like." He flashed soup-stained teeth.

"You dirty sod," the waitress hissed, outraged. Then she turned violently on her heel and stormed off to the kitchen.

Lone Diner leaned back in his chair, chuckling. A reaction was all he'd wanted. Just an acknowledgement. Being ignored was not an option. It never was.

He looked across at the couple still working through their starters, to see if they'd witnessed him in action.

The woman had moved her chair so that she no longer faced him. The couple were once again engrossed in conversation, heads tipped towards each other, backs turned from him. Her hand, he saw, was on her date's thigh.

Lone Diner's triumphant mood slipped.

He felt a moment of wild, raw jealousy for their intimacy.

He'd wanted to make more than a slight dent in their happiness. Their body language indicated he'd failed.

The kitchen doors swung open with force, banging into the wall beside. Lone Diner jumped. The waitress came back into the restaurant with two men in tow: the chef and the barman. They marched across the restaurant and stopped at his table, crowding in close, no proximity hesitation now, the men scowling down at him, arms folded. The chef was a big man with a beard and massive tattooed forearms. He loomed over Lone Diner angrily.

"I've been told you were disrespectful to a member of our staff," the chef said, curtly.

"I'm sorry?" Lone Diner blinked, feigning innocence. He kept his tone mild and polite. "I'm afraid I have no idea what you're talking about."

"Oh, yes, you do," the waitress snapped. Her voice was low. She did not want to disturb the other diners. "You made a joke about my tits. You were fucking staring at them! You made hand gestures!"

"I think you must be mistaken," Lone Diner said, calmly.

The chef and the barman both tensed.

"We don't take kindly to inappropriate conduct in our establishment," the chef said. "I'm afraid I'm going to have to ask you to leave, sir."

Lone Diner blinked. Outrage stung like smoke in his eyes.

"What, you're going to take her word over mine?" he said, incredulously.

"Yes, sir, I am."

"But… look at the way she's dressed, for god's sake! It's not my fault she's put everything on show like meat in the butcher's window!"

The chef bent down, pushed his face into Lone Diner's.

"Out," he hissed, and Lone Diner heard knuckles crack, one by one as the large man prepped his hands for a fight.

He had a moment to assess his situation, calculating the likelihood that he could get the better of the two men, realising quickly he couldn't. Not without a weapon. And not only was he at a physical disadvantage, and likely to get his face beaten in, he was also at an aspirational disadvantage: there was more that he wanted to do with his evening than just eat mediocre soup and wind up the waitress. Much more. If he made a fuss, his plans would be fucked. The men might call the police, and if the police came, they might lock him up for the night for disorderly conduct, or worse, search his car. He had no criminal record to date, no history of misdemeanour, and he intended to keep it that way until he'd achieved a few more personal goals. He had no desire to sacrifice his fingerprints to the great databank in the sky. Or the body parts in the boot of his car. Not now. Not when he was finally coming into his own.

Lone Diner held his hands up in a gesture of surrender.

"Alright," he said, as if the notion of leaving had been his idea all along. "I'll go. There's no need to be so aggressive about it."

He gathered his phone and slipped it into his pocket. Then he pushed the dead bouquet of flowers towards the waitress.

"Here," he said, smiling affably. "These are for you. A peace offering. Roses are red..."

"Get the fuck out of here, you prick," the barman interrupted savagely, and the chef cracked his knuckles again.

The waitress stared at the flowers as if they were a bouquet of poisonous snakes. They'd be in the bin before the night was through.

Lone Diner left, but not before he shot one final look at the couple in the window.

Neither of them acknowledged his parting, but he thought he saw the woman's face partially turn in his direction, so he knew she had registered him leaving.

Don't worry, sweetheart, he told her, silently. *You'll see me again before long.*

He was escorted back through the maze of corridors and out into the car park, the staff taking no risks that he would slip free and somehow get back into the restaurant to continue his mischief.

"Thank you so much," Lone Diner said on exiting the building, for all the world as if he'd had a wonderful evening and had chosen this moment to depart.

"You stink," the chef hissed, slamming the pub door in Lone Diner's face.

Out in the cold once again, the man considered getting his shotgun from the car, marching back into the pub, unleashing himself on the staff – but as he had this thought, he heard a bolt draw across the heavy oak door from within. They were locking him out, just to be on the safe side.

Wait, he told himself. *Save it.*

The right opportunity will present itself soon enough.

The couple in the restaurant couldn't stay in there forever, he reasoned.

Soon, they would be drunk, tired, full of food. Slow-witted, even more so.

He looked around and saw one other car in the car park, probably belonging to a member of staff.

It made sense. The couple would have taken taxis out here. They were both drinking too much to drive.

All you have to do is wait, he told himself again.

Lone Diner went back to his car, humming a jaunty tune to himself. His breath came out in thick, white plumes. The cold had somehow gotten colder, which he didn't think was possible. There was already a thick crust of ice on his car, newly formed in the hour he'd been away.

Good, he thought. *Good.*

A plan was forming.

Alone at Last

Connor let out an exasperated noise.

"What's happening now?" he said, no longer trying to hide his irritation as Amandine craned her head over her shoulder to watch Lone Diner being escorted out of the restaurant.

"He's gone," she said, relief washing over her. Her body sagged. "Thank god."

Connor turned to check.

"Really?"

"Yeah, I don't know what happened, but he got escorted out by the staff."

She turned back, feeling a hundred pounds lighter now that Lone Diner was no longer watching her every move.

Connor seemed happy with the turn of events, too.

"See? Now you can focus on what really matters," he said, trying on a winning smile for size.

Amandine said nothing – but thought many things to herself.

She moved her chair away from him, back to her original position.

Reset

"So," she said, the urgency to run home having died down with Lone Diner's departure. She still wasn't completely comfortable, but was willing to at least eat her dinner before leaving. She was hungry and had little food in her fridge. The wine was good. She knew the path of least resistance to an enjoyable remainder of her evening lay through flattery and attention. "Tell me about you. About your childhood. The real stuff."

Connor shrugged but seemed pleased with the line of questioning.

"Not much to tell, really," he began, shaking the now empty wine bottle and looking around for the waitress so he could order another.

"Modesty doesn't suit you," Amandine said, dryly. "Come on, this is what first dates are for, isn't it?"

"Fine, fine. I grew up in a single-parent family. My mam... ah, my mother sort of, um... gave me up when I was very small. She left just before Christmas."

Amandine sat up straighter. She had not been expecting this.

"Left?"

He nodded, just once. It was not a memory he enjoyed reliving.

"Said she was going out to do some last-minute Christmas shopping. Never came back." His mood shifted. Amandine caught a slight hesitation. There was more to this story, clearly.

"I'm sorry," she said.

He shrugged. "Don't be." A deep breath. "It was for the best."

Here it comes, Amandine thought.

Connor swallowed. Loosened his tie, unbuttoned his collar by two holes.

"She gave me this before she left, see."

Beneath the neatly pressed cotton, Amandine could see scarred tissue, pink and shiny. An old wound, it skirted around the base of his neck just above the collar bone, like a thick necklace.

Amandine's hand went up to her mouth, a brief, involuntary motion.

What the fuck, she thought, brain scrambling for words, *is the right thing to say in response to that?*

Her mind wheeled. She felt instantly, horribly sad for Connor and guilty for assuming the worst of him.

"That's quite a lot for anyone to go through," she said, grateful for her own mother. "Let alone a child."

Connor quickly buttoned himself back up. He seemed ashamed of his wounds. He slid the tie's knot back to its rightful place, adjusting it several times before it sat just right. His hands, she noticed, were very dry and red, like he washed them a lot.

"I don't blame her in any way," he said. "At least, I don't think I do. She was just a kid herself really. Got married too young. And if she'd stayed, who knows how much worse it might have gotten."

Amandine nodded. "That's a valid point. But–"

He cut across her, knowing what she was going to say. "Oh, I'm not blasé or anything, I know it was abuse. I considered it a lucky escape; I still do. But her leaving the way she did had lots of implications, right? She left my dad in the shit when she ran off. Well and truly. He had to do all of it. Be mam *and* dad. He never remarried. Trust issues, he said. As a result, I'm not..." He held up his hands. "I guess I'm not too good around women. Or rejection. Or emotional stuff in general. I tend to avoid it. Feelings. The big ones, at any rate. I get anxious, too. When I let myself."

"I'm sorry." Amandine was struggling. She'd got him all wrong. In the context of his childhood, wasn't some adult insecurity, neediness, unpredictability... inevitable? Forgivable?

Connor shrugged again. "Probably a very different upbringing to yours," he said, defensively. A knee-jerk reaction to making himself vulnerable. "I must come across as a right fuck-up, compared to you."

She was brought up short by this.

"Wait. Why do we have to compare ourselves to each other? Life isn't a competition, last I checked."

Connor shook his head. "Of course it is! *All* of life is a competition. That's the whole point. That guy's car or dick is bigger than mine, that dude makes more money than I do, that house is nicer than mine..."

Amandine rolled her eyes. "I think you're forgetting that not everybody's motivations or lived experience is universal. What makes you think my life is so perfect?"

The waitress came back into the restaurant looking relieved. Connor waved at her. He held up the empty bottle by way of explanation, and the silent order of a replacement was acknowledged.

"I get it can't be easy that both your parents have gone, but…"

"But?"

"It's just… the whole package you present." He gestured, a circular motion meant to incorporate her entire being.

"Package?" It felt like an odd choice of word.

"Yeah. You seem so cool, collected. Your dress, your jewellery. You just look…" He scratched his head. "Put together. Like you've got your shit in line."

She considered that.

"You ever feel like you're wearing a mask, Connor? To help you fit in more?"

He nodded.

"Yeah, I guess I do," he said, uncomfortable. "Every day, in fact."

"Well, me too. Some days," she said, "it's hard to get out of bed. Really, *really* hard."

The waitress returned with the fresh bottle of wine. She poured, filling Amandine's glass first, then cleared away their starter plates.

"Sorry for any commotion," the girl said as she left. "It should be nice and quiet in here for you now."

Amandine smiled, waited until they were alone again before continuing. She only wanted an audience of one.

She spoke haltingly, as if compelled.

"When I do manage it, I find I can't… *do* anything."

Connor examined his wine in the candlelight. "What do you mean?"

"Just that. It's like… I'm stuck. Not just some days, actually. Most days. I don't function like other people. I can't do things. Not one single, useful thing. On the really bad days, I can't even dress myself, wash my hair, brush my teeth. I don't look like this all the time, is what I am getting at."

"Okay..." Connor's face was closed, hard to read. She had an idea he didn't like how she was spoiling the illusion of her he'd created in his head.

But honesty was the only way this was going to work, she told herself, so he was going to get the real version of her, not the carefully curated version.

"If I'm lucky," she continued, "I'll fall out from under the duvet and end up on the couch, horizontal, where I binge watch some dumb TV show that I don't really care about or absorb or get into properly because I'm too busy playing a shitty game I've played hundreds of times before on my shitty old laptop, because I can never just do one thing at a time, even though I can't do anything at all. Does that make sense?"

"Not really."

"If anyone calls, I ignore it. Same with texts, most of the time. It's just too much effort."

Connor stared intently at his wine.

"And I often find it hard to feed myself, so I'll either starve, or binge eat junk food, which I can just pull out of a packet, you know? This meal is the most nutritious thing I've eaten in weeks, in fact, and so far, it's been mostly booze."

"Okay," Connor repeated, monotone.

Amandine kept going like a freight train with no brakes. "I also pull my eyelashes out repeatedly on this eye – see? I hide it with mascara, but the lashes here are missing. Look."

She pushed the candle to one side and leaned over the table, putting her face close to his so she could show him the noticeable gap in the line of otherwise long, curling lashes framing her eyes. The skin of that eyelid was sore, a little puffy. She pointed to the tiny blunt stubs where the eyelash hairs had snapped off near the base.

He frowned.

"What's that all about?" he said, finally.

Amandine settled back in her chair.

"It's called stimming," she explained. "I think. That's what the internet says, anyway. I don't pull them so much as I kind of, like, tap them and use my thumbnail to fiddle with them until they break off and go all stubby like this. It's a compulsion that makes me feel calmer, but then I get a sty or an eye infection that means I have to wear an eye patch to force myself to stop doing it. Fidget toys help. So do hobbies: painting, sewing, sketching, anything that keeps my hands busy, but those require energy and patience, and I have neither. If I start anything new, I can never stick to it for long enough to make any real difference."

"I see."

"Oh, I pick my scalp, too."

"Right."

Amandine felt like really thrusting the point of the truth dagger home. It was the only way to have a meaningful relationship, she realised. Everything out on the table at the start. If he was still around after this, then…

"I also have frequent panic attacks, and I get anxious and overwhelmed a *lot*." She started to feel panicky even talking about them. "I can't stand bright overhead lights or repetitive noises. Or loud noises. I can't get too hot, or too cold. I'm easily overwhelmed. It makes me hit myself in the head, when it all gets too much. Not hard enough to do any lasting damage, but sometimes I have bruises and lumps. I use walls or doorframes to bang myself against. Anything hard with a corner or edge. I'm used to the sight of my own blood. It's oddly reassuring. The pain helps make things manageable again."

Connor had gone very still, and very quiet. This was no longer fun, for either of them.

Still, Amandine didn't stop.

"I drink a lot of alcohol, because it helps tone the world down to an acceptable level. It's like… without booze the dial is always turned up to maximum in my body. My brain is too noisy without it."

The words dried up as suddenly as they had spouted out. Amandine had nothing left to share, so she closed her mouth and waited to see what Connor would do.

Disappointment followed as she saw he had shut himself off, powered down. It suddenly felt like she was on a date with a boulder or a brick wall. The change in his demeanour was deeply upsetting.

"Excuse me," Connor said eventually, pushing back his chair. "I need to use the bathroom."

Then, without another word, he left.

Amandine sat in the now deserted restaurant, whiplashed by the turn of events.

That's done it, she thought.

What had possessed her?

She sank her head in her hands and wondered if Connor would come back from the toilet at all, or simply use the opportunity to make his escape, leaving her to foot the bill.

Too Many Truths

Amandine waited. Connor didn't return. One minute stretched into five, then seven.

She couldn't blame him, she supposed. When it was out in the open like that, she sounded like an absolute freak.

Amandine felt a greasy sensation inside.

She was all too familiar with it.

With feeling routinely, unrelentingly ashamed of herself.

For being weird.

For spoiling things.

Amandine questioned her motivation for being so brutally honest. Any sensible girl would have kept all that information to herself on a first date.

Too intense.

Too much.

Was she deliberately trying to frighten him off, she wondered?

Or was it a test she was subconsciously trying to administer?

Can you cope with my brand of freak, Connor?

Whatever.

It doesn't matter. He isn't coming back.

But then, Connor returned to the table.

All Out on the Table

"Sorry," Connor said as he got settled again, but he seemed even more distant than he had before. They were back to square one, perhaps further back even, back to their wary, insulated selves, safe from harm.

Amandine shrugged.

"It's fine."

Best behave as if nothing had happened. Get through the date. Delete his number as soon as she got home.

Save face.

Mask back on.

"Like I said, I found ways to live with it."

More silence stretched between the couple. The greasy feeling in Amandine's guts remained.

"You okay?" she asked him, eventually. She wondered how much battery her phone had left. Enough to call a taxi, she hoped.

Then, Connor surprised her. He seemed to make a decision, and visibly came back into the room, back into the date.

"You said you feel bad some days," Connor resumed their conversation as if nothing had happened. "It's not like that every day for you?"

Amandine no longer felt safe sharing things with him. The mood was spoiled almost beyond recall.

She put on a false, bright tone.

"It's fine," she said. "Let's change the subject."

Connor shook his head. "I don't want to. I just needed a moment, that was all."

"You were gone for ten minutes. I thought you'd bailed."

"I told you, didn't I? I don't deal well with this stuff. It's not like I was encouraged to share feelings much when I was a kid. Quite the opposite."

Amandine softened slightly. "I thought… I just wanted you to know that it isn't easy for me, either."

Connor looked her dead in the eye. "I appreciate you sharing that with me. Now answer the question. You don't struggle like that every day?"

"No." She smiled, although it was a brittle smile that never reached her eyes. "It comes and goes. The upside is that when I *do* crawl out of the dark patches, it's like… like the sun coming out from behind clouds. Like someone injects fuel straight into my bloodstream. I can do anything, after. I feel like a superhero. Run a marathon, climb a mountain, write a book, paint pictures, learn a new software… I'm kind of invincible, in the good bits."

"That must be very tiring. The ups and downs, I mean."

Amandine tried to keep her composure, keep talking, because otherwise, she realised, she was about to cry. Another absolute "don't" on a first date.

"It's about learning to take the good with the bad, even when the bad really, really sucks." She drew a deep breath. "But… it doesn't lend itself to relationships, my way of life. Now perhaps you understand why *I'm* single."

"So, what is it? Grief? Trauma? Autism? ADHD?" he asked.

Amandine laughed. "As if I fucking know. Do you have any idea how long it takes to get a diagnosis for anything vaguely neurospicy in our healthcare system?"

"Neurospicy?" He coughed, amused. Dabbed at his wine-beaded chin with his napkin. "I've never heard that term before."

"It's a thing," she said, defensively.

"But seriously," he replied, "grief can do odd things to the human body, I've heard. How… how did your parents die?"

Oh, fuck no, Amandine thought to herself.

We're not doing that, not today.

"I… I, ah… I can't," she apologised. "Sorry. Too much."

He nodded. "Fair enough. You started it, though."

A small twinkle had returned to his eyes.

"I know."

"If you're neurospicy, does that make me… neurobland?"

Her guard wavered.

"Not even remotely," she said, amused. "Neurospicy people tend to move in herds."

"Like Jurassic Park?"

"Like Jurassic Park."

"So, wait, does that make me Malcom or Grant?"

His humour was a good sign, but she'd been around funny men before, men who used jokes to hide their real intentions with stunning efficiency.

"Definitely Malcom. Anyway. The waiting lists for assessments are years long, literally *years,* and I can't afford to go private. I can't hold down a regular job. I'm actually a disaster human, Connor. To go back to your earlier assumption that I have my shit in line. I know I shouldn't be saying all this on a first date. Offices and desk-jobs are death sentences to me; they exacerbate all my symptoms. I had to sell a ton of stuff to be able to buy this dress, and the jewellery, both of which are second-hand. The shoes… I rented these, can you believe that?"

"Your shoes?"

"They have websites for people who don't want to fork out lots of money for a pair of designer heels, so you just rent them for a night, then post them back. And my hair... I haven't been to a hair salon in five years. I just tie it up and hope for the best."

"So, what's your point?" Connor folded his arms, mirroring her posture.

"The point is... I *don't* have my shit together, Connor, that is the point. Not even remotely. You should know that before... before this goes any further."

"For real?" he said, eventually. "They let you rent shoes for one night?"

Amandine sagged back in her chair.

"Wow."

"I know. Made you smile, though." He tipped his glass at her, winking.

She realised she couldn't figure Connor out at all. He was as changeable as the wind. She wasn't sure if that was a red flag, her own inability to understand people, or both things at war with each other.

"Does none of this bother you?" she asked, genuinely curious.

"A successful business model built entirely around designer rental shoes bothers me enormously." He took a swig of water. "*And* the fact that you don't know what you're actually struggling with. Wouldn't a diagnosis of some sort help?"

"I don't think so. I just assume that certain things about me are true, and act accordingly."

"Self-diagnosed."

"No, nothing as presumptive. It's more like... I pay attention to what's good for my brain and what isn't. So, I socialise, but only as far as I feel comfortable, which isn't often. As soon as I get overloaded, I take myself off somewhere quiet, to be alone. Like you just did, I guess. Music helps. Headphones. I make things when I can and try to walk every day. I take a lot of baths. Something about the quiet, womb-like experience, maybe, I don't know. And I have these pills… you get them off the internet, it's like a funky mushroom microdose compound. They help too. As do boundaries."

"Boundaries?"

"I only trust who I trust. And I only like to be touched in certain ways."

"I see."

Amandine jutted her chin out defiantly. "You never answered my question," she said.

Connor smiled. "Am I bothered that you're a bit weird, you mean?"

Amandine waited.

"Honestly?"

"Yeah?"

Connor's smile widened.

"It helps, to be honest. To know I'm not the only one."

Amandine swallowed.

"The Emotionally Unavailable Man and the Chronically Overwhelmed Woman," she said, voice edged with feeling. "We sound like shit superheroes."

"We do."

Any lingering tension left the room. In its wake, Amandine felt one thing only, surprising and visceral: arousal.

The waitress came back, then, with their mains.

They used the new course to draw a line under things and move on.

And somehow, despite everything, the rest of the date went very, very well indeed.

Without a Ride

The waitress began to make not-so-subtle noises as midnight approached, clattering plates and moving chairs around impatiently in a bid to get them to hurry up.

"We're the last ones here," Connor murmured, stroking the back of Amandine's hand gently. He touched her this time as if it was a privilege he didn't want to forgo.

She retaliated by moving her other hand slightly further up his thigh, pressing her left leg into his right under the table.

"We were the only ones here to begin with," she replied. "Excluding the gross angry man with soup on his chin."

They checked behind them, a habit. Lone Diner's cellophane-wrapped roses still lay on his table, a lingering reminder of his unpleasant presence.

The waitress, failing to rouse the couple into any apparent sense of urgency, disappeared out back in a huff. She switched off the background music before she went, which left the restaurant in a deep, agreeable state of quiet.

Amandine looked at the dead roses.

"Fucking creep," she muttered, remembering the porn on his phone, and the odd, intense, furious stare he'd directed at her.

"He wasn't *that* bad," Connor laughed. "Just a skeevy, lonely dude with nothing better to do than perv over the only beautiful woman in the restaurant."

Amandine scrunched up her nose. "No, I told you. There was more to it than that. I can't explain it, but he set all my senses off."

"Well, he's gone now. We don't ever have to see him again or even think about him."

"True."

Connor leaned in.

"All by ourselves," he said softly. "You know what that means, don't you?"

"What?" Amandine had a good idea. She could feel heat radiating off her date. She smelt his aftershave again, sandalwood and soap and clean, fresh things.

She bit her bottom lip.

"Oh, don't do that," Connor murmured, staring at her mouth. "The lip thing… it sends me crazy."

"I can't help it." She chewed harder, exaggerated the gesture.

"Right, well. You're in trouble now," Connor said. He leaned in even closer.

The candle had almost burned out, the flame guttering on its final nub of wick. The lights in the restaurant were dimmed, another tactic to encourage them to leave. Through the panoramic window next to her table, Amandine could see dozens of stars in the cold winter sky, and the soft tips of reeds rippling in a gathering breeze.

Then Connor pressed his face into hers, blotting out everything else.

Their kiss felt like she was kissing someone she had known a very long time for the very first time. It was a peculiar feeling, at once a complete novelty but also comforting, familiar. Like walking into a strange house in a strange neighbourhood and finding it full of people you knew.

Hesitant at first, the kiss got heavier as they both learned what the other liked. A bit of tongue here, a nip of the lower lip there. Harder, now softer. Breath came heavier. Hands came up to caress. Hair got mussed and tousled.

They were interrupted by a cross throat-clearing.

"Guys, *please*," the waitress said, as they broke apart, panting a little. "Take it outside, would you? We want to go to bed."

Behind her, the bartender and a huge, tattooed man dressed in chef's whites leaned against a wall, looking tired. The bartender was rolling a cigarette and grinning. The chef rolled his eyes, unimpressed.

Connor pulled out his wallet.

"Bill, please," he said, voice unsteady. There was lipstick all over his mouth.

Connor paid the bill, leaving a generous tip for the staff's trouble, and the couple were ushered out. The waitress almost slammed the pub door on them in her haste to close up.

"Thanks for a nice evening!" Connor said, as the heavy front door swung closed.

"Welcome!" was the short response, and then, they were alone again.

The bitter air outside was like a slap to the face. Amandine remembered the weather warning on her phone: *extreme cold*.

They weren't fucking kidding, she thought, shivering as her body temperature rapidly plummeted.

Amandine, now thoroughly drunk and horny, turned to Connor, running a hand through his thick hair.

They kissed some more, eager to taste each other again and share body warmth. White breath-mist surrounded them, illuminated by the many fairy lights adorning the pub's exterior. The night felt almost solid, pressing against Amandine's skin like the flat of a blade. She shivered.

Connor slipped a hand around her waist, let it travel down her backside. In response, Amandine slid her own hand over his crotch, found an erection growing.

The sound of tyres pulling aggressively past them out of the car park broke them apart again. Gravel crunched. The waitress honked her horn as she left the restaurant in her small Ford Fiesta, the chef and bartender both leering out at them through the cramped Ford's windows.

Amandine and Connor grinned sheepishly, waved.

Then they kissed some more.

"Fuck," said Connor, pulling back once more to try to catch his breath. "I need to get you home."

But what about the Miracle Word? Amandine remembered, suddenly.

The one painted on her belly with blood.

If I'm naked... I can't let him see that!

But then Connor cupped her face in his warm hands and gently licked her top lip.

Her knees went soft, like butter.

"Your place or mine," she replied, in a slightly strangled voice. Then she laughed.

"What?"

"I've always wanted to say that," she explained.

"Yours," Connor decided. "I'll get us a taxi. What's your address?"

She told him. He pulled out his phone and tried to order a cab while Amandine shivered in her thin jacket beside him. It was the coldest night she could remember in a long, long time. Glittering frost crunched under her heels. The stars were brilliant, the sky a deep, brutal black. An almost-full moon, replete with a distinct halo, lit the pub car park, which was handy, as all the other lights apart from a distant streetlamp had been switched off. That was the problem with country roads and pubs, she thought, especially around here. It really was the middle of nowhere once darkness fell. Buses didn't run, no lights, no pavements, no nothing.

Just moonlight and reeds and barn owls hooting softly in the night.

Romantic, if a person's idea of romance was being completely alone and barely able to see.

Amandine smiled. It was.

And the moon was undeniably beautiful, the halo rainbow-tinged and clear. Amandine, who found she was far more drunk than she'd realised on leaving the warm restaurant, lost herself staring into it, reflecting on the evening she'd just had even as she felt herself getting rapidly chilled to the bone.

"Hey," Connor said, apologetically breaking into her reverie. "I don't suppose you could try, too? I can't get anyone to come out on mine."

He showed her his screen. *Locating driver... Unable to...* A location marker jumped crazily around the map of the area as the app searched for a ride and was unable to find one.

"Sure." Amandine drew out her own mobile and ran a cold finger across the screen, but there was no familiar glow in response.

"Oh, shit," she said, eyes wide. "I think it's run out of power."

"Ah, fuck," Connor swore softly. "Mine's only got a little bit left too. Don't worry. I'll keep trying."

"What happens if nobody comes? A lot of the cabbies knock off at ten out here."

"Yeah, but it's unusual for them *all* to have stopped for the night. It is Friday, after all. I'll keep trying. We'll get one eventually."

He sounded confident, but she knew enough about him now to understand that how he sounded and how he actually felt were two very different things.

"But," said Amandine, playing devil's advocate, "what if we don't?"

"Guess I'm carrying you home, then."

She grimaced. "You're such a bullshitter," she said, poking him in the ribs.

He winked.

"What? It's only a few miles to my place. I'm closer. Well, about seven. Can't expect you to walk all the way back in rented heels, can I?"

She leaned on him for warmth, trying not to think about how much her feet were hurting and how tired she suddenly was.

Connor kept trying to order a taxi until his battery ran out.

"Ah, shit. Phone's dead," he said, dejectedly.

By then, Amandine was too cold to reply. She shook violently, failing to hide her discomfort. She didn't want to spoil a good night by coming across as high maintenance, but it was well below freezing. She could see frost patterns on puddles in the car park, and her fingers and toes had gone numb. Her nose and ears hurt when she rubbed at them.

Connor looked her up and down, concerned.

"Look at you. We have to get you home before you freeze," he said, and then he squatted, motioning for her to jump, and hoisted her up onto his back. Amandine shrieked in glee, convinced she was about to squash him entirely, then clung on for dear life, like a shell on a turtle's back (*isn't there a joke about this? Michelle?*) legs wrapped around Connor's waist, arms locked about his shoulders.

"You can't carry me like this the whole way!" she gasped, secretly delighted. He was a lot stronger than he looked.

"Just watch me!"

He set off like a horse at the races, galloping along the pitch-dark road away from the pub, using the faint gleam from the cat's eyes set into the tarmac to keep himself in a straight line, and stop them both from rolling off into the deep drainage ditch that lined both sides of all the country lanes.

"Let me *down*!" Amandine hooted, half laughing, half serious, after only a few hundred yards of being bounced and jolted around. "I'm going to be sick on the back of your head if you keep going like that!"

"Ooh, kinky," Connor gasped. But he stopped, shifting his grip on her as she slipped.

She smacked him gently on his left shoulder. "I mean it! You have to let me down."

Panting, Connor did as he was told. "Maybe you're right," he said, wheezing as he let her slide down off his back. "Maybe I can't carry you the whole way. Peaked too soon, didn't I?"

"It's okay." She patted him on the back of his hot neck and ran fingers through his hair again, which now felt crispy, covered in a light film of ice. "I'm a big girl. I can walk. Really, I can. These shoes aren't that bad. Just let me lean on you."

Connor straightened up, still trying to catch his breath, and took her hand, slipping it into his own pocket and keeping it there.

"You know, if you ditched the heels, we'd be the same height, I reckon," he said, giving her a side-eye.

She shook her head. "I can't believe that's all you're thinking about at a time like this. If my height was a problem, you could have said something a lot earlier."

"It isn't a problem," he chuckled. "I'm into it."

"Humpf," Amandine said.

They hobbled on, Connor's shoulder bearing the load as Amandine leaned on him.

He remained encouraging, despite their snail's pace.

"You're taking this a lot better than many other people would," he said after they'd gone a little further up the road. "I wouldn't blame you for being annoyed. I feel like a fucking idiot for letting my phone run out like that. A gentleman would have ordered a taxi inside, before we left. I feel awful."

"Hey, I let mine run out too," Amandine replied, focusing on balancing in her heels in the dark without turning her ankle over and spraining it. There was ice on the road, lethal if she placed her foot down in the wrong way. She slipped every second step and had to correct herself constantly. She felt like a stork landing on ice, all long legs and fluttering wings.

"Besides, a little exercise never hurt anyone," she panted, as much to herself as to Connor. "And it means we get to spend longer with each other, if you think about it."

She felt, rather than saw, him shaking his head.

"Where have you been all my life?" he asked, squeezing her tight with one arm.

"Burning through vibrators at an alarming rate," she stated, dryly. "I've got one in my handbag. My emergency vibrator."

He shook his head again. "You're ridiculous," he said.

"I know."

Their good humour only got them a mile down the road before Amandine had to stop and rest her feet again. They had begun to bleed in several places where the inflexible patent leather of the rented shoes pinched and rubbed. There were holes in her tights too, and multiple ladders snaked all the way up from her feet to her knees.

"Oh, god, the state of me," she said, softly, examining her legs in the moonlight. "I look like a scarecrow."

"Your shoes still bad?"

Amandine walked a few more steps, then hissed in pain.

"Ahh… yes," she confirmed. "Really bad."

"Let me carry you again," Connor offered, but Amandine turned him down.

"No, I can manage. Maybe… maybe I can take them off, walk barefoot," she said, resting on a long metal crash barrier cradling a hairpin bend in the road. "You'll finally get your wish," she panted. "Heels off, so you can look me straight in the eye."

The barrier was jarringly cold, sharp-edged and uncomfortable. Amandine was aware she was probably getting her new dress filthy with the second-hand exhaust-fume-muck coating the metal barrier, but she didn't care. She needed to get the weight off. Her legs were about to give out entirely, she realised.

"You'll get frostbite on that perfect arse of yours if you sit on that too long," Connor warned. "It must be arctic temperatures out here now." He rubbed his hands together and jumped up and down on the spot, slapping himself to try and keep warm as he waited for her to recover a little.

"The forecast said minus fourteen, in some places. Record-breaking temperatures for this time of year."

"Yeah, I saw that. Weather's so fucked up these days. Global warming and all that shit. Doesn't feel very warm now though, does it?"

Amandine's shivering became once again pitifully pronounced now that she was no longer moving. She reached down and tried to hook off her shoes, but stopped when she realised doing so would expose the raw, blistered flesh on the backs of her ankles to the cold. She wasn't sure she could bear that, no matter how sharply the leather rubbed.

"I don't think I can take these off without making things worse," she said, feeling increasingly exhausted.

"Ah, shit," Connor said, now thoroughly dejected with how things were going.

He came over to her and slotted himself in between her legs, opening his coat wide and closing it over her body to make a heat seal. "I'm so sorry, Amandine. You deserve a better first date than this."

"Shut up," she replied, shaking and shuddering. "I've had a great time."

"Serious? I feel like it's been a giant disaster."

"Serious. I wouldn't say it if I didn't mean it."

He kissed her again, then, hard and urgent, and Amandine let herself get lost in it despite her discomfort, tongues clashing, teeth crashing into teeth, and she could feel him getting hard again, and she thought, despite the cold, that maybe they would do it right here, that he was about to spin her around and bend her over and fuck her there on the side of the road, pinned against the crash barrier, he felt so desperate for her, but just as hands began to wander with real intention, just as they both began to warm up and forget about the cold, a light came upon them, accompanied by a deep purring noise.

Two lights.

Headlights.

"Ah shit, flag it down, flag it down!" Connor said, blinking and ripping himself away from Amandine. He jumped back from the crash barrier, out into the road, and started waving his arms like a lunatic, shouting. He was barely visible even as the headlights approached, and Amandine had a sudden vision of the car rounding the bend and ploughing straight into Connor, knocking him into the ditch, leaving him bloodied and broken in the trench as it sped off into the night.

"Careful!" Amandine cried. "You'll get hit! Connor! Get out of the road, you idiot!"

But the car, which cornered the sharp hairpin carefully, slowed, the headlights – which had been on beam – dimming.

"Oh, thank fuck," Connor breathed, then he turned to Amandine, his face brightly illuminated. "There's hope for us yet," he said, a cocky grin back on his face.

Amandine was not so sure.

Red Flags

The car pulled up next to them and sat in the road, engine idling.

Connor went to the driver's-side window. Tapped on it.

The glass slid down, only an inch: just enough of a gap to talk through.

"Mate! Thank you for stopping," Connor effused, bouncing up and down on the balls of his feet with nervous energy. "You don't know it, but you're a lifesaver."

Silence from the interior. The engine filled the conversational gap, turning over crankily.

Amandine frowned. Was this car familiar?

Connor tried again, clearing his throat.

"Listen, I'm sorry to ask this, mate," he continued, "I'm *so* sorry. But we were having dinner at the Boat, and they kicked us out before we'd managed to order a taxi, and our phones have run out of juice, and we could not get one single fucking cab to come get us."

More engine noise. The car sounded as if it hadn't passed its last MOT. The whole thing rattled and juddered as it sat there idling.

Connor's voice went up, became pitchy.

"Anyway… We're stranded in the cold. My girlfriend can barely walk. If we could possibly get a lift… just up the road, like, not far…"

Connor trailed off, waiting anxiously.

Girlfriend, Amandine thought, feeling numb.

Chugchugchugchug.

Then, from the dark interior:

"Can't you call someone?"

The voice was soft-spoken, hard to hear over the engine.

Connor spread his hands. "I told you. Both our phones died. I'd ring a cab from a phone box if I could find one that still worked, but I don't think I could remember a taxi number if you paid me. I promise we're for real, mate. We're in dire straits. It's freezing out here. If you could just give us a lift to the nearest taxi stand..."

More silence. The driver was probably considering his options, Amandine thought.

Connor had a brainwave and tried one last thing.

"I can pay you!" he cried, desperate. "I have cash."

Connor pulled out his wallet to demonstrate that he did, indeed, have money. Amandine thought he might even get down on his knees and beg.

Does he really want to fuck you that badly? she wondered.

Begging turned out not to be necessary.

A resigned sigh came out of the small gap in the window. It made a cloud of white in the night.

"Where do you need to get to?"

Connor fist-pumped in victory, then clasped his hands together as if praying.

"*Yes!* Thank you, mate. Thank you!"

"Where?"

"The other side of Hickling Green, a couple of miles up the lane. Not far from Sea Palling Beach. It's only about a fifteen-minute drive. You're saving our lives, mate!" Connor resembled a small child, bounding about in enthusiasm.

Amandine winced. The word "mate" was starting to feel a bit overcooked.

Evidently the driver thought so, too. He leaned over and opened the passenger-side door.

"Get in," his voice said, still barely discernible above the engine noise. "I'll give you a ride. You won't find any taxis running tonight. Or a phone box."

Connor was still in full labrador puppy mode.

"Ah, mate, that's *incredible*! I can't thank you enough, really. I owe you one!"

A large hand motioned behind the window, gesturing for him to hurry up.

"You're letting all the heat out."

Connor beckoned Amandine, who still rested against the crash barrier.

"We have a ride, come on!"

But Amandine didn't feel so good about their new ride home.

Perhaps it was something to do with the way their rescuer spoke, in a soft, resigned voice that was hard to hear, or the fact that the car's interior was too dark for her to properly see the driver, only his indistinct, bulky shadow; or perhaps it was the speed at which he had agreed to help them, almost as if he'd expected to find them out here like this; or perhaps it was the niggly feeling that she'd seen the car before, somewhere, although she couldn't say where.

Whatever the reason, her internal warning system was yelling loudly at her to pay attention. *Redflagredflagredflag!* it said, the words a babble of urgency that grew more hysterical with every passing moment.

The hand came out of the car, gestured again.

"I'm not waiting all night," the driver said, raising his voice slightly.

"Amandine!" Connor urged, growing irritated. He didn't want to risk their ride slipping away any more than he wanted them to walk the entire seven miles back to his house during a record-breaking winter night and freeze themselves to death in the process.

Amandine knew this, and she knew that accepting the ride was the only sensible way out of their predicament, which could, given the weather, turn dangerous the longer they were out in the cold, but still she hesitated. She didn't want to get into the stranger's car, not one bit.

But she was also cold, and tired, meaning she couldn't say *why*, exactly, she didn't want to accept the lift. She knew she was drunk, and emotional, and she desperately needed to be somewhere warm again so she could start thinking properly, rationally. She could feel ice settling in her lungs. Her nose had lost all feeling. Her cheeks hurt. Her feet were two raw, throbbing wounds.

"Amandine!" Connor was staring at her, annoyed.

Regardless, she still hung back, motioning to Connor to come closer to her instead, unwilling to move without discussing things properly first.

Connor made an exasperated noise, told the driver to wait a second.

"One minute," came the reply. "Then you're on your own."

Connor nodded and jogged over, misinterpreting Amandine's request and holding out a hand to help her stand. "Come on," he said, briskly. "We'll get you warm in no time."

Amandine shook her head. "Wait a minute," she said, softly.

"What? Why?" Connor was pulling on her arm. She snatched her hand back.

"Because I'm not sure I like this, Connor," Amandine hissed. "Being in a stranger's car… I don't know if it's such a good idea. He could be anyone."

Connor reached out for her hand again. She refused him.

He made a noise.

"Look, it isn't ideal, I get it," he said, frustrated, "but we don't have a huge amount of choice, do we? Besides, it's fifteen minutes. Max. I promise. That's no time at all."

Amandine stared up at him, feeling small and tired.

"But it feels wrong," she said, miserably.

Connor threw his hands up in exasperation. "Fine, I get it! Woman's intuition! But what choice do you have? Stay out here with your intuition and freeze to death? Or trust me, and get in the fucking car?"

She didn't like how he spoke to her.

He's right, though, she acknowledged reluctantly.

She stood, wincing as she put weight on her ruined feet.

Connor sighed in relief.

"Plus, you're with me," he went on in a lighter tone, guiding her away from the barrier. "What harm could come to you with me around?" Connor grinned. He sounded so sure of himself.

She shot him a dirty look that he couldn't see.

Then she saw the cloud of heat coming from the car's exhaust pipe.

It is very, very cold, she told herself.

And it is only for fifteen minutes.

What's the worst that could happen in fifteen minutes?

"Fine," she said. "But if he turns out to be a psychopath, I'm going to haunt your every waking moment from here on out and say, 'I told you so.'"

"Atta girl," Connor replied, and he escorted Amandine over to the car, opened the nearest rear car door, and deposited her inside unceremoniously.

Soft Spoken

Amandine tried to get a look at the driver as she sat down, but the car's interior light only gave off a weak, sickly orange glow that barely illuminated anything at all. All she saw was the impression of a man, hunched, impatient, over the steering wheel.

"Thank you," Amandine said, politely. Her voice was a calm lie. She didn't feel thankful at all. She felt deeply, nauseatingly uneasy. All traces of the excitement and flush of romance she had felt earlier well and truly dissipated. Now she wanted the night to be over as quickly as possible.

The driver said nothing. He didn't even turn his head to acknowledge her.

It is well past midnight, she reasoned. *Too late for idle conversation.*

Even so.

Amandine's internal warning system was still going berserk, the same phrase repeating itself over and over in her head:

Redflagredflagredflag!

Connor had no such qualms. He flung himself into the seat next to the driver and clunked his seat belt into place.

"All in?" the driver asked.

"All in," Connor replied in relief.

Amandine, however, had not yet pulled her door shut. She planned on leaving it open until the very last minute.

She left her seat belt unbuckled, too, just in case.

Still time to run, she thought, but that moment was fast disappearing. The driver's hand was on his gear stick, ready to shift into first and Connor had buckled himself in, eagerly.

We're committed now, she realised, with grim resignation.

Reluctantly, she grabbed her door handle and pulled.

The interior light finally flickered off as her door clicked to.

Amandine couldn't be sure, but she thought she heard the driver snort gently in acknowledgement then, as if he had been holding his breath in anticipation, or had found something amusing, or both.

She chewed hard on her bottom lip, drawing blood. She doubted Connor would find this nervous action sexy, now. She was gnawing away at herself like a rat gnawing through wires. Soon she'd be down to her chin.

"Good to go?" the driver said, quietly. He said everything quietly, which irritated Amandine. It felt like a calculated choice, speaking beneath the engine's register.

"Please," Connor nodded, desperate to go. "And thank you again."

The driver flipped his lights back to beam, ground the gear stick into first.

"It's no problem at all," came the eventual reply, and the car pulled away.

Love Bug

Amandine felt warmth slowly envelop her. Her shivering subsided. The driver had cranked up the heating as high as it would go, and the temperature change was bliss, until the car's interior smell, musty and odd and sour, properly sank in. Her nose wrinkled. There was a strong chemical tang to the air, too, that Amandine attributed to the air freshener dangling from the rear-view mirror. The cardboard accessory, which swung like an erratic pendulum as the car surged forward, was shaped like a love heart, the words 'LOVE BUG' printed in the middle. It looked like the sort of tacky gift a wife might buy for her husband on a whim.

Amandine had a hard time imagining the shadow behind the wheel as a married man.

For a while, nobody spoke. The night whisked past the windows. Amandine felt increasingly claustrophobic, assaulted by fierce warmth in the car. The unpleasant smell worsened. Her fingers tingled with painful pins and needles. She envisaged herself thawing out like a frozen leg of lamb.

"This is really good of you," she said, attempting conversation. The car rattled back along the road they'd only just walked down, covering the same distance in seconds that had taken them much, much longer on foot.

"Yeah," Connor agreed, but the driver said nothing.

Amandine tried once more to get a better look at him, hoping fervently that he was as he presented himself: a good Samaritan helping them out of a tight spot.

The driver kept his head resolutely turned from her, trained on the road ahead.

Amandine left her seat belt unclipped.

The driver flicked her a glance in his rear-view.

"Better belt up," he said.

"Whoops," she mumbled, scowling. "Sorry."

"Better do it quick. It's icy out tonight."

Sighing, Amandine reached for her belt. Hesitated. The driver's eyes went back to the road. She surreptitiously pulled the neighbouring belt across the rear seat and clipped it into her buckle. Then she took her own belt and carefully pulled it around so it sat behind, not in front of her body, and fitted it into the neighbouring slot, hoping this would fool the driver without her having to physically restrain herself. It was dark enough in the back that he wouldn't be able to tell which belt was clipped where, she hoped.

"All clipped in," she lied, brightly. The driver grunted, steering around a large pothole in the road. Amandine enjoyed her silent, small victory while simultaneously trying, in whatever way she could, to calm her now shredded nerves.

You're going to be fine, she told herself, firmly.

Just ten more minutes.

No time at all.

Then Amandine felt something pull on her right-hand side, and realised her dress was caught in the door.

"Oh, wait a moment!" she said, opening the door a crack as they drove along. Air whistled through the gap fiercely.

Was it her, or had the driver picked up speed?

The interior light switched on, and the car dinged a dismayed warning alert, registering the open door while moving.

Dingdingdingdingdingding!

"What are you doing back there?" Connor laughed, looking round as if to say: *settle down, would you?*

"Sorry, my dress is caught."

She yanked the fabric free and slammed the door quickly, cancelling the alarm, but not before she finally got what she wanted: a split-second glimpse of the driver's face in the rear-view mirror, right before the interior light flicked off. He was checking to see what she was up to, and it meant a good portion of his face was visible above the swinging LOVE BUG sign.

It was just a split-second reveal, in poor light, a blink-and-miss-it moment, but it was enough.

Amandine saw smudged glasses.

A familiar, malevolent gaze.

Hair pulled back into a greasy ponytail.

Then the car was plunged back into darkness.

Amandine only stopped herself from swearing out loud at the very last moment, biting her tongue instead, hard.

She knew, with a sick, hollow feeling in her belly, that if she'd had longer to look at the man, she would have seen a bowtie, old-fashioned and dirty around his neck, encrusted with soup.

Fuck! she screamed in her head, loud and shrill.

Fuck!

Fuck!

Lone Driver

Amandine's mind raced as fast as the car, which now pushed along the back country road at sixty-five miles an hour. The man behind the wheel *had* put his foot down, there was no denying it.

He knows that I know, Amandine thought, frantically.

Connor remained ignorant, the odd one out.

What now?

Amandine tried to work through the implications, fighting the overwhelming urge to open the rear car door and fling herself out.

That's why I recognised the car!

She remembered now: this was the Nissan parked in the pub car park.

Did he wait for us?

Did he wait for us to finish, knowing we had no ride?

It was too much of a coincidence for him to just happen upon them the way he did, hours after being evicted from the pub.

He'd been waiting for them.

Intent.

Planning.

But why?

The car's headlights illuminated hedgerow rushing past on either side, adding to the impression of speed as the Lone

Diner pressed on. Beyond the hedges, a dark night sky loomed, pierced with stars. Amandine could no longer see the moon. She felt as if they were racing through an endless, thorny tunnel. She watched the needle on the speed dial creep further around its axis.

The endless barrage of shrubbery sprinting past at warp speed made her increasingly car sick.

As did the smell, which continued to gather strength. It was a powerfully unpleasant combination of the highly artificial pine-scented air freshener – and something else, some other stench that intruded, cloying and noxious. Alcohol, rich food, and anxiety warred with motion sickness as Amandine's stomach cramped painfully.

She passed a hand over her eyes, feeling her heart thump hard in her chest. Swallowing, she tried to focus on something stationary within the vehicle, rather than the dashing scenery outside.

I can't be sick in his car, she thought. *I can't.*

Her body, however, would not cooperate with her brain.

She felt a hot surge rising from her belly to just below her ribcage.

Amandine knew she was going to vomit.

She scrabbled for her window button, intending to crack it open just a fraction, just wide enough to get some fresh, cold air, but found with horror that the button was missing from the back door panel. Her hand felt for a crank-handle, instead.

The socket where the handle should have been mounted was bare, only a thin, sharp metal joint remaining.

The back window couldn't be opened, Amandine realised, swallowing more urgently.

She searched for something to catch her sick. She spotted her handbag on the seat beside her.

Then she remembered the rape alarm she packed earlier.

The nausea subsided momentarily.

She opened her bag and pulled out the palm-sized oval object as discreetly as she could, hiding it beneath folded hands on her lap. There was a small pin with a looped cord in one side of the object: pull it out, and the alarm would go off, shrill and insistent. No great use in the middle of nowhere, but it might buy her a second or two if it came down to it.

And that's better than nothing, she thought, feeling a fraction calmer.

Meanwhile, Connor slurred away amicably in the front, oblivious to her struggle, oblivious to Lone Diner's relentless accelerator foot, filling the uncomfortable silence with well-meaning, drunken small talk about the weather and the food in the restaurant. Amandine couldn't believe he hadn't made the connection between driver of the car and the Lone Diner. She also couldn't believe how much more intoxicated he seemed in the car than outside. The heat must be getting to him, too. They had drunk a fair bit of wine. Plus the cocktails, his beer... Her stomach cramped again. She couldn't find a discrete way to signal her newfound information to Connor without spewing a mouthful of regurgitated creamed potato all over him, so she kept her lips tightly sealed, hoping that the "fifteen-minute journey" would be over, soon.

And so what if it is the same guy? she told herself, needing logic more than she'd ever needed it before. Nausea curdled her insides.

So what if he was waiting to pick you up on some remote, dark country road in the middle of nowhere?

It doesn't necessarily mean anything bad is going to happen.

Even if he was staring at you like shit on his shoe in the restaurant.

Amandine's brain flooded with memories: the hate-filled glare, the food and saliva dripping out of his mouth, the porn playing on Lone Diner's phone, the leering expression on his face as he'd filled his mouth with soup, the shifting colours of his screen moving across his features, red and orange, flesh tones, more red.

What else had he been watching?

And why had he taken such a dislike to her?

Or perhaps, she told herself, it was actually Connor he had a problem with.

Or maybe both of them, as a couple: what they represented.

He had been alone, after all.

Red roses, ungifted on the table.

She knew they'd made a colossal mistake in climbing into his car.

She wasn't safe, and neither was Connor.

The sky took on a faint glow up ahead: a village, she realised.

A couple of miles away at most.

Just a few more minutes, she kept telling herself.

Not long at all.

She tried to work through the sequence of events leading her here.

Lone Diner had left the restaurant some time before they had settled their bill. Rather, he'd been thrown out by the chef and barman.

But *how long* before, exactly, felt important to remember. Was it after her main course?

Before, she thought, *I'm sure of it.*

Well before.

Which meant he'd been gone from the restaurant for a minimum of an hour before they'd found themselves kicked out into the cold.

An hour's continuous driving would put him easily ten, twenty miles away from the pub and the spot where he'd picked them up from, if not more, depending on how fast he drove. Yet, somehow, he had come past them just as they were walking along the road, not far from the pub at all. Less than a mile, in fact, if she had to judge, because her shoes had made it impossible to get very far.

Had he gotten lost?

Or had he just parked up and waited around the corner for them, on the side of the road, maybe?

And why was he even at that restaurant in the first place?

Nobody went to the Boat for a casual meal or to dine alone.

You went to the Boat for a first date, for a special occasion. Everyone knew that. The pub marketed itself on that basis, loud and proud: *Norfolk's most romantic restaurant.*

He must have known, going in, what sort of establishment he would be eating at.

Amandine remembered papery, browned roses in cellophane.

Her own rose was lying on the side of the road by the crash barrier.

"You from around here?" Connor asked.

More hedgerow flew past.

"Not far," Lone Diner replied eventually, in his soft, low voice. "I'm over Peterborough way."

He pushed his foot down harder on the pedal.

"That's not that close either," Connor said. "What brings you out here, to the sticks?"

"Business," Lone Diner said.

"What kind of–"

The Lone Driver reached up behind his head, moved the ceiling switch for the interior light over.

The pathetic orange glow filled the car once again.

"That's better," Lone Diner mumbled. "Can't see a fucking thing in here."

Then he took one hand off the wheel, bent forward, pulled a strange, curved, serrated object from the footwell of the car and swung it downwards, as hard as he could, in Connor's direction.

The weapon, which Amandine saw in the brief, split-second-long glimpse she had of it, was like a scythe, with a short handle and wicked, jagged teeth. It sank into Connor's thigh.

Connor screamed, his body lurching with shock. His arms flailed about, almost knocking Lone Diner's glasses off his face. The car swerved. The large man behind the wheel struggled to correct its trajectory one-handed, dragging them back into a straight line just barely before they went off the road and hit a ditch.

Enraged, Lone Diner angrily yanked the scythe's blade backwards out of Connor's thigh, as if he were cutting through a tree limb or a thick, stubborn weed.

Blood spurted, hit the dashboard with shocking velocity. Lone Diner had hit something significant. Connor screamed once again in pain and horror.

"Now shut the fuck up," Lone Diner said, slowing the vehicle and pressing the blade's wickedly pointed tip to Connor's neck, "both of you, and do as you're told. Else I'll cut your fucking head off, okay?"

Out, Out

Connor scrambled to press both his hands on his opened thigh, where the scythe's blade had left a long, ragged gash. The Nissan's interior felt as if it were all red, the orange lighting accentuating the glistening blood's rich hue.

Amandine heard nothing but the frantic pounding of her pulse in her ears.

Wompwompwomp, her blood said,

wompifuckingtoldyouso!wompwompwomp…

She couldn't keep it down anymore. The sight of Connor's wound, the confirmation of all her suspicions and fears, the food, the alcohol, the motion sickness… it flooded her system with adrenaline and raw, foetid fear, and she vomited, spraying the back of the Lone Driver's head liberally with hot, stinking chunks of a half-digested and highly expensive romantic dinner for two.

Off-Road

Lone Diner roared in disgust. Connor used the momentary distraction to let go of his leg with one hand and lunge for the steering wheel, trying and failing to wrench it out of Lone Diner's hand.

Lone Diner swore, reared back. Swung the scythe again.

Connor slumped forward, hitting the dashboard hard.

The car veered around a sharp bend in the road.

Amandine found she was screaming.

There was blood all over the front of the car, on the ceiling, running down the windows beside her.

Is he dead?!

Is Connor dead?

Lone Diner reversed the blade, cracked Connor over the back of his unprotected skull with the wooden handle of the tool.

"Should have listened to your girlfriend," he sneered, keeping the wheel steady somehow. "She's smarter than you."

Connor didn't respond. His head lolled on the dashboard. Amandine had an absurd, wild urge to put the windscreen wipers on, even though she knew the blood was on the inside of the car.

Lone Diner had large chunks of vomit nestling in his hair. The smell of it now mixed with the other pungent aromas in the car to make a truly nightmarish reek. Amandine felt dizzy, on the verge of hyperventilating. All her senses were being overwhelmed, one by one: sight, smell, sound. Every single part of her shrieked in the discomfort of danger.

What the fuck do I do? She pressed her fists into her mouth to stop herself screaming and vomiting again.

Amandine considered jumping from the back seat, remembering she was unbelted. She would have time, mere seconds before he stopped, to get up from where she landed and run for it. She would hurt herself badly at this speed, she calculated, but she'd have to take that risk, while she had the nerve.

She slipped off her shoes and readied her hands in preparation for grabbing the door handle, flexing and clenching them to warm up numb fingers. She realised she was still holding the rape alarm, and wished fervently that she'd listened to herself, listened to her instincts, paid attention to her body before she'd left the house earlier that evening.

She tensed her entire body, one hand now on the door handle, preparing to yank it up, push open the heavy steel wing, launch herself out into the rushing brown and black night, hope for a soft landing, but then she thought:

Connor.

I can't leave him behind.

Her grip on the handle faltered.

But why not?

Why the fuck not?

He's probably dead, Amandine. Look at the blood!

Her eyes filled with tears.

It's not your fault you ended up here, in this situation, is it?

She shook her head.

No, it's his.

He made you get into the car.

It's his fault.

Besides.

You barely know him.

You've only been on one date!

You don't owe him anything.

Get out now, while you can!

While the man is distracted!

Amandine didn't move. Her thoughts raced chaotically through her brain, and hesitation made room for more panic.

But where would I go? It's just fields and mud and…

Never mind!

Who gives a shit?!

First, get out of the car!

She hefted the rape alarm in her free hand.

And then what? If you don't break both your legs, your neck?

He'll just stop and come and find me.

He has a weapon.

It doesn't matter! her lizard-brain survival system shrieked. *You have to fucking try, Amandine! When you're out, you can push through the hedge, go into the fields, hide in a ditch somewhere until morning…*

But I'll freeze to death.

It has to be better than what this maniac has planned for you!

Now is the time!

No!

Go, now!

I can't!

Do it!

Amandine thought she might vomit her whole heart up, it was lodged so firmly in her throat. Another moment's dithering and she would be lost entirely, swept away.

Connor groaned. He lifted his head from the dashboard groggily.

"Whatever your plans are," he slurred, "leave her out of it. Just don't hurt her, okay?"

Amandine's internal voice silenced instantly.

She couldn't leave him behind. He was alive, he was hurt, and she would be killing him if she ran.

Kill, or be killed.

Amandine slowly untensed her body, releasing the door handle as surreptitiously as she could.

I can't leave him, she told herself, firmly.

Lone Diner made no acknowledgement of Connor's request.

He just kept on driving.

Crash

Amandine regained enough control of herself to start rationalising.

If he'd wanted to kill us, he would have done it already, she reasoned. Lone Diner only meant to disable Connor, not finish him outright, or he would have gone for the neck straight away.

"What the fuck do you want?"

Connor had his hands pressed back on his thigh wound. Amandine wondered how much blood he'd lost.

"Is it money? I don't have much left on me," he managed, "but you can have what I've got. Here."

He went to pull his wallet clumsily from his pocket, intending to offer it to the man.

The Lone Diner waved the scythe at him again. "Keep your fucking hands out of your pockets," he commanded.

Connor went back to pressing down on his leg obediently.

Amandine fervently wished she had a scarf she could strangle Lone Diner with from behind. The only thing she could use as a potential noose was her jacket, and she was not sure she could take it off and twist it into something useful in enough time without him noticing. He had the rear-view mirror trained fully on her now, she saw.

When had he done that?

"In the glove compartment in front of you, there is a Ziplock bag. Get it," he said to Connor, instead.

"I'm serious." Connor was visibly shaking, from fear, or blood loss, or both. "You can take my money, credit cards, I'll give you my PIN... Just leave her out of it, okay?"

"You're a slow learner. Get the fucking bag out before I slice your jugular open."

Connor stopped trying to offer his meagre life savings to the man.

"Okay," he said, trying to placate him. "Okay. I'm doing as you ask, just don't..."

The scythe waggled inches from Connor's face. The tip of the hook missed his eyeball by a hair's breadth. Connor reared back, crying out.

"Okay, okay! I'm doing it! Fuck."

Connor opened the glove compartment with blood-slicked hands.

The strange smell that had been bothering Amandine since she got into the car intensified.

Connor pulled the Ziplock bag out, held it in front of him.

"What now?" he panted. Both trouser legs were soaking wet, Amandine realised. He needed a hospital, or at the very least, a tourniquet.

"Please," she said, deciding to beg on his behalf. "Connor needs help. He's going to bleed out, at least let me..."

"Open the bag," Lone Diner said, coldly.

Connor did as he was told, using his teeth and one hand.

Inside, Amandine saw a folded flannel cloth, obviously wet. Condensation had built up on the interior of the bag.

Then she figured out what that meant.

The cloth was soaked in something.

Something smelly, and chemically.

"That won't work!" she blurted out. "It's not like the fucking movies; it takes longer than a moment to–"

Lone Diner looked at her in the rear-view mirror.

"I have a gun in this car," he said, calmly. "If you don't do as I ask, I'll shoot him. He can't exactly run away, can he?"

Amandine swallowed her protests. She couldn't see a gun, but that didn't mean he didn't have one.

"Take the cloth out, and hold it over your nose and mouth," Lone Diner instructed, changing up a gear as the road ahead straightened out again. For a split second, the hedgerow broke up, and Amandine caught glimpses of muddy, furrowed fields through the Nissan's windows before the wall of twigs and thorns returned.

Connor stared at the Lone Diner, and the penny dropped with him too.

"I'm not fucking chloroforming myself," he said, shaking his head. "Get fucked!"

"Do as you're told, or I'll shoot your girlfriend," came the reply.

"I don't see any gun. You're bullshitting."

Lone Diner's voice went hard with rage.

"Are you a fucking idiot as well as deaf?" he said, swiping at Connor again with the short-handled scythe.

"And I said, get *fucked*!" Connor roared. He dodged the hacking blade, the tip of which got momentarily tangled in the nylon string from which the heart-shaped air freshener hung, and lunged for the steering wheel again, arms stiff like a cartoon zombie, a blood-soaked ghoul rising from the deep.

Lone Diner cursed, dropping the scythe in the struggle. Connor was finally able to grab the wheel. He yanked it hard towards himself with slippery hands.

The car did a sharp turn and screeched off-road, slamming into the hedge on the right, barrelling through it, and landing nose-down in a deep ditch that lay just beyond. For a blurry, jolting second, just before they hit the ditch, Amandine thought they'd drown in icy cold water, but the dyke turned out to be dry. Then, her face smashed hard into the headrest in front of her, and she lost all sense of which way up she was for a few terrifying moments.

Rousing, she found herself pressed up hard against the passenger seat before her, body mashed into the upholstery. Her head was pounding, and her neck, she discovered, was horribly bent at a painful angle. Her hips and legs were jammed into the footwell. Something warm trickled steadily down her face.

Grunting, she examined her throbbing forehead, discovered a large wound.

That's what you get for not wearing your seat belt, Amandine.

The two men in the front of the car had gone quiet.

She peered blearily around the seat in front of her, hoping and praying that Connor was okay and that the Lone Diner was knocked unconscious.

The whole front of the Nissan was crumpled up like a paper bag. Lone Diner was pinned behind the wheel. He groaned, twisting about in his seat weakly. He didn't appear to be fully conscious. Amandine could see he'd headbutted the steering wheel hard – the car was so old it probably didn't have functioning airbags.

Then she spotted the scythe lying between the front seats, hooked around the gearstick.

Amandine clambered backwards, hauling herself up out of the footwell, hoping she hadn't damaged her neck permanently: a sharp, knifing pressure ran from her jaw to her collarbone.

She tried to get a better look at Connor, but he was slumped forward across the dash, away from her. For a moment she thought he was dead (again), but then she heard his ragged breathing. The air came out of his lungs wet and crackly, but it came out, which was the important thing.

She wasted no more time. She fumbled open her door, kicking it repeatedly. When it only cracked a few inches, she tried the far side rear door, which opened fully. She dragged herself out and jumped down into the deep ditch below, twisting both ankles violently in the dark.

She squealed but gave herself no time to feel anything further than the initial shock of impact.

Pain later, she told herself. *Survival first. Go, go!*

Scrambling up the steep bank of the ditch, she knew she had moments until Lone Diner came fully to his senses. She made it to the front passenger side of the car, which was a bent mess of metal and glass, and with difficulty, yanked open Connor's dented door.

She went for his seat belt clip, but it wouldn't budge. Connor sagged forward against the belt, his weight interfering with her efforts.

"Come *on*!" she panted, grabbing his hair with a fist, pulling back his head, and slapping his cheeks hard, trying to rouse him enough to help. His eyelids fluttered, and he focused on her with difficulty.

"I need you to help me with the seat belt, Connor! Now!"

He looked down at himself.

"I… can't… it won't…"

"Connor, if you don't help, I can't get you out!"

"He fucking… sliced my leg," Connor mumbled back. "Do you want to order dessert?"

"Oh, god," Amandine realised she was on her own.

Lone Diner coughed, spat out a wad of phlegm. Shifted again in his chair.

Amandine redoubled her efforts.

"It doesn't matter about your leg. You need to get out of the car *now*!"

"I'm trying..." Connor finally began to struggle with his seat belt clip. His eyes were full of reflected moonlight. He looked like a lamb off to slaughter. Helpless. Innocent.

Amandine started to cry.

"Fucking try *harder*!" she said, yanking on the belt clip to no avail.

"It's... stuck..."

Lone Diner turned to look at them. His eyes, no longer screened by his glasses, which had flown off, struggled to focus. He started to pat himself down clumsily.

"Where... the fuck..." He slurred like a drunk man, but his intent was sober enough.

He was looking for the scythe.

"Connor?" Amandine was sobbing now, in outright panic. "I don't want to leave you here, but he's waking up, you've got to try harder!"

Connor did as he was told, pawing at his belt with shaking hands, but he was so weak and blood-soaked he couldn't get a grip on anything.

Amandine looked at the hooked scythe hanging off the gear stick.

A light bulb went off.

She flung herself across Connor, got to the short wooden handle before Lone Diner could, and yanked the scythe up, lashing out at the man's flesh as hard as she could. She caught his forearm, felt resistance, and dragged the blade hard across his skin.

Lone Diner let out a howl of pain that was almost deafening, roaring unintelligible insults in the aftershock of the curving saw's brutal journey across his flesh.

Amandine lashed out again, making a series of vicious cuts on Lone Diner's arms. He struggled to defend himself, huddling into a ball on the far side of the car, bellowing in anguish like a speared bull. *Pussy,* Amandine thought.

Fucking pussy.

Amandine then used the serrated edge of the scythe to saw through Connor's seat belt.

By the time she'd broken him free, Connor had fainted again.

She moved to one side, intending to catch his weight as he lolled heavily towards her, but she couldn't move fast enough. He toppled hard to the left and plummeted out of his seat, almost knocking her off her feet, and landed straight in the ditch beside her.

In horror, Amandine realised she was going to have to carry or drag him to safety.

Sorry

Lone Diner, still trapped behind the wheel of the Nissan, continued to holler and yell abuse as Amandine grabbed the back of Connor's jacket. She figured her best bet was a fireman's-lift-type carry. She squatted low, whimpering at the excruciating pain in her twisted ankles and half-pulled Connor out of the ditch enough to struggle under him, then shuffled and dragged his weight over her shoulders with enormous difficulty.

Once she had him in place, a desperate Amandine tried to stand up.

She managed a low crouch, making it mere inches from the bottom of the ditch before her legs gave way. Connor was heavier than he looked, a dead weight when she was already disoriented and exhausted with pain.

Her feet slipped on the steep sides of the ditch, pitching her forward.

She toppled over, dumping them both back in the ditch.

"Connor!" she yelled, clambering off him and slapping his unresponsive body. "Wake the fuck up! Please!"

But Connor didn't wake. He just lay in the ditch like a discarded, rolled-up mattress, and Amandine was faced with a horrible choice.

Stay with him and risk her life or leave him and risk survival.

She chose the latter.

"I'm sorry," she sobbed, clawing her way up and out of the frozen trench. "I tried. I'm sorry, Connor."

Then she was on the road, lurching away from the crashed car, on towards the dim glow of the village up ahead.

Almost

She hadn't gotten far before she heard a car door slam.

A boot pop.

Then, a loud *crack*!

I have a gun in this car, he'd said.

Crack!

Another gunshot boomed out across the night.

Projectiles whizzed past her, off to the left. She heard things smattering into the hedgerow. It took her a second to process: not a single bullet, but lots of small objects hitting the vegetation, like gravel.

"He'll die if you run!" Lone Diner shouted, his voice malicious, the pronunciation mangled. It sounded like he was swallowing blood, or spitting teeth, or both.

"I cut him in the leg, near the femoral artery! He hasn't got long left, and you know it!"

Amandine kept stumbling forward, not falling for his tricks.

"He's going to bleed out in this ditch!" the Lone Diner shouted. "You want that on your hands?"

"Fuck you," Amandine sobbed, staggering on. She wasn't going back, not for anything. She just needed to get to that village. Or she needed a break in the hedgerow. Or a car. Yes, that was it. All she needed was one single car coming in the opposite direction, and then she'd be safe.

Just one and the nightmare would be over.

But what about Connor?

"If you keep running, I'll shoot you!"

Amandine didn't think Lone Diner could aim straight for shit, not in the dark, so soon after the crash, with the wounds she had given him over both arms. The gun sounded big, heavy, it would need a strong grip and a steady aim. He'd be losing blood like Connor, and he'd be concussed, disoriented.

She just had to keep going. The dark was her friend.

The moonlight, a traitor.

Her suspicions about Lone Diner's aim were proven when he fired again. A huge report ripped through the night, a cracking sort of boom, followed by more spattering, tearing sounds in the hedgerow, this time off to her right.

Amandine willed her body to move faster, knowing that shortly, Lone Diner would accept he couldn't shoot her from afar and would give chase. She wished fervently that she'd cut his hamstrings with the scythe instead of his arms, or gone for his throat. She kept listening for sounds of pursuit but heard nothing above the blood pounding in her ears. The not knowing where Lone Diner was terrified her, so she threw a look over her shoulder.

The car's interior light was still on. The orange glow leaking out of it made a puppet show of her ordeal. From the brief glimpse she got of the scene, she could see a black cut-out man with a ponytail, fumbling with a long, barrelled object. The shotgun.

What was he doing?

Trying to reload it, she realised.

Cursing floated down the road after her.

I can do this, she thought.

I can escape. He has no idea what he's doing. He has no real plan.

"Are you really that cold?" he screamed after her. "He'll die; I mean it! If this nice lad doesn't bleed out in the next ten minutes, I'm going to tie him up and torture him until he does. Do you hear that? It'll be your fault, bitch! You'll have to live with that for the rest of your life! You'll never have a moment's peace again!"

I don't care, Amandine thought – but she did. Every step she took towards her own freedom felt heavier and heavier.

Torture.

Kill.

Nice lad.

Your fault.

She faltered, only for a moment.

"He bought you a nice meal and what did he get in return, huh? Fucked over by a greedy whore!"

Was his voice closer? She thought it might be.

"You're all the same, you know! Selfish bitches!"

Not by a great distance, but enough to mean he was on the move, headed in her direction.

"His mother will know it's your fault. Everyone will. It will all be on you!"

Amandine remembered that Connor's mother had abandoned him at a young age. Left a scar around his neck like a torque as a parting gift.

Connor was a survivor, she told herself.

She started limping faster again, guilt cobbling her steps.

She remembered blood on Connor's hands as he tried, and failed, to unclip his seat belt.

She remembered the look in his eyes as he'd stroked the back of her hand in the restaurant, *there's a good girl, can I touch you?*

Fuck, she thought.

FUCK!

If you go back, you'll die.

More steps, hesitant.

Away. She just needed to get away.

He'll win; it's what he wants.

Connor's eyes pierced her heart: round with fear, soft, filled with his own inevitable end.

Fuck.

She stopped again, struggling for breath. Her ankles were on fire, the pain travelling all the way up her body. She knew she couldn't outrun her pursuer for long.

"FUCK!!" she screamed, to the stars, who didn't give a shit.

She just needed one car.

It was unlikely, in the dead of the night, in the dead of the worst winter they'd had in years.

An owl hooted a response in the distance.

Amandine turned, despite every bone in her body telling her not to.

Steam leaked out of Lone Diner's nose and mouth, illuminated by the flickering, muted beam from the Nissan's half-buried headlights. The gun, Amandine saw, was still levelled at her. He didn't look like he knew how to hold it properly. The cuts on his arms were making it difficult to aim straight.

"Get back here, bitch," the man yelled, as the moon high above looked down on the unfolding drama with an aloof, brilliant disdain.

He had to lift his voice above the rising noise of the car engine to be heard.

Wait a minute.

Car engine.

Not Lone Diner's car.

His was nose-down in the ditch.

Amandine's heart leapt.

Another car!

Lone Diner's outline grew even more distinct. A bright halo formed around him, like the halo around the moon.

Someone is coming!

Lone Diner spun around, holding his gun behind his body as best he could, and started waving at the approaching vehicle with his free hand.

Amandine thought of Connor, waving Lone Diner down as he came around the bend, back before the nightmare had truly begun.

"Help us!" Lone Diner yelled, his voice suddenly feeble and reedy with false distress. "Please! Help!"

Amandine's heart plummeted again.

What is he… Oh, shit!

The car slowed to a stop.

"Don't!" Amandine croaked, her fleeting moment of hope now a horrible, jagged stone lodged firmly in her windpipe.

But it was too late.

Lone Diner had limped over to the driver's side.

The window rolled down.

"Oh, my god, are you alright?" a woman's voice asked.

"Don't!" Amandine screamed.

Lone Diner clasped a hand to his head in mock gratitude. "Help us, please! We… we had an accident; our car went in the ditch…"

"Don't!" Amandine screamed again, but Lone Diner didn't listen. He couldn't even be bothered to finish his sentence. Instead, he took several steps back, brought the gun out from where he'd been hiding it behind his body, and shot the driver of the car at close range in the side of the head.

Expectations Versus Reality

Shooting someone up close was not as enjoyable as Lone Diner had hoped it would be. He didn't know what he had imagined – perhaps an exploding skull, like they showed in the movies – but the reality was considerably less dramatic.

He opened the stranger's car door so the interior light flicked on. The damage sustained to the side the female driver's head was significant, but not deadly. This was what the man in the gun shop had been trying to tell him: aim, distance, size of pellet. It all made a difference.

With disappointment, Lone Diner saw he'd made a hole in the woman's temple, one that looked like a rat had chewed its way through her skin, and he saw the rest of her face peppered with pellets, but beyond that, the woman was still conscious and able to move, even if she was disoriented and rolling her head around on her shoulders as if drunk.

Lone Driver looked back to the dark road, to the shadow of the other woman, who was hobbling along the road as fast she could. She was going to get away unless he acted fast.

And so fast he was. He stepped forward, unbuckled the wounded driver's seat belt, and pulled her out into the road.

Groaning and dazed, she lay on the ground like a rabbit in her own headlights, eyes wide, hands clutching her ruined face. Lone Diner had a brief moment where he felt conflicted.

This had never been part of the plan. He considered leaving her alive, for his energy was fast dwindling and his real prey was still getting away, but he couldn't risk letting a witness survive, so he made sure to swerve and slowly roll over her with her own car as he commandeered it to chase after his original target.

The body breaking under the wheels of the vehicle didn't sound or feel like he'd thought it would, either.

Ditch

Amandine wheeled and frantically started limp-stumbling away.

Behind, she heard a car door open once again, something heavy hit the road, and a car door slam shut.

She heard the engine rev.

The car bounce and thump.

Amandine heard things crunch.

She tried to run.

Her weakened right heel turned almost immediately, folding her entire foot beneath her. She had caught a pothole in the road, invisible until the last moment.

Amandine felt something snap in her ankle. Pain streaked through her foot and up her leg.

She fell forward, hitting the road hard.

The car drew closer. Louder. More inevitable.

Winded, the stolen vehicle almost upon her – *he is going to run me over, I know it, he's going to fucking run me over* – she desperately tried to get up, knowing she was moments from death, and then it occurred to her that what was happening was wrong, it was all wrong: she hadn't planned on going out like this, not at all, and that thought suddenly coagulated into a bout of unexpected, furious, final-reserve energy.

I'm not dying like this! she thought. *I told Mum and Dad I'd live to be a hundred!*

Fuck you!

And with that, she crawled to her knees.

Tried to stand.

Fell down again and hit the tarmac for a second time, face smashing into the frozen surface, teeth driving through her top lip, which promptly split open – and now, she was so angry she could feel blood roaring in her ears, could feel pins and needles all over herself.

The noise of the engine filled her consciousness.

She got to her knees again, shaking with rage.

Scrambled to the side of the road, where the ditch lined the tarmac.

The car was mere feet away.

She rolled herself into the ditch.

Brakes squealed on the icy road.

The car came to a skidding halt, tyres thumping into the same pothole that had tripped her up.

She reached up above her head. Thick, thorny hedgerow bordered the ditch. Amandine struggled to find a gap wide enough to crawl through. It was almost impenetrable, a dense and vicious formation. Wicked needles and branches stabbed at her face and hands and neck, tore at her clothes like hungry teeth and claws.

She kept pushing, finally managing to squeeze her head through a gap. A thorn ripped through the top of her right ear. She felt the skin and cartilage tear. Amandine squealed and wriggled forward until she was up to her shoulders in hedgerow.

She could taste her own blood. It spurred her on.

Almost…

Sounds came to her, distinct and laden with horrible intent.

A car opening.

Feet, purposefully clopping along.

He was limping, his gait like morse code on the tarmac: step, drag, *step*, step, drag *step*, dot dash *dot, SOS bitch, I'm coming to kill you.*

A voice, muttering: "Stubborn fucking slut, stay put, won't you!"

There was a grunt.

A thud, the feel of impact behind her.

Lone Diner was in the ditch.

FUCK YOU FUCK YOU FUCK–

Amandine was almost through. Her shoulder snagged on a thick stem, but she kept wriggling, heaving her body against the wall of pain. It was only a plant; she could conquer it if she just pushed hard enough.

I'm going to make it, she told herself, delirious with the promise of freedom. *I'm going to–*

Lone Diner grabbed Amandine by the ankles.

He yanked her back through the hedgerow towards him.

She felt her momentum reverse, somehow managed to grab onto a thick root stem, thorns piercing the palms of her hands, her fingertips, lodging under her fingernails. Her backslide stopped abruptly. Amandine clung on for dear life.

"Come *on*!" Lone Diner growled, and pulled again, hard. Her sprained ankles screamed in protest.

Fuck.

YOU!

She kicked and flailed, feeling her heel connect with something soft: she'd caught him in the face. She kicked again. Lone Diner yelped in pain, and she used the second of reprieve to surge forward.

But Lone Diner had had enough.

With one massive heave, as if she were a rope in a tug-of-war battle, he hauled Amandine fully out of the hedge.

The force of the movement propelled them both backwards into the ditch. Amandine crumpled into a heap, feeling his body beneath hers, horrified by the sudden proximity, by the heat he gave off, and the smell of him, foetid, overpowering, and awful. She screamed, rolled, clawed up the side of the dyke, made it back onto the road.

She tried to run one last time.

She got three steps away before she rolled her ankle again. Amandine flew forwards, twisted, landed on her side, and lay like a felled tree, stunned.

And the anger went out of her, quick as it had flourished, its purpose – survival – thwarted.

She'd been so close.

So close.

There was no time to try to run again.

She wasn't even sure she could stand anymore.

I can't, she thought, exhausted.

I just can't.

And then Lone Diner was upon her.

Grunting with victory, he flipped Amandine over and straddled her, the entire weight of his body pinning her painfully to the road. She felt her hips creak under the pressure. She didn't even try to squirm away.

He had her, and now, all she could do was submit.

"Stupid bitch," he said, chest heaving with exertion. "What was the point of that?"

"Why are you doing this?" she spluttered weakly, only the words didn't come out too clear. Her lip was swollen, her mouth filled with blood. The tip of her front tooth was sharp. She'd broken it falling over.

Lone Diner put paid to any more questions with a swift punch to her ribs, followed by a heavy clout to the side of her head, where her torn ear flared in agony. Emboldened by Amandine's cries of pain, her attacker swung for her again.

This time, his fist connected solidly with her right eye and the bridge of her nose.

Her head cracked backwards, smashing into hard tarmac.

Amandine felt herself give up completely, in that moment. Any last vestige of hope she held that she might be able to get away from the nightmare evaporated like steam in cold air.

Her body, now heavy as a rock, lay still upon the road in a way that felt very final.

Cold above, and cold below.

The moon shone down on her, its halo like a doorway to another place.

A safer place, where things were luminous and shimmering, where Lone Diner didn't exist.

This is it, she thought, sadly.

You tried.

Her parents' faces swam into view. Not the living memory of them, for she'd lost that, but the memory of a photograph on the dressing table in her bedroom.

Is this how they'd felt before they died?

No, they'd had no warning. It had been sudden, absolute, wet...

I tried, Mum, Dad, I did. I'm sorry...

The words meandered through her consciousness, but she could no longer attach any significance to them.

Lone Diner pulled something from his pocket, leaned over and pressed it onto her face. It was the stinking cloth from the glove compartment. It smelt awful. Amandine struggled weakly against it, gagging, trying to hold her breath, desperately trying not to inhale, but she couldn't hold out forever. Lone Diner was stronger than she was, and he kept pressing until, eventually, things in her head went even softer and fuzzier than they already were. It took a long time, during which she fully comprehended the awfulness of her impending death.

Then, she felt woozy, like she was floating on a large body of water.

Is this… how… they felt…

Her body eventually relaxed.

And Amandine, a born survivor, even if she didn't yet know it, stopped fighting.

SATURDAY

Wake Up

"Wake up, Amandine."

The pleading voice roused her, slowly.

"Please, *please* wake up."

Amandine found herself too tired to answer. Her head pounded. Her throat was dry, sore, and scratchy. Her legs hurt. Her stomach ached fiercely and began to cramp the more awake she became. Her bottom lip was swollen and crusted with blood. She ran her fat tongue slowly over her teeth and found broken jagged edges. Her muscles screamed at her. Her face was on fire from a network of scratches and lacerations and thorns embedded deep in her skin. Her torn ear throbbed.

"Amandine!"

The voice, groggy yet urgent, came to her again. "Please, wake up!"

"Leave me alone," she slurred, trying to roll over, away from the demand. "Leave me be."

Only she couldn't roll over. She wasn't lying down, for one thing. She was half sitting, half lying, her back propped up against something cold and hard, arms behind her body, encircling a thick, cold object.

Why were her arms behind her back? What was she holding onto?

There was something weird going on with her legs and feet, too. She couldn't separate them.

Couldn't feel her toes, either.

Or her fingers.

Frowning, she tried to open her eyes.

Her eyelids wouldn't part.

There was a film of something glue-like on her eyelashes, sticking them together.

"Come on, Amandine!"

The voice would not let up.

"You'll freeze to death; you need to wake up!"

Freeze to death.

Her brain moved slowly through the word and on to its implication.

Eyelashes crusted with...

Frost.

She kept trying to blink, rolling her eyeballs and fluttering her lids until the persistent rime cracked. She once again attempted to turn over, but it was no use.

She was stuck in a single position, the hard, unyielding thing against her spine. Her arms ached fiercely in their unnatural position, the sockets raw and screaming on both sides of her body.

My hands are tied together, she thought.

Panic flooded her system.

My hands are tied behind my back!

Amandine came fully to with a dreadful burst of awareness, and discovered how cold she was.

So cold she barely felt human.

She moaned, flailed, willing her legs to move, to part, to do anything. They felt numb, unresponsive, as if she didn't have legs at all.

Her eyelids ripped fully open, painfully breaking the last remnants of frost seal.

Do I still have legs?

Her vision struggled to adjust. The world was an incomprehensible mess of fuzzy shapes, soft, muted lights, blurred lines.

Fuck!

Do I still have legs?!

"Amandine!"

Who the fuck is that? Why don't they leave me alone?

"Sweetheart, please talk to me! Come on, you have to snap out of it!"

She ignored the voice. It would have to wait.

She blinked, over and over.

She could hear birds, she realised.

Seabirds.

Slowly, her vision focused.

She looked down at herself, desperate to see.

Relief washed through her, hot and visceral.

She had legs.

They were swollen; she could see that well enough even through her laddered stockings, and they were arranged at odd angles. Her ankles, bound tightly, were bloated and huge. She appeared to be constrained above her anklebones with something narrow and plastic that cut into her flesh, but she still had legs.

Okay, good, she thought.

Now test them.

She willed her right foot to move. It twitched feebly.

She clenched her thigh, activated her knee.

Right leg, check.

Now the other.

She repeated the sequence of signals on her left leg.

This time, she only managed a slight twitch in her left big toe, nothing more.

No circulation.

Amandine concentrated hard and attempted to activate both legs at the same time, proving to herself that she could do it, gritting her teeth and drawing up her knees as far as she was able, then flopping back down, a weak mermaid's-tail movement.

Got to get the blood flowing, she thought.

Then, the voice spoke again. She'd forgotten about it momentarily.

"Amandine? Talk to me!"

Connor, Amandine remembered then, the fog in her brain slowly clearing.

She let that sink in for a moment.

Connor is here.

Wasn't he dead?

A surge of hope raced through her.

It died quickly, a tidal bore of optimism that was gone before it had really started.

Connor is alive.

But why does it sound like he's crying?

Bound

A vignette of horrible facts fell into place in quick succession as Amandine struggled to locate Connor.

The sky, bruised with dawn's blush.

Water, brown, still, stretching out around them. Frost patterns on the surface.

Birds, singing. Flocks in the sky, moving inland.

Reeds, an ocean of them, furry-tipped, golden against the grey-pink, moving, hissing, trembling as if they were cold too.

I'm deep on the broads, she thought, with some wonder. *How the fuck did I get out here?*

About ten feet away, a hulking structure rose above the reeds, leaning sharply to one side. It was an ugly, rotting shed cobbled together with slimy wood and rusted iron. A slipping thatch roof lay on top of it, infested with thick, green cushions of moss that capped a dark, yawning mouth. It was a disused boathouse, double doors hanging wide open and lopsided on ancient hinges. She couldn't see if anything was inside.

She took in her surroundings with mounting despair.

Wooden planks formed a platform underneath her – she was lying on an old jetty, or pontoon. It was raised above the icy water on stilts, laid out in an L-Shape that led from the boathouse into the middle of the broads and off through the reeds.

"Amandine, I'm here. I'm here, look at me, *please*."

Amandine's eyes slid back along the jetty.

And, finally, she saw Connor.

Her heart lurched.

He was slumped on the pontoon about six feet away from her, tied to a large wooden post that looked like a tree-trunk thrusting up through the boards. The post was huge: taller than a person, solid, driven deep into the mud below. Used to moor boats to, once. Now used to anchor a human in place, stop him from drifting away. Her own screaming shoulders made immediate sense: Connor's arms encircled the post behind his back, his wrists tied on the opposite side of the trunk behind him. His legs stuck out uncomfortably straight in front. They were bound at the ankles like hers, with a bundle of cable ties.

"Connor," she whispered.

"Hey, gorgeous," he replied, weakly. "Welcome to the party. I'm so fucking happy you woke up."

Amandine could see he was in a bad way. His face was bruised and blackened. One eye was swollen so much he couldn't open it. Blood soaked his entire right trouser leg, and there was a sizeable red stain on the wood beneath him. Someone had tied a tourniquet of sorts tight around his right thigh, presumably to stem the flow, but it looked like a half-hearted attempt at first aid at best. Connor was deathly pale around his bruises, confirming that he'd lost a lot of blood. His lips were blue, and his hair was white and stiff with frost. There was ice on his eyebrows and eyelashes. Pale air puffed out of his nostrils.

"Connor!" Amandine leaned weakly against her bonds, more to keep moving than because she thought she could break free. "What the fuck is happening? Where the fuck are we?!"

"Up shit creek," came the response.

Amandine started to cry.

"I thought you were dead."

The tears melted away the residual frost on her lower lids, trickling down her cold skin, cooling, solidifying once again on her cheeks.

"Nah," Connor croaked. "He made a mess of my leg. I hit my head in the car crash… There are holes and cuts all over me. I'm bad. But not dead yet."

"Where the fuck are we, Connor?" Amandine repeated. She tried working against her wrist bonds again, now that some small strength was returning to her limbs. They were so tight the most she could do was clench each fist over and over, hoping to create space between the hard plastic and her soft skin. She could feel panic rising inside her like dirty floodwater. Soon it would roar through her entire system and wash her sanity away with it.

Then, the pins and needles hit.

Gasping, she bucked and jerked as horrible sharp pains flooded into her hands, wrists, forearms, and elbows, which had been motionless until now. It was the blood moving around her body again, she knew, sluggishly reacquainting itself with her circulatory system, but it felt like a million tiny deaths, as if she were being invaded, vein by vein.

She groaned, cried out. "Ahh! Oh, god!"

She could hear Connor, distantly, but his words didn't make sense. The pain kept stabbing, each of her nerve endings a crucible of fire.

"Oh, *god*!"

And then the memories came back.

Her body yanked about like a maggot on a hook, writhing, thrashing in discomfort as if her reawakened blood were carrying recollections in like flotsam on a hot tide.

Getting ready, in her house.

Blood on her abdomen, a word, lipstick on her mouth.

The taxi to the pub.

Meeting Connor.

Drinks. Food. Lingering looks.

The sour presence of the Lone Diner, three tables away.

Walking in the freezing cold.

Kissing, fumbling at each other.

The car.

The moon.

The chemical smell.

The struggle.

The crash.

The ditch.

Gunshots.

A body hitting the floor.

A foot to the ribs.

A foot to the head.

Blinding white pain.

A cloth over her mouth and nose.

Amandine continued to shake violently, and not just with cold.

No way out, she heard herself think, over and over as reality caught her up in its uncompromising fist.

No.

Way.

Out.

In the wake of this thought, a terrible impulse.

Hurt yourself to survive, it instructed.

It's the only way.

Amandine obeyed the voice, as she always did. The pathway out of hysteria was through the forests of harm, an old route she was familiar with. She fell headlong into the coping mechanism she'd developed following the death of her parents and began to beat the back of her skull repeatedly against the hard wooden post behind her.

Slam!

You're tied up!

"Amandine!" Connor yelled, scared. She heard him clearly enough this time, despite the ringing in her ears. "Stop it!"

She could not.

Lone Diner!

Slam!

"Amandine! I mean it! Stop that!"

Slam!

He shot someone, right in front of you!

Slam!

"Fucking stop it!" Connor yelled.

Slam!

Slam!

You're going to die here.

Slam!

Amandine's vision became spotted with small bright lights.

The man with the ponytail and bowtie is going to rape and murder you.

Slam!

"Please!"

Probably torture you, too.

Slam!

"Listen to me! You need to stop before you knock yourself out. Jesus!"

Connor's going to die too, and it will all be your fault.

Slam!

Your fault.

Slam!

Like the person he shot and ran over, that was your fault too.

Slam!

"*AMANDINE!*" Connor roared, straining against his ties. "If you die out here, I die too, don't you get it?!"

His desperation finally sliced through her panic, triggering a fierce anger response in Amandine, a response that overrode the instinctive desire to beat her own brains out.

"Quit yelling at me!" she screamed back, furiously.

But she stopped banging her head against the post.

Connor sagged back.

Moderated his tone.

"I'm sorry," he said. "But I can't stand to see you hurt yourself. Not when he's done so much damage. You're letting him win. We can't let him win, alright?"

Amandine's head throbbed viciously. Her eyes were filled with strange, swimming things.

"Just don't yell at me," she panted, feeling sick.

"Amandine, I promise. We're in a world of shit, and I know it's hard, but I need you, okay? Just… don't do that again."

Amandine trembled all over. "I've stopped," she said, with difficulty. "I've stopped."

She thought she meant it. She was temporarily back in control.

Until she remembered she was tied up.

Then she burst out crying again.

"I want to go home," she spluttered. "Why is this happening to us, Connor? What did we do?"

She wanted answers he didn't have.

It didn't matter. Deep down, Amandine knew. She remembered Lone Diner's face in the restaurant.

He'd looked at her as if he'd hated her very existence, and she believed now that he did.

They hadn't done anything except be in the wrong place, at the wrong time.

"'Why' isn't important," Connor said, weakly, and she could tell he was forcing himself to be patient. "What matters is that we survive."

Amandine fell silent, glaring at Connor in dull comprehension. Around them, the sky turned tangerine bright, the colour of a new day.

Acceptance

Connor waited for Amandine to reach the same stage of acceptance that he had. He knew it was a terrifying reality to grasp, but he needed her to do so as quickly as possible.

After her panic attack, Amandine seemed to lapse into a state of zombification.

He tried to keep her engaged in conversation.

"Amandine, talk to me. Come on, sweetheart. You have to snap out of it."

But she didn't want to talk to him. Amandine had gone statue-still and looked as if she were trying hard to will herself out of existence. Her eyelids were the only things that occasionally moved on her body: they shuttered and opened, lizard-slow, periodically exposing rolling whites.

Connor kept trying until it became obvious she was falling back asleep. He watched her eyelids slide shut, then stay closed. It was horrible to witness the life and emotion drain from her face so completely. Horrible to see her mental anguish. She'd been so animated on their date, he remembered. So funny, reassuring, odd, and honest. As comforting a presence as she'd been annoying, as vulnerable as she'd been full of fire.

Now, she was a ghost.

Her head flopped forward.

And a few moments later, to his continued amazement, she started to snore.

That's one hell of a coping mechanism, he thought, and he was momentarily gripped by jealousy. How nice to just sleep through all the shit. How nice to close one's eyes and be in a better place.

The sun continued to rise above them, its pink fingers lingering on Amandine's broken-doll form through a gap in the reedbeds. It looked as if she were a performer on stage, resting in a spotlight's coloured pool. Any minute now, she would leap to her feet, smile fixed and bright, head held high, arms and legs poised for action, then the band would start to play, and…

Connor shook his head.

Fucking Christ, Connor, he told himself. *Keep it together.*

But it was hard. He was alone again. She'd left him alone. Alone with his own spiralling thoughts, freezing and desperately thirsty and in tremendous pain.

It won't be for long, he told himself. It was too cold and uncomfortable to sleep deeply; Connor knew from bitter experience. Amandine would manage a fitful doze at best, but hopefully one that allowed her overloaded brain some recovery time.

When she came back, they'd talk, they'd form a plan.

He just needed to let her rest for a little while longer. But not too long.

He needed Amandine awake. He needed her focused and sharp. Compos mentis. Because their best way out of this situation, he knew, was through her. *His* best way out. Amandine, despite her mental state, was in far better physical shape than he was. She was stronger, taller, had not lost as much blood. As far as he could see, she had no major injuries beyond the cuts and scrapes she'd gotten trying to escape. Her ear looked horrendous, ripped into two distinct flaps at the top, and her face was swollen, her mouth beaten up, but these were superficial wounds in comparison to his leg.

This got Connor thinking about the difference in their encounters with their captor. The brunt of Lone Diner's violence had, so far, come his way, not hers. This felt calculated: take the man out first. But it also had to give them an advantage somehow. He couldn't put it together properly, but he knew it did. They weren't dead yet, and there was significance to that, and the significance, he was sure, was wearing a green dress and lying tied up and snoring to a post a few feet away.

Amandine was his ticket out of here, he concluded.

An asset, one to be protected.

Nurtured.

It was all on her, now.

The thought came with some considerable shame, tempered by the only desire that mattered.

The desire to live.

Waking Nightmare

Connor used the sun as a guide to help mark the passage of time as Amandine slept. More specifically, he used the shadows cast by the sun as it worked its way across the sky. The post he was tied to acted as a crude sort of sundial. It left a black shadow on the planking of the jetty that crept in a circular motion around him. He arbitrarily decided, for want of a better rationale or system, that a half foot of movement equalled roughly an hour of time passed, and regardless of whether that was accurate, this calculation anchored him a little. Time was familiar, a brace against horror and violence. He was used to the digital clock on his phone, but that was long gone, he presumed. Probably still in the ditch they crashed into, or, if Lone Diner was clever, sitting at the bottom of the broads surrounding them, weighed down in a bag with a brick, just to be sure.

That's what I would do, after all, he told himself, and the thought almost made him laugh.

Almost.

He waited until the shadow had crept a whole foot along, then coaxed Amandine awake once more, as gently as he knew how, acutely aware of hypothermia. Inactivity was deadly, in cold conditions like this. He had to keep her moving her body around, keep that circulation flowing. She'd had the right idea, the first time she'd woken up, but then her brain had taken a hike. He had to get her back on track, back to some sort of antifreeze regimen. This was the kind of cold a person could lose fingers and toes to quite easily.

He knew this, because he could feel the skin on his little fingers going hard.

"Come on, Amandine!" he crooned, his throat raw and crackling. "Waking up time!" He spoke to her like his dad used to speak to him when he was a kid, drawing the curtains and poking him gently in the ribs to rouse him for another day at school.

"Amandiiiiine!"

Amandine twitched and groaned. Connor persisted.

"Wake up, baby. We need to talk."

It took a while, but he kept nagging at her until she emerged slowly from her vegetative state. He could see how much more difficult she found it this time. She had dissociated violently.

"Kidnapped," she muttered, as she came to the surface of reality once more. She was speaking to no one in particular.

"Wake up, Baby," Connor repeated, gentle and bright. Desperation tickled at the edges of his resolve and his patience. He was not sure how much longer he could keep the facade going, how much longer he could hold his shit together for the both of them. It was going to be a twice-onerous death, if he had to carry the whole burden of their demise.

"Baby. My mum used to call me Baby." Amandine's eyelids fluttered and spasmed.

"That's good." Connor kept a check, just barely, on his mounting agitation. "What else did she used to say?"

"She used to say… I don't know." Amandine frowned. She had a weird, dopey expression on her face, like she'd been drugged. "I can't remember."

Connor knew he had to keep her talking. Had to keep himself talking, too. He was feeling unsteady, the effort of rousing Amandine was draining his own minimal reserves. So was the cold. He worried about how much blood he had lost from the severed vein in his leg. He didn't think it was the femoral artery, or he'd be dead by now, but whatever the scythe had cut had been significant.

"What was her name, again?" he asked, as much to distract himself as anything else. "What else do you… uhhhh…"

He trailed off as a surge of nausea washed over him. He fought it back, clenching his jaw. He'd already been sick on himself once and didn't want to repeat the experience. The vomit had frozen to his clothes. He could see small chunks of icy, undigested steak glued to his once-clean shirt and tie.

"Wake up," he slurred, struggling to maintain the conversational thread.

"I'm awake," Amandine replied, less drowsily. "I'm sorry, I'm awake."

"Good girl." Connor bit back more bile. "Come join me. We need a plan."

Amandine finally focussed on him.

Her eyes travelled the length of his body. Her expression sharpened in concern.

"You look worse," she said. "Your lips are completely blue."

"I'm fine," he lied, even as hot liquid climbed back up his throat. He swallowed it down forcefully. "I need a hospital, but I'm alive. The bleeding stopped a while back. Looks worse than it is. If I was going to die, I would have by now."

"The crash… the car… were you hurt in it?"

Connor could see she was still piecing the sequence of events together.

Atta girl, he thought. *Let's get those wheels turning again.*

"I have a concussion, I think..." He cut himself off. He couldn't hold it back anymore, the foulness cramping his insides. Connor spluttered, choked, bent forward painfully, as far as his bonds would allow – aimed to one side of himself, away from his injured leg – and ejected a thin steam of hot, stringy bile, stained with red.

The wine from last night, he thought, as he heaved and strained. He watched the vomit leak out of him and onto the frosty boards below. *A good vintage. Forty quid, down the drain.*

I wanted so much to impress her...

"Connor?"

It took him a little while to recover. Once he was sure there was no more puke, he sat up straight again. He could tell from Amandine's face that he looked terrible.

"You're a funny colour now," she confirmed. "Your eyes don't look right."

"I'm okay," he lied again, trying to snap out of it. "I hit my head hard. Been puking since I woke up."

"I'm sorry I... lost it like that, earlier..." Amandine whispered. Connor got a handle on his emotions with some difficulty.

He could be angry with her later.

For now, they only had each other. They had to work as a team.

"It doesn't matter," he said, gently. "It's okay. We need a plan, Amandine. Together, we can figure this shit out."

She took in a shaky breath.

"I'm so cold," she said, miserably. "I can't... I can't... think straight."

"You need to move around, Amandine. It's the only way. You need to get your circulation going."

"How?"

"Just move your body, any way you can. Every single muscle you can. Like you did before. Just move."

Amandine started to rock, side to side, like a metronome hand, leaning to each extent of the post as far as her bonds would allow. The motion offered slight relief on her joints as she rocked, judging by the expression on her face and the way she grunted when she hit a certain point.

"Good, that's good," Connor said, encouragingly. He started to do the same, mimicking her movements. "Let's have a little workout."

Amandine tensed her stomach. Tried to lift her bound feet off the wooden platform again. This time she barely managed an inch from the jetty.

"Come on, Amandine," Connor encouraged, but he could see the weird, desperate light fire up in her eyes.

Don't you dare, he thought, savagely. She was about to freak out on him again.

We don't have fucking time for this.

"Don't give up," he said, out loud. "You can do it, Amandine!"

She strained and grunted, arching her back with effort. Connor could see the extent of her cuts and bruises more clearly as she manoeuvred around. She still had thorns sticking out of her arms and legs, one embedded in her cheek. There was a long gash running along one arm and scratches all over her breasts and shoulders. Her thin fake leather jacket was ripped in dozens of places. He was overcome with a surge of pity for her as she pitched and grunted and flopped about like a clumsily controlled puppet. He had another brief flash of memory: Amandine across the table from him in the restaurant, eyes lit by candlelight, hair gleaming, lower lip gripped by her front teeth as she listened to him intently.

She was so beautiful then.

It was his fault she was here.

If he hadn't asked her out…

"Oh, what's the point?!" Amandine wailed, and Connor's short-lived faith in her resilience died.

"No, don't give up! Keep moving!" he cried. "You have to!"

Rage contorted her face. "Why? There's no fucking *point*! We're going to die out here! He's going to leave us here to die, don't you get it?"

"Of course he's going to leave us to die out here! But it doesn't matter. We won't give up. Someone will come. He crashed his car in the ditch, right? It's probably still there. Someone will find it and know something happened. They'll see all the blood."

"We probably aren't anywhere near that place anymore," Amandine hissed. "If he's smart, he drove us miles out into the broads, away from the crash."

"It doesn't matter," Connor repeated. "Sooner or later, people will realise we're missing. They'll start piecing things together. We were seen at the pub. They'll come looking. Send helicopters!"

This made Amandine pause.

"Nobody even knows I went out on a date with you," she said, quietly. "I don't have any family. Few friends to speak of. I could be out here and nobody would be any the wiser for weeks. It's like… I don't exist."

Connor licked his dry lips, thinking: *My dad will miss me, but…*

He's away.

He'll wonder why I haven't texted, though.

But it'll take him a while. When he's at a work thing…

They both fell silent.

"Nobody's coming for us, are they? Let's be real." She said it matter of factly.

Connor found himself despising Amandine suddenly.

"They have rangers out here," he replied, mind scrabbling for hope. "Police boats. I read about them."

Amandine shook her head. "It's the coldest winter in decades, Connor. Rangers are volunteers, my dad had a friend that did it. They don't work at night, or in extreme weather. The police have to know someone is missing to go out and look for them. How long do you think we can last tied up in the fucking dead of winter, seriously? How fucking long? I'm so cold." Amandine hung her head, defeated.

"I don't care," Connor said. "We don't *need* anyone to come for us. We can do this ourselves."

"I'm so cold," Amandine repeated. Then she burst into tears again.

Connor closed his eyes despairingly, letting her cry, thinking it best if she drained herself once and for all before he laid some hard, sharp truths on her. She needed to work through all the emotions he'd gone through while she was unconscious, but she also needed to get a fucking grip. Their time was running out. Lone Diner would be back soon, Connor knew it, back with more than a shitty old hunting rifle and a scythe. The man had designs on them.

The shadow marker had crept another half a foot along when Amandine eventually dried up. Connor resented every increment.

When he was sure she'd stopped weeping for good, he laid it out for her.

She listened properly this time, watching him with swollen, reddened eyes.

Teamwork

"If you don't get a grip," Connor said, voice now hard and uncompromising, "we will die out here. Do you understand me?"

A few small hiccups leaked out of Amandine's mouth, but beyond that, silence.

He continued.

"We might have a chance to keep each other alive, Amandine. As a team. Something about this guy, I don't know… he strikes me as chaotic. An amateur. As if he doesn't really know what he's doing. The way he's put together, the clumsiness… But we can only figure it out together, you got that? If you give up, if you keep letting it all get on top of you, I'll die. And that will be your fault, not his. You understand?"

More silence.

He kept going.

"You're in better shape than me, and we're in this together, for better or worse, alright? We have a responsibility to each other, Amandine, whether you like it or not."

Her face remained blank. He wondered if the words were filtering in.

"Now. We're alone for the moment, but he's going to come back soon. What would be the point, otherwise? Why bother with all this? Think about it. This is some fuckin… deranged fantasy he's living out. Amateur or not, he knew exactly where to bring us. He has the gun, whatever the stinky chemical shit soaking that cloth was, the cable ties. The fucking sickle thing. People don't just drive around with that stuff in their car, do they? He's done some preparation. He saw us in that restaurant and came back for us. And for all we know, he might have done this before, had a practice run with someone else."

Something sparked in Amandine's face, but Connor ploughed on, mercilessly. No time for detours.

"If he's coming back, it will be to hurt us, or torture us, or rape us, or kill us. He has to get a kick somehow. He's a kicks kind of guy. I bet you were right about him watching porn in the restaurant. It won't be pretty, whatever he has in mind. It's important you wrap your head around that. A beautiful woman, tied up and vulnerable, in the middle of nowhere? It's a fucked-up kidnap fantasy. And he's keeping me around to be the audience, I reckon. But none of that matters. The details don't matter. What matters is that he's coming back, and that gives us a chance, you see? An opportunity. He wants us alive until he's done whatever it is he has in his sick head. Which means we have a window of time. But the only way we can get out of this is if you get your shit together, you hear me? Don't leave me alone with this, Amandine. Don't you fucking leave me alone with this. I haven't been through the shit that I've survived only to die, here, at the hands of some fucking pervert."

His voice broke on the last sentence. He had reached the limit of . He tasted bile in the back of his throat once more. There was blood on his teeth, too, a thick red gunk ridging the bottoms of his incisors. He worried at it with his tongue, trying to work the gunk away, and failing. He hated dirty teeth.

Amandine's eyes bored into him, finally understanding her situation. He saw the pieces slot together in her brain, piece by piece.

They were alive, for now. If they wanted to stay that way, they needed to act in unison.

They had a responsibility towards each other, she saw, a commitment. They were bound by circumstance until they got free.

She nodded, her first definitive, calm movement in a while. Her face was stony, and set, but there was a flourishing resolve that came out in her posture, in the tilt of her mouth.

"I hear you," she said at last. Her eyes went to the old scar around Connor's throat, reappraising him.

And Connor could feel, with enormous relief, that she meant it. Finally, for better or worse, Amandine was back on his team.

Taking Stock

"So now what?"

Amandine asked, returning to her sitting exercises. Keeping the cold at bay was their top priority, and she set to work immediately, shifting her body about with determination, reigniting her sluggish circulation.

Connor did the same, more tentatively. He didn't want to open his leg wound any further, but he had to keep moving. The cold gave him no option. His toes were hard blocks of pain on the ends of his feet. He tried his best to wriggle them, scrunching his feet, activating each toe in turn, but it was agonisingly difficult. He wondered if any of them had started to turn black yet. Surely he would be able to feel his own anatomy turn necrotic, but then again, maybe not. He just had to keep wriggling every digit and hope for the best.

"Let's take stock," he said, and Amandine sat up straighter.

"Alright." She winced as she tried to work her arms up and down awkwardly along the length of the post at her back, rubbing the cable tie around her wrist against the rough wooden trunk, hoping perhaps to weaken it, or catch it on a knot or nail. It was not a bad idea. Connor studied her post carefully, looking for something that might help.

As his eyes travelled up, he was rewarded. He spotted something buried deep in the wood of the post not far above Amandine.

"What's that?" he asked, squinting at the object intently.

Amandine stopped moving. "What?"

"On your post. Up above your head."

She craned her neck back as far as the post allowed, peering up the length of the trunk.

"I think it's an old hook, or nail or something," she said, eventually. "I can't see very well from here. It looks rusty. Yeah, I think… I think it's a hook."

"Think you can reach it?"

"And do what?"

"These cable ties. They won't break unless weakened. Maybe…"

Amandine caught on quickly. "I could maybe hook my wrists over, hang my whole weight off it… maybe rub them a bit against the metal…"

Connor felt a spark of hope. "The locking mechanism, the square bit on the ties, that has to be the weakest bit, right? Try and pull on that, maybe, if you can manoeuvre. Maybe you can poke the tip of the hook into the lock, release it somehow…"

Amandine shook her head. "With my arms behind my back?"

She had a point. She would have to be a contortionist to manage that level of fine motor control with her arms bent backwards that far.

"Well, start by trying to stand up. Then go from there."

Amandine looked in despair at her stiff, unresponsive legs stretched out in front of her on the wooden jetty. Her ankles were like two balloons tied together. "I don't see how."

"Use the post behind you as a leverage point. Try and hug it tight to you while pushing back against the wood. Use your core and brace."

She shot him a sceptical look but tried to do as instructed, her heels skidding on the icy wood of the jetty. Her head whammed back, unintentionally this time, against the post.

"Ah, fuck! It's too slippery…" she grunted, as her stockinged feet scrabbled for purchase. "I can't get a grip!"

"Keep trying," Connor urged, "I know you can do it. You just need to brace your stomach muscles, use your arms as an anchor. Keep trying."

"If it's that fucking… easy…" Amandine snapped back, aggravated, "then why the fuck don't you do it?!"

"Fine!" Connor said, thinking: *Good, more fire. That's it, Amandine.* "I will. Let me show you–"

He pretended to move as if preparing to stand, but Amandine wasn't fooled.

"Oh, stop being a cunt," she replied, sharply. "You'll fuck up your leg again. I'm doing it, alright? I'm fucking doing it."

She gritted her teeth, drew her stomach muscles in, inched her heels back slowly, squeezed her arms into a tight circle around the post, and somehow, whether out of sheer spite or desperation, or both, she managed to shuck her feet into a position where she could brace her back properly against the timber, working her core and going stiff as a board, and then slowly, like a bear hugging a tree as it climbed, only in reverse, arms behind her back, she grappled the trunk and finally shunted her way into a standing position. Connor fed her exuberant praise throughout the entire gruelling exercise, and his triumphant cries almost made her smile as she wobbled on her bound feet. Almost.

"There," she huffed, when she could talk once again. "I can feel the hook against my back."

"Move round a bit, away from it," Connor instructed.

She did as she was told. Now she was upright, the hook stuck out at chest level.

"What now?" Amandine stared down at Connor. "My arms are still behind my back."

"You'll have to go around the post until your hands meet the hook behind you, then sort of hoist your wrists up onto it. I'll direct you."

"Pull them up behind me?" she panted. "I'll dislocate my fucking shoulders, I'm not that flexible."

"We'll cross that bridge when we come to it."

"This," Amandine started to edge clockwise around the post, "is like the worst… fucking… team-building exercise… ever."

"Shut up and stop moaning," Connor said, although there was no sting in his words this time. "At least you didn't get a fucking scythe to the leg."

"*You* shut the fuck up," Amandine retorted. Connor found he preferred this version of her to the one that wouldn't stop crying or trying to beat her own brains out in despair.

This might just actually fucking work, he thought, incredulously, as Amandine rotated clumsily around the pole until her body was on the other side of it, her bound hands now facing him. He could immediately see she didn't have long to get out of the cable ties: her fingers were bloated, swollen, and a deep, shiny red in colour. He winced and wriggled his own fingers in sympathy, then his toes. *This little piggy went to market, this little piggy stayed home…*

"Am I close?" Amandine said, and Connor could see she was tiring, standing awkwardly tight up against the pole. "Tell me where to go."

"A little to the left," he instructed, whereupon Amandine moved to the right.

"No, not your left; my left!" he corrected, biting back a laugh at the absurd dance playing out before him. He had, again, a sense of everything being performed upon a stage, for someone else's pleasure. For all he knew, Lone Diner was watching them through the reeds, or with binoculars.

That thought sobered him considerably. If he was watching, this was all for nothing.

They had to keep trying, though.

Amandine moved her hands in the other direction, arms shaking with effort.

"Now up a bit."

"My arms won't go up any higher!" she wailed. It was true. Her arms could only move as high as her shoulder blades when they were tied together behind her back, no higher.

"Stand on your tiptoes, then!"

"I'll fall!"

"Just do it!"

She wobbled up onto the pads of her feet, giving herself another inch in height. It was just enough.

"That's right – there! It's right there!"

Amandine's wrists almost brushed against the hook.

"I can't reach it!" She gasped, dropping back to the flats of her feet again. "My arms don't bend that high up!"

Connor almost bit his own tongue off in frustration. "Amandine, you're *so* close, you just need one final push, okay? Now, I'm going to count to three, and you're going to go up on your toes, and you're going to bounce and hoist yourself up onto that fucking hook, or we'll freeze out here and die, you hear me? Your fingers are already going bad, Amandine. If you don't do it, you'll lose them."

"They are?" He could hear the horror in her voice. "I can't feel them, it's so fucking cold, I–"

"Up on tippy toes, *now*!"

She obeyed, lurching up onto the balls of her feet again.

"Now, on the count of three, bounce and hook! Ready?"

"No!" she wailed, but Connor didn't care.

"One, two, three... bounce, and *hook*!"

Amandine pushed herself upwards against the post with a small, explosive burst of her knees, bouncing a good space higher than she had on her previous attempt. At the same time, she forced her bound arms up painfully, shrieking with the effort.

She missed.

"Fuck," Connor muttered, in despair. She'd been so close.

But Amandine tried again, positioning her body in just the right spot, squatting her knees like an awkward ballerina, lowering herself down and then surging up against the post, and somehow, miraculously, in a feat she could probably never repeat even after a hundred tries, she managed to snag her hands, and the cable tie, over the protruding iron hook.

And then she hung there, exhausted, moaning in pain as her shoulders constricted, as her arms bent so far up behind her they looked likely to pop out of their sockets at any moment. Stunned, Connor looked at Amandine, who now resembled a joint of meat on a butcher's hook.

"You did it, baby! You did it!" Connor crowed in triumph and disbelief. "You gorgeous bitch, you did it!"

Tears ran down Amandine's face. She was in tremendous pain, letting her whole weight dangle from the hook as her knees buckled in fatigue.

Suddenly, one of the slender ties bundled around her wrists broke under her body weight.

Stupid fucker brought the wrong type of zip tie, Connor thought.

"Oh, my god!" Amandine cried, joyously. "It's working! One of them snapped!"

"Keep going!" Connor said, feeling sick once more, but this time with excitement.

Amandine leaned further forward, face down to the jetty, rearing back up and then repeating the downward slump, over and over, weakening the remaining ties as they rubbed against the rusted metal hook. Connor prayed the hook would hold, that it was embedded deep enough into the post to stay firmly lodged. His prayers were answered, the final ties snapped, pitching Amandine forward as her arms broke apart, and unceremoniously dumping her back onto the platform, where she knelt, panting in triumph.

Too Easy

Stunned, Amandine examined her raw, red wrists. The Reminder Words were still there, faded but present. CELERY, she read. CONNOR. She worked her screaming shoulders, flexed her bloated fingers and rotated her arms until the fiery pain burning down each length of them subsided a little. Her digits were like scarlet sausages, the skin on each of them hard and shiny. She made crabbed fists, tensing and letting go, over and over, willing the blood back into each finger.

The pins and needles came after, as she knew they would. She rode out the pain more easily this time. Besides, it represented one thing: the flesh on her hands was still alive. Barely.

When Amandine experienced some true sensation in her fingers once more, she sat up fully and stared at Connor in shock, feeling as if she were being pranked.

"Seriously? It was that easy?" She felt distrustful, unable to fully enjoy her moment of victory.

Connor started to laugh.

"I told you he was a fucking amateur," he wheezed, letting his whole body succumb to mirth. "Now get over here, would you?"

Brief Freedom

With blood singing again in her tortured arms and hands, Amandine slithered across the jetty to where Connor was tied up. Her ankles were still bound together, but she could deal with that later.

First, she wanted to look at his wounds, make sure he was really okay. She had a feeling he was playing down the extent of his injuries. Amandine needed to know what she was dealing with.

Before that, more than anything else, she wanted to get close, close enough to share body warmth. Although the sun was growing brighter, it gave out no heat. Perhaps if they sat close to each other, they could generate some between them.

She caterpillared her way over the platform awkwardly, dragging herself up to a sitting position and coming to rest with her head on his shoulder.

"Hi," she said, eventually, resting her a hand on his uninjured thigh. "Fancy meeting you in a place like this."

He kept chuckling. He hadn't stopped since Amandine had broken her ties.

"Can I touch you?"

Connor nodded. "I thought you'd never fucking ask."

She rested her head on his chest and sat like that for some

time, thigh to thigh, pressing every part of her she could manage into him so they'd warm up.

It was the best almost-hug Amandine had ever experienced.

When Connor's lips had turned from blue-tinged to purplish again, she untied his tourniquet, peeked at the wound underneath.

The damage inflicted by the sickle's serrated blade was significant: Connor's skin was shredded, a deep gash going inches down into his flesh and muscle, and there was a good deal of dirt and grime in the mix too. He needed to be cleaned up and bandaged before it got infected. And the wound would need stitches.

"I wish I had some superglue," she said, peering at his leg.

"I wish I was on a beach somewhere hot getting my dick sucked, but we can't always get what we want, I guess," Connor wheezed. His teeth were chattering again. Amandine had read somewhere, long ago, that teeth chattering was good in extreme cold. When you stopped shaking, stopped feeling the cold, things got dangerous.

"The cut might open again when you put weight on it. I'll put the tourniquet back on. It'll be tighter this time, I warn you."

"Can't wait," Connor said, voice flat.

"Could be worse," Amandine soothed, refolding the blood-soaked, filthy tourniquet fabric. "He shot someone. A stranger who stopped to help. Right in the face."

"I know. I was awake for that bit."

Amandine stopped what she was doing.

"You... you saw?"

Connor let out a short, bitter laugh. "As well as I could from the bottom of a ditch. But I saw enough."

Amandine bowed her head. “I thought… I thought… I wouldn’t have left you if…” Shame washed through her.

There was no getting around it.

She’d left him because she knew it was the only way to save herself.

Connor gave her a look that she struggled to meet.

“It’s alright,” he said, eventually. “It all happened so fast. I know you tried to carry me. I don’t blame you for not being strong enough. I’d have run too.”

The words stung worse than her frost-bitten fingertips.

She fumbled a knot into the tourniquet, pulling the ends of the fabric tight and hard with her teeth.

Connor grunted.

“Sorry,” Amandine whispered.

“It’s a hunting gun,” he said, eventually. His hands shook so much he looked as if he had palsy. “I only got a glimpse from the ditch, but I’m sure. The sort you use to take out rabbits and pheasants. I doubt he killed whoever it was with six-shot.”

Amandine didn’t tell him about the car thumping over the body in the road. If he hadn’t seen that part, she didn’t want to burden him.

“I cracked a tooth on a piece of shot, once,” she said instead, remembering. “Dad brought home a pheasant from the market. It was riddled with pellets. Chipped a whole chunk off my tooth. I had a crown. Guess what?” She spat to one side. “Chipped it off again.”

Connor didn’t care.

“Can you free my hands?” he asked, eyes fluttering shut. Amandine could see his colour going strange again. A sheen of sweat had popped out on his brow.

“I’m on it.”

She looked around her for a tool to break Connor’s cable ties.

"If I can find something..."

She trailed off as her eyes landed on the dilapidated boatshed nearby. There was bound to be something in there, she reasoned, an old tool or fishing hook, or even a rusty nail or screw would do. All she needed was something hard and sharp enough to jab into the plastic locking mechanism, to depress the little rigid bar that kept everything held tight on the zip tie.

But she couldn't reach the boathouse while her ankles were still tied. The planking between her and the shed was slippery, thickly coated in ice, and she didn't want to risk slithering off the edge of the boards and into the water.

"Amandine?" Connor sounded odd; his voice dreamy.

"Hush, I'm thinking," she replied, but her thoughts were interrupted by a noisy cloud of birds that erupted up from the reeds a little way off: a warning cloud.

Fuck! He's coming back, she thought. *He's coming back!*

Connor heard it, too. He became instantly more alert, fear slapping him out of his disoriented state.

They strained to hear footsteps.

Sure enough, moments later the distant sound of heavy feet clomping carefully along rickety, slick wood planks came floating to them across the tips of the reeds.

"Fuck," Connor breathed. "Go!"

Amandine didn't need to be told twice. *If he finds me like this, he'll have the advantage,* she thought, hurling herself away from Connor and slithering back towards her own post. Her best bet was to get her back against the trunk again, put her arms behind her and pretend she was still tied captive.

But what about the frost? He'll be able to see drag marks in the frost!

No time to care about that now.

She reached the post with moments to spare, kicking the snapped zip-ties into the water so Lone Diner wouldn't find the evidence of her jailbreak.

She hurled her arms behind her, crossed them at the wrists, interlocked her sore fingers to keep herself in place, and waited.

When Lone Diner finally emerged, and saw her sitting, awake and waiting for him, he smiled.

"Hello, lovers," he said, and Amandine braced herself for the worst.

Phone Proof

He held an empty bucket in his hand with a rope tied to the plastic handle.

"You're awake, I see." He spoke pleasantly, as if his next statement was going to be about the weather. "Shame the same can't be said for lover boy."

Amandine glared at him, then over at Connor, who was slumped, unresponsive, against his post. He was pretending to be asleep, she realised. Why, she didn't know.

In daylight, up close, Lone Diner was far more dishevelled and far less of a threatening proposition than he'd appeared in the restaurant, or in the driver's seat of his car. Perhaps this was because he was very visibly injured, which meant, to Amandine, that he was no longer the shadowy, evil phantom figure her brain had constructed in his absence. His arms were wound with dingy bandages and strips of cloth. Blood from the cuts Amandine had inflicted seeped through. His tux was shredded from the serrated scythe blade. He limped, and when he came to a standstill, he wavered unsteadily on his feet. His bowtie was crooked, his ponytail had slipped. He had large humps of greasy hair sticking out in all directions from his scalp. He had found his glasses, but they were so smeared and cracked she wondered if he could see out of them at all. A massive bruise flowered across his forehead: a leftover from the crash.

Lone Diner, Amandine thought, was every bit as human and fallible as she and Connor. Tired, too. He had deep lines around his mouth and between his eyes. His face was puffy, as though he hadn't slept. She had a sense he was not used to physical injuries. He favoured his arms in a strange, posturing way, as if he was showing the lacerations off for sympathy. Like a kid with a grazed knee, milking the scab for all it was worth.

It was a strange relief to find that beneath the odd clothing, the filth, the glasses, and the blood, Lone Diner was otherwise unremarkable. The type who could easily hold down a dull desk job, who had a library card and a mortgage. She was shocked by how mild his voice was, how neutral his expression, how ordinary his stance and build. There was nothing distinctive about his appearance once you stripped away his wrinkled tuxedo, stained bowtie, and greasy ponytail. These were all just elements, she realised, of a carefully curated costume he wore to make himself stand out more. Even the smell and the filth he adorned himself with was an outfit, the type adopted by a villain from a comic book. A signature scent. A malfeasance USP. Take that away, and you would be left with an average-looking man of medium height, medium stature, medium age, medium everything. The man had the sort of face you would struggle to remember in a crowd.

He desperately wanted to be remarkable, so he was trying to become so with his actions.

With violence, with fear.

It was all about getting attention, that was it.

Strangely, she understood this. She understood wanting to be more.

But it wasn't who Lone Diner was, down at heart. He lacked conviction, Amandine intuited, as she watched him assessing his captives, working up to his next move. He might think this was his true calling, but none of this came naturally to him.

He was a tourist in the Badlands, nothing more.

Amandine felt fierce contempt and had a hard time keeping it off her face. Her lip curled, an involuntary disgust response. She controlled it.

How do people like him survive, when my parents were taken? she thought.

How was that fair?

It wasn't.

The truth of this burned in her.

Lone Diner stood and looked at Amandine for a long time, a buyer scrutinising a new purchase, only he hadn't paid for her, he'd stolen her. She saw a variety of emotions slide across his face in quick succession. He was at war with himself.

But why did he have to make that my problem?

Amandine was shivering again now that she could no longer move around. She was convinced she would never feel anything but cold for the rest of whatever life remained for her. She could not remember how it felt to be warm, comfortable. Her bones ached. Her fingers were almost completely numb again. Her lips had grown so chapped and raw they had developed large splits that she worried with the tip of her tongue. She hurt, everywhere. Every single part of her.

But somehow, she knew the worst was yet to come.

He would have to make up for his mediocrity somehow, wouldn't he?

Warily, she waited for Lone Diner to move. Speak. Do anything.

He carried no weapons this time, only the bucket.

She wondered if it was intended for use as a toilet. Which made her think, suddenly, about her period. Almost immediately, as if relieved she had finally remembered it, her stomach cramped. She tried to remember when she'd last changed her tampon. She was wearing a pad, too, but she'd need to get rid of both soon; she had been wearing them for well over eight hours. The pad would bleed through before long anyway.

How would Lone Diner respond to that? Would he even notice?

But the bucket wasn't for use as a toilet, as Lone Diner demonstrated when he finally stopped staring at Amandine, blinking rapidly and jerking into action as if waking up from a trance. He busied himself filling it, using the rope to lower it off the edge of the jetty and down into the waters of the broad. He threw a rock down first, to break a hole in the ice, ice that seemed to get thicker with each passing hour, despite the climbing sun.

The empty bucket bobbed, then filled.

Amandine considered using the time Lone Diner was distracted to hurl herself at him, shove him sharply off the jetty, but then she remembered: her ankles were still bound.

You could roll into the water, she thought, frantically.

Except for the fact that she couldn't swim. Especially not with bound feet.

Although she was sure, given the right impetus, she could learn fast.

Just not when the waters are freezing over all around you, idiot. You'd be dead from shock in seconds.

Besides, Amandine had read once that the water out here was bad, toxic. The algae on the broads was poisonous, and swimming was prohibited.

Still. Death by drowning or toxic algae still felt preferable to whatever it was Lone Diner wanted to do to her.

She tensed her body, preparing to inch closer to the platform edge, but then her sights landed on Connor, who was still pretending to be asleep. Maybe he didn't have the mental energy to engage with what was going on, or maybe it was a ploy, to create the impression he was worse off than he was.

Or maybe he wasn't pretending at all and was fading fast. If that was the case, they didn't have long.

You can't leave him behind again, she told herself.

Patience, Amandine.

But it was hard. Her arms were free, and that gave her an advantage. Freedom was a great deal closer than it had been when she'd first woken to find herself tied to a post.

Closer, but not close enough.

She waited and watched.

What was the strange fucker up to?

Lone Diner let the bucket fill to the brim with water, then heaved it back up onto the jetty with some considerable effort. His injured arms gave him obvious discomfort as he worked. Amandine held her breath, hoping that Lone Diner might put a foot wrong, perhaps slip and topple forward into the reeds, but he didn't. He kept his balance.

Then he turned, looked at them both again. He was panting with effort, and his breath plumed fast and ragged in the cold. A hand subconsciously massaged the left side of his chest, as if it hurt.

"I hope you're not thinking about trying to escape," he told Amandine, when his breathing had calmed down a little. He still spoke in that deceptively pleasant voice, a salesman making a telephone pitch. False bonhomie and charm. *Would you be interested in learning about our special deals today, madam?*

She had a sudden mental image of him at a desk, with a headset perched on his head.

Amandine found she couldn't look at him. Her arms shook with the effort of pretending they were still tied behind her back.

"Because if you did, I would have to punish you," Lone Diner continued, lightly.

Amandine said nothing.

"Like I did the last pair."

This was not the gotcha moment he expected, however. Amandine had already put two and two together from something Connor had said earlier: *maybe he's done it before.* She'd remembered the alert on her phone, the headline about the missing couple. They were engaged, she recalled, but she hadn't wanted to dive into the article to find out more.

Now, she wished she had.

What were their names?

Her continued silence and lack of reaction annoyed Lone Diner.

He stretched his back, cracked his neck, feigning nonchalance.

"Yeah, I'm afraid it didn't end too well for either of them," he continued, drawing a single finger across his throat, an unmistakable gesture. "Especially for her."

Then he winked, and Amandine kept her face as expressionless as she could, refusing to give him the attention he was fishing for.

God, he is so needy, she thought, disgusted.

Lone Diner's aloof mask slipped, briefly.

His body language grew odd and stiff.

He's annoyed, Amandine thought.

No, more than that.

He was offended.

He was putting on a show for her, and she wasn't appreciating it.

Appreciating him.

Good.

Lone Diner recovered, sighed, shook his head and pointed to a patch of water in front of the boathouse, still trying to draw her in. "They're both down there," he said.

Amateur machismo, amateur everything.

"I thought they might like some company, so I brought them you."

Amandine stopped short of rolling her eyes.

Lone Diner's lenses flashed.

"Want to hear her begging for her life?"

Amandine turned her head from him. She didn't care about the other couple, not at that moment. She found it hard to care about anything when she was this cold, this desperate.

I just want to go home! she screamed, internally.

I want to go home and lock the door and climb into my bed and never leave it, ever again!

A sound started to play: the tinny, unmistakable clamour of a phone playing media with its volume up to max.

Now what? Amandine was slow to comprehend. More porn?

No.

At first, she thought she was listening to an animal of some sort, squealing, a horse or pig or…

It was not an animal.

It was a woman.

A woman's voice screamed in miniature.

"Please, don't, don't, please! *Don't! Fuck! Fuck!*"

Amandine realised, then, that she'd made another mistake.

She'd underestimated Lone Diner because of the pitiful way he presented himself.

Pitiful and amateur could still be dangerous, though.

Give us a Hand

The woman in the phone squealed and screamed and swore. Vile expletives fell from her lips as frequently as the pleas for her life, pleas that grew more hysterical and desperate as the video played out. Amandine didn't think a human could actually make such noises. She fought hard to keep her composure.

Focus on something else, her brain told her.

This is a tactic.

Don't fall for it.

She concentrated on using her right index finger to lightly trace a Miracle Word onto the palm of her left hand, as surreptitiously as she could.

SAFE, she wrote, letter by letter.

It helped, a very small amount, until Lone Diner thrust the phone screen in her direction. He had sensed her distancing herself. He wasn't going to allow it.

"Want a closer look?"

Amandine reared away. She didn't want to look, but Lone Diner's hand followed her head no matter how she positioned it. He wouldn't quit trying to make her watch. The best thing was to let him think he was in control. If she looked, he would get bored, move on to the next nasty treat he had planned.

She stopped trying to get away from the video and turned her gaze purposefully towards it, falling back on an odd little trick she'd learned as a kid: she could focus and unfocus her eyes at will.

It worked, momentarily. Amandine let her gaze fall, loose and fuzzy, and saw nothing but a chaotic mix of images and movements and colours.

She couldn't make her ears stop working, however. The sounds slicing into her eardrums were awful. They ate at her brain.

Her finger kept writing.

SAFE, SAFE, S-A-F-E.

Connor remained silent, maintaining his pretence of being asleep, propped up against his post. She wondered if he could hear. Of course he could hear.

What was he thinking?

The squealing cut off, suddenly.

Other sounds became apparent: fleshy sounds, meaty sounds, thumping and grunting and something metallic scraping on something else that wasn't.

Amandine's eyes snapped into focus, unbidden.

The cracked and smeared phone screen was right up close, now. Lone Diner had shoved his cinematic creation practically under her nose. Amandine thought about breaking her pretence, whipping her arms around, snatching the phone, dialling 999 in the seconds she might have before he took it back – but then she saw the smaller version of him in the phone sawing at something that looked a lot like a human wrist, with a hacksaw, the metal type with the rounded steel frames like surgeons used in historic movies, and Amandine almost screamed, *almost*, but managed not to give him the satisfaction, as the human hand came completely free from its owner and fell out of shot and then a little, instantly recognisable icon popped up on the screen, momentarily blotting out the horrible details on the video still playing:

Lone Diner had a text message.

When are you coming home, sweetheart? it read.

I made that curry you like.

Amandine wheezed, choked, and then started to laugh. A high, pealing laugh wholly disconnected from sanity.

Lone Diner frowned.

"Your wife is texting," Amandine said.

Lone Diner's face became an almost cartoonish study in consternation and disbelief.

He flipped the phone round, cancelled the video, jabbed at something else on the screen, then pocketed his phone.

The laughter dried on Amandine's lips as quickly as it had bubbled out. Lone Diner was really angry, now. He'd been interrupted in peak villain-flow, and he didn't like it.

Not one bit.

Pouting, two hotspots of pink burning on his cheeks, he took something lumpish and misshapen out of a different baggy jacket pocket. Whatever it was, the thing was wrapped in a plastic bag, one that had seen better days: the bag was tattered and full of ragged holes.

Stained red, too, Amandine realised. She had a feeling she knew what it was, from the size and the shape.

Lone Diner hefted the object for a moment, then unwrapped it and threw it at Amandine.

It landed heavily on the boards between her and Connor.

Amandine peered down, then bit back a cry of disgust, using her legs to push backwards away from the thing, but the post at her back blocked her way. She very nearly let her shaking arms drop again, barely managing to keep them behind her in mock-restraint from sheer force of will alone.

Connor's voice spoke out.

He was no longer pretending to be asleep.

"Jesus fuck, you sick bastard."

Lone Diner smiled and folded his arms. Order restored, control reasserted.

Amandine gagged but couldn't look away from the thing.

The nails were long, and painted red.

An engagement ring on the fourth finger glinted in the rare winter sun.

She remembered the video. The hacksaw on the delicate wrist, like a branch from a silver birch.

And Amandine's opinion of Lone Diner continued to evolve, adapt.

Because he might be amateurish at some things, and childish in other ways, and he might be a pathetic figure to look at, an Average Joe of the highest order, but maybe all of that made him *more* dangerous, not less. There was something desperate about him, in the way he was so performatively violent. It reminded her of stories she'd read of people smearing faeces on the walls of prison cells: protest behaviour, all of it, and it spoke of a massive, deep-rooted sense of anxiety, of fear, fear of rejection.

The whole reason he'd thrown the hand down on the deck was to show his strength, reinforcing how much of a threat he thought he represented. It would make her cooperate more, but also, it made for a good show. It was all part of the plan: subjugation, cooperation, control. Response.

Validation.

Applause. Cheers. Encore.

She looked at his face.

His lips hung loose, and wet, as if…

As if he's aroused, she thought to herself, in revulsion.

Connor made an appalled noise deep in the base of his throat.

“You fucking bastard,” he spat, unable to contain himself. “I read about them, you fucking, cowardly freak!”

Lone Diner’s mouth turned down at the corners.

“Shut up,” Lone Diner replied. He grabbed the bucket, stepped forward, and unceremoniously dumped the ice-cold contents all over Connor.

Water for Fools

Connor was instantly drenched.

The shock of the freezing marsh water hitting his skin slapped him hard and brutal as a giant open palm. What little breath he'd been able to muster before was snatched away. He might as well be drowning. For a moment, he thought he was. His lungs closed. There was water in his mouth, in his nostrils, in his ears.

Unintelligible sounds filled his head.

His skin became a tapestry of stabbing points of pain.

Connor understood, distantly, beyond the agony, what Lone Diner was trying to do.

He was going to give Connor hypothermia.

Make him literally freeze to death, if he could.

His plan, such as it was, had changed. Lone Diner didn't have the patience to wait for days on end for Connor to die of exposure. He was going to escalate things.

Connor blinked frantically. There was something heavy and white on his eyelashes.

Ice. The water had already frozen.

Lone Diner smiled, hefted the bucket, and returned to the side of the jetty.

He's going back for more.

"Stop it!" Amandine shouted, but Connor knew shouting was futile. Nobody could hear them out here apart from the birds and the gathering clouds in the sky.

Lone Diner ignored Amandine, lowering the bucket into the water once again using the rope tied to its handle.

He filled the bucket, humming to himself, just a busy man going about his chores.

Hauled it back up.

Returned.

Looked down at the shivering, gasping wreck of a human he had captured.

Threw the water.

It hit Connor with a meaty *smack!*

Full in the face this time.

Connor tasted strange things on his tongue, unclean things, metallic and earthy at the same time. He thought about bugs and larvae and bacteria and faeces and algae and chemical spills and dead people rotting below the surface of the broads and tried to puke, but he had nothing left in him to regurgitate, so he started to cry instead.

"Connor, you need to move your body!" Amandine pleaded.

He could barely hear her. His ears glugged loudly as he wept.

"Connor! Don't give up! You need to keep your body moving!"

The words leaked through, distorted but stubborn.

She's right, he thought, weakly. Lone Diner's feet retreated as he went back for more water.

Connor responded by slowly flopping around on the deck like a dying fish, desperately trying to keep his drenched, struggling body going before the next bucketload hit. He sobbed and gasped as he writhed, knowing how absurd he looked, visualising his own piteous end on the rotting stage in brilliant, vivid detail.

Lone Diner returned, the bucket heavy again, and watched this display of clumsy energy with a weird, fixed intensity, chewing the skin around his thumbnail on his spare hand, the other swinging the bucket in gentle arcs around his legs.

"That's it!" Amandine told Connor, as encouragingly as she could. "Keep moving!"

Lone Diner grew bored of Connor's exercises. He shook his head, grunted, and threw another freezing-cold load of water.

Connor clenched every muscle he could, but nothing could prepare him for the agony of assault as the third load drenched him.

He wondered distantly what it would feel like to be burned alive.

Worse or better than this?

Death ran down his skin in rivulets. Delirium nibbled the edges of his mental faculties.

Roll up, roll up, come take a peek at the Human Eel, folks! This week only!

His flopping and flapping grew more erratic. His lips made a strange, stretching O shape, and Lone Diner frowned, lowering the bucket. Connor saw the expression on his face and redoubled his efforts. He was a fish. Flip, flop, flip. His leg wound opened, letting out fresh, hot, seeping blood that smeared all over.

Look, ma, I'm a fish out of water!

His legs bound together only reinforced the imagery.

It was all so fucking hilarious.

Poor Timing

Amandine could see Lone Diner thinking, *What the fuck?*

She didn't know if Connor was deliberately trying to distract their captor or had legitimately lost his mind at that point.

It didn't matter.

Amandine saw a window.

She didn't care that her ankles were bound.

Connor would die unless she did something. He was bleeding again; he would get hypothermia and pass out and die.

And if he died, Lone Diner would turn on her next.

While Connor was alive, she had a chance.

Amandine broke her pretence, pulling her arms round in front of herself, flipping clumsily over away from the post, curling her body up into a bunched hoop and then flinging herself forward across the jetty with as much force as she could muster, ready to grab Lone Diner's legs like a rugby player, ready to try pull him off balance and off the platform into the broad below – but he saw her coming at the last moment.

Swearing, he swung his now empty bucket in a wide arc. It whacked Amandine in the side of the head, not hard, but hard enough to put her off balance, and she hit the planks hard and awkward, then found herself slithering and sliding forward on slick white wood. She scrabbled frantically for purchase on the slippery platform as her body skidded towards the edge of the jetty, trying to dig in her useless feet to slow herself down, but it was no use, and suddenly her head was over the edge, facing down into the dark waters, then her shoulders, and she knew she was about to fall headlong into the broads, and she would drown with her ankles tied.

A hand grabbed the back of her dress and hauled back, hard.

She felt a second of relief, and then, realising who had her, renewed terror.

"*No!*" she screeched.

Amandine landed in a tumbling heap on the jetty once more, wailing in frustration, flipping herself over and trying to crawl away.

Lone Diner brought the bucket around for another brutal swing.

This time it hit her nose, hard. There was a crunching sound, and she fell back, dazed, ears ringing, clutching her face, which spouted fresh blood.

Another bolt of impact battered her across the side of the head, and then on the other side, and again, and again, until everything grew dark.

First Base

Lone Diner waited until he was sure the woman was unconscious, then turned and hit the thrashing man still doing fish impressions in the face with the empty bucket until, eventually, he also stopped squirming and wriggling and laughing like an idiot. Instead, he lay without moving, breath coming in frantic little bursts.

"That's better," Lone Diner said.

"Fuck you," the drenched man spat. His cheeks were splattered with blood and ice crystals and broken reed strands and rotten leaves from the broads. A small brown worm wriggled across his chin, and strands of oozy pond weed were entangled in his hair.

Lone Diner kicked the man in the stomach twice with his good leg, sending agonising pain up his injured leg. He kept kicking until the man was completely subdued.

"No," he then said, feeling much better now that he had them both back under control. If nothing else, he would learn from his mistakes. "I wouldn't dream of it. Not when you're both on a date."

"What?" The captive man could barely speak. "What… are you fucking talking about?"

"First base," Lone Diner replied, cheerfully. "I think you've both waited long enough, don't you?"

He brought the bucket down for one last blow.

Shared Warmth

He tied them together this time. He stripped them of their clothes first. This was harder than he'd thought it would be, because they were both dead weights unconscious, almost impossible to manipulate, but Lone Diner persevered, wrenching their clothes off and bundling the garments into a sodden pile to dispose of later.

One thing at a time. It was hard to think straight. He was excited, his heart galloping. The girl's attempted escape had not angered him. Rather, it invigorated him. She'd tried to get the best of him and failed. He'd been quicker, stronger, better. He had needed that reminder, badly.

He rubbed his crotch absentmindedly as he worked.

Lone Diner used a new batch of cable ties to secure his captives, positioning them so they lay on their sides, facing each other, nose to nose, hands up behind the other person's head, as if they were bringing each other in for a passionate kiss. He wanted them to breathe in each other's mouths, sour and acrid with the lingering scent of bile and vomit and broad water. He pushed their heads together, so their lips were touching, *first base*. He was sure the woman's nose was broken. She breathed noisily through bubbles of blood, which burst and splattered onto the man's face every time she exhaled.

Ankles and knees bound together with a system of interlocking zip-ties like a daisy-chain around their limbs.

He had seen a picture, once, an image of two skeletons archaeologists had uncovered lying together in a dusty tomb. "The Lovers of Valdaro", they had come to be known as, and as much as he hated the saccharine joy that image had provoked across the internet, the picture had stuck with him. Why, he couldn't say, but it had. Recreating his own version was tricky but rewarding. He felt like a sculptor working on a masterpiece. His life's work, manipulations in frigid flesh.

He photographed the final result as he straightened his back. His leg throbbed wildly, but the joy mingled with hate he felt looking at the couple outweighed the discomfort.

It was perfect, he thought, as he lined up the marbled lovers in the shot so the reeds and lowering sun made an attractive backdrop.

They look dead already.

He scooped up the dismembered hand before he left, wrapping it lovingly back in its tatty plastic bag, and patting it affectionately as it resumed its place in his pocket. He wondered idly if wood varnish would slow the decay, if he could pick some up from the DIY store. He could get some fresh bandages for his arms, and some antiseptic and painkillers. Maybe swing past the crash site of his own car, see if it was still there or had been towed yet. He'd cleaned it out of all his belongings, transferring them to the stolen vehicle, having ripped the licence plates off it first, but it might not hurt to double check.

Lone Diner's nostrils flared as he walked back to his car.

Smells like snow, he thought, happily.

Bound

Amandine figured out her situation as soon as she woke, this time. There was no burgeoning awareness, no slow, horrifying realisation. She could smell Connor, feel his skin on hers. Feel the familiar cut and bind of fresh cable ties at her joints. She shifted, groaning in pain, and he moved in a corresponding way. She felt the weight of him and knew they were conjoined, realised immediately what Lone Diner had done.

Their nakedness was not a shock either. She had expected something like this well before now.

Amandine didn't struggle or fight. She lay still, taking mental stock of the damage that had been done to her. She scanned herself, starting at the head and working down methodically.

This was difficult, because everything ached.

Everything felt broken and bad.

Everything felt cold, cold, cold to the bone.

The injury tick list grew longer and longer.

Fatigue. Weighing her down, pressing her body hard into the wooden platform beneath her sore buttocks and hips.

A fierce headache, gripping the space between and behind her eyes.

Her nose, a horrible, screaming lump on her face coated in congealed blood and snot. Probably broken. If she pressed into Connor's nose, she heard a grinding noise. Cartilage.

A sharp, stabbing pain at the back of her throat, which was dry, swollen, almost completely closed up, but she still needed to cough. Coughing directly onto Connor felt absurdly rude, so she tried her best not to, but fighting it made her want to cough even more.

Her guts churned, the leftover remains of adrenaline ravaging her insides.

Below her belly, blood lay sticky on her skin: it didn't dry as quickly as the miracle word had. It came in slow little gouts between her legs, warm, the only thing about her that was.

Lone Diner must have taken her tampon out when he undressed her, because she could no longer feel the swollen bulk of it down there.

She felt so suddenly, terribly ashamed at the thought of bleeding while being this close to another human being, like a child who had wet the bed, unable to exert even the most basic control over their bodily functions. She wanted so desperately to be able to clean herself up. Restore some dignity to her body.

She was grateful Connor was still unconscious.

Or was he dead?

Her stomach dropped. Her breath quickened.

He was cold enough to be dead.

She was too close to get a proper look at him.

Oh, god. Oh, god!

Amandine panicked, thinking she had been tied to a corpse, and trying to jerk away from him.

His head lolled between her forearms. There was a worm on his face, wiggling around.

"Connor!" she shouted, but he didn't respond.

Then she heard a crackling hitch, felt his breath on her lips.

No, not dead.

What would you do if he was?

Tied to a dead body in the middle of nowhere. Naked.

What would she do?

She didn't know the answer.

Don't focus on that, she told herself, trembling spasms running along her naked limbs.

Focus on survival.

It was hard to think coherently. Her mind slopped around here, there, everywhere, wrestling drunkenly with unknowns.

Will we make it?

Will I make it?

Will I die?

Will anyone ever find my body?

At least my parents don't have to deal with the aftermath of all this. Thank god.

Focus, idiot!

She squeezed her eyes shut.

Survive.

How?

One step at a time.

Identify the threats and face them in order of immediacy.

The biggest threat to her at that moment, she worked out, was the cold.

Hypothermia.

Amandine leaned into Connor, trying to share body warmth, but found his knees, bound at the joints, formed a barrier. They felt weird and knobbly against hers, and the pressure of them leaning into each other put stress on the cable ties, which cut savagely into Amandine's flesh.

Suddenly, she lost all concept of her own parts, of what flesh she was composed of. She knew she had limbs, but she couldn't feel them very well and got them mixed up in her head with Connor's. It was like they had absorbed each other.

Calm, she told herself, catching another rising wave of panic and slapping it away before it could get a hold of her.

Calm.

She started the process of re-scanning herself, searching for her own arms. Her warped proprioception made this difficult, but she eventually located her hands behind Connor's head. They were secured with cable ties again. Of course. All that hard work of getting free, nearly dislocating her arms at the shoulders, for nothing.

Don't give up.

You're both still alive.

For now.

If you got free once, you can do it again.

But get warm first.

Get warm, then get away.

Amandine carefully pulled her bound arms, so they slipped down behind Connor's head, and then worked them along his spine, dragging her embrace downwards until she was wrapped tightly around his bare ribcage, which rose and fell with shallow, sickly bursts of breath.

Poor Connor, she thought, through a fuzz of dissociation and despair.

Amandine held onto him as closely as she could, feeling her breasts press into his chest, feeling his face smush into the hollow at the base of her neck as she brought him closer, shifting their bound knees up at an awkward ankle to ease some of the pressure, feeling, just barely, his heart thumping weakly in his ribcage, and she held him, rubbing his back with bound arms that felt like tree branches, hoping against hope that she could share some of her meagre heat and restore circulation and life to him, into them both, before it was too late. She didn't know if it would work, maybe the whole skin-to-skin thing was a myth, a trope reserved for the movies, for romantic novels, but it didn't matter, she had nothing else at her disposal except her own body, and his.

So, she would use them the only way she could: the friction of flesh on flesh her last chance of survival. She would be his life jacket in the cold, and wear him like one too.

She felt him stir, as she worked at him.

Yes, wake up, she thought. *Don't leave me alone with this.*

Amandine whispered in Connor's ear, a joke, meant to soothe, meant to rouse him from his stupor.

Humour would do it, if anything would.

"I bet this is not what you had in mind when you said you wanted to see me naked," she murmured, still rubbing his back vigorously. His skin felt less livid already.

Connor said nothing, but she thought she heard a small, weak grunt.

It was a start.

Amandine took a brief pause from massaging Connor to trace a Miracle Word onto her palm with her opposing thumb.

LIVE, it said.

The sun passed over them, remote, and as unimpressed as the moon.

Curry

Lone Diner got back to his car and tried to burn the lovers' drenched clothes, using lighter fluid to speed things along. They didn't take, only smouldering momentarily before fizzling out. He gave up, eventually, bundled them into the boot of the car. He'd burn them when they were dry.

Then, he climbed in behind the steering wheel and checked his phone. His wife had texted again.

When are you home?

Curry sounds good, Lone Diner texted back, wearily. *Don't know what time I'm back. Save the leftovers.*

Truth was, he didn't want leftovers.

Truth was, he hated his wife's curry.

Truth was, she was a terrible cook, with a limited repertoire of terrible recipes.

Agitated by his wife's unwelcome intrusions into the fantasy he was living out, he decided to comfort scroll through his various social media accounts until enough time had passed for the couple tied up on the jetty to be thoroughly broken. This would take an hour, maybe two, tops. Plenty of time to sow some chaos online.

Then he would go back and finish what he had started in the real world.

Maybe the cold was starting to get to him, or maybe it was his low boredom threshold, but Lone Diner found, for some indefinable reason, that he didn't want to draw this scenario out as long as he had with the others. He found that he wanted a more immediate conclusion, something deeply dramatic and gratifying. Throwing water over the man had been fun, but he wanted to see that special kind of desperate light in their eyes again: pure, unadulterated panic. And knowledge, knowledge of what was coming, of the inevitability of it, of the nastiness of their impending end. His hand itched for blades and for cutting. He wanted to make another video to add to his collection.

His thumb swerved away from his social icons, grouped together in a neat folder, and went back to his hidden folder instead.

Maybe he could soothe himself before going back out there with another viewing of his special gallery, but his phone suddenly went black before he could tap the folder.

He stared at it, perplexed.

Jabbed the dead screen.

It remained dark, unresponsive.

Anger flooded his veins.

But I just charged the battery.

Then he remembered: cold sped up battery loss.

He searched around for his portable battery charger, but he couldn't find it.

He had left it in his old car. Damn!

He banged the dash in frustration, searching for a charging port in the new car.

Nothing.

Not a cable, not even an adaptor socket.

He threw his phone as hard as he could against the windscreen of the car.

It bounced back, hit him square on the forehead.

Lone Diner scrambled out of the car, threw the phone on the ground, and stamped on it repeatedly, screaming as the screen splintered underfoot.

"Fuck you! Fuck you! *Fuck you!*"

A tight band of pain gripped his chest and radiated down one arm, forcing him to stop. He clutched at himself, hissing.

The pain subsided.

Then, whining like a dog, Lone Diner collapsed back into the car, slumped in the driver's seat and stared up at the horizon.

It didn't matter, he thought, when all was said and done. A phone didn't make much difference. He would still have the memories to go back to.

When he had his strength back, he would end it, he told himself.

Suddenly, curry didn't sound so bad after all.

Later

Amandine continued to rub her arms up and down Connor's spine. The motion soothed her into a sort of semi-conscious state, and she drifted in and out of bouts of exhausted awareness as wild scenarios ran through her mind. They eventually settled, like swirling snowflakes, on a clear and vivid vision of her home. The scene filled every remaining space inside her and produced a visceral response, a helium punch to the gut and lungs that left her fighting for her life, struggling to breathe as she choked on a better, safer world beyond the waterlogged broads.

She thought about the gas fire in her living room, hissing and crackling, blue flames giving out longed-for heat.

Candles flickering on the mantelpiece.

Soft furnishings, a deep-pile rug.

Pictures and photographs on the wall.

Potted plants, soft fronds – not straight, sharp, unforgiving reeds.

Cushions.

Steaming mugs of tea–

No, hot chocolate, with tiny marshmallows bobbing on the top.

Thick stew, with crusty bread sliced doorstop-style, slathered with yellow salty butter that melted just so.

Wine glasses, filled with crimson delights.

A podcast on the go, or perhaps a movie, a cosy comfort-style TV show with autumnal leaves and wholesome characters with perfectly assembled outfits, hair and makeup, everything easy on the eye, no aesthetic brutalities. The plot would be holey, the storylines banal and unchallenging, and she would treat herself to a hot bath after bingeing multiple seasons. The bath would have salts sprinkled in it. There would be more candles. A face mask. Some sugar scrub…

I just want to go home, she thought, miserably.

Connor shifted, groaned into the hollow of her throat again.

Her eyes filled with tears.

She blinked them away, furious at herself.

You don't have time for this.

It was getting darker.

The temperature, Amandine knew, would drop further when the daylight went, even though she couldn't imagine how that was.

Connor was still unresponsive. Amandine wriggled her fingers behind his back, something she was trying to do on rotation, to a count of twenty that she kept going in her head, a grounding technique that she kept running along behind the scenes of her chaotic visions of being back home in the warm and dry, with the doors and windows locked. Her hands, she could tell, were worse after their second stint of immobility. Her fingers felt tighter, more swollen than ever, and they were oddly hot to the touch.

She hoped nothing had turned black, yet. She thought she would be able to tell when they did. Even though they hurt, even though she felt like they would burst at any minute, the skin splitting under internal pressure, she could still feel *something*. Complete loss of sensation was the point of no return for living skin.

She was not ready to say goodbye to any parts of herself, not yet.

Wriggle, wriggle, wriggle.

LIVE.

Tell Me a Joke

Fresh blood running down her leg brought her gracelessly back into the world.

Her period. Still going strong. She'd hoped it might go away with the shock, with the stress, with the cold, but if anything, it was getting worse. Her cramps only grew more painful.

"Fuck," she muttered, instinctively trying to uncoil and realising for the dozenth time that she couldn't.

At least she was a bit warmer than she had been on first waking. The rubbing had done them both a favour, but it was paltry defence against the coldest winter in decades.

Time to go, she told herself.

"Wake up, Connor," she urged, shaking violently. They needed to get up, get moving, and fast. Amandine thought she could smell snow in the air. From the corner of her eye she could see thick clouds gathering, soaking up the remaining daylight "We have to go. Night is coming. I think it's going to snow."

In the silence between them, bitterns boomed.

She knew he could hear her. She felt his eyelashes flutter.

He just didn't want to face the world anymore.

"Tell me a joke," Amandine said, suddenly. She was tired of being alone and yet feeling so invaded at the same time. If Connor didn't wake up soon, he would give up, and he would die, and she would be bound to a dead weight for real.

She nudged him with her forehead while still working her tied arms up and down his body, generating as much friction and heat as she could.

She wondered if he would thank her later for keeping him alive.

"Come on, you bastard," she growled. "Wakey-wakey time."

She nudged him again, harder.

"Don't," he mumbled.

"Wake up!" she insisted.

"I'm awake. I just don't want to be," Connor whispered.

"You don't have a choice. It's time to go. Now."

She kissed him on the lips, then bit his bottom lip, hard.

Connor roused slowly, squinting into her face.

"Ow," he croaked.

She could see he didn't have much left in him.

What was the euphemism?

Turn your face to the wall.

He was already halfway there, she thought.

They needed to find a way out of their ties. Amandine understood that of all the things Lone Diner could have done, binding them together was actually the most helpful thing when it came to their likelihood of escape.

Shared body heat was better than none, and two pairs of hands were also better than one.

It would require some contortion and effort, but she began to figure out the human Rubik's cube they had become, working through each limb movement in sequence in her brain.

First, she had to get Connor back in fighting form.

"Tell me a joke," she insisted, lowering her tone to make it both comforting and almost flirtatious – remarkable in the circumstances. She kissed him again, felt him stir.

He blinked painfully. "Are you out of your fucking tree?" he rasped, but a response was an improvement on no response, so she took it as encouragement.

"Any joke you can think of. Tell me a joke," she repeated, shuddering.

Connor shook his head in a tiny, bewildered movement. His eyes seemed to get bigger by the second. "What the fuck are you asking me?"

Amandine kept at it.

"Just do as I ask. Tell me a joke. Please. I need one."

"Amandine, I–"

"What, you have somewhere else you need to be?"

"Fuck you."

"Later," she said.

He growled in frustration, but he kissed her back, suddenly, and she could feel something in him shift.

"Knock knock." He sounded so weak. So diminished.

"Who's there?"

But he couldn't remember. Connor cleared his throat, opened his mouth, shut it again.

"Go on," Amandine urged.

Connor tried again, but nothing sensible came out beyond a ragged squeak.

"Keep going," Amandine urged, relying on his stubbornness to come through.

It did. She could almost *hear* Connor's mind wheeling through several alternative, poorly constructed knock-knock jokes until it finally settled on the one he could remember.

"Knock knock," he managed once again, spitting out the words like mouthfuls of bad fruit.

"Who's there?"

A streak of pain shot up Amandine's legs suddenly, and she

writhed, trying to shake out the sudden, unexpected cramp, crying out in agony.

"Oh, god!"

Connor tensed, strained forward against his bonds. Her pain seemed to wake him up almost completely.

"Are you okay? What's going on?"

"Jesus fuck, just tell the fucking joke!" she cried. *"Who's there?!"*

Connor swallowed.

"Howard," he said.

"Howard... who?" Amandine panted. The cramp slowly subsided.

Connor smiled then, she felt it, and she automatically smiled in response, feeling the action crack the dried blood on her cheeks, split her lips anew.

"Howard you like to be my valentine?"

Amandine started to laugh, and laugh, and laugh, to the point where she thought she was going to be sick, she could feel it all shifting in her guts, climbing up her gullet, but instead, Amandine started crying again, the sound of her desperate, exhausted sobs ringing out across the water.

"Hey," Connor pleaded, blinking away his own tears. "Don't. Don't! I can't bear it."

Amandine tried to catch her breath. "But I need to," she explained. "I need to get it all out before it rots me away on the inside."

He saw then why she'd needed the joke: she'd been building up, like a pressure cooker. He was the gauge that allowed her to vent the steam.

"Knock knock," he said once more, licking his own dry, cracked lips for the thousandth time.

Then he felt something wet and warm spreading under him.

"Connor, stop," Amandine said, in a tiny, shame-filled voice. "I have to tell you something."

"Now?"

"I pissed myself," she whispered, almost inaudible. "You made me laugh and…"

Connor thought about this for a moment.

"It's warm," he said, eventually. "Thanks."

Amandine exhaled.

"You're not shivering anymore," she said.

"I don't feel as cold. Did you put the bins out?"

"You're not making any sense, Connor."

"Yeah, I know."

The water around them crackled as ice spears on the surface grew thicker. Another flock of birds moved in a feathered mass across the sky, heading off to roost and chittering as they went. Amandine took hope from the murmuration. There were so many free, living things out here in the marshes that it felt inevitable they would eventually join that number.

At least it can't get worse than this, Amandine thought, bitterly.

Then, something cold and soft drifted down, landed on Amandine's cheek.

Amandine turned her head a fraction, to face the clouds. *Is the sky falling down?* she thought, sadly. *Like Chicken Licken said it would?*

Another furry, wet object settled on her lips, melted.

"It's snowing," she murmured, and it was.

Escape

"We have to get out of these ties before we become next spring's top news story," Connor whispered.

The snow made tiny, soft *plat-plat* noises on the planks around them.

"So, what's the plan?" Connor asked next, as she knew he would.

"We start with the arms," she replied. "They're tied behind our heads but not tied *to* our necks or heads. So we can…"

"What?"

"Just do as I say," Amandine said, unwilling to waste any more energy explaining. She dragged her arms up in reverse along the length of Connor's spine, working them back up over his shoulders and over the top of his head, the zip ties on her wrists dragging through his hair so he hissed in discomfort, until she was able to bring them down, in between their bodies, and fold them to her chest. The change of position was an immense relief, easing the ache in her shoulders considerably.

"Now you do the same," she said, panting slightly from the effort.

He did, slowly, laboriously working his tied embrace up towards her neck and back across her hair, until he stopped suddenly.

"What?" Amandine asked, shaking violently as more snow settled on her bare skin.

"You have something in your hair," he said.

She felt him fumble clumsily at a matted lump that had formed on the back of her head.

Realisation struck.

"Hairpin!"

Amandine felt genuine excitement, an emotion that was as incongruous and out of place in their bleak, cold surroundings as it was welcome.

"Can you get it?"

"I'll… try… my fingers don't work very well…"

More fumbling at her head.

A sharp pull as Connor yanked at strands of her hair.

"I can barely feel anything, my hands… I'll can't use my thumbs. The other fingers are going bad too."

"Take your time. But not too…"

A grunt.

"Got it!"

"Don't drop it," Amandine hissed through clenched teeth. "Don't you dare fucking drop it. We can use it."

"If… you say so… boss."

The snow started to fall faster.

Connor got his arms up over her head and down in front of his own chest, so they looked like two people praying, now, face to face.

"Your thumbs," Amandine said, eyes wide.

His thumb tips were turning black.

"Never mind that," he said. She saw he was on the verge of tears again.

She looked for the hairpin in his right hand, the unexpected key to their freedom. He was gripping it as hard as he could between his index and middle fingers, which were crossed, as if for luck, the pin jammed between them. She had to get it before he fumbled it and lost what could be their last real chance at getting out alive.

"Hold still," she said, dipping her head and grasping the pin gently between her teeth. Then she transferred it to her own right thumb (bright red, but not necrotic) and index finger, pincering the hairpin in as tight a grip as she could manage.

"Now show me your wrists, hold them up a bit."

"There isn't enough room," he said, struggling.

Amandine arched her back away from him, creating a fraction more space. Cold air rushed into the new gaps formed between their bodies and threatened to undo all her good work of cuddling and massaging Connor's unconscious body. Cold was a weapon, cold was a way of life, cold was everything, the unmaker, the destroyer; cold, she understood, was something she would never underestimate again.

"Okay?"

"I… yes…"

He held his bound wrists before her face with difficulty. Only one cable tie this time, tightly zipped around his wrist bones just below the heel of the hands. Lone Diner had been running low, she realised, using dozens of ties elsewhere to secure their bodies to each other.

"What are you going to do?" Connor asked.

It was a stupid question.

"Shh," she murmured, so he did.

Focusing harder than she had on anything in her life up to this point, Amandine carefully located the cable tie's locking mechanism and looked for the tiny flat nylon pin that kept everything securely in place.

She guided her hairpin hand in as carefully as she could, given the cold. It proved impossible to get a good trajectory. She was shaking so hard she missed her target once, twice, three times.

"Shit," she swore. "I can't keep still enough."

"You can do it," Connor said.

Amandine searched frantically for a distraction while she attempted time and time again to jam the end of the hairpin under the locking mechanism and release the tie. With each fail, her resolve strengthened, a deep, primal stubbornness rising up like rainbow-swirled oil to the surface of marsh water.

"My parents both died in a car accident," she said, grimacing as the pin slipped once more and almost came flying completely out of her grip. The problem was, once she managed to even get it near the mechanism, the bent end of it was too large to jam into the lock.

Connor watched silently as she reversed her hands, brought the hairpin back to her mouth, and used her teeth to unfold it, pull it out into one long, straight piece of metal. It was easier to grip like this, there was more length to get hold of.

Amandine went back to the lock.

"They drove into a ditch filled with water," she continued, peering at Connor's wrists so intently in the fading light that her eyes watered. She felt momentarily grateful for the snow, which was extending their daylight in a muted, reflective manner as it settled.

Connor kept quiet, holding his breath, mesmerised by her attempts to pick the zip-tie lock.

"I remember the sound of the crane whirring when they hauled the car out of the ditch the next morning. I was there to help identify them."

The end of the metal pin inserted clumsily into the zip-tie lock.

"Mum's hair was over her face, but I remember her hands."

Gently does it, Amandine told herself.

"They were all wrinkled and white, like she'd… like she'd been in the bath."

This is the most important moment of your life, Amandine.

Don't fuck it up.

Amandine stopped talking.

Held her breath.

Slowly manoeuvred the hairpin down the side of the lock, pressing against the plastic tongue holding everything tightly in place.

When it was pushed in far enough, she let out her breath, slowly.

"Move your wrists apart," she whispered.

"When I was five, my mam slammed my head into the dining tabletop so hard I passed out," he replied.

Amandine could not afford to burst into tears, not now.

"Do it. Pull your wrists apart, sharp."

Connor did as she asked.

The cable ties released and began to slide loose as the hairpin kept the locking pin open.

"Not too fast!" Amandine warned, as a fierce triumph blazed in her chest. "Don't lose the pin!"

Connor's wrists came entirely free with a deliberate, almost joyous motion that Amandine was sure she would remember forever.

Amandine started to laugh, victory filling her body until she felt fit to burst.

"Easy peasy," she said, and Connor leaned in to kiss her out of sheer gratitude.

Free Again

Amandine instructed Connor on how to break the ties around her own wrists. There was a certain knack to inserting the metal pin in exactly the right place. Releasing her was a much tricker prospect because of the state of Connor's hands. After multiple failed attempts to manipulate the hairpin, he gave up.

"I don't think I can do it," he said, his voice loaded with bitter disappointment. He was letting the side down, and he knew it.

"Here," Amandine said. She blew onto his hands, cheeks inflating frantically while he looked down at her, the bent-out hairpin now clasped between his own front teeth so he didn't drop it.

After a few minutes, he muttered, "Stop. That's enough. I think it helped."

Connor put each hand under his armpits, humming to himself in desperation until, eventually, he was able to restore just enough sensation to pull the pin out of his mouth, and guide it into the locking mechanism. Once it was in the right place, Amandine curled the fingers of her left hand across the back of her right, just enough to push the pin at her wrist joints down into the right spot, release the lock, and open her ties, just the same way she had Connor's.

"Where the fuck did you learn how to do that?" he asked, as her hands separated. Amandine let out a huge groan and immediately shoved her red, stiff fingers under her own armpits, desperate to stave off frostbite, if she could. She thought she had caught it just in time. The ends of her fingers were almost completely numb, and hard to the touch, but she could still feel things, like the stubble growing in her pits, sharp and scratchy.

"TikTok," she shivered, offering no further explanation.

Her hands tingled as they warmed, only a fraction, but enough to trigger the stabbing pins and needles again.

Together, they started working on the rest of their bonds.

Lone Diner had used a total of fifteen cable ties to bind them together at the knees and ankles. Amandine and Connor got through most of them before the light vanished, taking regular breaks to blow on their fingers and rub each other's extremities back into life. Three ties remained tightly wrapped around the bottoms of their calves as darkness fell.

"We lost the light," Connor said, stating the obvious. A bat flitted across the sky, not far from his head. A bird of unknown description screeched in the distance.

Stars began to poke through gaps in the thick cloud cover above, which was gradually breaking up.

"I can't see much," Amandine said, leaning forward. There was more light than there should have been, thanks to the snow still drifting in around them, but it was not enough. Amandine wished she had a torch, but there was no chance of that; she would have to feel her way instead.

"Talk to me," she pleaded with Connor as she worked, but talking was once again beyond him. The snow and the cold and the advent of night had overcome any temporary burst of energy he'd managed to summon while they picked their ties open, and Amandine could hear his breath, ragged and uneven. His lungs sounded wet and crackly.

Amandine stopped fiddling with the ankle ties and reached out for him in the fresh silence. The snow muted all the sounds they had grown used to: birdsong, reeds whispering, water moving. The world had become thickly insulated.

"Come here," she said, wrapping her arms around him once more. This was easier now that they were both mostly untied. Their ankles were still secured together, but they could lie one atop the other and rub each other's bodies to try and keep some circulation going. It was agony for both of them, but they did it, Amandine's teeth chattering, Connor's chest rising and falling in shallow breaths.

He felt like a cold slab of beef bought fresh from the butcher.

She told him so.

"Fuck off," he managed, then he spoke no more for some time.

Everything hurts

Amandine kept tending to Connor until his teeth started chattering again. She rubbed his chest and back, knowing that most heat was stored in the middle of the body. He weakly returned the favour as far as he was able.

"How… do you feel?" she croaked, when he started making gentle groaning noises. "We can't stay here much longer, Connor."

"Fucking terrible," he replied in a hoarse whisper. "Everything hurts… I'm naked… think I'm going to lose my thumbs… huge hole in my leg."

"If everything hurts… it means you're still alive."

"The rubbing…helps. Just… a bit more."

Amandine did as she was asked, begrudging the time but knowing she had to get Connor's body functioning again. She started back under his armpits, vigorously manipulating the flesh, and worked down his chest, to his stomach, then the tops of his uninjured thigh. Her hand brushed his cock by mistake, and she hissed an apology.

"While you're down there…"

Amandine tsked but knew he was back with her, if only for a moment.

Her mind went to their next task, after breaking the final ties – shelter. That, and some sort of clothing.

Maybe they could even start a fire, although she didn't want to risk revealing that they had broken free.

Unless they could get undercover somehow.

Amandine remembered the boathouse.

Perhaps if she could try to start a fire there...

With what? her brain asked.

Wet wood and reeds?

Shut up, she told herself.

One thing at a time.

She felt for the remaining cable ties, located the locking mechanisms with what were now expert fingers. She pushed the pin into each lock, wedged her sore index finger under the strap, and worked it loose. She repeated this, by a stint of blindly feeling her way, twice more.

Then she used her hands to pull apart the bonds – and suddenly, they were free.

Completely, definitively free.

The mental burden of being tethered to another human dissipated. Amandine felt lighter.

"You're incredible," Connor whispered.

"Save it," she replied. "Can you sit up on your own?"

"I think so."

He did, slowly.

"Guess what," he said, and she could feel the smile in his voice.

"What?"

"It stopped snowing."

She held out her hands. He was right.

"Thank Christ," she breathed. "Now if only the moon to come out."

Five minutes later, a breeze picked up. Clouds shifted. More stars popped into view.

The moon came out from where it had been hiding, casting the now white world into brilliant relief against the dark night sky.

"Well, fuck me," Amandine said, tears prickling her eyes.

"You have writing on you," Connor croaked, staring at her abdomen.

Amandine looked down at herself and thought back to a time when this would have embarrassed her. The miracle word had flaked, but most of it remained: LOVE, it said.

She'd been a different person when she'd written that with her finger.

Love no longer seemed important.

In fact, it seemed the least important thing of all.

"Is that… blood?"

Amandine decided she didn't want to have this conversation. There was blood quite clearly covering her thighs, but this was what he focused on?

"Lipstick," she lied.

He struggled to remember. "Miracle Word?"

They didn't have time for this.

"Let's get out of this shithole," she said instead.

Amandine used one of the posts for support, dragging herself upright. It took far more effort than she would have liked, but eventually, she found herself on her feet.

This was a mistake; her screaming body told her this in no uncertain terms. Her ankles, bound for so long they had swollen up to the size of small balloons, gave way. Her numb feet tried and failed to carry her weight.

With a cry, she toppled forward like a felled tree, landing on the jetty with a hard *smack!*

"Hey!" Connor cried. "You okay?"

She wasn't, but she had no choice but to persevere. She doggedly got to her knees and hauled herself up again.

This time, she swayed like a drunk person on her fat ankles, but stayed standing. She began to stamp her feet, over and over, alternating each one, doing a strange, stilted on-the-spot march, wincing as pain tore up her shins and calves; she remembered twisting both ankles badly trying to run away on that potholed road. No wonder the tops of her feet would be black and blue and green from bruising.

Amandine willed her blood to move faster through her veins, telling her brain to send signals to each unresponsive part of her body. Enough was enough, she was done being weak, she was done being cold, she was done being a prisoner, it was time to go. Action was required.

Eventually, her body did as she asked. Blood returned to her feet, and she felt stronger the longer she stamped, not even self-conscious that she was stark naked in front of Connor.

At least he's naked too, she thought. *No secrets here anymore.*

When she felt ready, she tested herself with a few stumbling steps forward. These went okay, so she walked in a small circle, getting more confident with each step. The snow proved useful: it was fresh, crunchy, easier to navigate than the rotting boards beneath.

Then she bent down, hooked her hands under Connor's armpits, and tried pulling him to his feet.

She may as well have tried pulling a truck along the road with a rope gripped between her teeth.

Connor couldn't stand. He wanted to, but he couldn't.

He made it a couple of inches off the planking at best.

Snow squeaked beneath Amandine's feet as she strained.

"I'm sorry," Connor said, thumping back to the jetty with a cry. "I... can't."

Amandine had been patient long enough.

She stared at him in the moonlight, then slapped him hard across the face, twice.

"Then try harder!" she shouted.

Connor stared up at her in shock.

Amandine did not apologise. She was trying to keep him alive.

She tried lifting him again, muttering and swearing under her breath.

This time he stood, like a newborn fawn, limbs awkward and shaking like a leaf.

"I'm up," he panted. "Now what?"

Amandine looked around.

She didn't know.

What could they do if Connor couldn't walk? She couldn't carry him.

And where was Lone Diner?

He could be anywhere, she realised. He could be hiding in the reeds, watching, letting them think they had another chance before jumping out and putting them right back to square one.

An owl hooted in the distance. The same one as before? It sounded like it was mocking her.

"We won't… last long… without clothes," she managed. "We need shelter, a weapon… something to wrap ourselves up in."

Connor's eyes went to the boathouse. "In there?" he said, nodding to the dilapidated structure.

"Let's go."

"What… what if he comes? He'll find us… I can't run." Pain was making it difficult for Connor to explain himself.

"Yes you fucking can," Amandine retorted, lifting an arm to drape across his shoulders. "Let's go."

She managed to drag him forward one single step before he cried out in pain, sagging so heavily against her she thought he'd fainted again.

"Come on," she said, refusing to give up.

They took another step. Then another.

Connor stumbled on something beneath the snow, his injured leg catching on an uneven plank on the jetty. He doubled over and tried to vomit again.

"For god's sake, Connor!" Amandine cried, shaking him in desperation. "You need to fucking try harder!"

Connor let go of her and sank back to the platform.

"No, no, no!" Amandine cried, almost kicking him in frustration. "Get the fuck up! We have a chance, don't you see? Don't fuck it up for us!"

She could feel herself getting angrier and angrier.

"I can't," he whispered, head in the snow. "I can't put any weight on it. I can't walk without a stick."

Amandine stared at him, furious. "But…" Words failed her. They were so close. She'd overcome so many hurdles, just to get to this point.

And he was going to let her down, at this final, vital moment.

Every second they remained here was a second wasted.

Every second they didn't run brought them closer to the possibility of Lone Diner's return.

She bent and grabbed hold of both his hands.

"Then let's find a fucking stick," Amandine said, through gritted teeth. "We're in the countryside, how hard can it fucking be?"

She dragged him, thanking the sky above for the snow, which was beginning to freeze over now that the fall had stopped, creating a surface like an ice rink. Connor's body slid easily, the snow compacted beneath her bare feet, and as she inched backwards along the jetty towards the boathouse, tits swinging wildly, leaving little drops of dark menstrual blood in the snow behind her, she thought once again how fucking absurd this must look if anyone were to see her from a distance.

If Lone Diner is lurking somewhere, watching, he's probably laughing his ass off, she thought, savagely.

Let him laugh.

She was going to win, no matter what it took.

She was going to win, not him.

She dragged Connor like a sack of potatoes across the jetty and along the boardwalk leading from it until the boathouse loomed, dark and forbidding, behind.

Then Amandine leaned Connor against the boathouse wall and told him to keep moving his feet while she looked inside for something useful.

"I won't be long. I want you to keep moving. You got that?"

"I'll try," he replied. He didn't look like he could commit to the statement. He leaned against the wall like a giant doll someone had discarded. He was so pale in the moonlight he looked as if he had been sculpted from marble.

"You'd better," she said.

Connor's face drooped.

"Some first date, huh?"

Amandine made to leave him.

"Trust me," she said, hobbling off on frozen feet. "I've had worse."

Lone Diner

He slept – and dreamed.

Of his couch back home, eating him with ruthless appetite, only the couch covers were made of flayed and stretched skin, not fabric.

Of secateurs, clipping off his fingers, one by one.

Of laughter, insistent and mocking, pouring into his ears like acid.

Of swallowing the end of his shotgun, awkwardly reaching down, somehow managing to pull the trigger with a piece of string he'd tied to it.

Of words, scrawled in blood on snow in confident capital letters: *LIVE, LAUGH, LOVE.*

Of tomato soup, with globules of spit floating on the top.

Of holding hands with a woman in the moonlight, walking among fluttering reeds, being led to an open expanse of water that reflected a dazzling blanket of luminous stars, where the woman removed her clothes and then his and bathed him, in the cold water, carefully, attentively, a mysterious smile on her lips as she fondled all the sensitive parts of him gently, so gently…

Of his wife, ladling large, gloopy spoonfuls of bright orange curry into a bowl with practised boredom. It looked like diarrhoea, and the rice beneath it moved, because it wasn't rice at all but a bowl teeming with maggots.

Of eyes watching him, always, following no matter where he walked, how he acted and behaved, what he said, what he wore… the eyes were framed with long eyelashes coated in mascara, eyeshadow heavy in the creases of the eyelids, and he tried to remember what it was his father had told him again about women who wore makeup, but he couldn't remember; he could only remember…

Of his wedding day, only instead of his wife, he was facing the woman who now lay at the bottom of Hickling Broad in a bag. As he slipped a wedding band on her hand, it fell off, and the fingers came to life, carrying the hand away down the aisle as if it were a spider scuttling off, and…

He woke to find he was sucking his thumb, a leftover trait from childhood that he sometimes reverted to in times of stress.

No, not his thumb.

Hers.

Boathouse

Amandine once again took mental stock of herself as she searched for a way into the boathouse: apart from the cold, the hunger, the raging thirst, and worsening headache, her swollen, bound ankles, her period cramps, the scratches and thorns in her face, hands, arms and shoulders, her broken nose, her torn ear, which hurt more than she could describe, the encroaching hypothermia…

She was doing alright, all things considered.

The main double doors leading into the boathouse were inaccessible, hanging directly above the water, but Amandine spotted a side door towards the back of the structure, almost concealed completely by a wall of reeds she had to push through. When she got to it, the door was old and swollen, sticking on rusty hinges, but Amandine managed to get her fingers round one side of it and pull until, eventually, it screeched open far enough to allow her to slip through.

Inside, it was almost completely dark except for the thin, reflected glare from the moonlit snow outside. The weak light highlighted the cracks in the wood, along with more water, coming right up through the middle of the boathouse. When Amandine's eyes had adjusted, she could make out a narrow ledge running around the boathouse walls. The ledge was slippery with pondweed.

Amandine made a hopeful noise as she saw something breaking up the shadows on the water, right then and there: a hulking shape floated, almost indiscernible, but she could make an educated guess – a boat. She edged closer. The boat had oars. She thought she could see them sticking out of one end, as if they'd been propped there and left untouched since its last outing.

This is it.

This is how we get away.

No need to traverse the rickety, lethal jetty and risk being seen. She doubted Lone Diner had gone far.

If he spotted them and still had his gun…

But now they wouldn't have to navigate the boardwalk at all. All she would have to do was load Connor into the boat, and they could row out into the broads and over the nature reserve to eventual safety. He wouldn't even have to walk on his bad leg.

They were saved.

Then she got closer, heard the slap of moving water, and saw something was not quite right about the wooden vessel. Hope turned to ash in her mouth. The boat wasn't floating at all like she'd thought: the rotting shell was half-submerged, the rest wedged against a splintered plank of wood holding it up on one side, a small bank of silt that had gathered on the other.

If she pushed this old heap out into the broad, it would sink in seconds.

They would need to find another way.

Connor's voice came to her faintly from the jetty.

"Hurry Amandine!" He sounded bad. "I can't… much longer…"

Something rustled in the boat as she jiggled it experimentally with one foot. Carefully lowering herself into a squat, she grabbed hold of an iron joist jutting out of the boathouse wall, and leaned into the boat, feeling with her other hand. It brushed against something scratchy, that made a loud noise under her fingers: a covering of some sort. A tarpaulin, maybe. It was cold, and wet, but it was something she could wrap herself in. Anything was better than nothing when there was snow lying everywhere outside.

She retrieved the tarpaulin, brushing it down as vigorously as she could in the gloom, trying not to think about spiders and leeches and anything else that had made a home in it, then wrapped the covering around her shoulders, gasping as the cold, resistant material met her skin. It felt awful, like putting on a horrible, dirty raincoat with no protective layers beneath, but her skin gradually warmed the material and it began to give a little, moulding better to her shape.

It'll do, she told herself.

Now, what else can we use in here?

Her hopes of being able to build a fire had faded completely, but that didn't mean she couldn't find something to use as a walking stick. She considered one of the oars, but it looked too heavy to lift out of the boat, much less use as a weak man's walking aid.

Then, Amandine spotted something leaning against a wall that was mostly moss and cobwebs.

She shuffled closer, mindful of the gaping boat bay mere inches from where she stood.

It was a long, slender pole, she thought, with some sort of fixture on the top.

Perfect.

She edged forward, putting one hand out to feel her way carefully along the left-hand wall so she wouldn't accidentally step out into the dark, algae-scummed water. Her hand kept reaching, and she inched along the small ledge until her fingers brushed against the pole.

And something else, hanging from a nail on the wall next to it. It rustled but had weight to it. A bag, holding something.

Maybe some rags, or bait, or something else we can use or burn for warmth, she thought.

She unhooked the bag, transferred it to her free hand without looking at its contents, and reached for the pole. Grabbed it. Backed up and exited the boathouse with some effort, given the length of the pole. She got stuck several times in the doorframe, eventually scraping her way back into the night with extra splinters in her arms for her trouble.

There was just enough light to examine her find. She assessed the pole, realised it was a boathook, six feet long, topped with a brass double-hook end that was pitted with spots of corrosion but otherwise looked and felt solid. Useful.

A weapon and *a walking stick,* she thought, smiling.

"Here you go," she said, emerging from the reeds after using the boathook to thrash them out of her way. "I found thi–"

A bright beam of light clicked on and shone directly in her eyes.

"Drop it," Lone Diner said. "I have my gun pointed right at his pretty, dumb head."

Less Than a Man

I've had worse.

Her words echoed in Connor's mind, bouncing around and around. His face still stung from where she'd slapped him. His leg… his leg was its very own entity now, one made of fire and pain, a pain he'd never experienced before. It took his breath clean out of his lungs whenever he moved. He poked it with hands that didn't work properly, and heard squishy, squelching noises. He thought he could smell, it, too, the wound: it smelt off, unclean. An odd smell, and an unsettling one. He thought about infections, about dirty water, about wriggling things and maggots getting into him and eating him from the inside out.

Despair trickled down his body like rain now that he didn't have Amandine around to keep him buoyed.

How the fuck were they going to escape when he was in this state?

The answer was stark: *they* were not going to escape.

She probably was.

His thumbs felt odd. He carefully shuffled his hands up on the boathouse wall to head height, so he could take a look without having to let go. They'd been turning black, earlier. God knows what they were like now, after scrabbling around in the snow.

I guess my career as a pianist is over, he thought.

He could hear Amandine moving around in the boathouse behind him. He wished he had the courage and strength to stand, to run with her, but he was finding it hard to keep his head up, never mind anything else.

Move your body around, he told himself half-heartedly. *Circulation. That's what she said.*

But why? What's the point? he thought, dully.

She will be pissed at you if you don't, his brain countered.

She wouldn't be long, she'd said.

He would try his best.

He went through the motions of keeping himself active, staring at the moon as he worked through his exercises. With Amandine gone, the wildlife around him grew bolder. Things rustled in the reeds: he hoped they were birds.

Suddenly, a pair of otters appeared on the landing nearby. Connor heard them squeal and chitter before he saw them. As a thin cloud scudded across the full moon, he watched one of the slick, wet creatures gobble up something long and wriggling: an eel. Connor, who had not eaten for a very long time, imagined himself lunging at the animal, wrestling the slippery brown fish from the otter's jaws, gobbling it down himself, choking as the eel slid down his throat. He wondered if it would wriggle in his belly. He wouldn't care. Food was food, alive or otherwise.

He found himself suddenly alternating between fantasies: hot pies, roaring fires, amber pints, thick quilts, steaming showers. He realised sadly that all those things belonged to other people, other lives. He would never feel warmth again, and he mourned for the once hot and healthy version of himself. For sweat and flushed cheeks and mediterranean breezes from childhood vacations with his dad. He mourned for his father, who would have no idea what had happened to his son. He felt sad for all the times he had not appreciated what he'd had: a home, central heating, a full fridge.

Something Amandine had said earlier came to mind, then. What did she call them? Miracle Words. She said they helped.

Connor was desperate enough to try anything to make himself feel better, so he tried the words. He had a limited repertoire, and drew them into the snow on the jetty boards with the nail on his left big toe:

HOT.

WARM.

SUN.

For a brief second after writing each word, he fancied himself filled with fire, coursing through his veins, thawing him out, burning away the infection in his leg; but he must not have been doing it right, for after he finished writing, the otters suddenly plopped back into the water of the broads, the reeds rustled, and a tall shadow emerged on the jetty, a shadow that limped, that had rounded shoulders. The figure was burdened with several things Connor couldn't distinguish, and one thing he could: a gun.

Choice

It was a head torch light. Lone Diner trained it to shine right in Amandine's face, so it obliterated her vision.

She held up a hand to ward off the glare. Brilliant spots danced under her eyelids. False stars, unreliable as her freedom.

Her hands tightened on the pole.

"Drop it," Lone Diner repeated.

Even though he had the upper hand, he sounded like he was reciting a line from a movie, as if he needed a script for reassurance. She thought about telling him he was a cliché, a stupid fucking trope on legs. Just a cartoon baddie, a kid who'd somehow gotten hold of Daddy's cigarettes and was choking on a lit one, trying to hide it so he still looked cool.

Was he telling the truth? About the gun pointing at Connor?

She heard a muffled groan.

Yeah, he probably was.

But we were so close! she wailed, in her head.

"You don't know how to use that thing anyway," she spat out loud, blinking furiously and reluctantly letting go of the pole, just in case. It clattered to the jetty and lay tantalisingly close to her right foot.

"Maybe," came the response, "but I don't think I can miss from here, do you?"

The beam of light moved. Amandine's vision cleared.

She saw Connor in the spotlight instead. Right where she'd left him, head tilted back at an unnatural angle.

Lone Diner had the end of the gun barrel pressed deep into Connor's eye-socket.

He was right. There was no way he could miss from there.

Something rustled in her hand.

Lone Diner's beam of light whipped back, highlighting the object she held.

Amandine looked down, discovering, as she'd thought, that it was another plastic bag. It was a Ziplock bag, she realised, the sort used to store leftovers in a freezer. Amandine recognised the plastic as identical to the wrapping around the severed hand Lone Diner had shown them earlier.

Her heart sank. If this was one of his, then…

She saw, in the beam of the torchlight, a bloodied cock lying at the bottom of the bag, which was moist on the inside with condensation and gore.

No balls, just the shaft.

There were maggots crawling along the length of it.

She stared at it, hearing the blood pound nightmarishly loud in her ears, imagining the scenario that had played out and resulted in this sad deposit of rotting meat in a bag.

It looks like a dildo, she thought, a crazy bubble of sound squeaking out from her lips.

It looks like a fucking dildo.

Why had he hidden it in the boathouse?

What else was in there that she hadn't seen?

Amandine shrieked suddenly and panicked, as if realising she was holding a live snake.

"Don't," Lone Diner barked, but it was too late.

Amandine threw the bag violently away from herself, out

into the broads. Her hand burned with the remembered weight of the bag's contents.

The bag landed with a small, definitive splash in the waters.

"The fuck did you do that for?" Lone Diner roared, and she heard Connor whimper as Lone Diner jammed the end of the gun into the other man's eye with renewed fury.

Amandine struggled to get herself under control.

It doesn't matter, she told herself. This was fast becoming her most useful mantra. Nothing mattered, except escape.

Her hands suddenly itched to write that last word down, turn it into a miracle word.

No time, no time.

Get moving, Amandine.

If you run now, you can make it.

It's dark.

He can't shoot straight.

You can't save Connor now, he's too weak.

But she didn't run. She stayed, frozen by indecision.

Lone Diner was wearing something different, she realised. Something that rustled. A plastic coverall.

It was white and had a hood.

She put this piece together with other things the torch beam illuminated.

A canvas tool bag by his feet. There was a hacksaw in it, and a pair of secateurs. Together with the suit…

Amandine felt white-hot contempt swill around in her guts.

And anger.

At herself, for wasting the time they'd been given.

She should have dragged Connor off into the reeds, hypothermic or not, useless leg or not.

She was angry at Connor, for not being able to walk, for leaving the burden of freedom to her.

She was angry at Lone Diner, for being a pathetic fucking lunatic who'd ruined her life irrevocably.

Her eyes went to Connor. *Do something, you piece of shit!* she pleaded with him, silently. *Fucking do something!*

All Connor had to do was grab the end of the gun, yank it out of Lone Diner's hands, and swing hard with it to knock him off the jetty. Amandine saw it play out in her mind, step by step, it would be so simple – grab, yank, twist, shove – but Connor did none of those things. He sat with his head lolling back, his chest heaving erratically, the gun like an odd telescope to his eye. He had accepted his fate and was waiting for Lone Diner to get on with the final act.

Amandine felt betrayal, then, deep and irrational. Connor had left her alone to deal with this shit.

He had made her responsible for him.

He could have shouted a warning, anything, so she could have heard in the boatshed, but he hadn't.

He'd let her down.

As if on cue, Connor mumbled: "Run!"

"Shut up," Lone Diner said, kicking Connor viciously in the side. "That's my line."

Then he gave Amandine an unexpected gift.

He gave her a way out.

"Run," he repeated, reclaiming the word from Connor.

To Run, or Not to Run

Amandine blinked, swallowed and pulled the dirty tarp closer around her body.

"What?" she whispered.

"I'm giving you a chance," the disembodied voice behind the torch glare said. "Run. You can leave. Now."

Amandine didn't move, wondering instead what his play was.

Lone Diner shifted his weight impatiently from foot to foot. The boards beneath him creaked.

"Didn't you hear me? Go on," he said. "Run."

Amandine couldn't. Lone Diner shifted again.

"Look, I'll give you a head start. You can't both survive this, but surely one is better than none?"

Amandine still didn't understand.

What the fuck is he talking about?

"You are a slow bitch, aren't you? Run," Lone Diner said, exasperation heavy in his voice. "I won't shoot. I promise. All you have to do is turn around and go."

"I can't." Amandine looked at Connor. It was as if Lone Diner had been reading her mind.

Lone Diner poked Connor with the gun again, hard.

"Leave him, he's finished. Run."

Amandine's knees braced, then relaxed. She clenched and unclenched her fists.

The boathook still lay within easy reach.

Why would he let her go?

Or was that the point?

Take something that was in her control, and make it his choice?

His preference?

Yes, she thought that was it.

He wanted to own everything, even her escape.

Amandine weighed up her options as Lone Diner continued to encourage her to run. She didn't trust a word that fell from his horrible, chapped lips. If she turned her back to him, he'd shoot her in the back, she was sure, despite what he said.

And yet if she stayed…

She remembered the severed hand.

The member in the bag.

She had a very good idea of what he had planned.

She eyed up the dark waters on either side of the jetty, reminded herself that jumping in would be a swifter death sentence than staying put. It would be painful, too, drowning in water that cold.

"Do as he says," Connor muttered. "Go."

But Amandine didn't go.

Amandine couldn't.

She didn't know what to do, or say, what to think, how to act.

If she ran, if she somehow avoided the gunshot that would surely follow, the pellets that would pepper her skin, not lethal, but destructive enough to maim, if she then managed to navigate the snow-coated boardwalk without slipping and falling to her death, if she found a way through the reeds in the middle of nowhere to a road or some sort of safety…

Connor would die.

But if you stay, you both die.

Lone Diner's face was a stinging bright insult that hurt her eyes. He looked like a poster for a horror movie she'd once seen. There had been snow in that movie, and she remembered a line from it, plucked from the part of her brain that dealt with the old version of her, before her date with Connor.

Nobody trusts anyone anymore.

I don't need his permission to run, she thought, then.

I've got the better of him already.

I escaped twice.

He's trying to take it back. What I won.

"Better hurry up and decide. Your window is closing."

She ran.

But not away, this time.

Instead, she bent, picked up the boathook, and ran towards Lone Diner, charging like a mediaeval knight with a lance.

Lone Diner side-stepped her clumsy advance with ease, and Amandine, propelled forward by her own desperation and refusal to die on his terms, ran clean off the edge of the jetty and fell into the black, icy waters of Hickling Broad.

Deep, Dark

She couldn't breathe.

She couldn't see.

She couldn't think.

Every part of her body shut down, instantly.

She had no awareness of her imminent death.

There was only the cold, absolute, and terrible.

SUNDAY

Romantic Setting

Is that… fire?

Crackling, snapping twigs breaking under heat.

Woodsmoke.

Skin, reacting to real, true warmth. Muscles relaxing. Hair, sopping wet and stinking of marshwater, curling.

An orange glow made its presence known.

Fire.

Definitely fire.

Amandine sat up, slowly.

I'm dreaming…

She coughed, spat out a mouthful of nasty brown liquid, gagged, heaved, spat some more, coughed up a huge ball of phlegm, recovered.

Nope.

Fuck.

With mixed relief and disappointment, she understood that she was still, somehow, despite everything, alive.

Alive, and at the mercy of Lone Diner.

Her captor and, she realised, now saviour – for who else had dragged her out of the broad?

Not Connor.

Lone Diner had rescued her.

Why?

He had also built a fire, a big one, from dry wood he'd scavenged from who knows where. And rags and something that smelt strong, some chemical to make it burn brighter and fiercer.

Amandine looked across the flames and wondered why she wasn't dead.

Why hadn't he let her drown?

More pieces of the grim jigsaw fell into place as she blinked smoke out of her eyes.

Because he had more he wanted her to do. That's why.

She turned her head.

Saw Connor, wrapped in a blanket, waiting once again for her to wake up. He seemed relieved she was alive, but also apprehensive. In the firelight, she could fully appreciate what an awful state he was in. He was gaunt, hollow-cheeked, huge bags under his eyes, and his skin was a strange colour. He shook violently and held his hands out to the fire. His thumbs were completely purple. He shifted, and his blanket opened just wide enough for her to see his leg, which was swollen and bright red and still leaking blood.

She was not sure she had let herself acknowledge, before this, how bad things had been for him. She'd gotten it into her head that he just wasn't trying as hard as she was to live.

It was more complicated than she'd allowed for. Connor was very, very sick indeed.

Something rustled as he tried, and failed, to get comfortable in front of the fire. His feet brushed against something shiny and conical. Amandine's eyes travelled to it wearily.

A fresh bunch of roses, plastic-wrapped, laid at Connor's feet.

There was also a bowtie around his neck, one Amandine recognised.

She looked down at herself. She was wrapped in a blanket too, a cheap scratchy one that matched Connor's. A pair of ornate earrings swung from her lobes, and she could feel a heavy necklace clasped tightly around her own neck.

Something else lay nearby.

A box of chocolates sat on the jetty before her, the price sticker clumsily ripped off the corner of the box.

A throat cleared loudly behind her, a hacking noise. Amandine looked over her shoulder to the shape of Lone Diner sat cross-legged on the jetty. His shotgun lay across his knees. Amandine had been so focused on Connor she had neglected to look for the man.

"Welcome back," he said calmly, watching her through the reflected flames in his lenses. Amandine thought she saw hell in the glass, then remembered she didn't believe in things like that.

Amandine said nothing, simply watched Lone Diner, waiting for the next words, which he delivered with a flat intensity, licking his lips as he spoke.

"Are you ready for your second date now?" he said, eye-flames flickering brightly.

Coupling

"What?" Connor stared, aghast. "What are you saying?"

"You heard me."

Lone Diner stood up, awkwardly, using the shotgun for support, then pointing the weapon at Connor's head.

"I want you to fuck her, in front of me. By the fire. I made it nice and romantic for you."

"No!"

Connor began to shake harder. Amandine could not tell if it was through fear, anger, cold, or all three. She thought he might be about to shake himself into pieces, the tremors were so intense.

"Go fuck yourself!" he spat, with difficulty.

The stranger smiled.

"No, see, that's the point. I don't want to fuck myself. I want *you* to fuck *her*. Right now. On the ground, in front of me. Or I'll empty this into your face. Then hers. How about that?"

Amandine shook her head.

A small, bitter smile grew on her lips.

It was all so predictable.

So tawdry.

So fucking small and mean and petty.

Saving her from drowning so they could act out his weird, grubby fantasy in front of him. Like a pair of barbie dolls illicitly laid on top of each other by someone who didn't fully understand the act yet.

How grim, yet pathetic.

That was all this was about. All it boiled down to.

The most disappointing of grand masterplans.

Sex.

All the pain and fear and suffering he inflicted, just to watch them fuck.

So he could record it, she presumed, to get off to.

She had a sudden memory of the man she once dated who wanted to push her down the stairs. *To get off,* he'd said. Is that how things like this started? An impulse, blurted mid-thrust. Was it a slippery slope, after that threshold had been crossed? How long before the request became an action, before a woman went tumbling without consent? How does a person get to this point in their life?

Amandine calmly realised that he was likely going to tie them up again afterwards and let them die out here. Their copulation would be the denouement. He would climax, or maybe he wouldn't, couldn't, maybe that was the whole point. It hardly mattered; what mattered was the completion of the scenario as he had scripted it, and once the last line was delivered, that would be the end of it for him. Curtain call.

Like the very worst kind of movie.

"I'll fucking kill you!" Connor muttered, and Amandine could see tears sliding down his cheeks.

Poor Connor. His will was broken, which is precisely what Lone Diner wanted.

To take a good thing and corrupt it beyond recognition.

Just because he could.

Lone Diner shook his head, sighing.

"You won't kill me, but you *will* fuck her. You'll do it, because you don't have a choice, do you? If you don't, I'll shoot her, so you'll be saving her life; think of it that way."

Connor said nothing further, his breath coming in pained, shuddering bursts.

Amandine had heard enough of Lone Diner's spiel to last her a lifetime, two lifetimes. Three.

"You're a child," she said.

The gun moved in her direction, but it didn't frighten her anymore.

Nothing frightened her anymore.

She was done with everything.

Weary to her core.

"Just a lonely, spiteful little boy," she continued. She gazed into the fire, dreamily.

Lone Diner's lips curled into a cruel smirk.

"Feeling brave after your baptism, is that it?"

Amandine would not be put off. The flames were encouraging. Bright sparks shot up into the night sky like fireflies.

She thought they were beautiful. She wanted to roll in the embers.

"Did you shave the hair off your sister's dolls when you were little? Draw over their eyes? Stick nails in their private parts? I bet you stole her underwear when she was out."

Lone Diner worked hard to conceal a succession of emotions on his face. Indignancy, anger, a mean amount of guilt.

Amandine knew she had touched a nerve, perhaps several.

She no longer cared.

Getting cheap shots in wasn't the goal.

Being better than him was the only worthy path ahead.

"Careful," Connor breathed, so faintly she barely heard it.

"Go on." Lone Diner straightened his back, waved the shotgun once again at Connor. His patience was failing, but he still had a weapon. "Get on with it. Fuck her."

Connor shook his head. "No. I can't."

"Do it, or I'll shoot her, right now."

"It's okay," Amandine said, trying to get Connor to look at her, but his eyes darted all over, seeking escape.

"I can't," he repeated.

"Connor, look at me," Amandine replied, with more force.

His eyes were as dead as a statue's.

"Listen, Connor. Listen."

Lone Diner took a step closer to them.

"Didn't you hear me?"

"It's okay," Amandine told Connor, as though Lone Diner did not exist. "I don't mind."

Connor was horrified. "What… I don't… but it's…"

Amandine swallowed back something. More marsh water? It tasted cold and bitter.

"It's just sex," she said, as nonchalantly as she could.

Her eyes communicated a different message.

Her eyes said:

I would rather it was you than him.

She hoped desperately that he would understand.

He did.

He understood and shook his head helplessly again.

Amandine shifted sideways onto her hip, then lay down on her back on the wet deck, where the fire's heat had melted the snow in a large, dark circle.

Lone Diner made a funny sound deep in the base of his throat.

Shifted his grip on the gun, changed hands.

Amandine opened her blanket, showed her body. Looked down at herself. Saw her ribs sticking out. Saw her public hair, matted with menses.

The word LOVE was now only one letter, the letter V, standing proud on her belly. She told herself V was for Victory, and then she remembered the phrase *lie back and think of England*. Suddenly she felt as though she was going to lose her temporary grip on the situation if Connor didn't make a move soon.

You'll never be the same again after this, Amandine, she thought.

"Come on," she said out loud, smiling at Connor encouragingly.

Again, Lone Diner moved towards them, another shuffling half-step, and again, she showed no signs of acknowledging his existence. She behaved as if there was only one man left on Earth, the one she was really on a second date with, pretending to give Connor the go-ahead, feeding into Lone Diner's fantasy, but twisting it on what she believed would be her last night alive to become a gentle, soft thing, a plot and narrative of her own making, not his. If he wanted to see them fuck, then she would do it, and it would be the most tender, honest, considerate moment of her life, a reclamation event, because she owed herself that, and she owed Lone Diner nothing.

Nothing at all.

Connor stared, stricken.

"I *can't*, Amandine."

Still, she persisted. She knew this was the right way. She knew it in her cold bones.

For when were people more vulnerable than when they finally got what they wanted?

She would give Lone Diner what he wanted.

And then some.

"Just try, okay? For me, just try. He is going to kill you if you don't try. Then he is going to hurt me. I'll be all alone with him, do you hear what I'm saying? You need to try."

"*You need to try,*" Lone Diner mocked in a high-pitched, short-tongued drawl. The gun intruded further on their territory, its long nose sliding into Amandine's peripheral vision. "*You need to try, I don't want to be alone with the nasty man, save me, Connor!*"

"Please, Connor," Amandine begged from where she lay, letting her eyes fill with tears. "Please, trust me."

She held her arms out.

Connor went to her as if hypnotised.

"I don't understand what the fuck is happening," he said, eyes wild, shivering as if he had a palsy.

"Shh," Amandine said, reaching up to slide her hands through his thick, filthy hair. She dragged his head close to her mouth. "Just pretend," she whispered softly into his ear. "Just pretend, okay? I don't want to die like this."

Lone Diner went very still on the edges of her vision.

Connor crouched over Amandine, clumsily. His mouth dripped with blood and saliva. He'd lost a tooth somewhere along the way. He positioned himself with great difficulty so one knee was on either side of her, the blanket dangling down to form a tent, but he couldn't put any weight on his damaged leg, so he was tilted, lopsided, his face suspended over hers. She could see the broken veins in his eyes, the damage to his face. He looked like a ruined mask hanging from the ceiling in a museum.

Amandine felt something awful unlock in her mind.

"I love you, Connor," she whispered, and was secretly appalled to hear words she didn't mean slip out into the cold night between them.

But it felt like the right thing to say, in their last moments together.

It did not have the desired effect. Rather, it triggered something in him.

He shook his head.

"No," he said. "No. Not like this. Not… like…"

The tap of the shotgun's barrels on the back of his head signalled Lone Diner's proximity.

"Ah fuck, ah fuck!" Connor swore, shaking now from the effort of not collapsing on top of Amandine. She had to use her forearms to prop him up, so he didn't crush her.

"Yes," Lone Diner said, his breath ragged and urgent. "Yes."

Amandine knew they didn't have long.

"Say it back!" she hissed, in a panic.

"Say what back?" Connor's body lowered an inch as he lost strength.

"Say you love me! Say it back! You have to!"

"Fuck, stop it, Amandine, fuck!"

She saw it in his face.

The limit, she discovered, was this.

The line he could not cross.

She thought of other men she'd known, men who had thrown around the L-word as if it were confetti, brilliant and celebratory in the moment, dissolving in the rain like weak promises come morning.

Connor was not like that.

He wouldn't say it, couldn't say it, not even to save her life.

"NO!"

He reared up and back, his entire body whip-tight, like a rod. "Not like this, do you understand?! I can't, fuck, *fuck*, not like this, *FUCK!*"

His face stretched into a violent display of denial and revulsion that was barely recognisable as human. He became, in that horrible, cold, lonely moment, a parody of a person, and Amandine's heart broke for him, even as she celebrated the fact that he'd finally, finally found his balls.

And she thought about the faded Miracle Word on her belly, love backwards, *EVOL*, now just V, and she knew what power there was in this word, and she knew that Lone Diner would never understand that, never understand the feeling that came over her in those last vital moments out on the cold and frozen marsh, where the air tasted of mud and ice-skinned water that crackled and snapped all around as birds, oblivious to this human drama playing out beneath the moon, whistled and called and hopped from stem to stem or slept, huddled together, for warmth.

But she also knew, because Connor couldn't say it, not even to save her life, that they had lost, and spoiled the fantasy, and so, this was the moment they died. All her bravery, all her resilience, all the effort it had taken to survive, all wasted, all pointless. Done was done, and now, Amandine accepted, she was dead.

Amandine closed her eyes and waited, fully expecting the crack of the shotgun to tear through the air.

This was as good a time to go as any, she supposed. A deep, profound sadness washed over her.

But the shot never came.

She waited a moment longer.

Still no gunfire.

Amandine opened her eyes.

The shotgun had withdrawn.

She found Lone Diner bent over them, smelled his stink as it assaulted her nostrils, felt the heat he gave off in fetid waves.

His face was squashed up tight next to Connor's, so they were cheek to cheek. Amadine recoiled, banging her head against the wooden planks below.

"Now you know how it feels," Lone Diner's voice said. "Now, you know how it fucking feels. It isn't just me. Do you hear? It isn't just me."

Fuck Them

Lone Diner had never hated anyone more than the woman and man cowering before him on the jetty at that precise moment in time. The instructions had been simple enough. The last couple had given it a decent enough shot, but these two?

Disappointment flooded his whole body, quickly followed by rage, then a crushing sense of his own impotence. Along with the anger came a searing pain, a tight, horrible band of it across his chest. He massaged it, only thinly aware of what he was doing. The pain served to make him angrier still. His mind filled with a haze of grey, thick hatred. It obscured his vision, disorienting him, making him question his own sense of reality, obliterating the lingering elation he'd felt when he'd first tied the pair up to their respective posts on the jetty.

That already felt like a thousand years ago, and none of this had gone the way he'd hoped since. The man had bled too much right from the get-go and been virtually fucking useless throughout the entire performance. As for her… the silly bitch had freed herself, fallen in the water and never once, throughout the entire course of this special encounter with him, showed the requisite level of fear in his presence that he desired. Of terror. Of submission. She had defied him at every turn. She didn't seem to care that he could kill her, and this confused him, hurt him, and made him afraid of himself, for some reason. Inadequate. Incompetent. He was not the same man who had sent body parts sinking, in a brick-weighted sack, to the bottom of the marsh only a short time before meeting this new couple.

The band of pain across his chest squeezed again, ripping the breath from his lungs. The grey fog thickened, cleared, returned. Lone Diner wondered, suddenly, what was happening. Was this defeat? Hopelessness? Despair? Indigestion? Was he dying?

He was suddenly afraid.

He couldn't die, not before he'd finished what he started. It wasn't on the agenda. It wouldn't be fair. He'd only just begun to come into himself, discover his capabilities, even if there were teething problems, these were all things he could learn from; it wasn't his time yet.

Resolve straightened his spine, despite the pain and breathlessness.

He had a job to finish, and he'd see it through.

Starting with the uppity bitch who wouldn't do as she was told.

Her hand, he thought, would look splendid in the cool box alongside the other already lying there, waiting for his return.

Fuck her. And fuck him, too.

Fuck them both.

Denouement

Lone Diner straightened up. Spat.

A wad of hot sticky phlegm landed on Amandine's collarbone.

She did not flinch. She stared right up into the sky, instead.

Reaction was what he wanted.

Reaction was what he fed from.

She would not give it to him.

Lone Diner shouldered his shotgun. He seemed almost proud of himself, Amandine realised. Like he'd pulled off a great heist of some sort. Won some great battle, without even going to war.

"Did you think I was serious?" he said as Connor collapsed backwards, crying. The words confirmed the growing suspicion in Amandine's mind.

That he didn't actually kill the other couple.

That he had just let them die, instead.

Sure, he gave them a ride, lured them into his car, brought them out here.

Tied them up.

Tortured them.

But he didn't kill them.

He couldn't.

She was sure of that, now.

They'd died of exposure.

Of the cold.

Or starvation.

Or dehydration, or all of it.

He'd cut them up *afterwards*. To hide them. To make them harder to identify. To keep trophies.

He was responsible for their deaths, but he had not definitively, by terms that now suddenly mattered – mattered a whole lot – committed the final deed of taking their lives.

Murder did not come naturally to him, despite his posturing.

Despite the coveralls.

The tools.

The woman in the car, the one who had stopped to help them?

A mistake.

An anomaly.

He'd panicked.

Amateur.

Lone Diner rubbed his chest absentmindedly, as if it hurt, then turned and made his way unsteadily over to the assortment of tools he'd brought with him from his car, boots stomping like the goat from the Billy Goats Gruff fairy tale, *trip trap, trip trap* on the wooden planks. Amandine wondered if there were more cable ties in there somewhere.

"I see you!" she shouted after him, her lips cracking with hate. "You're a fucking fraud!"

A heron, dislodged from its hunt by Lone Diner's ungracious passing, lifted up into the sky, its enormous wings beating hard against the air. It dragged itself up to a higher height with great effort, and then flew off into the dark wetlands, legs trailing beneath it. Amandine thought it looked like a dinosaur, then wished for a time when man did not exist, where the most hostile things were natural and driven by instinct, not whatever motor drove Lone Diner's engine inexhaustibly on.

Connor crawled back beneath his blanket, and rolled himself tightly into it, like a worm.

Amandine knew she was as alone as she could possibly be, then.

She thought about her parents, drowning in the ditch.

She thought about her grandma, making her stand before the mirror as she recited Miracle Words.

With a stiff, trembling finger, Amandine wrote another word on herself using Lone Diner's phlegm. Real tears now started to slide down her cheeks, not performance tears.

DIE, it said, his spittle cold and vile like slug trails on her chest.

It would be invisible when it dried, but she would know it was there.

She would know, and that would be where the magic was.

It wasn't a Miracle Word, not this time.

It was a Murder Word.

DIE.

She went back over it, frantically tracing and retracing the word to reinforce its potency.

DIE.

DIE.

DIE.

Lone Diner reached the pile of things, his kidnap kit, and bent over to rummage.

The act of bending down seemed to trigger something in him, some pain, some discomfort. As Amandine's fingertips worked, he made a funny noise, a strangled gasp of pain.

DIE.

DIE.

DIE.

And then, miraculously, without preamble, he did.

Exit Song

Amandine watched with wide eyes as Lone Diner clutched his chest, right where his heart was. He'd been massaging it earlier, she realised. In fact, if she thought about it, he'd been persistently worrying at that part of himself, kneading at himself as if that would make any difference to the rot within.

DIE, she wrote again, one last time, when she realised what was happening.

Lone Diner's jaw clenched.

His arm went limp, the one holding the gun.

He dropped it.

Slowly lowered himself to his knees.

His breath came fast and short.

"Connor!" Amandine hissed. "Connor, look!"

Connor did not respond from his blanket fort.

Lone Diner vomited, suddenly. The vomit splattered into the column of light under his head torch. It looked dark and unhealthy, almost black in colour.

"Connor!"

Lone Diner crashed face-first to the jetty. His cracked glasses came skittering off, and landed on the planking, lenses shattering on contact. The head torch light, now pressed into the boards, dimmed.

And Lone Diner went very, very still indeed.

Is This Real

At first, Amandine didn't know what to do.

At first, she thought he was faking.

Another prank, to fuck with their now shattered sense of reality.

If she went to him, he would grab her ankles at the last minute, the jump scare satiation he'd wanted all along.

Amandine scrabbled over to Connor, shook him.

"Connor!" she said. "Look! Look!"

Connor's face peeked reluctantly out of his blanket cocoon.

She pointed at the dim shadow of Lone Diner, lying face down on the jetty, still unmoving.

"I think he's dead!" she whispered, gleefully. "I think he fucking died!"

Connor sat up.

They sat side by side by the fire, swaddled in cheap nylon, staring at the motionless form of their tormentor in disbelieving silence.

Garbage Disposal

He remained motionless for what felt like hours but was probably only several minutes. Measures of time beyond day or night had long lost all meaning for the couple out among the reeds.

The fire kept them company during the uncertainty of waiting, crackling, and fizzing as it burned lower.

When all continued to be still, Amandine made a decision.

Whether Lone Diner was faking or not, this was an opportunity.

One she was not going to waste.

"Come on," she said.

"You know I can't."

Amandine *tsked,* went over to the boathook which Lone Diner had propped, she saw, against one of the twin posts. It struck her that maybe he'd used it to save her life when she fell into the water.

She handed it to Connor, dragging him to his feet.

"Use this," she commanded.

The blanket slipped from his shoulders. Amandine retrieved it, and knotted it in place around him like a Roman toga.

Then they went to check on the fallen man.

Amandine retrieved his gun from where he had dropped it, nudged the large body with the end of the barrel.

Nothing.

Or was that…?

Amandine jabbed the man with the gun again so that he rolled, partially. The head torch assaulted her eyes. She used the barrel tip to slide it up Lone Diner's head so she could see Lone Diner's face.

Drenched in sweat, his skin was a grey colour. His eyes were closed, his lips loose. He looked, for all intents and purposes, unconscious. Not dead. A thin, faint breath leaked out into the night.

Amandine prodded Lone Diner's lips with the gun.

Inserted the barrel gently between his teeth.

Thought about pulling the trigger.

Still, the man didn't react.

"It would be so easy," she breathed, finger hovering over the trigger.

"Don't," Connor said. "Not like this. Not you. Let him die in the cold, like he wanted for us."

Amandine thought about it. Her finger twitched again. She wanted to pull the trigger so very, very much.

"You're right," she said eventually. "Let's go."

She bent down and ripped the head torch from Lone Diner's forehead with such force that the elastic snapped. His head came up with the vigour of the pull, then thumped back hard to the jetty as the torch came free.

Still no reaction.

He wasn't faking.

He was really, truly out for the count.

After everything he'd put them through.

The pathetic bastard was going to die of a heart attack. She felt for his pulse. It was weak, barely there. She held her fingers to him until it seemed to stop altogether. The world was quiet around her.

Then she spat on him, returning gesture for gesture. It landed on his cheek.

She wrote no words this time. They were not necessary.

"Come on," Connor whispered, exhausted. "Come on."

They held hands as they left the jetty behind them.

Wait Here

They found the car easily enough. The boardwalk wound for a mile or so through the reeds and then widened out into a rough, potholed expanse of dirt that had only one vehicle in it: the stolen one they'd been transported here in.

Convinced it would be locked, Amandine went to the driver's-side door and saw it had been left wide open.

Moments later, she intercepted the smell.

"Oh, god," Connor said, dragging one corner of his blanket over his nose and mouth. "Is that–"

The headtorch showed the truth of it.

Shit.

All over the car interior. On the windscreen, the dashboard, the seats, even the ceiling and the interior light. Lone Diner had been thorough, his gifts copious.

Is this what he had been doing all those times he left them alone out on the jetty? Painting his own excrement all over the inside of the car in case they escaped and found it?

"He's fucking insane," Connor whispered, revulsion on his face.

"Doesn't matter," Amandine said, determinedly. "You want to walk home?"

Connor gazed at the car, the corners of his mouth dragging down with misery.

"Nope," he said, wearily. "I suppose we've been through worse, right?"

Amandine nodded. "Right. Now, where do you think he put the keys?"

She searched the car's interior, disregarding the shit as easily as she'd disregarded the man who'd excreted it. No keys dangled from the ignition, or lay wedged behind the sun visor on either side, nor in the recess in the central control panel, nor in the deep wells on each door interior.

Which left only the glovebox.

Gritting her teeth, Amandine opened this last compartment and found what she was looking for.

Car keys.

Resting innocently in the upturned palm of a severed hand.

Red nails gleamed in the torchlight.

And rage welled up in Amandine's heart.

"Wait here," she told Connor, wheeling around and stumbling back along the path they'd just traversed, the gun clutched tightly in her hands.

"Where are you going?!" he shouted in desperation, but Amandine didn't answer.

She had one last thing to attend to.

Goodbye

He lay as she'd left him: on his side, twisted, unconscious, breathing in irregular, shallow bouts, eyes closed, jaw slack.

Amandine watched him for some time, thinking of the awful things he'd done to those other people.

She'd had no room for sympathy before, not with her own survival in question, but now, with the upper hand, with him incapacitated, with a loaded gun (or what she assumed was a loaded gun, she realised she hadn't checked, didn't really know how to) pointed at his body, she had plenty of space to feel. The indignity of what he'd done to that other poor woman who had come before her.

To the man, too.

Lopping off parts of them and keeping them to play with, to accessorise his pathetic little life.

Amandine bent closer.

Her nose wrinkled in disgust.

"Jesus," she whispered, staring down into his face. "You fucking stink."

Lone Diner's eyes remained closed.

Amandine had never, in that moment, hated anyone or anything more than she hated the sight of his face, closed to the world, cut off from the consequences of all that he'd done.

She shone his head torch over to the pile of things he'd brought, presumably to help erase all traces of her eventual demise. She saw a toolkit, the hacksaw, and on closer examination, a pile of large, blue, plastic rubble sacks, more zip ties (she'd been right), and a pile of large, heavy stones.

And suddenly, she knew what she had to do.

It took several large bags to form a big enough shroud, and she had to get creative with them, slitting several down the side to enlarge the surface area of the plastic, but Lone Diner lay dead to the world while she worked, and even though she thought every second she wrapped him up that he would wake, that his eyes would bolt open, that he would smile that horrible lascivious leering, loose-lipped grin and say, "Gotcha!" in his best cartoon-villain voice, he never did.

She wrapped him and secured him with dozens of cable ties punched through holes she pierced in the plastic, and with each new layer of blue she applied, she wedged a heavy stone into the shroud.

He's still alive, a tiny voice said in her head. *It's not too late. Don't be like him.*

You're better than this, Amandine.

It sounded like Connor's voice, but she ignored it.

She knew she wasn't better. The old Amandine was.

But the old Amandine was gone forever.

When he was wrapped, a bundle of meat and nothing more, she stood back. Assessed her handiwork.

Put her foot on the bundle.

Pushed.

Nothing happened.

She bent down, put both hands on Lone Diner's body, and pushed again.

Lone Diner's rolled-up body flipped, reluctantly, slid off the side of the jetty and landed, with a colossal splash, in the dark waters beneath.

Amandine looked down into the broad.

The large blue bundle floated in the water, air trapped between the layers of plastic keeping Lone Diner temporarily buoyant. He looked like some sort of wrapped mummy from another era, at first, which made Amandine giggle. Then she wiped her streaming eyes.

Now he looked like so much refuse, dumped. She thought of flotsam, debris, junk. Sodden and stained, unwanted.

Drown, you fuck, she thought, over and over. *Drown. Drown. Drown.*

The bundle never twitched, not once.

If he was still alive in there, he was unconscious, and his death would be more merciful than the death of the others whose bodies he was about to join.

Connor's voice spoke up again. The imagined version of him told her, very quietly, that the water wasn't too deep.

That she still had time, if she hurried, to jump in after him, drag him to safety, cut the wrappings away. Mouth to mouth might save him, despite the likely heart attack that had made him collapse. Perhaps he was only concussed. Hypothermia would be a risk, but…

She ignored the voice.

Lone Diner didn't want to be saved, she reasoned.

Not really.

Not judging by the state of the car.

He'd gone too far, crossed bridges he knew he couldn't retread.

And besides, Amandine found, as she watched the bundle slowly sink, she had nothing left.

No energy, no strength, no ability to react.

And so, with a mouthful of bitter saliva, she watched Lone Diner float peacefully at first, then sink, like a boat with a hole in the hull, and slowly disappear beneath the surface of the water, which was beginning to change colour, as was the sky above. Amandine imagined his lungs filling with water. Mud settling beneath him. Eyes invaded by small wriggling things.

It took a little while for him to sink completely, for the trapped air to fully escape the packaging, but eventually he was gone.

And Amandine sank to her knees, weeping, as dawn broke.

Return

Connor couldn't sit in the car and wait. He doubted he would ever be able to sit in a car again, after this was over.

Instead, he leaned on the bonnet, blanket tightly tucked around himself, suspended in a stupor of exhaustion and trauma and pain and the lingering, pervasive fear that Amandine wouldn't come back, that the reeds would part, revealing the familiar, shambling figure of Lone Diner instead.

The sky lightened. Noises carried on the distance: other cars, Connor realised. Far away, but a main road. It was morning.

His skin screamed at him.

It was another day, and they were still alive.

They were almost there.

Amandine returned as the sun peeked over the snow-coated hedges lining the parking area.

When she came back, limping, face set and resolute, he knew he would never be able to ask her about whatever had happened.

They exchanged looks.

"Can we go now?" he pleaded.

She nodded.

"Guess I'm driving," she said.

"We could hitchhike."

"No."

"We could, Amandine. Then we wouldn't have to..."

"No. I won't get in another car with a stranger. I won't."

"We could wait," he whispered. "For the right car. For a woman. Or an elderly driver. They'll be less likely to... to... We'll get them to take us to Queen Elizabeth Hospital. Or a phone box, so we can call the police."

"No. The last woman who stopped to help us died. And we aren't calling the police."

Connor started to shake violently, his whole body spasming. He seemed to have no way of controlling it. His breath misted around their faces.

"No police? But–"

"Just get in the fucking car, Connor. If we don't get to a hospital soon, you'll die."

Connor found himself doing as he was told, gingerly lowering himself into the shit-smeared car without another word. Truth be told, he was in awe of Amandine, the kind of awe reserved for prey when they realise they are about to be devoured by something faster, stronger, and deadlier.

As they pulled out of the clearing and found a narrow, decaying road grown over with weeds and grass, the sun broke free of the surrounding vegetation, throwing Amandine's profile into high relief, turning her hair to spun gold – but it couldn't smooth the deep creases in her face; it only enhanced them, bloody furrows of pain like furrows of fresh dirt in a ploughed field.

Connor thought, regardless, that he had never seen her more beautiful. More determined. More ferocious. She was his life raft on the broads, warm and safe and capable. She would carry him to shore.

In that moment, he knew he would have given up anything for her, done anything she'd asked.

Which was fortunate, because what she asked of him later was a pretty fucking huge request, all things considered.

No Police

They kept the windows down as they drove.

"We need to go to the police," Connor said, after a short while. He was drifting in and out of awareness, the final release of escape having weakened him to the point of collapse. He kept blacking out around the edges of his vision, feeling his eyelids droop, only to snap open again when Amandine changed gear or hit a pothole.

"I have no fucking idea where we are," she muttered. "I'm just going to keep driving till I find a sign."

"We have to go to the police," Connor repeated. "There were others."

They both glanced at the now closed glovebox, inside of which the hand still sat.

Amandine's jaw tightened. "And what if they don't believe us? What if they think we did it?"

"You're a mess. I've been stabbed and shot. I think they'll believe us. Plus, DNA, forensics… there's nothing to tie us to them."

"Except the hand. Plus my fingerprints are all over that gun of his. I ditched it, but…"

"They'll believe us. We have to tell someone about him. About…" Connor drifted off, roused himself with increasing difficulty. "…what he did."

Amandine slammed the palm of her hand down onto the dash, suddenly furious. "Listen to me! We can't go to the police, okay? We just can't."

Connor began to suspect that she had other reasons for not talking to the law. He understood that it had something to do with why she'd left him at the car.

Connor didn't want to think too much on that. His entire body felt alien to him, like he'd been scooped out and replaced with something rotten and weevilled.

He gave up. He slumped forwards, drunkenly. Amandine's hands shot out to grab him by his blanket before his head hit the dash.

She dimly recalled, as a fresh wave of cold air blasted in from the open window, how smart he had looked back in the restaurant, when they'd first met.

"Tell me why," Connor slurred. "Why."

Amandine cradled his wilting body with one arm, her free hand gripping the steering wheel tightly.

"Because we deserve better," she whispered.

"I don't... I..."

"Do you want this to be our lives?" Amandine asked, not expecting an answer. She struggled to see through the glass they'd managed to scrape clean before starting out. "Because if we go to the police, this experience... what he did to us... it will become our entire story, don't you get it?"

Connor's eyes fluttered shut. He was too tired to talk anymore, but a part of him listened, from a distance, even though a loud ringing sound had begun building in his ears.

Amandine continued, not really caring whether Connor heard her or not. She was free to say what she wanted for the first time since her capture, and the words bubbled out of her.

"Our entire futures, reduced down to being his victims. It will be all over the news in days, Connor. It'll be everywhere. You know what this country is like. Our ordeal will be public domain in a matter of hours. And they'll find his body. He'll get dredged up. The papers will tell stories about us, but I guarantee they'll lose interest in us pretty quick. They'll hound us at first and then it'll turn, you watch. It'll shift. The whole thing will be all over social media, only it won't be our faces they care about anymore. It'll be *him*. Every single time you open an app or try to google anything or open your emails. *His* face. They'll write long opinion pieces about him. They'll fucking salivate over him; you know how it works. There will be books. Podcasts. YouTube specials. Cringey Tiktoks. Instagram. Reddit threads deep-diving his motivations, his psychological MO. He'll become some sort of cult villain, elevated from a sad, pathetic fuck who smelt like sour spunk to a deranged, sophisticated, evil killer; he'll get that Bundy makeover, you know? That Fred West treatment. And years from now, you'll turn on the TV and you'll find yourself confronted with a gritty, high-budget six-part Netflix special about him. Some A-list actor who only played nice guys up until that point, looking to 'push themselves', strutting about in the role like he didn't cut that guy's dick off at all, or that woman's hand, like he didn't leave them to die out there, alone and freezing and vulnerable, all their fucking hopes and dreams now at the bottom of the broads. And it'll get rave reviews and it will be all about how difficult his childhood was, how he was beaten by his mother or father or how his parents got divorced and he wasn't loved enough, how kids at school were mean to him, and *he'll* be the victim, he'll be the star, and people will start to talk unironically about how hot he was, and we won't feature at all. They'll get Nick fucking Cave to write the theme song,

Connor. Nobody will care about us, but *he* will earn a place in fucking history, and they'll make T-shirts with his fucking face on them, and we'll have to live with that… and… and…"

Connor reached up, put his hand on Amandine's shoulder as she trailed off.

"Okay," he whispered. "We won't tell. But… I don't feel too… good…"

Connor's eyes fluttered shut. The drone of the car's engine grew, mingled with the ringing sound already grabbing his skull like a hot vice, filling the huge space between the earth and the sky in his head. Connor, no longer sure of anything, started to mumble something.

"Goodness gracious me!" said Henny-penny, "The sky's a-going to fall; I must go and tell the King!"

He wished, for one bleak, cold, desperate moment, that he had not survived at all.

Wounds

At the hospital, Amandine gave false names for both of them. The nurse who wrote her details down didn't argue. She couldn't. The couple had no ID, no belongings to identify them at all.

And neither of them, at first, were in a fit state to answer questions about anything beyond: "Does it hurt? Do you need more pain medication?"

To which the answer was always: "Yes."

WEDNESDAY

No Crimes Here

Amandine recovered faster than Connor, who went straight to intensive care, desperately ill with sepsis, hypothermia, pneumonia, and blood loss. There was intermediate-stage frostbite on the thumbs on each hand, the tips of which he lost, and on his big toes, where his skin went a deep, angry red colour and blistered, but they managed to save those.

Nurses assured Amandine that Connor would not lose any more digits. The skin was not necrotic anywhere else, they said. He would recover.

Amandine herself underwent surgery on her nose, which was badly broken, and her ear, which was torn right down to the concha. She was cleaned and provided with sanitary goods and fresh underwear and soft, clean night things, and then hooked up to some intensive antibiotics and a variety of other plastic bladders that fed healing liquid directly into her veins.

She was asked again and again, after her surgeries, what had happened – and every time she told the same story: it was an accident. They had been drunk, stoned. Had driven a car into a ditch on the edge of the broads. The story was plausible, just. Her other injuries, she said, came from trying to outsmart nature. They'd gotten lost on the waterways trying to find help, turned about by the cold and the dark, and the rest she left for the nurses to piece together.

They hadn't meant to do it, she said. It was a stupid car accident.

She could tell none of them believed her, but Connor wasn't awake or cogent for long enough to contradict her.

They called the police anyway.

"I have a duty to report it," a senior doctor told her two days after her admission. "With wounds such as yours, and given that your boyfriend can't answer any questions for himself…"

Amandine started to cry.

"I thought… I thought as patients… we had confidentiality…"

The doctor shook his head. "If it helps," he said gently, "my obligation only extends as far as telling the police that someone has been hurt, in an accident. I don't have to tell them anything else, although it will be obvious from the state of you both that something… *extreme* brought you here. Besides, I assume you left your car in the ditch."

Amandine thought about the car she had actually crashed in. The dead woman lying in the road not long after, shot in the face and then run over. Of course the police would know about these things. That made it doubly important not to be questioned by them now.

The doctor waited for a few moments, giving Amandine the opportunity to elaborate.

She didn't.

The doctor sighed.

"So, once I've informed the authorities, someone will likely come to talk to you. They'll question Connor if he's awake in time, but I imagine you'll be first."

"But I don't have to tell them anything, right? Being injured… it's not, like, illegal?"

The doctor stared at Amandine, hard.

"Technically not. Depends if you hurt anyone else in the process. Did you?"

Amandine dodged the question. "They can't force me to say anything if no crime has been committed."

The doctor sat down gently on the side of Amandine's bed, being careful to keep his weight away from her.

"It has though, hasn't it? Drink driving, driving under the influence, for starters. I can see how scared you are."

She said nothing, holding her breath.

The doctor examined the backs of his hands. "You know, that other couple that went missing round here a while back… they were in the news, I'm sure you saw… they were about the same age as you. You kind of look like each other. The missing woman and you, I mean. Strange, huh?"

Amandine stared at the bedcovers.

"Let the police help," the doctor pleaded, gently. "There's no shame in talking if you did nothing wrong."

Amandine swallowed her tears with brutal determination.

"I'm not a victim," she said, her voice hard and cold. "I don't need any more help. I just made some dumb decisions, is all. We crashed in a ditch. We escaped the car, injured, and wandered off into the broads. Then we got lost. That's it. I don't want to go to jail for a stupid car accident."

"You both have cable tie burns on your wrists and ankles. Not to mention you were heavily dehydrated, clearly hadn't eaten for a long time and…"

"Please," Amandine begged, closing her eyes. "Please stop."

The doctor rose. He folded his arms, trying one last time. "It's obvious whatever happened, you were not at fault," he repeated, and she could tell he was disappointed. He'd been hoping to crack her.

But Amandine wouldn't be cracked.

Besides, she thought, as he left with a solemn shake of the head. She knew she wouldn't have long, after that. He was a man on a mission, and that mission was to get to the truth of the matter.

It was my fault. All of it.

I went on the fucking date in the first place.

TWO MONTHS LATER

Too Much, Too Soon

Amandine realised, after two months of living with Connor, that moving in with each other immediately after their ordeal had been a huge mistake.

An understandable one, fuelled by their shared experience and the knowledge that no one else would ever understand what they'd been through, but a mistake.

A decision made out of fear, as all the worst decisions were.

They had been afraid, she realised, of facing the world alone after what they had suffered, but Amandine discovered that being alone now scared her, after Lone Diner. She was used to being alone, after all. She'd lost both parents at a young age, had few friends, and had spent vast amounts of time by herself up until the fateful night of her first date with Connor. It was not as if solitude was a new conceit.

And yet, the thought of waking up safe in her bed after everything she'd been through, with a head full of nightmares and memories and kaleidoscopically gruesome images, sounds, sensations… it all proved too much for Amandine in the early days. Connor clearly felt the same, staying glued to her side, relying on her as he had from the second she freed him from his cable tie bonds. After his discharge, and hers, they'd packed up his things and Connor's dad had helped him move in to her house, utterly confused as to the weird turn of events that had occurred in his son's life during his absence on a prolonged business trip, and completely ignorant as to the real reason why his son had suddenly shacked up with a girl he'd only just met. A girl he didn't like much or approve of. A girl who had dragged him off on a drunken, drug-fuelled escapade that had ended with his son losing his thump tips and needing a blood transfusion. Amandine never tried to win Connor's father over or correct him. There was no point. She didn't want him to know the truth about her, about what happened to them. Let him think Connor was impulsive, that moving in with her was a romantic gesture on his son's part. Let him believe in puppy love. They put on a good show on the rare occasions he visited, upholding the myth, because the truth was too awful and too bleak to lay at his feet like wilted roses, like cheap, cut-price chocolates.

They renewed their pact to tell no one about what happened, and for a while, the secret brought them even closer together, especially as they both scanned the internet for missing persons reports featuring Lone Diner's face, but that closeness angered Amandine. She thought it was obvious to anyone with half a brain cell, including the policeman who had come to talk to her, and the plainclothes person who had later come to lean on her some more, especially when they couldn't find the car where she said she'd crashed it, that they were lying about their injuries and their identities. Lying, but nobody could tie either of them definitively to any particular crime. Without a car, she couldn't be charged with reckless driving. There was another car, of course, written off in another ditch – a coincidence, Amandine said, a lot of ice on the roads that night, the coldest night in decades – and a lot of blood, and a dead woman in the road, and a missing couple of honeymooners... but somehow, miraculously, nobody got as far as the doctor did in piecing any, or even some of it together. A spate of post office robberies started up and resources, already stretched thin, were directed elsewhere.

Connor had come round, they had left the hospital shortly after, and that was that. They'd gotten away with it, and Amandine should have been happy about that, but she wasn't.

She wasn't happy at all.

She was furious.

She went looking for answers online, read an article about diminished police numbers in the wake of the pandemic, about problems recruiting and training new officers, about dwindling resources. Another article told her that Norfolk Constabulary had reduced the number of frontline police officers on call so drastically it could no longer properly investigate burglaries, assaults, and other incidents, and they were calling for an increase in its share of council tax to compensate. There was a statement from a police and crime commissioner who spoke about rising costs and cutbacks.

Amandine didn't care about cutbacks.

She had killed a man, and she had information about three murdered victims, and as relieved as she was about this, the fact that nobody had come knocking also felt wrong. Not one single person seemed to care.

She knew it was irrational, but she felt a wild and deep sense of injustice about this, a sensation that worsened as she stumbled across an article about the woman Lone Diner had shot at close range in the head. The woman who had stopped to help. She had been called Jean, and she was an active member of the local wildlife and wetland charity. She had a dog called Francis, and a sister living in Ely.

Catastrophic damage by vehicle…

Brutal and unprecedented…

Police are still looking…

Amandine stopped reading in disgust.

Meanwhile, the worst winter in decades gave way to an early and unseasonably warm spring.

The severed hand in the glove compartment bothered Amandine more and more as the nights and days ground on, as the space between themselves and the horrible experience on Hickling Broad grew wider. Somewhere out there, a mother was missing her daughter. Or a father was missing her, or a brother, or a friend. Amandine swung wildly between self-preservation and deep, deep guilt that she knew the fate of the missing couple when nobody else did.

Jean's stolen car was discovered, eventually, by some teenagers who found it dumped in an abandoned car park half a mile away from the hospital, where Amandine had parked it, a spot chosen deliberately far from any obvious or visible CCTV cameras. The hand was found and quickly identified. That, at least, had been all over the news for a while. *Foul play* was the phrase most commonly used to reference the grisly discovery. Connections were made to the dead woman found in the road. Jean. It was her car, after all. Why there was a missing woman's hand in it, nobody could fathom.

Amandine thought then for sure that the police would continue to connect the dots, that the silence would be broken, that the knock on the front door would eventually come. The police, forensics must have combed every single inch of that vehicle. They would have collected pieces of her and Connor from the shit-stained interior: fingerprints, DNA, hair, saliva… but nobody came for them. And as the weeks went on, she had to accept the trail had gone cold again for the Norfolk police. Neither Connor nor Amandine had ever been fingerprinted, as far as she knew. Their DNA was not on file, no records existed in that sense.

It didn't matter how much evidence was collected if the police didn't have other data to reference it against.

Soon, the furore died down, and another case took all the attention: a murder-suicide, a man in debt up to his eyeballs and his wife and child. The media machine rolled on. Resources were once again diverted elsewhere.

And Amandine discovered, as she cooked meals and washed and folded underwear and made the bed and hoovered the floor and put the dishes away and wiped out the fridge, that bad things didn't stop happening because the ordeal was over.

There were no rolling credit screens, or curtains to cut that experience off from the rest of their lives.

Rather, the bad things were still there, imprinted in memory, like frost patterns on the layer of thin ice covering the surface of a deep, unforgiving body of water. They would melt, in time, but never go away. They would simply be absorbed into the main and become part of the scenery, invisible, but fundamentally, awfully permanent, thanks to entropy.

Coping

She found herself staring into space a lot. Her body felt confused much of the time, as if she were walking around in the wrong skin. Her guts churned continuously, preparing her for something terrible that never occurred. Her shoulders felt sore, heavy, and ached from the tense, braced positions she held herself in.

At first, Amandine drank to medicate, as a means of quieting her nervous system down, but quickly realised the booze made her feel ten times worse after. She found herself constantly swallowing back tears, and she carried a permanent headache. After she quit drinking altogether, she tried regular, old-fashioned pills from a doctor, but they made her horribly breathless and sluggish, so she quit those, too, after only a week or so.

It wasn't long before she began to feel like a prisoner once again, only this time, she was a prisoner in her own form. Her house seemed twice as small and claustrophobic as it had before she met Connor, who quit his job entirely and began drinking Scotch like it was juice. He spent a lot of time lying down, scrolling on his new phone, bought for him by his dad. He slept poorly, and kept Amandine awake a lot.

He also required a lot of reassurance, in the form of physical touch, which Amandine hated giving, because skin on skin felt like rough sandpaper to her soul. She had to restrain herself every time he reached out and tried hard not to shudder as his fingers met her body.

Despite this, there were some tender moments. Sometimes they took walks together and felt lifted by simple things like blue sky or dappled sun on leaves or ducks on the pond or live music in the park, but these were temporary moments of reprieve. When they got back into the house, the ordeal came back to them with a grim, abrasive predictability that wore them both down.

Amandine began to find grey hairs in her parting line.

Connor developed worry-jowls and an eyelid twitch.

They never once, neither of them, considered going back to the police.

Safe From Harm

The first time they made love was horrible. Amandine could only picture that night on the jetty, when Lone Diner had insisted Connor fuck her in front of him. She could not, for that reason, lie under Connor. The first time he attempted it, she had a violent panic attack. Connor rolled off and sat to one side while she hyperventilated, stroking her hair and her back softly with short-thumbed hands until she calmed down.

Then they tried again.

This time, she was on top.

This suited her better posture-wise, but Connor found it difficult to stay hard because her weight pressed down on his damaged leg, which had significant nerve trauma.

Eventually, they settled for doggy style, which felt the exact opposite of what either of them wanted: it was an animalistic position, no space for eye-contact, and after a few urgent thrusts Connor collapsed back onto the bed, frustrated and distraught.

"I don't understand," he murmured, staring up at the ceiling. "I didn't think it would be this difficult. We love each other. We're safe, now."

Amandine lay down next to him. "It was always going to be difficult, Connor," she said. "I didn't expect fireworks, not the first time. And we aren't safe until our brains tell us we are. That's going to take a long while."

They decided the setting wasn't right, so they did everything possible to dress it up, make their next time as far removed from their awful experiences as possible: soft music, heating turned up as high as it would comfortably go, candles, freshly laundered sheets, a bottle of expensive wine. They were both determined to erase Lone Diner from the lexicon of their love language, but it was difficult.

They kept at it, though. Relationships, they'd been told, were hard work.

Especially one with such unusual roots as theirs.

A therapist with a series of online tutorial videos on YouTube told them to start small, work up to the big event.

No pressure.

Focus on foreplay, on having fun.

On feeling safe.

So, they learned to play with each other's parts in non-threatening ways, which felt in equal measure absurd and humiliating for Amandine, but she stayed with it because she didn't know what else to do.

And then she realised that pandering to her trauma was only making it worse. Being gentle, playing, all the faux sensuality… it hadn't been her style before, so why would she enjoy it now?

She asked Connor to be rough with her, she begged him, tears running down her cheeks, and he didn't want to at first, but then he did. They found themselves tumbling onto the floor with a savage urgency they'd not yet experienced. Connor grabbed her naked hips, and she slid down onto him so hard she felt him bend, at first, but they kept going and found a rhythm. A feeling grew in Amandine's belly, a slow, building fire, and she rode him faster, losing herself to the sensations, leaning forward and putting her lips close to Connor's ear.

"Pull my hair," she begged, and Connor did as he was told, and then she asked him to slap her, and he did that too, and she came ferociously, her entire body quivering, as Connor stared at her in shock, wondering what the hell was going on.

Amandine climbed off, once the tremors had subsided, and used her mouth to take the questions out of his eyes. His own cries as his warmth jetted down her throat were as desperate and confused as hers, and he crashed back onto the carpet after like a felled tree, chest heaving.

He lay motionless for some time, staring into space, his face haunted.

Amandine went into her ensuite bathroom, gently closed and locked the door, grabbed a towel, sat on the toilet, and sobbed and sobbed into the thick fabric until she almost threw up, hoping against hope that Connor wouldn't hear her.

He did.

Flames

The next morning, Connor found Amandine at the breakfast table with a lit candle held to her hand.

She held her palm over the flame until her skin blistered and blackened.

He slapped it away before the damage got too extreme, and shouted:

"Why did you do that? What the fuck, Amandine? Haven't you been through enough?"

"I needed to check I was still alive," she said.

Connor bit back his reply. Stared at his own hands, shiny skin covered the places where his thumbs had been sliced down. He'd been offered prosthetics but hadn't had the mental energy to consider that, yet.

"Are you?" he asked, trying to be patient, but wondering the same thing of himself.

"I'm not sure," she replied. "I'm really not sure."

Weak Glue

Any genuine connection Amandine and Connor might have once had got buried in the mundanity of their forced commitment to each other. It was hard to thrive, Amandine found, when every single thing they did was tainted with terrible memories.

It wasn't going to be enough, she realised. Their terrible glue.

After everything, there were still broad, dead waters between them.

She was not a life raft.

She was an island of her own.

Space

"What do you mean, you need space?"

Amandine gave Connor a flat stare. "It's obvious from my choice of words, isn't it? I need some space from you."

His face was an open wound.

"I don't understand. How can you need space from the one person who knows what you're going through?"

An open wound, but she had wounds of her own to tend to.

"Because that's just it, isn't it?!" she snapped, standing up abruptly. They were in the bedroom again. "You understand too much! Every time we look at each other, we see *him*. Every single time I hear you call my name, I think of *him*. You are the only person in the whole wide universe who understands what I'm going through, and that is exactly *why* I need space from you. You remind me of that jetty, that boathouse, that shit-stinking car every single waking second that I'm around you. Whenever you open your mouth, my skin starts to crawl. Whenever you touch me, *he* is touching me. Whenever we hold hands, I am holding hands with you on that boardwalk, and we're both covered in our own blood. I can't do it anymore! I just *can't*!"

Connor continued to stare at Amandine as if the world was ending. Hurt and anger battled each other, but bewilderment was the emotion that finally won out.

"But what will I do on my own without you?" he said, in a small, small voice. "I'll have nobody left to talk to."

Amandine bit her lip before she said something truly dreadful.

Something neither of them could come back from.

The small drop of blood she tasted on her lips calmed her, if only a little.

"It's not your fault," she continued, after considerable internal struggle. She spoke in a soft, placatory tone. "It is not your fault. Neither of us asked for this. I know that. But Connor... I can't bear it. I can't bear to be around you. Not until I've had some time to... process all this. My only frame of reference for our relationship is pain, and suffering. We don't have any other type of memory or foundation."

"But... I thought... you loved me."

Connor probably knew how pathetic he sounded, but he couldn't help himself.

Amandine threw up her hands in exasperation.

"I can love you and need you to be far away from me at the same time, do you understand that? We don't have to live in a world of black and white. I can love you and need distance from you in the same breath. There can be nuance. I don't have to operate in absolutes. Especially not now. I love you... but I can't have you around me right now, Connor."

She let that sink in. It felt worse than when she'd been forced to take the car keys from the severed hand. Worse than watching Connor being doused with ice-cold water. Worse than seeing an innocent woman get shot, then run over deliberately.

Worse than any of it.

It was the most painful feeling she'd ever encountered, largely because she knew that she was right.

Connor sunk his head into his hands.

"So, what do we do now?" he said, and the words were muffled as they came out past his fingers.

Amandine let out a sigh of relief. Her posture softened. She was getting her way, and that meant she could relax a little. Connor, she was sure, hated her at that moment.

She was relieved to be getting away from him.

She was not sure he would forgive her for that.

She questioned herself, briefly, one more time.

Weren't people in love supposed to want to be near each other all the time?

In marriage, you said for better for worse, in sickness and in health. They weren't married, but didn't the things they'd survived together mean anything to her?

"Now?" Amandine repeated, thinking about it.

"Yeah. This very moment. What... what do you need?"

"Now," she said, after some considerable silence, "you leave. It's that simple, Connor. You leave me alone. You pack up your shit and you call your dad, and you leave me with a kiss, and a hug, and I shut the door, and you walk away, and you let me be for a while."

"Let you be?" She thought he might be sick.

"Let me be alone. With my thoughts. With my silence. I need silence. You let me be, and we'll take it from there."

She was so calm about it. So reasonable.

Connor started to cry.

"And what if... you don't come back? Where the fuck does that leave me?"

"I don't know," Amandine said, and she just managed to stop herself from shrugging, although it was hard. The barricades, he could tell, had gone up already. She was impenetrable, and no amount of effort would get him inside the compound walls.

"You don't know."

"Stop repeating everything I am saying." She was getting annoyed.

"I'm sorry, I just..." Connor finally ran out of words.

Amandine took a deep breath, softened momentarily.

"I know," she said. "I know it's hard."

"I'll tell someone. I'll tell the police. I'll tell them everything."

She smiled sadly. "No, you won't. I need this. Please. I can't be what you need right now. I can't."

"Alright," Connor said, admitting defeat, and although there were tears in his eyes, and although his jaw was set in anger, and although she could feel him tense and harden up as they hugged, he did as he was asked: he kissed her, just once, on the mouth, a chaste, almost brotherly kiss, they embraced and then he left.

Amandine changed her locks, blocked him on her phone and email, ripped up the letters he pushed under her door unread, and didn't speak to him for a year.

She did a lot of scrolling, though.

How to Get Over Your Ex.

How to Let Go of a Toxic Relationship.

How to Overcome Trauma.

How to Confess to a Murder.

How to Say Sorry.

How to Learn to Trust Again.

Ten Things to do to Feel Less Lonely.

How to Overcome Fear.

How to Escape a Trauma Bond.

In the end, all it took was time.

ONE YEAR LATER

Third Date

It was a new bar. Tapas, lanterns, upbeat music. It was popular immediately, tables booked out for weeks in advance.

Amandine thought it suited Connor very well, when she saw him seated at the table in the window. He had a large glass of something bubbly in front of him and was wearing a new suit jacket with jeans and sneakers.

He was with a woman who looked, she realised with some amusement, a lot like herself. Buxom, taller than him, long, dark hair. Broad shoulders. Big hands. Handsome, not beautiful. She smiled a lot and had a deep laugh.

Amandine walked up to their table and stood, waiting to be noticed.

Connor's face on seeing her was one of absolute shock.

"What the fuck are you doing here?" he breathed, but there was joy on his face, too.

He'd missed her.

She'd missed him too, she realised.

She saw he was wearing prosthetic thumbs.

"I don't think we can move ahead until we dredge them up," she said, without preamble. Guilt had led her here. That, and curiosity.

"Dredge… them up?" Connor blinked. "All three? Or just…" He trailed off, shaking his head.

"Um, excuse me?" the woman said, icily.

"This is fucking typical of you," Connor spat, angrily. "Turning up in my life when I was partway to getting over you. With this, of all things. The time for that has passed, don't you think?"

The woman at the table with Connor bristled, looking back and forth between them.

"I'm sorry," she said, "who the fuck are you, again?"

Amandine ignored her.

"Just the two of them. So they can go back to their families. Not him. He can stay down there where he belongs."

"How is that going to make anything better?" Connor was getting angrier and angrier. "Fuck off, Amandine. I wrote, you didn't answer. I called, you blocked me. You made yourself very clear. We're done here."

"They deserve funerals."

Connor slapped his hand on the table, hard.

"Enough!" he shouted, while his new girlfriend looked on in shock. The other punters in the restaurant glanced over, smirking.

"You push me away, you tell me to fuck off, you don't speak to me for a whole fucking year, then you turn up when I'm finally moving on with my life and tell me I owe it to you to tell the world the truth? You really are a fucking treat, Amandine."

Connor's girlfriend narrowed her eyes as they darted from her date to Amandine, back and forth, back and forth, trying to figure out what exactly was taking place before her.

"Anyone going to fill me in on what this is all about?" she asked – and was ignored.

Amandine lifted her chin.

"I'm going to dredge them up, Connor."

"And do what with them? We can't..." He lowered his voice to a hiss. "We can't do this, not now. Not after such a long time. It would look terrible. We don't even know for sure they are down there. We only have his word for that, and he's dead."

"I'm going back there. I can't leave them out there anymore. Their families deserve better. We should never have left it this long, but I'll face the consequences of that when it's done. I'm going. With or without you."

Connor's girlfriend pushed her chair back, stood up.

"Connor?" she said, her cheeks red with mounting ire. "What's going on? Who is this?"

Connor cleared his throat.

"My ex," he said eventually, in a low, shaky voice. "This is Amandine. Amandine, this is my girlfriend, Jo, and you're fucking everything up–"

"I don't care," she replied, smiling sadly. "I'm sorry, but I just don't care. I'm going to dredge them up, Connor, and then I'm going to leave them somewhere for the police to find. Somehow, anonymously. Come with me, or not. I just wanted you to know."

Amandine turned to leave, conflicting emotions battling inside her. Disappointment was the easiest and most immediate to name.

Connor stood hastily, reaching out to stop her from going.

"Don't," he said, in a broken voice. "Don't leave me again, I can't..."

In his urgency, he knocked over his glass. The table flooded with liquid, most of which spilled over onto Jo's shoes.

She squealed and stepped back, but Connor didn't notice.

He grabbed Amandine's shoulders from behind, held them tight.

"Think about what you're saying," he pleaded, and she could feel the love still there in his touch. He'd never stopped caring about her, and somehow, she had known that.

"Think about what this will do to us, to our lives. Our future. You're about to do something irrevocable, don't you see?"

Amandine was unswayed.

"It doesn't matter," she said, gently. "It's the right thing to do."

"It matters to me!" Connor cried. "It fucking matters to me! When are you going to stop acting like it only happened to you? Huh? It didn't only happen to you! It fucking happened to me, too."

His voice cracked.

"So, let's do it together," Amandine said, eventually. She turned back to him, placed a hand gently on his cheek and stroked his mouth with her thumb.

Jo made an angry noise that the other two ignored.

Connor shuddered, and bowed his head, leaning into Amandine's hand in defeat.

"Come with me and we can make it right, together," she said.

"Why did you have to come over here?" he mumbled, eyes still closed. "I was finally doing okay. I was finally getting somewhere."

"You'll never get anywhere while he still has a hold on us. You know that. You can pretend, you can bury it deep, but he's still down there, isn't he?"

Connor knew she was right. He just didn't want to admit it out loud.

He let out a shaky breath instead.

Amandine could see she was finally getting somewhere.

"Let's own it, Connor. Let's own it, instead of hiding from it. In our own way."

He opened his eyes, wiped them with a trembling hand.

His girlfriend, furious and wine-splattered, pulled on his sleeve.

"Connor!" she hissed, eyes boring into him. "What the fuck is going on?"

He shook her off, gently.

"I'm sorry," he said, his voice robotic, his words formal. "I don't think this is going to work out, Jo."

The woman's lip wobbled.

Her eyes were disbelieving saucers.

"What?" she said, shocked. "What the fuck are you saying?"

Connor turned away.

Slipped his hand into Amandine's.

"I'm sorry," he said again, as he slowly started walking to the restaurant door. "I can't be in a relationship with you anymore. I have to go dig up some dead bodies with my ex."

Dredge

The still, brown, reed-choked waters of the Norfolk Broads are home to a great many things.

Birds, a wide variety.

Eels.

Otters.

Sometimes, a seal that's lost its way.

They are also home to a great many secrets.

Sunken boats.

Lost treasure.

The bodies of drowned animals, of discarded fish.

Of rotting matter, of silt and clay and insect carcasses and rusty, long-defunct military equipment, and even the occasional unexploded bomb, mud-slick and patient.

And, of course, the waterlogged corpses of lovers.

Three such corpses lay at the bottom of a particularly remote creek just off of Hickling Broad, not far from a jetty that leads to an ancient boathouse roofed with thatch. The bodies, as far as bodies can go, were in a bad way. They had been down in the marshy waters for a year, give or take, left to rot in a sack and a bundle of blue wrappings weighted down with bricks and nuggets of slimy concrete. The sack, which housed the furred bones of lovers, was tied tightly at the neck with a rope. The end of that rope had caught, unbeknownst to Lone Diner, upon a nearby tree root poking up out of the mud like a broken finger aimed at the sky. Birds often rested on this root, unaware of the decaying matter that was snagged just below it.

One secret of many, that the broads swallowed whole.

Dawn Dive

They went at dawn, which was the time, Amandine recalled, when they had finally escaped from the Lone Diner. That felt both seconds and lifetimes ago, and she found herself trapped between two versions of herself: past and present, victim and survivor, both of whom were formed in very different ways.

Connor stood a little distance off from her as the sun's burning cap slowly emerged from the golden reed-line. He was very visibly trapped in two states in the same way Amandine was: he longed for comfort but did not want to be a burden. He held a thick pair of rubber gloves in his hands, and twisted them around and around, over and over, his nervous eyelid tic pronounced as he contemplated the task ahead. Amandine wondered if his new girlfriend had accommodated these little spasmodic peculiarities of his, or if she'd found them frustrating: *can't you ever sit still?* She knew the tone.

No, I can't, he would reply silently, because trying to explain eternal restlessness to a person who fundamentally couldn't understand it was a thankless waste of energy.

Amandine understood it, though.

She had always understood what sort of person Connor was, because sometimes, you meet someone who is a reflection of yourself, for better, for worse, and it isn't like meeting a new person at all, but more like walking up to a mirror and embracing your own throwback.

She knew what motivated him, pleased him, scared him, thrilled him, made him happy, made him sad, made him stressed, made him cum. She'd thought about it a lot, while they were separated. She knew where he liked to be touched and how he liked to be held and what he liked to think about when he drank his morning coffee and what temperature he felt comfortable sleeping in and how tight he liked his shoes laced.

She knew what his dreams for the future had been, before their first date, and she knew everything about his family, his past, his childhood, his disappointments and triumphs and abuses, the other women he'd fucked, and how much he had cried when his childhood dog Winter had been put to sleep, and how he still had nightmares about that, occasionally, when he was stressed, because his mam had done it to punish him, a cruel and unfathomable thing.

She knew how much he loved her, still, in his own way, and she knew what that love felt like for him, and how she'd hurt him, and she knew that he also blamed himself for what had happened to her, blamed himself for not taking the threat seriously enough when Lone Diner had made himself known to them in the restaurant, for not listening when Amandine had been reluctant to accept Lone Diner's offer of a lift. He blamed himself for having needed her too much because she, unlike anyone else he had ever met in his whole life, saw him – really *saw* him – for who he was, and he didn't know how to let go of that, and she saw that he understood how selfish that made him, inherently selfish to the detriment of another person's happiness and ability to breathe, and she knew that he was working on that part of himself, that neediness, working on pressing it down and reframing it, and she knew that if anyone could learn lessons from rejection, it was Connor, because she knew a lot of things about him.

She knew a lot of things because he'd written long letters telling her all these details, letters she'd read, eventually, but never answered.

She understood that she couldn't explore the depths of that knowledge while the barrier of the dead couple's rotting corpses hung between them.

The wan light gathered around them, signalling a new day, a day in which to finally take control of some of the ghosts that separated Amandine from her own future. They'd formed a plan, on the way here. They would lift the remains, wrap them, lay them carefully in a nearby field, then make an anonymous call to the police to report the bodies. If nobody took them seriously, the bodies were by a footpath, used frequently by dog walkers and farmers. The couple would be found eventually, she was sure. The rest: identification, informing the families… that was up to the experts. She lifted her head, breathed in the boggy air. In the distance, beyond the old jetty and the sinking barge in the decaying boathouse, Amandine could see rows of stacked, tufted pyramids lining the narrow waterways. Those were new. Cutters had been reed-harvesting recently. She frowned. This meant the area might not be as deserted and quiet as she would have liked. The cutters would be along soon to collect their bounty, or harvest more, and she didn't want any interruptions. People started their days early round here, especially those who worked the land, and she didn't think it would be long before they would lose their window.

"We should get on with it," she said, softly, as a warbler burbled away nearby in soft agreement.

Connor didn't move.

"Are you sure about this?" he asked. His face was turned to the rising sun, seeking warmth, seeking reassurance. His chest rose and fell with anxious intakes, and his hands would not stop twisting the gloves. "What if we're seen?"

Amandine let out a small whistle of annoyance.

"Then we tell the truth," she replied. "But only if they find us."

"What if they don't believe us?"

Amandine moved to the end of the jetty. "I don't care," she said, stripping off her clothes to reveal a bathing suit underneath. "I can't sleep while they are down there."

Amandine shivered slightly, for the day was fresh and goosebumps rose on her arms as she stared down into the black water beyond the edge of the pontoon.

Water she'd almost drowned in.

"I think he said it was around here, somewhere, right? Near the boathouse."

Connor stared down into the murk. "I can't really…" He swallowed.

The memories were flooding back into his brain like wet sludge jettisoned from a blocked drain. His eyelid twitch was now so bad his whole face contorted with it.

"I think… it's hard to remember exactly, but I think…"

He pointed at an old decaying root protruding from the water about six feet from the edge of the boathouse. "Is that a rope?" he asked, peering in.

Amandine dragged a pair of goggles down past her hairline and onto her eyes, then lowered herself in without further discussion. Her pale flesh was swallowed by the gloom of the broad water, which was a deep brown colour and had a sheen of iridescence on the top: natural oils released by the mud that lay thick below.

Then, she struck out towards the root Connor pointed to.

"Are you okay?" he called, concerned as he watched her swim. Perhaps he was worried she would drown from the weight of the memories.

It took her some time to grab the end of the rope. "It goes down!" she said, eventually. "I think... it's tied to something heavy!"

"Hey!" Connor said suddenly, calling out to her across the water.

Amandine looked over, treading water. Connor was on the edge of the jetty, tapping his eye lightly with one hand. He still held his weight off his injured leg, she saw. He probably always would.

"We don't even have a song, you know," he said.

"A song?"

"Yeah. You know. Most couples have one, don't they?"

"We're alive, Connor," Amandine said. "We don't need a song."

Check out another Gemma Amor mystery from Datura Books, The Folly

Read the first chapters here.

One

He shuffled out of the prison door in a daze, a small bag of belongings clutched to his chest. I saw him pause as the early light of day embraced him. He closed his eyes briefly, and dragged in a deep, full breath, up through his nostrils, out through his mouth. I had haggled for his release to be set at five in the morning, to help us avoid attention from the press. I had not accounted for how surreal exiting into an empty, quiet street must have felt for him. Like exiting onto the moon after a long flight.

The sky overhead was drenched in pink fire that morning, bright streaks of blue raking through. The prison walls, tall, thick, built of Victorian red brick, caught the weird dawn glow and hung on to it. It gave the complex a surreal, artificially lit aspect, as if it were a movie set or a paint and canvas creation, not the brutal bricks-and-mortar structure that had stolen my father for six and a half long years.

Prison had not been kind to Dad. That release day, I could not believe how much older than his true age he looked. Of course, I had visited him every week while he was inside, but now he was out, I could see clearly how diminished he was. White-haired, he stooped, which didn't suit him. My father had always been a straight-backed sort of man, a man who had once been proud of his height. Now he moved as if he were an inconvenience, as if he were actively trying to lessen the amount of space he took up in the world. He was thin, too, cheeks saggy. I was glad I had a shepherd's pie waiting for him at home, calorie-dense, smothered in cheese. I had made an apple tart for dessert, which I would serve with custard or clotted cream, or both, depending on how hungry he was.

Dad took a few more hesitant steps across the carpark. I went to him. We had been apart for a long time. I didn't want to waste another second.

"Hello, Dad," I said, gently taking his bag. It wasn't heavy, but he was having a difficult time with it. His arms shook. I swallowed back tears. My heart was pounding. I was determined not to cry in front of him. He had enough to deal with. He didn't need my sentimentality on top of everything else.

"Hello, love," he replied in a gravelly voice. "You didn't have to come get me. I could have got a taxi."

I shook my head, wondering when he would hug me. "With what money?" I scolded. "Come here." I could see he wasn't going to make a move, so I made it for him, wrapping him in a tight embrace. He stiffened at first, then slowly returned it. I drank in his smell, which I had nearly forgotten. Bones dug into me through his clothes. I estimated he'd lost at least thirty pounds, maybe more. He didn't feel like my dad, not yet, but he would soon enough. I would make sure of it.

We leaned into each other for a minute, then broke apart.

"Right then," I said, clearing my throat. "Let's get out of here, shall we? Before the media shows up."

"Yes, please," he replied, and I could see ghosts in his eyes.

Two

Dad's sentence had originally been a fifteen-year sentence. He served just over six of that, give or take thirteen months, which we both begrudged. I had hoped the furious media interest in his appeal and retrial would expedite his release, but, if anything, it had slowed things down. Bureaucracy, paperwork, logistics... the system wanted to hang on to him, an innocent man. A victim of a miscarriage of justice, although the press wouldn't communicate it that way. Dad's trial had been a trial of public opinion. It had not taken me long to learn that the truth, the real truth, as far as anyone could ever know it without having been present, was nowhere near sensational enough to drive clicks and sell papers. Accidents didn't make money, murder did. The best I could hope for now was a version of events that meant we could live our lives together again in peace, lives that had been disrupted beyond all belief after a simple trip, a split-second tumble. I tried not to feel angry about how things had gone, although I was. I was angrier than I knew how to cope with, but I squashed it down. Anger wasn't useful. Patience, I had found, was the only useful virtue. And acceptance. True, my family life had imploded in the space of an hour, but now...I had my dad back. That was all that mattered. Now was the time to look forward, not back. I could change none of the past.

I could change our future, though, for the better.

"There are still a lot of forms to fill out," I told him, putting the car into reverse and awkwardly three-point turning in the narrow street outside the prison. An approaching car barreling in the opposite direction jerked to a halt and honked, the driver motioning for me to hurry up. I waved back calmly. City drivers were all bluster, nothing more. The trick was not to back down, not to show that they had gotten to you.

"And we have a lot to discuss," I continued, eventually pointing us in the right direction and letting the other car squeeze past aggressively. Our wing mirrors clipped. Dirty looks were exchanged. The other car's exhaust belched and roared, and the vehicle sped off. Just another encounter in a world full of aggravation and stress, par for the course for the times. The pandemic had brought out the very worst in people, I thought, but I didn't say so to my father.

I pulled away from the prison for what I hoped would be the very last time. I felt as if I knew every aspect and contour of the place, every brick and slab. I hated it.

Dad, meanwhile, watched the building grow smaller in the rearview mirror.

"You know," he said quietly, "I've waited so long for this moment, and now it's here, I'm afraid."

"Afraid of what?"

"Everything. All of it." He waved a hand at the world passing slowly by: shuttered shops covered in graffiti, cafes, bakeries, vomit-splattered bus stops, greengrocers, pubs with tables and chairs stacked atop each other on the path outside, a church, a supermarket, pound stores, designer boutiques, estate agent offices, second-hand furniture stores—a relentless commercial jumble, a chaotic urban kaleidoscope that must have been a lot to absorb after the sparse and spartan world of prison. Even if it was all closed doors, now. To me, it felt like a zombie town.

The city had been in lockdown for so long it was hard to remember what life had been like before. For Dad, though, it must have been a siege upon the senses.

"Want me to put you back in?" I joked, although the joke hurt my heart. "I could drop you off in time for lunch."

He chuckled, just one short burst of hard-won mirth, then hung his head as if he did not deserve to laugh. I could almost see the hefty mantle of guilt sitting heavily on his shoulders as he began to process his freedom. He didn't feel he deserved it, even if it had been granted by law. He had been so conditioned to his own worthlessness inside, it would take time to reprogram him as a blameless man, I knew. Patience would be necessary. We would have to rebuild him, brick by brick, from the ground up. It wouldn't be quick or easy, but time would play its part. And space to breathe. Peace. Fresh air. A change of scene.

I had a plan for all of that.

He could sense my mood, in that intuitive way he'd always been able to with me.

"You don't have to do all this, you know," he said, patting my hand as it rested on the gear stick. "You don't have to put me up. I can find my own way. My own place."

"I'm not so sure about that."

He shook his head. "A parent should look after his child, not the other way around. Not at your age."

I shook my own head in mild exasperation. "At my age? I'm pretty sure most people my age are looking after at least one parent, if not both. You aren't a spring chicken anymore, Dad. This is how it works, isn't it? It's why people have children."

He sighed. "That cynical brain came straight from your mother, didn't it."

I pursed my lips. "Don't. I can't, not today."

"You know what I mean. I should be able to look after myself."

"And you would live where exactly? You know how difficult it will be to get a job. Especially at the moment. People are losing their jobs left, right, and centre. And it'll be a nightmare trying to get insurance. *And* you don't have the money to rent, you lost all your savings."

"Jobseeker's allowance," he muttered, a little cowed. "Universal Credit."

"Those will only get you so far in this city. Do you know how expensive it is to rent these days? You want to live in some mouldy old hovel with a bunch of addicts? Or a tent in the centre of town? Camp out in the Bearpit? Stop being silly. You're my dad. Of course you're going to live with me."

"I could, you know. Put myself back in. Commit another crime. Find a police officer, assault them. That's a thing, you know. Some of us get so used to being inside that we walk right up to the first copper we can find after release and–"

"Dad!" I was horrified, for he sounded half serious.

"I could. Then I wouldn't be any bother."

"Dad, stop it. We fought for this, for years. You're free now. Free to live your own life. I'm just helping you get back on your feet is all."

Dad was silent as he pondered the word *free.*

"I suppose you're right," he said eventually.

"Now, stop spoiling things. This is a day to celebrate! I have a hot meal waiting for you at the house. A freshly made bed. Let's get you away from town and settled in. Then we can talk properly."

"Shepherd's pie?" he asked, meek and humble, a mode I never liked that much in him.

I smiled. "Of course. Your favourite. Just the way Mum used to make it."

He thought about it. "Got any beer?"

I smiled. "A celebratory bottle of Tribute, and your favourite glass."

He sighed. "You're a good girl, Morgan," he said. Then: "It will be nice to see the old house again. I've missed my home."

I kept quiet. He didn't know yet that it wouldn't be his home for much longer.